Wicked Whiskey Love

The Whiskeys

MELISSA FOSTER

ISBN-10: 1948004887
ISBN-13: 978-1948004886

This is a work of fiction. The events and characters described herein are imaginary and are not intended to refer to specific places or living persons. The opinions expressed in this manuscript are solely the opinions of the author and do not represent the opinions or thoughts of the publisher. The author has represented and warranted full ownership and/or legal right to publish all the materials in this book.

Cover Design: Elizabeth Mackey Designs
Cover Photography: Golden Czermak, FuriousFotog

WORLD LITERARY PRESS
PRINTED IN THE UNITED STATES OF AMERICA

A Note to Readers

Bones Whiskey is the most mysterious of the Whiskey siblings, and I loved getting to know him better. He's a powerful, compassionate man who lives within the eye of a storm and unleashes his wrath only when absolutely necessary. Sarah Beckley brings out his best qualities, and her painful past brings his introspective nature to a whole new level. Bones and Sarah are a perfect match, and if you're female, be ready for an ovary explosion when you see him with her children. The man is a romantic, loving force of nature, and he is exactly the man Sarah needs. I hope you love them as much as I do and that you enjoy their sexy, emotional love story.

Each of Sarah's and Bones's witty and wonderful family members and friends will also be getting their own happily ever after. Several books are already published and available for your enjoyment (TRU BLUE, TRULY, MADLY, WHISKEY, DRIVING WHISKEY WILD, and RIVER OF LOVE). If this is your first introduction to the Whiskey family, each book is written to stand alone, so dive right in and fall in love with the Whiskeys.

Remember to sign up for my newsletter to make sure you don't miss out on future Whiskey releases:
www.MelissaFoster.com/News

For more information about my fun, sexy romances, all of which can be read as stand-alone novels or as part of the larger

series, visit my website:
www.MelissaFoster.com

If you prefer sweet romance with no explicit scenes or graphic language, please try the Sweet with Heat series written under my pen name, Addison Cole. You'll find the same great love stories with toned-down heat levels.

Happy reading!
~ Melissa

Chapter One

THE RUMBLE AND roar of the Dark Knights Motorcycle Club cut through the cheering crowd as they led Peaceful Harbor's Halloween parade down Main Street. Even in costumes the Dark Knights were an intimidating bunch, but Sarah Beckley wasn't afraid. Two months ago Bullet Whiskey, a Dark Knight, had rescued Sarah and her family after they'd been in a horrendous accident. In the months since, the Dark Knights had come out in droves to assist them. They'd pulled together a fundraising rally to help pay for their medical bills, helped her find a job and babysitting for her two children, and drove her brother, Scott, to physical therapy when she was unable. Sarah didn't know much about bikers' lifestyles, but she'd learned a few things lately. Their families went well beyond bloodlines and birthrights, extending to *claiming* and *protecting* the friends and families of each and every member of the Dark Knights. To be included in such a group was an honor.

Sarah glanced ahead at her three-year-old son, Bradley, riding in a sidecar attached to Bones Whiskey's motorcycle. She couldn't see Bradley's face, but she knew her sandy-haired warrior was grinning from ear to ear as he waved at the people on the sidewalks. He had been excited about the parade, but the prospect of riding with Bones had left him too elated to sleep for the past two nights. Her gaze shifted to Bones, the all-too-hot physician/biker, and her heart raced. He had taken to her children like an adoring uncle and to *her* like a hungry, protective *man*, as if she were *his* to protect, rendering her not only sleepless, but hot and bothered, for weeks.

Not in a million years had she imagined sitting on a float waving to a community of people who treated her and her children as one of their own, much less catching the eye of someone like Bones. But here she was, sitting atop a giant cupcake-shaped chair Bones had insisted he and his overprotective clan of biker brothers build for her, surrounded by a gaggle of new friends who had embraced her family and brought them into the fold of the close-knit community. Not for the first time since moving to Peaceful Harbor, Sarah took stock of her life, thanking the powers that be for her good fortune—powers that until now she had been sure were evil.

How had she gone from homeless to happy?

Twice?

If all these people knew the truth about her background, would they still be as accepting? Or would they hide their husbands and children, treating her as the pariah she'd often felt like?

As the float rolled to a stop, Dixie Whiskey, Bones's sister, tossed her red hair over her tattooed shoulder, straightened the seashell bikini top of her mermaid costume, then shimmied to adjust her shiny green sequined skirt. Ever the biker, she'd paired the outfit with chunky black leather boots. "Finally! If I have to smile for one more second, I'm going to scream."

"I loved every second," Sarah said honestly. She knew what it felt like to be alone, hungry, and scared, and she treasured every second that she wasn't. Bathing in the warmth of good feelings, she gazed down at her eleven-month-old daughter, Lila, looking precious in her red onesie with THING 1 printed on the front. Her little hand rested on Sarah's burgeoning baby bump, which proudly displayed THING 2. At five and a half months pregnant, Sarah felt good, and maybe more important, for the first time in her life she was truly, deeply happy.

Therein lay the problem.

Every time Sarah had dropped her guard, her world came crashing down around her. She knew better than to let the comfort of these warm, welcoming friends sway her into believing she was on solid ground.

Sarah glanced at Bones as he climbed off his motorcycle. Denim strained over his powerful thighs. He whipped off his helmet, and his sexy dark eyes sailed over the sea of heads separating them, landing on her with the heat of a volcano. His lips curled up into a panty-melting smile that made her forget she was a pregnant mother of two and caused her to think about all the dirty things she'd like him to do with that beautiful mouth. Because of her history with men, his attention was as disturbing as it was comforting. She constantly battled the urge to dig deeper into his comfort versus hiding her and her children away from the rest of the world *just in case...*

Bones tossed her a suggestive wink. Her stomach dipped, and she looked away, her cheeks burning. But his draw was too strong, and she had to steal another glance.

Her heart thundered as she took in his handsome, rugged features and a body that put every other man to shame. She noticed several women watching him. He didn't seem to pay any mind to the attention he drew as he talked with Bradley, Sarah's *real* Thing 1. Her boy was as enamored with Bones as she was. He'd refused the Dr. Seuss–themed costumes in favor of matching Bones.

Bradley hadn't even batted an eye when four-year-old Kennedy, the daughter of their friends Truman and Gemma Gritt, had convinced all the guys in their group to dress up as cheerleaders while she dressed up as a football player—with a pink tiara, of course. Bradley carried his pom-poms proudly and had even been willing to wear the skirt. The men, however, weren't quite as open to the idea. They'd donned denim shorts, white T-shirts that read TEAM KENNEDY across the front, black leather vests with the Dark Knights emblem on the back, and their biker boots. Pom-poms were *not* optional, and most of the men had them crammed in their back pockets.

Bones seemed to enjoy taking her family under his very sexy wings. He had insisted on buying Bradley a little leather vest and boots. The tattooed, burly bikers had revealed their hearts of gold, and her little boy had been over the moon to be included. Bones did a lot for them. He was helping Scott finish their basement, and he helped Sarah with the kids when they went out as a group. Sarah was still learning to accept such generosity and was slowly coming to understand that not all gifts were given expecting something in return.

As her friends moved toward the edge of the float, their significant others appeared like the cavalry to help them. Bullet lifted his fiancée, Finlay, into his arms, kissing her on the way down. His thick arms and body swallowed her up as their rottweiler, Tinkerbell, who had ridden on the float with Finlay, whined for attention. Finlay owned the catering company for whom the float was built, and she looked adorable in a short pink skirt and white apron that proudly displayed *Finlay's* in fancy pink script, along with a big, puffy baker's hat. The petite blonde had been another saving grace for Sarah after the accident, preparing allergen-free meals for her day after day.

Bullet and Finlay were getting married next weekend. Although Finlay was as demure as a bunny and Bullet was like a beast ready to charge, they made love look easy.

Sarah had once believed love could be *something*, though certainly not *easy*. She'd since learned how treacherous even thinking about being in love could be.

On the other side of the float Scott helped Dixie and their friend Isabel climb down. He had that goofy look in his eyes guys got around hot girls. It was nice to see him involved and happy.

"Daddy!" Kennedy hollered to Truman as he approached. She clung to Gemma's hand. "Get me and Mama!"

Carrying Lincoln, their toddler, Truman reached for Kennedy. "Come on down, princess."

"I'm a footballer, Daddy!" Kennedy climbed down as Bear, Bones's younger brother, helped Gemma down, then reached for his wife, Crystal.

She noticed Bones holding Bradley's hand and heading her way. The love and support of the Whiskeys was beyond admirable. She swore their protective nature was woven into the very fabric of their beings. The crowd pushed forward, and she lost track of Bones and her boy.

Scott pushed through the crowd and reached for Lila. "Give her to me, and then I'll help you down." He didn't seem to care how silly he looked dressed as the Cat in the Hat to match their Dr. Seuss theme, and she loved him even more for it.

When they'd first reconnected, she'd seen hints of their

father in his facial features. She'd mentioned it to Scott, and he'd stopped shaving and had let his hair grow out. Sarah didn't think that mattered now that she'd gotten to know him. There was no hint of her father left in him.

"I'm not sure I should give up my baby to a giant cat-man," Sarah teased as she handed him the sleeping baby.

Scott had kept a heavy hand on Sarah's shoulder during the entire parade. No doubt he worried that this life they were creating could go up in smoke at any moment and she'd disappear again. It would take a pack of wolves to separate her from the brother she hadn't seen in so many years she'd thought she'd lost him forever.

They'd only just reunited, and the first night they'd gone out to celebrate, they'd gotten into the car accident that had landed her babies and Scott in the hospital. Lila had scars on her face and arms, and Scott was still doing physical therapy to strengthen his legs, which had been broken in the accident. Thanks to Bullet's fast thinking, they'd all survived.

That seemed to be the story of their lives. *Surviving.* She wondered if any of the others were waiting for their own beautiful lives to implode, or if she was alone in that fear.

She hiked her baby bag over her shoulder and climbed down, taking Lila from Scott. They were quickly swept into the crowd as they made their way toward the motorcycles. Sarah peered around a heavyset woman and scanned the crowd, quickly finding the broad shoulders she'd know anywhere. Bones was surrounded by a group of women dressed in sexy costumes with short skirts and tight bodices. They were gazing up at him like he was the Wizard and held the answers to all their problems.

Sarah pushed through the crowd, and Bones turned, his

dark eyes locking on her so intently she stilled. She lowered her gaze, looking for Bradley, and her stomach took a nosedive.

A woman dressed as a witch grabbed Bones's arm, turning him away.

"Scott, where's Bradley?" Panic gripped her as she spun around, searching the crowd. In her heart she knew Bones would never put her children in danger. But her children's own father, the man who was supposed to protect them with his life, had put them in harm's way. She no longer trusted her instincts like she used to.

"It's okay. I'm sure he's nearby." Scott plowed through the mass of people, hollering Bradley's name.

With her heart in her throat, Sarah pushed forward, clutching Lila and calling for Bradley. Bones spun around and quickly closed the distance between them.

His arm circled her waist, hauling her and Lila closer. "What's wrong?"

She pushed out of his arms, panicked. "Where's Bradley?"

"He's with my mother, Babs, and Chicki. They're taking him to get cotton candy."

Relief washed over her. Babs's and Chicki's husbands were Dark Knights, and they were both as close as family to Bones. Babs babysat Lila and Bradley, and Chicki owned the salon where Sarah worked. She trusted them and Red, Bones's mother, explicitly, but that didn't stop her fear from tumbling out. "You've got to let me know before you let someone else watch him."

"You're absolutely right. I was just coming to tell you, but one of the nurses from the hospital cornered me. I'm sorry." He drew her closer and then held her even tighter. "You're shaking."

"Damn right I'm shaking," she said, trying to calm her remaining panic. "I thought my baby was lost. I need to see him. Can we—"

Bones was already on the move, barreling through the crowd with Sarah tucked against his side. He did that a lot, and she didn't think she'd ever get used to the pulse of heat seeping from his body to hers. He hollered to Scott as they passed, and Scott joined them, making a beeline for the cotton-candy vendor.

"He's with Red, Chicki, and Babs," Sarah explained. The relief on her brother's face was as pure and present as her own.

"Thank God," Scott said. "I told you it was going to be okay. Bones would never let anything happen to Bradley."

"Not a chance," Bones said fiercely. "I didn't mean to alarm you guys. I was heading over to tell Sarah when I got snagged by a nurse."

Bones pointed to Bradley sitting on Chicki's lap in the grass beside Red and Babs, dousing the last of Sarah's lingering panic. Bradley had sticky blue cotton candy all over his cheeks, and he was giggling as he held the sugary puff out toward Red. Red leaned forward, making a dramatic show of taking a big bite of the sticky treat, and then Babs did the same. Bradley giggled, and Chicki hugged him.

Sarah might be wary of fully trusting anyone, but seeing those women love up her son made her warm all over, and embarrassment for overreacting after Bones and his family had done so much for them nearly swallowed her whole. In addition to everything else the Whiskeys had done for her and her family, after Scott's injuries had cost him his new job, the Whiskeys introduced him to the guys down at the marina, where he now worked.

Before she could apologize to Bones, Quincy, Truman's younger brother, hollered "Scott" from across the street. He was with Isabel and Jed, Crystal's brother. "Dude, want to hang with us?"

Scott glanced at Sarah. "You okay? I'll stay if you want me to."

"I'm fine. Go have fun. We'll catch up later."

As Sarah watched Scott cross the street, she noticed his limp was a little more pronounced and was glad he had his cane in the car in case he needed it. He had a permanent plate and pins in one leg. He'd been fortunate in his healing, and his doctors no longer anticipated future surgeries. He still had days when he couldn't do as much as he would like, but at least he was out of the woods.

"Sarah, I'm really sorry," Bones said, pulling her back to the moment.

When he looked at her as he was now, gazing deeply into her eyes like he meant every word, it was hard to concentrate. She liked to look at him *too much*, and she found herself trying to put the pieces of his life into some semblance that she could understand. He didn't look like a biker, and yet the club was a huge part of his life. He was tall and clean-cut, and he didn't have any tattoos like most of the other bikers did. At least none that she'd seen. Then again, Bones didn't need ink to underscore his badassery. He had a commanding presence made even more powerful by the angular cut of his jaw and his piercing dark eyes. He was the kind of man women lusted after and men looked up to.

She shifted her gaze back to her son and said, "I know. It's okay. I'm just overprotective."

"As you should be. When I saw the fear in your eyes, I felt

horrible."

The emotion in his voice drew her gaze back to his. She had no business noticing anything about him, much less letting her overactive imagination run wild. Bones could have any woman he wanted. She wasn't fooling herself into thinking he'd be crazy enough to want a pregnant woman with two children. Besides, she'd made the mistake of trusting kind words and sexy eyes before. She couldn't afford to fall into that dark place again.

"How about a smile from this pretty little lady's beautiful mommy?" He tickled Lila's chin, earning sweet baby giggles.

Her insides melted when he did things like that. It was no wonder she was a mess of confusion around him. She desired him so much she ached with it, but her mind continually threw out warnings and barricades in the form of painful memories.

She flashed a quick smile and then headed for Bradley before her hormones had a chance to overreact again. When Bones's hand landed on her lower back, she forced herself to focus on Red, who was tickling Bradley's cheek with a blade of grass, instead of the delicious warmth his touch created inside her. It wasn't an easy task, distracting herself from such an enticing creature, but she was determined. She studied the three women, who acted like sisters although they looked as different as could be. There was one thing about their appearance they had in common, though: They emanated strength and resilience like Sarah had never before seen. Maybe it was because they were bikers' wives, or maybe they were born that way.

Sometimes Sarah felt strong, but at other times she felt like she had a magnet on her back, drawing bad shit from every direction and it was all she could do to duck and cover.

"THERE'S MAMA AND Sissy," Babs said to Bradley as they approached. Bones had known Babs his whole life. Her long blond hair always looked windswept, and her clothes were constantly disheveled, but she was as warm as she was tough.

Red smiled up at them and said, "Escorted by my big, brave boy." With her fair skin and short hair, it was hard to believe she had birthed three dark boys. But like them, she was a biker through and through, and she almost always dressed in black, from her T-shirt and jeans right down to her chunky leather boots.

Bones ruffled Bradley's hair, and Bradley flashed a sugary-blue toothy grin.

"Hey, Red. Ladies." Bones leaned down and kissed his mother's cheek. "Will I ever graduate to being called a *man* instead of a *boy*?"

"That's what *other* women see you as," Chicki said, her legs tucked beside her. She was the most fashionable of her friends, exotic almost, with olive skin, dark hair she often pulled back in a severe bun, and a penchant for colorful blouses and zipping around on sky-high heels. "No matter how big and bad you are, to us you'll always be the boy who toddled around naked in the backyard, saying, 'Check this out!' and then doing a hip swivel to make your willy swing around."

Christ. He was in his thirties. Would they ever stop bringing up this shit?

Sarah snort-laughed as she sat down beside Chicki, quickly covering her mouth. Her beautiful brown eyes flicked up to his, dancing with amusement. Damn she was gorgeous. Sometimes those eyes of hers looked troubled and haunted or a million miles away, and other times, like now, they were carefree and innocent, even if it lasted for only a few brief seconds. He wanted to capture those seconds in a glass, treasure them, and give her more reasons to feel that way.

"You think that's funny, do you?" he said to Sarah. "I bet your mother has some embarrassing stories about you, too."

Sarah's face blanched, and pain appeared in her eyes.

"My grandma is in heaven," Bradley said matter-of-factly. He thrust his cotton candy at Lila, who grabbed a fistful and began sucking it off her fingers.

Man, I'm batting a thousand today.

Bones touched Sarah's shoulder and said, "I'm sorry. I didn't realize…"

"It's okay," she mumbled just as Lila shoved her sticky fingers into Sarah's mouth. Sarah gently moved her daughter's wrist, keeping her from putting her sticky hand elsewhere, and smiled lovingly, the pain instantly disappearing. "*Mm.* Thank you, Lila boo."

It was *that* smile, the one she shared only with her children, that had first captured Bones's attention when he'd seen her in the hospital after her accident. Sarah was as guarded as a wounded bird, but when it came to her children, she was strong, open, and loving. He wondered what had happened in her life to make her so untrusting of others.

"Here come the troops." Red pointed across to the sidewalk, where Bullet, Finlay, and Tinkerbell led a pack of their siblings and friends, a motley crew of princesses and the worst-looking, hairy, thick-legged cheerleaders Bones had ever seen.

Babs nudged Chicki. "They look like they're ready to go have some fun before trick or treating. Come on, girls. Let's let these young'uns do their thing."

"Thank you for watching Bradley," Sarah said. "Bradley, say thank you, honey."

Bradley threw his arms around Chicki's neck and said, "Thank you!" His high-pitched voice rang out as he scrambled off her lap and into Red's, doling out more hugs and kisses. Then he threw himself into Babs's arms.

Bones wondered if he missed his own grandmother.

Sarah went up on her knees, and he helped her to her feet, drawing her body against his and holding her there for a beat just to see her blush. As if on cue, her cheeks flushed, and she put space between them. If she blushed when he held her, what would she do when he got his mouth and hands on her? When he poured his desires into pleasuring her?

I can't wait to find out.

He'd always found pregnancy a time of wonder and beauty, but he'd never been attracted to a pregnant woman before Sarah. There was something about the sweet, sexy blonde, pregnant belly and all, that had drawn him in from the start. She was feminine, and yet she resonated inner strength like a watchful soldier who had seen too much darkness. The thought made his blood simmer, though he had no idea if he was reading her right. He had all types of women vying for his attention, but he rarely dated women from Peaceful Harbor, preferring to keep his conquests far away from his turf, protecting his reputation with the same vehemence he protected his family. But with Sarah, he had no choice. There was an unstoppable force driving him toward her—and for once in his life it wasn't his head, but his heart.

"Thank you for letting Bradley ride in your sidecar and monopolize your attention during the parade," Sarah said as she adjusted Lila on her hip.

"He's a great boy. I enjoy having him around." He raked his eyes down her body, lowered his voice, and tried to earn the sexy blush he loved. "I'd like to take you for a *ride* sometime." Her eyes widened, and he worried he'd pushed too far, so he added, "In my sidecar."

His mother and her friends rose to their feet, watching him with a spark of intuition, as if they sensed his feelings for Sarah growing right before their eyes. Damn, he hated that spark. He swore they had some kind of truth radar, having caught him and his siblings weaving stories on too many occasions to count when they were kids. He shifted on his feet, turning away from them and toward Sarah. He didn't know much about her background. She evaded questions about her past and the children's father—or *fathers*—like armor deflected bullets. She'd mentioned an *ex*, but he didn't know if she was married and using *ex* figuratively, hiding out from an actual *ex*, or if she was just cautious in general. She had two beautiful children, was pregnant with another man's child, and *still* she had invaded his darkest fantasies and provoked protective urges well beyond what he was used to. There was no denying the burn of attraction he felt, but the idea of messing around with another man's woman wasn't even on his radar.

He glanced down at the precious girl in Sarah's arms, who was watching him with smiling blue eyes. The difference between Lila's trusting gaze and Sarah's guarded one was inescapable. He hoped to fix that, but first he needed answers.

An embarrassed smile lifted Sarah's lips, and she said, "I'm sorry I freaked out about Bradley. My greatest fear is something happening to my children."

"I should have realized. I'll never give you a scare like that again."

Bones was a protector by nature, but his desire to protect Sarah and her children was like a bone-deep ache he couldn't, and didn't want to, shake. He didn't know if it was because he'd watched each of his brothers find love and they'd never been happier, or if what his mother had told him so long ago was really true. *When you find the one person who you're meant to be with, nothing can change it.* All he knew was that if Sarah was married, if she was spoken for on any level and all he could do was admire her from afar, he'd do whatever it took to show her that she could trust him.

"Who's ready for trick or treating?" Finlay asked as Tinkerbell pulled her toward Bradley.

"Tink!" Bradley stood up, and Tinkerbell pushed her big head forward, licking his face so hard he plopped down on his butt, giggling.

Bones crouched between them and grabbed Tinkerbell's collar. "You okay, B-boy?"

"Yes," Bradley said through fits of giggles. "Let her go!"

"How about we get you on your feet first?" Bones helped him up and put one arm around his waist as Tinkerbell bathed him in doggy kisses. The boy needed a puppy his size, but Bones imagined the last thing his mama needed was another mouth to feed, train, or care for.

Red and her friends said quick hellos before heading off to find their husbands.

"Looks like your boy's got a bodyguard," Finlay said to Sarah.

Bones glanced at Sarah, who was watching him warily. It was rare for him to be on this end of scrutiny. He saved lives for a living. Most people looked up to him, valued his word as if it were golden, and he tried to live up to that. What would it take to earn Sarah's trust? And where the hell was the lucky bastard who had earned her heart and fathered her children?

"Come on, B-boy," Bones said as he rose to his feet. "Let's show these guys how trick or treating is done."

"Shoulders! Shoulders!" Bradley jumped up and down, arms stretched up toward the sky, earning an excited *woof* from Tinkerbell.

As Bones lifted Bradley onto his shoulders, Sarah touched his arm and said, "You don't have to…"

Bones winked. "I don't usually do things because I have to. I do them because I want to."

"Uncle Be*ah*, I want a shoulder ride like Uncle Boney is giving Bradley. *Please?*" Kennedy pleaded, looking precious in her little football uniform complete with shoulder pads, cleats, and a pink tiara. Truman had taken her to a high school football game, and she'd been enamored with the sport ever since. Kennedy was such a girly-girl, so they'd all been floored when she decided to be a football player for Halloween instead of a cheerleader.

"Sure thing, sugar pop." Bear hoisted her up to his shoulders.

Bear was the most emotional and lighthearted of his siblings. Bones had no idea how, with all he'd been through over the years. His affable personality had saved their family in more ways than one. When Bones had been away at school and Bullet was on tour with the military, their father had suffered a stroke. Bear had just graduated high school, and he'd put his life on hold to take over their family business, Whiskey Bro's, and eventually, after their uncle passed away, Whiskey's Automotive. He'd not only kept them solvent over the years, but he'd helped them flourish, all while taking care of the homestead so

Bones could put focus on becoming a doctor and Bullet could give himself over to their country. Now it was Bear's turn to follow his dream, and Bones couldn't be happier for him. He'd married Crystal several months ago and was currently designing motorcycles for the elite Silver-Stone Cycles. And because he loved the business so much, he continued working part-time at the auto shop as well. Bones was in awe of each of his brothers and their accomplishments, and he would forever be thankful for Bear's selfless generosity.

Kennedy set her pink tiara on Bear's head and said, "Now you *weally* look like a cheerleader!"

"Only for you, Ken," Bear said with a shake of his head.

"Where's Dixie?" Bones asked.

"Penny and Izzy dragged her off with Jed, Quincy, and Scott," Crystal explained.

"Penny said they were going to do *single-people things*, which was quickly followed by a waggle of Quincy's brows," Gemma said.

Bones glanced at Sarah. *I'd like to do single-people things with you.* As if she'd read his thoughts, she blushed and looked away.

Bullet grunted something Bones couldn't make out. Like the rest of the guys, he looked ridiculous in his cheerleading outfit, with two pom-poms sticking out of his back pocket, but he was six foot five, and there wasn't a man alive stupid enough to make fun of him. And like all the Whiskeys, there was nothing they wouldn't do for Kennedy.

"Shoot. I forgot the stroller," Sarah said.

"I'll carry her." Bones reached for Lila. "Come here, peanut."

Sarah turned her shoulder toward him. "You've already got Bradley."

Bones reached up and put one hand on Bradley's back and waved his other hand. "And I've got a free arm."

"Mommy, he's a good holder," Bradley said, patting Bones on the head. "He's holded me a lot."

She blinked up at Bones with an apology in her beautiful brown eyes. "It's okay. I can carry her."

Lila reached for Bones. He stuck his finger out, and she wrapped her tiny fingers around it, pulling it toward her mouth.

"I don't doubt that you *can*," Bones said. "But this is what friends are for, lightening the load." Didn't she have close friends wherever she'd moved from? Or had they scorned her? The thought made his muscles constrict. "If you're not comfortable with me holding her—"

"No, it's fine. I'm just being—"

"A responsible mother." *Which makes you even more alluring.* "It's an admirable trait."

Sarah shook her head. Her pretty blond hair billowed around her shoulders. "But really, Bones, you can't carry them both."

"Oh boy," Finlay said, glancing knowingly at Gemma. "You haven't learned not to question the manhood of a Whiskey. They'll always prove you wrong."

"Darlin', you've got a bun in the oven and you've been out here all afternoon." Bones extended his arm. "Now, please hand over that pretty little lady. We'll walk over to your place and pick up the stroller if you'd like, and then we'll trick or treat in your neighborhood. We should probably get her hedgehog and blanket, too, in case she gets fussy." Sarah lived only three blocks away. It wasn't a long walk for him carrying the kids, but he worried about Sarah lugging a baby on her hip all evening.

Sarah gave him an incredulous look, her eyes full of wonder.

"Her hedgehog…"

"I have no idea how you got out of the house without it." Bones had given Lila a stuffed hedgehog when she got out of the hospital, and from what he'd seen, Lila rarely let it out of her sight.

Gemma sidled up to Sarah and said, "They say you can tell a lot about a man by how he treats his mother." She turned loving eyes to Truman and said, "I think you can tell more about a man by the way he treats other people's children."

Bear had befriended Truman when Truman was a teenager. A few years later, Truman had taken the fall for a crime Quincy had committed and had spent several years in prison. Shortly after being released, he'd rescued Lincoln and Kennedy, siblings he hadn't known existed, from a crack house where their mother had overdosed. He'd met and fallen in love with Gemma, and they'd since married and adopted the children, raising them as their own. The kids had come a long way. Kennedy had been afraid of everyone and everything. Now she was in preschool three mornings a week and loved being the center of attention. Truman was a good man who had been through hell and given himself wholeheartedly to others. Bones was proud to call him his *brother*.

Sarah finally relented, handing Bones her sweet baby girl with an appreciative smile. "I hate feeling like I'm taking advantage of you. You're always helping us out. One day you're going to spin around and wonder where all your free time went."

"Take advantage, darlin'." He couldn't keep the double entendre from sounding like one, and the widening of her eyes told him he'd better pull back or she just might run scared. But he wasn't great at pulling back from something he wanted, and when he caught Sarah stealing a glance at him—a very *heated* glance—he added, "As often as you'd like." Then he tipped his chin up and said, "Hang on tight, B-boy. We're about to get our trick or treat on."

Chapter Two

ALMOST TWO HOURS and several trick-or-treat stops later Bradley was fast asleep in the stroller, clutching a bag of candy, and Lila was in Bones's arms, bundled up in her favorite blanket and hugging her hedgehog. Kennedy was fighting sleep on Bullet's chest, but Lincoln was wide-awake in Truman's arms, tugging on his beard. Crystal and Bear had taken off about a half hour ago. If Sarah tried really hard, she could pretend she belonged among this close-knit group. But she'd spent a lifetime pretending, and no matter how good she was at it, it was exhausting. She'd give anything to have been born into a different family, to be free of her past without lies or fears of what people might find out about her, but she wasn't blessed in that way. She *was* blessed, however. One look at her beautiful babies, or her brother, was all it took to remind her of how lucky she truly was.

"We should probably get your little ones home to bed," Bones said as they strolled down the sidewalk. "You must be exhausted, too."

She glanced at him, and her pulse did that sprinting, crazy thing that she'd dreamed of finding as a little girl—and that fervor made fear rise up inside her. She'd screwed up once and could not afford to do it again. If it took everything she had, she was bound and determined to give her children a happy, normal life. What exactly *normal* meant, she didn't know anymore. But walking along the sidewalk with Bones, talking about the parade and her children, felt like a start, and it was surely much more *normal* than how she'd spent too much of her life—on the run, doing things she'd never imagined to keep food on the table, and believing in a man who only let her down, leaving her to start all over again.

She'd had such a good time today, she didn't want the evening to end. But she couldn't put her selfish desires before her children's need for a good night's sleep. "This has been really fun. Believe it or not, I've never been to a parade."

"You've never been to a parade?" Finlay spun around in front of her, her pink and white outfit lifting in the wind, sending Tinkerbell into a frenzy. The pup's big head swung back and forth, assessing the threat.

"Tink," Bullet said sternly, giving his thigh a single sharp slap. Tinkerbell cocked her head, whimpering at Bullet, then looked at Finlay again.

"It's okay, Tink." Finlay petted her head and said, "Parades were a staple of my youth. Where did you grow up?"

Sarah was pretty sure the response *in hell* would incite too many questions, so she said, "Florida." The last thing she wanted to do was talk about her childhood. She was sure they'd all had perfect childhoods filled with parades, parties, and pancakes with little smiley faces. The type of childhood she wanted for her children. She'd screwed that up, too, but it wasn't too late to start over. *It's never too late*, she reminded herself. That was the motto she and her siblings had lived by when they were young. A sea of longing moved through her with thoughts of her younger sister, Josie.

"Sunshine and beaches, like Peaceful Harbor. Most of the time, anyway," Gemma said with a happy sigh, pulling Sarah from her thoughts. "Well, now that you're here, you can join us for the parades and the club rallies and—" Her eyes bloomed wide, and she gasped. "When are your kids' birthdays?"

Sarah laughed softly at her quick change of topic. "Lila turns one at the end of next month, and Bradley will be four in April."

"Next month? What date?" Bones asked as they came to the corner of her street.

His lips quirked into a hopeful smile, and she wondered what he was hoping for. He had the most beautiful, full lips, the kind women paid good money to emulate. She often found herself staring at them, thinking about things she shouldn't think about, like how they'd feel pressed against hers or sliding along her neck and whether he'd kiss hard and demanding or slow and titillating. She shifted her gaze to her baby in his arms to try to distract herself from those thoughts. Lila's sweet little hand rested on his jaw. Her daughter had gone to Bones without hesitation from the very first time he'd tried to hold her. Sometimes Sarah was jealous of that easy trust, wishing she could muster it. But other times her daughter's trusting innocence underscored Sarah's responsibility to watch out for her children and protect them from snakes in the grass.

"Birthday?" he said with an amused grin.

Oh crap. She'd forgotten he was waiting for an answer. "November thirtieth."

"Dude," Truman said in a low voice. "Now, that's what Gemma would call *fate*."

"Fate?" Sarah had a love-hate relationship with ethereal things like fate. Before moving to Peaceful Harbor, her life had been too awful to believe some higher power was guiding it. She'd believed fate was something weak people relied upon. But then Scott had found his way to working on the oil rigs, she'd escaped her father's wrath, and eventually, Josie had, too, giving her hope that some guiding light would lead them all to happiness. But then she'd landed on the streets. Every time happiness was within her grasp, it was torn away, proving time and time again that fate was for the weak—and surviving was for the strong.

"That's my birthday, too." Bones pressed his tempting lips to her daughter's forehead, earning a sleepy murmur from Lila. "No wonder I adore this little lady so much."

The man was a walking ovary explosion.

"We have to throw a joint birthday party!" Gemma said. "I'll bring dress-up clothes for the kids." She owned Princess for a Day Boutique, where she hosted children's parties and offered a variety of costumes and themes. She'd hired Sarah to do the kids' hair for two parties recently, and Sarah had loved seeing so many happy, creative kids in one place.

Finlay clapped her hands. "That's perfect!"

"You don't have to do that," Sarah interjected. "I usually just make a cake and get them a little something."

"I think it sounds like a great idea," Bones said, gazing down at her daughter. "Turning one is a big deal. She deserves fanfare. Why don't we do it on Thanksgiving? Everyone will be there anyway. I'm hosting it at my place."

Everyone agreed, and as Finlay and Gemma talked about themes, Sarah touched Bones's sleeve to get his attention, speaking just above a whisper. "We can't just take over your family's Thanksgiving."

"Darlin', you became family the second Bullet pulled you from that burning car. Have Thanksgiving with us. You and the kids and Scott belong there."

She'd never belonged *anywhere*. He couldn't imagine the way that made her feel all gooey and happy inside.

"Of *course* they're going to join us," Finlay said. "I've got a whole allergen-free feast planned. I've been menu planning for the past two weeks."

Now she wanted to cry. *Stupid pregnancy hormones.* They made her overly emotional. And when Bones was around, horny as a cat in heat. Struggling to force those emotions down deep she said, "But it will take me a lifetime to repay you for everything you've already done for us. And you don't even know us that well. We could be bad people."

"What the fu—"

"Bullet!" Finlay cut him off, eyeing Kennedy in his arms.

Bones shook his head, looking at Sarah like she'd lost her mind.

"I think we'd know if you were a bad person by now," Gemma said. "At least our guys would. They have a sixth sense for trouble."

"But how does that work exactly? That sixth sense?" Sarah asked, but it came out like more of a plea, because she wanted to possess that skill desperately. Was she the only person in the world who didn't have that knack, or were they just too naive to realize some people were masters at hiding their true colors? "How can you tell if someone is bad or good after just a couple of months?"

Bones, Bullet, and Truman exchanged an incredulous glance.

"All I need is about two minutes," Bullet said.

"From what I've seen," Sarah said, "people can change without warning."

"That can happen," Bones said in a serious tone. "And sometimes good people do bad things and then redeem themselves and make things right."

He looked deeply into her eyes, and she wondered if he saw the dark memories of her past dragging her down. She was sure there was a special place in hell for men like her father and her ex. But what about people like her? She had to believe in redemption, at least in certain cases. If not, she was screwed.

"Don't worry, darlin'," Bones said. "You're one of us now. We'd never let anything happen to you."

"Thank you. That means the world to me, but I still wish I knew how to spot bad people."

"I'll show you." He must have seen a modicum of relief in her eyes, because he slipped his arm around her waist, pulling her closer as he lowered his mouth beside her ear and said, "Not all types of bad are harmful. Some are very, *very* good." Then he locked those dark eyes on hers, making her stomach go ten types of crazy, and said, "I can teach you to spot *all* kinds of bad."

Her jaw dropped open, and he gave her an *I didn't mean to go so far but I sort of did* crooked grin that made her *almost* laugh.

"Down, bro," Bullet said. "We don't need the dirty doctor making this sweetheart go into labor right here on the street."

Bones glowered at Bullet; then he turned that devastating gaze on Sarah again and said, "Say yes to Thanksgiving and a joint birthday party, darlin'."

"Yes," Finlay said. "Please do, Sarah."

"And don't mind these guys," Gemma added. "They always talk like that."

"If you're sure…?" she asked carefully.

"Absofrigginglutely." Bones leaned closer to Lila and whispered, "We're celebrating together, peanut."

Gemma peeled Kennedy from Bullet's massive chest. "On that adorable note, I think we'll get our babies home to bed, too."

Kennedy sighed, her sleepy eyes closing again as she cuddled in her mama's arms.

"I'll hit you guys up this week," Truman said to the guys.

"Sounds good, man," Bullet replied.

Finlay looked at Sarah and said, "I'll call you and we'll figure out a time to get together after the wedding to plan the birthday party."

"Okay, thanks. That sounds like fun." She glanced at her baby girl sleeping cozily in Bones's arms. *Turning one is a big deal. She deserves fanfare.* She did deserve fanfare, and Bones recognizing that fact made it an even bigger deal.

Finlay wrapped her arms around Bullet and gazed up at him with stars in her eyes. "I still can't believe we're getting married next weekend. Who plans a wedding that fast?"

"A gnarly, possessive biker who wants to get a ring on your finger before you realize what a mistake you're making," Bones said with a smirk.

"Damn right," Bullet said.

"Thank goodness Cassie has the time to cater," Finlay said. Cassie owned Messy Buns and Muffin Tops Bakery in the heart of Peaceful Harbor. "What kind of caterer can't take care of her own wedding?"

"A busy one," Sarah said. "I have no idea how you do as

much as you do, with working at the bar, your catering company, *and* planning your wedding."

Finlay leaned into Bullet's side and said, "The wedding planning was simple. As long as family and friends are there, nothing else really matters. We didn't even have to send out invitations. Bullet put out the word about the date, and it quickly spread to all of the Dark Knights members. We had more help than we could have ever needed."

"That's my girl." Bullet embraced her, and Tinkerbell shoved her nose between them. Bullet reached down to pet her, eyeing Finlay lasciviously. "Come on, Fins. Let's get home and have our own Halloween celebration."

The girls hugged, careful not to wake the little ones, and then Bones walked Sarah home, his arm firmly and protectively around her, as he'd been doing for weeks.

When they reached the house, she was filled with a sense of peace that had taken some getting used to. She'd never had a home where she'd felt completely safe until she'd found Scott and they'd moved here. Scott had texted earlier to tell her not to walk home alone and to text him when she was ready to leave. But she'd let him know she had an entourage watching out for her tonight, and she had to admit that felt good, too. And Bones's attention? That was right up on her Things That Feel Good but Make Me Nervous list.

Even with Bones making her as nervous as a teenager, feeling safe was such an incredible sensation, she wanted to linger in it and soak it up.

"What are you thinking about?" Bones asked as he lifted the stroller onto the small front porch.

"Nothing," she said, because how silly would she sound if she told him the truth?

"Here, let me." His big fingers wrapped around hers as he took the keys. "That wasn't *nothing*. Your eyes went soft, the way they do when you look at your children."

She shifted her eyes to her boy, sleeping in the stroller. She felt the same sense of peace and knew he was right. "Do you notice that much about everyone?"

He unlocked the door and pushed it open without responding. His gaze swept over the cozy living room of the two-bedroom rambler, separated only by a half wall to the kitchen. Plastic toys were spread over the coffee table and floor. Stuffed animals and kids' books littered the sofa.

"Oh gosh. I'd say excuse the mess, but you've been here often enough that you know this is pretty much how we live."

He smiled and said, "Your house is just how it should be. My mother always used to say that you should be able to tell who lives in a house with a single glance. That a lived-in house is a house full of love. It's the impeccably clean ones you have to worry about."

"No wonder I like Red so much."

"She likes you, too," he said casually, but there was nothing casual about the way he looked at her. His gaze turned serious, and he said, "I'm about ready to show up here with curtains for those glass doors. I know you have a fenced-in backyard, but you can't be too safe."

She winced. When they'd first moved in, they'd hung a sheet over the glass doors that led from the kitchen to the backyard. Curtains hadn't exactly been a top priority, though she'd heeded his worries, bought fabric, and had begun making curtains. "I'm almost done making them."

She bent to unbuckle the straps of the stroller, and Bones touched her arm.

"I'll carry him in," he offered.

He transferred Lila to Sarah's arms, tucking the blanket around her and her hedgehog. He started to lower his lips to her baby's forehead; then he looked at Sarah, silently seeking approval. She nodded, wondering if he'd kissed Lila earlier without realizing he had done it. Because he'd done it so naturally, and on several occasions, she imagined that was the case.

He closed his eyes as he pressed those beautiful lips gently to her daughter's head, and then he whispered, "Sleep well, little lady."

He gathered Bradley in his arms and followed her inside. Bones had been in her house many times, but as he followed her down the narrow hallway, she realized they'd never been alone.

BONES WAITED IN the doorway as Sarah changed Lila's diaper on a pad on top of the dresser. Too drawn to them to stay away, he stepped into the bedroom she shared with her children. That seemed to be the story of his life lately, *being drawn to Sarah and her children*. He stood beside her as she buttoned Lila's sleeper.

"I can't believe she stayed asleep through that." He gazed down at the baby with awe as Sarah lifted her into her arms, cradling her against her breasts.

She kissed the baby's head and said, "She's always been a great sleeper, unlike my little man. Believe it or not, he didn't sleep through the night until a few weeks after we moved here." She laid Lila in the crib, tucked her blanket around her, and set her hedgehog in the corner of the mattress.

"What about pajamas for B-boy?" Bones whispered.

She grabbed a set of Batman pajamas from a dresser drawer. "If you lay him on the bed, I can change him."

"Shouldn't he use the bathroom first?"

Her smile told him she knew all the tricks. "He'll wake up just enough to go while I change him."

Bones laid him on the bed and helped her carefully remove his little black boots.

As she changed him into his pajamas, Bradley's eyes fluttered open. "Mommy, where's my candy?"

Bones chuckled at his priorities.

"It's tucked away in a safe place until tomorrow." She helped him sit up and said, "Let's use the potty, and then you can go nighty-night."

Bradley's eyes shifted sleepily to Bones. "Can Bones take me?" he asked with a yawn, drawing out his words.

Sarah glanced at Bones, and for reasons he had yet to fully understand, he hoped like hell she'd trust him enough to do it.

"Only if Bones doesn't mind," she said.

"Not at all," he said as casually as he could. "Come on, buddy. Show me to your throne."

Bradley slipped off the bed and took his hand, leading him toward the hall. "What's a throne?"

Bones explained that throne was a cooler way to say *toilet* as Bradley used the toilet. Their house had only one bathroom, and though Bones tried not to be nosy, it was impossible to miss the netting of plastic toys attached to the side of the bathtub or the bottles of Johnson's baby shampoo, body wash, and bubble bath. Hanging from a basket around the showerhead was a bottle of generic body wash. A tiny black towel with the Batman insignia on the back, a hood, and ears hung on a hook on the wall beside a tiny pink towel with a hood and fairy wings.

He helped Bradley wash his hands, spotting a Batman toothbrush in a cute little holder with a bottle of SpongeBob toothpaste and a tiny paper cup dispenser with colorful designs on the cups. Sarah's and Scott's toothbrushes stood upright in a plastic cup, and a tube of store-brand toothpaste lay beside it. It didn't surprise him that while Sarah didn't have much, she took extra care for her kids.

"We should probably brush your teeth, huh?"

Bradley nodded, rubbing his eyes as Bones put toothpaste on the brush and handed it to him. He wrapped his little fingers around it and halfheartedly brushed one side of his teeth.

Bones crouched before him. "How about if I help you?"

Bradley relinquished the toothbrush and opened his mouth—obviously he knew the drill, while Bones was playing catch-up. He helped Bradley brush his teeth; then he filled a paper cup and handed it to him. "Do you know how to rinse without swallowing the toothpaste?"

Bradley nodded, filled his mouth with water, and then leaned way over the sink and spit into it, dribbling on his chest in the process.

"Good job, buddy. But I think we should take that shirt off before you go to bed." He took Bradley's shirt off, and Bradley wrapped his arms around Bones's neck and rested his head on his shoulder. Bones wondered again where the kids' father was. Other than Sarah's sister, who had visited only once, he knew no one had come to see them at the hospital. Was her husband a deadbeat? Or worse? Was he dead? He wondered again if there were more than one father to consider.

One thing was for sure. If these kids had a single deadbeat

father or two separate loser fathers, he'd wish he was dead if Bones got ahold of him.

He carried Bradley back to the bedroom and found Sarah gazing down at Lila again. She looked up as they walked in, her gaze sweeping over Bradley's bare back, and covered her smiling lips.

"We brushed his teeth," Bones explained.

"You didn't have to do that. I would have warned you. He can't spit without dribbling down his front."

She tossed Bradley's dirty pajama shirt into a hamper in the corner of the room and grabbed a clean shirt from the dresser.

Bones held Bradley as she put his pajama top on. Then he laid him in the bed and covered him with the blanket. He looked tiny and vulnerable in the big bed. "Does he get a stuffed toy?"

She shook her head. "He doesn't have a favorite. He likes to cuddle his blanket."

"Night, B-boy." He brushed his fingers over Bradley's forehead. "Sweet dreams."

They left the door open a crack as they left, and Sarah walked Bones to the front door. He didn't want to leave, much less leave her alone without Scott there. Hell, he wanted to lay his emotions on the line, ask the questions he needed answers to. But he had a feeling she'd shut him out completely if he tried, and he wasn't about to risk that.

"When's Scott going to be home?" he asked.

"Soon. He texted while you were in the bathroom. He's on his way."

Bones nodded, still reluctant to leave. He gathered the candy from the stroller and the baby bag she'd hooked over the handle and set them inside the door. Sarah yawned, looking adorable *and* exhausted. He saw so much in her beautiful brown eyes—love for her children, secrets, *warnings*—and even though she looked away quickly, as she'd done so often when he felt the buzz of electricity sparking between them, he hadn't missed the *desire* brimming in her eyes.

He touched his fingertips to hers, and her eyes flicked cautiously up to his.

"You asked me earlier if I noticed as much about others as I do you," he said softly. "I'm not sure of the answer. It's hard not to notice little things about you, like the way you blush when I touch you and the way your love for your children and your strength as a woman radiate like the sun." Her cheeks flushed, and he said, "I don't know what you've been through, but I want you to know you have friends here. Friends you can trust. And I hope one day you'll see more than that in me."

Her eyes skirted nervously around the room before finally returning to him. The haunted look in them was undeniable.

He lifted her hand and pressed a kiss to the back of it, and since that wasn't enough, he drew her into his arms and said, "Thank you for letting me help put the kids to bed."

He reluctantly released her and stepped onto the porch before he took the kiss he so craved. And holy fucking hell, she wore the most conflicted expression, like she was turned on and frightened at once. "Sarah…" *Who the hell hurt you? Tell me so I can slaughter him.*

She swallowed hard, and he thought better of it and said, "Don't forget to lock up behind me, okay?"

She nodded, flashing an *almost* smile as she closed the door. After he heard the lock sink into place, he sat on the porch step waiting for Scott to arrive.

Chapter Three

THURSDAY EVENING SARAH hung up her black hairdressing apron in the back room of Chicki's salon and gathered her things, mentally ticking off items on her to-do list. She loved working at the salon, and took pride in earning a living and showing her children that being self-sufficient was a good thing. It was also a great opportunity to get to know people in the community. Every time she picked up a pair of scissors, she filled with a sense of accomplishment for how far she'd come.

"Hey, baby girl," Chicki said as she walked in the back door. "Heading out for the night?"

Chicki, Red, and Babs had called her names like *baby girl* since the first time they'd met. While it had felt strange coming from women who barely knew her, now Sarah found herself tucking those endearments away alongside other small reminders—like their hugs and the love the three women lavished on her babies—that even though her mother hadn't been loving or even kind, she was worthy of both.

"Yes. I wasn't expecting you tonight. Are you shorthanded? Do you need me to stay?"

Though Chicki owned the salon, she worked only a few

hours each month. Regardless, she always looked perfectly put together, from her coiffed hair to her crimson lipstick and smoky eyes. She wore her hair down today, parted on the side. It fell in soft waves, skimming her shoulders and giving her a youthful appearance. Her black wrap shirt was belted around the waist, accentuating her ample bosom and rounded hips. She wore a pair of black skinny jeans and heels that Sarah would topple off of with her first step.

"No. I just came in to get something from the office. Your babies need their mama, and your feet must be killing you."

"Not really, and I had a great day. Isla came in for a trim." Isla was one of Chicki's daughters. She was in her early twenties and ran their family's flower shop, Petal Me Hard. She was also about as rebellious as a girl could be. Sarah envied women like Isla. Women with normal families and normal lives, where they chose to rebel instead of being forced to find a way out.

Chicki scowled. "That little rascal made sure to come in when I wasn't here. She's on my shit list at the moment."

"Uh-oh," Sarah said. "What did she do this time?" She'd seen Chicki and Isla knock heads on more than one occasion, but no matter how much of a hard-ass Chicki was, she never let her daughter walk out the door without a hug and an *I love you*.

"What hasn't she done? That girl has been skirting lines since she could bat her pretty, long lashes." Chicki pointed at Sarah and said, "You should hope you're having a boy this time. Girls can be snarky, secretive, and so emotional they can make you crazy, while boys might be visceral, but at least they don't keep you guessing. They tell you when you piss them off." She shook her head, going off on a tangent in Spanish that Sarah couldn't understand. Then she blew out a breath and said, "Right now baby Lila is as sweet as can be. But one day she'll discover boys, and then your whole world will be turned topsy-turvy. You'll go from worrying about whether she'll find friends at school to hoping she doesn't get herself pregnant."

Sarah thought back to her childhood. She'd never even had the chance to discover boys. From the time she was twelve and had gotten her period, her parents had called her horrible names, as if they'd assumed she'd been sleeping with every male within a hundred miles. She pushed those thoughts away as she left the salon and drove to the grocery store. She considered herself lucky for somehow innately knowing she wasn't the cause of her parents' hatred. She didn't know the sex of her unborn child, and she didn't care. She knew it was a survivor, and whether it was a rebellious girl or a headstrong boy, it would never know anything but love. She hoped that was enough for all of her children to keep them from ever being cruel to others, despite sharing their father's genetic makeup.

After making a quick stop at the grocery store, she picked up Bradley and Lila from Babs and headed home, listening to Bradley chatter about playing at the park with Babs and Red. Bones's motorcycle was parked out front. She should be used to seeing him, since he was there almost every evening helping Scott with the basement. Still, her pulse quickened as memories of the other night rushed back to her. She slung her purse over her shoulder and climbed from the car, trying to distract herself. But there was no distraction big enough to sway her overzealous pregnancy hormones, which had been on overdrive from the moment he'd followed her into the house on Halloween night. She could still feel his fingers brushing against hers and could smell his virile maleness. Her heart beat faster as she thought of the way he'd looked at her babies, like they were the most beautiful creatures in the world. When he'd *thanked her* for allowing him to help her put them to bed, she'd gotten all choked up. Their own father had seen them as an imposition for so long, so she'd always been prepared for the worst. Her body heated with memories of Bones imploring her to trust him, the feel of his warm, soft lips on her hand. She'd been struck mute, unable to do more than nod. It didn't help that Scott had told her that Bones had sat on the porch until he'd come home just in case she'd needed anything.

"Bones is here!" Bradley yelled as she opened his door to help him out. He tugged at the straps of his car seat. "Hurry, Mommy! Let me out. I want to help Uncle Scott and Bones!"

She drew in a deep breath to try to clear her mind as Bradley wiggled out of his seat and sprinted across the yard. "Don't get in their way," she called after him as she went to get Lila, who was waving her arms and kicking her feet excitedly.

"I've got ya, Lila boo," she said as she lifted her into her arms. "Do you want to see Bones, too?"

Lila leaned forward in her arms, as if she could propel her mother to walk faster.

"Hold your horses, little lady." *Little lady.* Had she spent so much time with hugely helpful Bones that she was picking up his vocabulary? She *had* noticed how much she liked the way it sounded when he said it, like Lila was special to him. She kissed her baby girl on the cheek. "Too much love is never a bad thing, right, boo?"

She grabbed the plastic grocery bags with her free hand and bumped the door closed with her hip, steeling herself against the wave of anticipation she was trying so hard to ignore.

Inside the house, she heard Bradley's high-pitched voice floating up from the basement, followed by Bones's hearty laughter. She set the grocery bags on the kitchen counter and then set Lila down on the floor with her toys in the living room so she could put up the baby gate at the top of the basement stairs. Lila wasn't walking yet, but she crawled like Speed Racer and she loved to pull herself up to her feet.

As Sarah toed off her shoes and gathered Lila's toys, she heard Bradley telling Scott and Bones about his day. Her remarkable little boy had settled in nicely to their new world. She wondered how much of their old life he remembered, but she was too afraid to ask, for fear of stirring up unpleasant memories. He hadn't seen her ex push her around, but there was no escaping the nastiness in his voice or the horrible, unfeeling things he'd said toward the end about the kids.

They had a good life now, and that's what she focused on.

"Come on, boo. Time to make dinner." She gathered a few of Lila's toys and brought them, along with her sweet girl, into the kitchen to play while she cooked.

Her nerves got the better of her as she made dinner and thought about Bones. It was silly, really. She was sure she had read too much into that kiss on the hand and the look in his eyes. *God.* Why was she so nervous? *Because you want the hand kiss to have meant something.*

Ugh. Did she? *No.* She'd been through too much to even entertain the idea of a man like Bones being interested in her. He was probably one of those guys who liked to rescue women, and she did *not* need rescuing, *thank you very much.*

She hoisted Lila onto her hip and headed downstairs.

Every step caused her stomach to dip like she was on a roller coaster.

Stupid pregnancy hormones.

As she descended the steps, voices became clear. They had been working on the basement for a few weeks, and the framing was already up for a bedroom and a recreation room. Scott was working on hanging drywall in the recreation room, while Bones was crouched beside Bradley in what would become the bedroom. Her pulse sped up, the way it always did at her first glance of the handsome man whose big body made her son seem even smaller. His hair was brushed away from his face, and he was totally focused on Bradley, who wore the toy tool belt Scott had bought for him and clutched a hammer in his right hand.

Bones placed his hand over Bradley's and said, "Remember how I taught you to hit the nail?"

"Square on my head," Bradley said proudly.

Bones chuckled. "Square on *the* head." He showed Bradley the head of the nail and patiently explained what he meant.

"Square on the head," Bradley repeated.

She watched as they banged the nail into the drywall, her heart filling with happiness for her boy.

"It's coming along, huh?" Scott said, jarring her from her reverie.

"Yeah. How's your leg?" Sometimes she worried that he was pushing himself too hard.

Scott made a face that told of his irritation at being mothered. She couldn't blame him. How crazy must it be for him after more than a decade of living alone to suddenly have a sister he barely knew anymore and her family move in with him? When the basement was finished, Scott was moving downstairs and giving up the master bedroom for Sarah. She hadn't asked for it and had fought him on the idea, but he'd insisted. He'd never once made her feel like an imposition, but he made no effort to hide the fact that he didn't need to be mothered.

"A better question is, how are you?" Scott asked. "You've

been on your feet all day."

"I'm fine." She'd always loved being pregnant, even the first few months when she was tired all the time. She hadn't experienced that fatigue with this pregnancy, which was probably because she had been so busy trying to scrape together enough money to stay off the streets with her children. Slowing down hadn't been an option. "Dinner's ready. I came down to get Bradley."

"Dinner!" Bradley tore out of the bedroom. "Come on, Bones! Dinnertime!" He bolted up the stairs.

"Slow down and wash your hands," she called after him.

Bones sauntered out of the bedroom, his eyes locked on her, and all her nerves flamed. Should she thank him for sitting guard outside her house the other night, or tell him she didn't need protecting? That would sound bitchy…and maybe untrue in some regards. There was no denying the comfort that Bones and his family had given her, embracing her the way they had. She'd have been in debt forever had they not hosted the fundraiser. But still, she didn't want to be seen as a damsel in distress. She hadn't survived all these years having others take care of her, and she was proud of that.

"It's nice to see you, darlin'," he said in a low voice as smooth as silk.

She felt her cheeks flush. *What is wrong with me?* She was acting like a ridiculous girl who had no experience with men. She knew how to flirt and seduce like a pro, but around Bones all the skills that had gotten her through the most difficult situations flitted away.

She shot a look at Scott to see if he'd picked up on the intimate sound of his voice. Scott flashed a knowing smile. *Oh God, you heard it, too?*

Scott turned back to the drywall, and Bones stepped closer, making her even more flustered. "How's this pretty little lady?"

He tickled Lila's foot, and Lila buried her face in Sarah's neck, giggling. Bones dragged his gaze down Sarah's body and said, "You look nice tonight."

She glanced down at her maternity jeans and white scoop-necked shirt. She'd gotten a long flowery blouse at a consignment shop, and she wore it open over her T-shirt, adding color to her outfit—and hoping to draw Bones's eyes away from her belly. It *was* a cute outfit, and she realized he was probably just being nice, not flirting. She was a little disappointed at that. "Thanks. Do you guys want some mac and cheese?" How many women would offer Bones Whiskey macaroni and cheese? Their schedules varied so much, their paths didn't usually cross at dinnertime, but what else could she do but prepare enough for all of them?

"One of my favorite meals," Bones said.

He must be a really good liar, because she believed him.

"But you're allergic to dairy," he added. "Aren't you eating?"

Just another thing to set her apart from normal people. She was allergic to dairy, gluten, nuts, and eggs. She never went anywhere without her EpiPen. "Yes. Even though my kids got lucky and they don't have food allergies, it's easier to cook for them using only foods I can eat, instead of making separate meals. Then there's no chance of contamination."

"It's delicious, dude. You should stay," Scott said.

"You sure you have enough?" Bones asked with that hopeful smile again.

She nodded, and Bones set down his hammer.

Lila leaned toward him, arms out. "Bababa."

"May I?" Bones asked as he reached for her.

Sarah handed him Lila as Scott set down his tools and glanced over, watching them intently. Could he tell Sarah was melting inside and at the same time telling herself to get the hell out of there? Or was Scott just happy that Lila was so loved?

"You look mighty good with that baby in your arms, Doc," Scott teased. "Better watch it. I hear they're contagious."

Bones scoffed. "That would take a female participant."

"What? No special lady in your life?" Sarah slammed her mouth shut, unable to believe she asked the question that had been burning in her mind for weeks.

Lila patted Bones's cheek. "Babababa."

Holding her gaze, he said, "Oh, I wouldn't say that."

BONES COULDN'T RESIST putting a hand on Sarah's back and nudging her toward the stairs. She was fucking adorable when she attempted to hide her nervousness. He followed her upstairs, trying not to stare at her gorgeous ass.

The minute they were in the kitchen, she took charge, settling Lila in her high chair and removing Bradley's plastic dinosaur from his plate. "Let's eat, then play," she suggested with a pat on his head.

Scott disappeared into the bathroom down the hall.

"Mind if I wash my hands here?" Bones motioned toward the kitchen sink.

"No. Go right ahead. Sorry about the mess. I usually do dishes after the kids are down for the night."

"No worries," he said as he washed his hands. "I've babysat Kennedy and Lincoln. I know you need eight arms to do it all at once."

He began washing the pots as she moved gracefully and purposefully, doling out peas and carrots onto Bradley's plate and Lila's tray and then scooping mac and cheese onto each. She set a tiny pink fork next to Lila. Lila blew bubbles as she grabbed the fork in one hand and a fistful of noodles with the other. She shoved the noodles into her mouth, pleasure washing over her tiny face.

"Not too much, boo," Sarah said, earning a wide, noodle-filled grin. As she grabbed two sippy cups from a cabinet, she noticed him washing the dishes. "Bones, I can get that. Please sit down."

"I think I can handle a few dishes."

"You're our *guest*." She filled the cups and set one in front of each child.

"Nah. A guest dresses fancy and brings wine. I'm dressed in jeans and brought a hammer. We're good. These hands can do more than healing," he said with a wink.

Scott came into the kitchen and reached into a cabinet for adult-sized plates. "Doin' my job?" He handed the plates to Sarah and then retrieved glasses while Sarah dished out their dinners.

Scott was a likable guy, a little rough around the edges, but he clearly loved his sister and her children.

"Just helping out." Bones grabbed a dish towel and dried the pots. "No dishwasher?"

"Got this place for a song, remember?" Scott had told Bones that he'd bought the house at auction when he'd first moved to Peaceful Harbor. In the weeks before the accident he'd done a nice job of painting and fixing it up. But like a typical guy, he didn't seem to mind not having luxuries at his fingertips.

Scott pulled open the refrigerator. "Want a beer? Iced tea?

Water?"

"I'll have a beer, thanks. I hear you're doing the girls' hair for the wedding Saturday," Bones said to Sarah as they took their seats at the table.

"I'm looking forward to it," Sarah said, and went on to give Scott a hard time about not letting her trim his hair.

Scott grinned and said, "Chicks dig shaggy hair. Gives them something to hold on to."

Sarah rolled her eyes and quickly changed the subject. Conversation came easily. Bones enjoyed the banter between them, and he loved watching Sarah care for her children. She wiped faces, caught a sippy cup midair as it tumbled from Lila's tray, and answered questions that Bradley seemed to pull out of nowhere—*Why are peas green? If I eat dinner, can we make a cake? Can I build a motorcycle with blocks?* It was a wonder she had time to eat anything at all, but if it bothered her, she didn't indicate it. She was patient and handled it all effortlessly.

"This is the best mac and cheese I've ever had," Bones said honestly. "But if you tell Red that, I'll deny it."

Sarah rolled her eyes. "I'm sure the dairy-free cheese tastes different from what you're used to, but thank you."

"It does taste different. *Better*," he clarified. "Where'd you learn to cook like this? Your mom?"

She shook her head and focused on Lila. "I've been cooking for myself forever. There are all types of recipes online for people with food allergies."

She was trying too hard not to look at him. He didn't like the vibe he was getting and wanted to ask more about their family, like whether her father was still alive and, if so, did she ever see him? But knowing her guard went up when he asked personal questions, he went for a safer subject. "Scott, you said you worked on oil rigs before coming here? How did you get into that line of work?"

Scott took a swig of his beer. "I worked on marinas down in Florida during high school, learned how to weld, do engine repair. Things weren't great at home, and one day one of the guys told me about this job on a rig. I took off at seventeen, got certified in welding and eventually diving, and found my way to being an underwater welder. Good money, a roof over my head, just dangerous as hell. But I survived." He glanced at Sarah and said, "It was a good move. How about you, Bones?"

"I graduated high school early, at sixteen, and went to college, but living on an oil rig? That was a brave move at that age."

"Not really," Scott said. "My sisters are the brave ones. Sarah left home at sixteen, and Josie at thirteen. I was an old man compared to them."

Bones's gut seized. Graduating early was one thing, but leaving home at sixteen and thirteen? Something must have been very wrong, which was made even clearer by the angry stare Sarah was giving Scott.

"You're not an old man," Bradley chimed in around a mouthful of peas.

Sarah's expression softened and she said, "Uncle Scott's just being silly, honey."

Sarah got up and wet a dishcloth. She busied herself wiping Lila's hands and face, her mouth set in a firm line. Bones tried to think of a way to defuse the tension, but he had too many unanswered questions—and he couldn't think of a single potential answer that wasn't bad. This new information made his protective urges surge even more. What had she been through?

Bradley wiggled down from his chair. "Can I go play?"

Sarah was still busy with Lila, so Bones snagged Bradley around the waist and pushed to his feet. "How about we wash those hands first?"

"Dude, you're lightning fast," Scott said as he got up to help. "Want me to get him?"

Sarah lifted Lila out of the high chair and said, "I can do it, Bones. You came over to help with the basement and got wrangled into dishes and everything else." She looked at Scott.

"Hey, I offered," Scott said. "The doc wants to help. Who am I to tell him no?"

Bones turned on the sink and set Bradley beside it. "We've got this, right, B-boy?"

Bradley nodded and stuck his hands under the water. "Can we work more?"

Bones looked at Sarah, who was busy stripping off Lila's dirty shirt, and said, "That's up to your mama." He finished washing Bradley's hands and dried them with a towel.

She glanced over with an apologetic smile. "Only if it's okay with you guys."

"Totally cool with me, little dude." Scott scooped him off the counter. "Bones, we'll meet you downstairs."

The tension when Scott left the kitchen was as tangible as another person in the room. Bones played over a dozen things to say, but when he went to Sarah's side, the wariness in her eyes told him there was only one thing he needed to know.

"Just tell me this. Are you in danger? Is your husband or your father looking for you?"

She swallowed hard, her eyes wide and watchful. She shook her head and said, "I've never had a husband, and I don't think my father looked for me when I was a teenager. I'm sure he's not looking now."

"Sarah," came out as a tortured growl. He reached for her, wanting to ease the pain in her eyes.

She pressed her hand to his chest, pushing him away. "Don't. I'm fine. *We're* fine. We don't need saving."

"I don't want to save you. I just want to—" *Help you? Be with you?* Fuck. Everything sounded like he wanted to rescue her. What the hell was wrong with that? There was no changing who he was, but just because he wanted to take care of her and protect her didn't mean she was just like everyone else he'd ever helped. He didn't want to get her to safety and be her friend. He wanted to be the man she didn't fear, the man she knew she could count on, the man in her bed. He wanted to be *hers*.

"We're *fine*, Bones."

She started to walk out of the kitchen, and he gently grabbed her wrist. "I'm not trying to save you. You're not one of my patients, Sarah. But I'm here, and I heard those things. That's not going to change." He glanced at Lila, anger and heartache intertwining. How long had Sarah been raising her kids alone? How had she managed? Did her children have the same father? And where the hell was her sister?

"Mommy?" Bradley hollered, his footsteps stomping up the basement stairs.

Bones reluctantly dropped her wrist, but he continued holding her gaze. "Let me in, Sarah. You won't regret it."

"Mommy, I need Bones to bonk the nail," Bradley said as he walked into the kitchen, looking completely put out by the delay in his plans.

"Okay, baby," Sarah said as she gazed down at Bradley, absently brushing her fingers through his dirty-blond hair. Then she looked at Bones for a long, silent moment with an expression hovering somewhere between a plea and a warning.

Bradley grabbed Bones's hand and dragged him toward the basement.

Bones looked over his shoulder at Sarah. She opened her mouth to say something and then closed it. A troubled and somehow also appreciative smile lifted her lips, and she mouthed, *Thank you.*

Chapter Four

SARAH LOOKED OUT Bullet and Finlay's bedroom window toward the fenced-in pond in their backyard Saturday afternoon, trying to catch sight of her children as she put the finishing touches on Finlay's hair for her wedding. They'd gotten lucky. Early November in Maryland could be cold and rainy, but the sky was clear and the air was crisp. Rows of white chairs faced a beautiful wooden wedding altar Bones, Bear, and Truman had built for Bullet and Finlay. Between Bones's job and how often he helped Scott with the basement, she had no idea when he had found the time, but the altar was breathtakingly beautiful. Pink and white roses adorned the top, and fall-colored flowers overflowed barrels on either side. The same flowers filled planters throughout the yard. Glass lanterns hung from tree limbs with white candles inside and pink, white, and peach roses around the top. The yard was packed with members of the Dark Knights and their families. Children ran around with balloons tied to their wrists, dodging adults who were mingling on the lawn. Finlay had planned the wedding perfectly. The enormous white tent they'd set up for the reception had space heaters just in case they needed them. A makeshift stage for the band and a dance area had been set up at one end. Round tables had pink and white tablecloths and beautiful floral centerpieces in vases in the shape of a motorcycle with a pink banner that had Bullet's and Finlay's names written in black. Sarah scanned the grounds, trying not to let her nerves get the best of her. She finally spotted Chicki and Red holding Lila and Lincoln beneath a big tree, chatting with Finlay's mother and her husband.

Sarah threaded more flowers into Finlay's hair and took another quick glance outside, searching for Bradley. Her pulse quickened as her gaze landed on Bones standing by the fence around the pond with Bradley and Scott. Scott was busy ogling Cassie, the caterer, as she came out of the reception tent, which was fine, because Sarah took a moment to ogle Bones, standing tall and broad, with one strong hand resting protectively on her son's shoulder. Like the other men, he was strikingly handsome in jeans and a black dress shirt, with a pink tie that matched the flowers in Finlay's bouquet, and his biker vest and boots. But unlike the other men, Bones took her breath away. *He could make sweatpants look like a million bucks.* Bradley had insisted on wearing the boots and vest Bones had given him. He was gazing up at Bones, and in that moment Sarah wondered if she was letting her children get too close to him. She'd spent a lifetime being disappointed in others, and the idea of anyone having the power to shatter her children's happiness worried her.

She focused on Finlay's hair, listening to the girls talk about their lives. As Gemma told them how often Kennedy emulated her, waving her little hands and fluttering her lashes, Sarah feared her worries that the other shoe was about to drop would somehow wear off on her children, no matter how much she tried not to let it.

She was tired of living every moment on guard, preparing for the worst. Just for one day she wanted to allow herself to be a normal twenty-six-year-old woman and enjoy the afternoon without those looming concerns. Lord knew Bones and his family had earned her trust.

If only her past would stop casting shadows over her present.

"Isn't everything gorgeous?" Gemma said as she came to Sarah's side, appreciation sparking in her green eyes. She looked beautiful in a knee-length mauve dress with shimmery sleeves. She had long legs for a woman of only five two or five three, a slim waist, and curvy hips.

Sarah placed her hand over her baby bump, trying not to be envious of the other girls' figures, but *hair envy* was another thing altogether. She had major hair envy for the girls' shiny, bouncy hair, from Gemma's natural array of browns and golds to Dixie's thick, flame-red waves cascading down her back. She knew stress could wreak havoc on skin and nails, and she swore her dull, sandy tresses were proof that it was hell on hair, too.

"Look at Bullet pacing like a caged tiger," Gemma said. "He's driving poor Tinkerbell crazy." Tinkerbell paced with Bullet, but kept stopping and looking toward the house.

"I begged him to let Tink stay with me," Finlay said as Sarah secured the last of the flowers into place. "Bullet worried she'd get in the way, but I know that's not why he kept her with him. Bullet needs Tinkerbell like other guys need a stiff drink."

Finlay pushed to her feet and gazed dreamily out the window. She was stunning in the white satin and lace wedding dress Crystal had made for her. It was long in the back, knee-length in the front, with two white satin bows at her waist. The skirt had a layer of floral lace that began as white and faded into gradients of pink as it reached the hem. The plunging neckline was shielded with pretty lace that matched the long lace sleeves. She wore her hair down. *The way Bullet likes it best.* Sarah had French braided the sides into a pretty horizontal braid across the back, which looked gorgeous with baby's breath weaved into it. She'd added little flowers to each girl's hairstyle.

Finlay turned around and said, "I *love* that about him. Bullet feels everything so deeply. I swear he's got the biggest heart of any man I've ever met." Her eyes glistened with tears, and she fanned her face.

"No tears!" Isabel hurried over from across the room. She was Finlay's best friend and one of her two maids of honor. Finlay had been unable to decide between her sister, Penny, and Isabel, so they were both walking down the aisle with Bones, Bullet's best man.

"No, no, no." Penny rushed over with Crystal and Dixie on her heels. She took Finlay by the shoulders and said, "Look into my eyes. If you ruin your makeup before the wedding, we have to start all over."

"I'm sorry. I'm just so *happy*. Bullet is..." Finlay fanned her face faster, blinking rapidly. "He was so gruff and such a dirty-talking, shameless flirt when I met him. And now all those things make me fall harder for him by the second. I just love him *so* much."

Penny pulled her into a hug. "When you marry a big, burly, tatted-up biker, you get the best of everything."

"Careful of my hair," Finlay said.

"I'm just glad you love Bullet for who he is," Dixie said as she looked out the window. She wore a short forest-green backless dress, with lace sleeves and sky-high heels. She was so tall and willowy, she could have been a model. Well, a *tattoo model*, considering she had so much ink. "I worried that he'd never let a woman into his head or his heart. I'm happy for both of you."

"He's so lovable, Dix," Finlay said. "I never stood a chance."

"Dixie is *happy* for you," Crystal said with a smirk. "But she's *happier* because one more of her brothers has another female to watch over besides *her*."

Dixie thrust out one hip and crossed her arms, amusement filling her keen green eyes. "There is some truth to that rumor."

"Why does that make you happier than Bullet and Finlay getting married?" Sarah asked.

"When you were growing up, did Scott scare off every guy who looked at you?" Dixie asked.

Sarah's nerves prickled. "I didn't really have guys looking at me back then." She'd done everything she could to avoid it so she didn't get a beating.

"Oh please. *Look* at you." Dixie waved her hand toward her. "Even after two babies—and with one in the oven—you've got Bones all tied up in knots. And he never goes out with women from around here."

Sarah. Couldn't. Breathe.

"Oh yeah, that man's totally into you," Gemma said. "On Halloween even Tru noticed it."

Unsure of what to say, Sarah went with, "He's just being nice."

"I don't know," Finlay said. "Kennedy and Lincoln have been coming here for a long time, and suddenly Bones decided the pond was a danger to little ones. He hired Crow, one of the Dark Knights, to put up that safety fence around it, and then he showed up at the crack of dawn *every* morning this week before going into work to make sure it got done."

"He's just cautious, and maybe spending time with Bradley lately has made him think more about kids in general," Sarah said.

"I think your kids have gotten to him in a big way," Dixie said. "Well, you and your kids, really."

Happiness bubbled up inside Sarah, but just as quickly the familiar dread of what he might expect in return tried to chase it away. She struggled to hold on to the positive feeling.

"It's not like that," Sarah said, but even as the words came out, his voice whispered through her mind. *Let me in, Sarah. You won't regret it.* She put her hand on her belly, thinking about her life. Women often looked at her like she had an enviable life, with two children and a baby on the way. They had no way of knowing what she'd been through. But men? When she wasn't pregnant, on the rare occasion she'd gone out without her children, she'd noticed a few glances, but now she was invisible to almost all of them. Why she wasn't to Bones she had no idea, although their friendship had definitely developed an electric charge lately. She blamed her desires on pregnancy hormones. But for him? It had to be some kind of passing attraction.

"Bones can have anyone he wants," she finally added. "I'm like a walking baggage terminal. He's a protector, like the rest of your family, and we're just new people to look out for."

Dixie and the others exchanged a look that loosely translated to *Has this girl lost her mind?*

"Fin!" Cassie's voice floated up the stairs. A minute later she appeared in the doorway. Her brown hair was piled on her head in a bun, and she was all smiles in a pretty peach dress. "If you don't hurry up, I swear Bullet's going to come in here and haul your heinie out over his shoulder!"

"Oh my gosh!" Finlay put her hand over her heart. "Why am I so nervous?" She turned to Gemma, Crystal, and Sarah and said, "Were you nervous when you got married?"

"Yes!" Crystal and Gemma said in unison.

All eyes turned to Sarah. She was so used to calling Lewis her *ex*, she'd forgotten that most people assumed she had been married. She wasn't embarrassed not to have been married. In fact, she thanked the heavens above, because it was one less tie she'd had to cut.

"I've, um, never been married," Sarah explained. "We just lived together."

"I'm sorry. I just assumed..." Finlay said as they moved toward the stairs.

"It's okay. I don't like to talk about him anyway." Grasping for a diversion, she said, "Why did you decide to get married so quickly?"

"Because I love Bullet wholly and completely," Finlay answered without hesitation. "I want to have his babies and get old and gray together. I want to hold his hand as we leave this life and pass into another. That's how sure I am about our love. And I'm equally sure that he needs this commitment even more than he needs Tinkerbell, so why would I ask him to wait for it?"

As Sarah followed the girls downstairs, she wondered what it would be like to love someone that much. She would do anything for her children, including putting her life at risk to save them, and now that she'd reconnected with Scott, she thought she might do the same for him. But he was her brother. He'd been there in the thick of the violence from their parents, trying to protect her and Josie, finding a way out that would benefit all of them, and when they'd reconnected after all those years, he'd changed his life to be with them and to try to rebuild their relationship. And even though Josie had shut them out, she knew she'd give her life for her, too.

But falling so deeply in love with a man that she couldn't imagine a life without him? She wasn't sure she was capable of healing enough to ever trust her instincts, or someone else, that much.

BONES WAS SURE Bullet was going to break into a sprint, haul his big ass down the aisle, and plow through Bones and everyone else to get to Finlay instead of waiting for the wedding procession to finish. Bear and Crystal had walked down the aisle first, followed by Truman and Gemma. Dixie was walking with Lincoln down the aisle now. Bullet was so close to Truman and Gemma's babies, he looked as though he was tearing up. Bones held tightly to Kennedy's hand as he crouched to fix the pink bow around Tinkerbell's neck, stealing a glance at the most beautiful woman in the yard—in all of Peaceful Harbor as far he was concerned. Sarah sat in a floral dress with Lila on her lap and Bradley beside her. He hadn't been able to stop thinking about her—about the three of them—since he'd seen them last. He'd helped Scott with the basement last night, but he'd only gotten to say a quick hello to Sarah before she'd disappeared to put her little ones to bed. He'd wanted to offer to help, but he'd been covered in drywall dust. When she hadn't appeared later, Scott had said she'd probably fallen asleep with the children. Bones wanted to believe that, but he'd seen how tormented she was when Scott had divulged parts of her past she'd clearly wanted to keep hidden. He wondered if she was avoiding him.

Knowing Sarah wasn't married had severed the tethers that had kept his emotions in check. If she was embarrassed, that would end *today*.

Bradley leaned across Sarah's lap, planting a kiss on his baby sister's cheek. Lila giggled, and love fell over Sarah's features like a moment in a movie, sending awareness rippling through Bones. She was really something. She'd been upstairs with the girls for hours doing their hair, and he swore he'd seen her looking out the window, searching for her children at least three times each hour.

"*Now*, Uncle Boney?" Kennedy bounced in her pink frilly dress, her pretty brown eyes as big as saucers as she tugged on his hand, bringing him back to the moment. A lace headband with large fabric flowers sat crooked on her forehead.

He straightened the headband and handed her a basket the girls had filled with pink roses. He looked her in the eyes as she bounced and said, "*Now*, sweetheart, but remember, try not to get Tink too excited, okay?"

Kennedy nodded vehemently. "Come on, Tink!" She began skipping down the aisle, throwing rose petals as she shouted, "Look at me, Uncle Be*ah*!"

"Mommy, look at Tink!" Bradley pointed at Tinkerbell. "Hi, Tink! Hi, Kennedy!"

Bradley waved wildly, and Kennedy ran over and put a handful of petals on his lap. Tinkerbell licked Bradley's face, and everyone laughed.

"Sit, Tink!" Bones snapped, and Tinkerbell plopped to her bottom beside Kennedy.

Sarah cringed, her cheeks flushing as she leaned closer to Kennedy and said, "Thank you, sweetheart. You'd better keep walking."

"*Fust* I have to give baby Lila some!" Kennedy tossed rose petals into the air, and they floated down over Lila. Lila grabbed at them, causing collective *aww*s and laughter to erupt around them.

Lila and Bradley played with the rose petals. Sarah smiled shyly, hugging her babies. It took all of Bones's restraint not to go to her.

"Come on, Tink!" Kennedy barreled back into the aisle and skipped all the way down to Bullet. "You're getting *mawied*, Uncle Bullet! I love you!" She threw her arms around Bullet's legs and then she ran to Gemma.

Tinkerbell barked, looking nervously between Bullet and Kennedy. Bullet patted his thigh, and Tinkerbell settled in beside him.

Bones couldn't stop smiling. This—*family*, *friends*, *happiness*—was everything good in the world. He glanced at Sarah again, and he knew she belonged in this picture, too.

Bradley was sitting sideways on the chair at the end of the aisle, watching him as he offered his arms to Penny and Isabel. Sarah had one arm around Lila, the other around Bradley. She lifted her head, and their eyes caught. For an unguarded second, she looked at him like she desired him, and in that split second his insides flamed. She dropped her gaze, and her hair blocked his view. But that sexy look was already etched into his mind. And damn, *that* was a look he wanted to see a hell of a lot more.

He and the women began walking down the aisle.

"Hi, Bones!" Bradley waved.

Bones winked at him.

"Bradley," Sarah whispered, but Bradley pushed to his feet and ran toward Bones.

Bones scooped him into his arms with a big-ass smile and

said, “Hey, B-boy. You want in on the action?”

More laughter rang out as Bradley hugged Bones around his neck, nodding. Bones glanced at Sarah, who looked mortified. He winked at her and mouthed, *It’s okay.* Then he said to Bradley, “You’ve got to hold this pretty lady’s hand, okay?”

Bradley nodded as Bones shifted him onto his hip. Bradley put his hand out for Penny to hold, beaming with joy, but it was the way Sarah was looking at Bones, with a mix of astonishment, embarrassment, and something *much* deeper and more alluring that had his heart thundering as they made their way down the aisle. He heard his father, who went by the biker name Biggs for his six-five stature, chuckling.

“Sorry, dude,” Bones said to Bullet as he took his place beside him with Bradley in his arms. Bradley buried his face in Bones’s neck in delayed embarrassment.

Bullet chuckled. “It’s all good, bro. It’s how it should be.”

The “Wedding March” played, and Finlay appeared at the end of the aisle on her mother’s arm. Nothing could have pulled Bullet’s attention from his beautiful bride, just as nothing could divert Bones’s attention from Sarah.

The ceremony was heartfelt, but Bones missed much of it. He was too focused on Bradley’s head resting on his shoulder and Sarah trying her best to look like she *wasn’t* watching them. He never lost track of her for a second, not after the ceremony when a mass of friends and family converged on the wedding party for congratulatory embraces and not as Hawk, the photographer, gathered them together for pictures. Bones got a kick out of the fact that Bradley would be in them. Sarah anxiously bounced Lila on her hip, looking like she wanted to plow through the crowd and relieve him of her son, but also like she didn’t want to cause any more distractions. When Hawk finished, Bones took a moment to speak with him and Bullet. Then, as everyone else headed for the reception tent, Bones blazed a path toward Sarah.

Her brows knitted, and an apologetic smile lifted her lips as he came to her side.

"Mommy! I was in pictures! Did you see?" Bradley asked excitedly.

"Yes, baby," she said to Bradley with a forced smile. Then to Bones she said, "I'm sorry. I didn't know what to do, and now Bullet's pictures are ruined, and—"

"No apologies necessary, and they aren't ruined. They're even better than they would have been." Bones draped an arm around her shoulder, guiding her toward Hawk, who was standing near the wedding arch looking at them through the lens of his camera. Did Sarah look as exquisite to Hawk as she did to Bones? He would love to see her through the eye of a lens, close up, catching every twitch and quiver of her beautiful face. Did Hawk notice the sweet curve of her belly, or the way she touched it often, like she needed her baby to know she was thinking about it? Or the way she kept stealing glances at Bones? Did he catch sight of the birthmark on her left wrist? Would he get a picture of her smile at the very moment when it reached her eyes?

"Bones..." Sarah said shakily, her eyes darting to the few guests still making their way toward the reception tent. "Where are we going?"

"How long has it been since you had pictures taken of you and the kids?"

Confusion riddled her brow. "Um...?"

"That's what I thought." He hadn't seen any pictures of her and the kids at her place, not even a stray picture hanging on their refrigerator, like Truman and Gemma had. Hell, like he had of Lincoln and Kennedy on his own fridge. Her phone was probably full of them, but he was sure she didn't have a photo printer.

"Bones, *no*," she said as Hawk lowered his camera and raised his chin in greeting. "He doesn't have to do this. You're going to make him miss Bullet and Finlay's first dance."

"No, he won't, Mommy," Bradley chimed in. "Bones asked Bullet to wait for us."

"Oh gosh, *Bones*…? Please tell me you didn't." Her beautiful eyes pleaded for it not to be true.

"I can't lie to you, darlin'. Lies make me twitchy." He glanced at Hawk, who was wearing mustard-colored pants and brown leather suspenders with a white dress shirt. His eyeglasses had multicolored frames, and though he had a few tats and a thick beard, his light-brown hair was shorn tight on the sides and longer on top, brushed back in a trendy style. Hawk was a highly-sought-after photographer and worked with magazines as well as individuals. He had made a name for himself when he published a photo spread of two A-list celebrities and their three children a few years back, and he was about as down to earth as a guy could get. "Hawk Pennington, this is Sarah Beckley and her daughter, Lila. You've already met Bradley."

Bradley waved.

Hawk nodded with a friendly smile. "Now I see why Bones asked me to hang back. You have a beautiful family."

"Thank you. But you really don't have to take pictures," she said.

"Pictures are my life." Hawk glanced at Bones and said, "How about if we get the kids comfortable first. Bones, why don't you carry Bradley beneath the arch with Sarah and Lila?"

Sarah's brows knitted again, as if she was puzzling a way out of this. Bones put a hand on her lower back and leaned in closer, whispering, "Relax and enjoy the spotlight, darlin'. If not for yourself, do it for your kids. Show them how special they are."

There must have been magic in his words, because the smile they brought nearly dropped him to his knees.

"Okay," she relented, nervously shifting from foot to foot beneath the arch. "Thank you. This was really unnecessary, but very thoughtful."

Hawk moved around them, taking pictures, and Bones tried to distract Sarah enough for her to relax. He tickled Lila's chin, earning a heart-melting giggle. "This pretty little lady has a big birthday coming up. Consider it your birthday present."

"It's almost Lila's birthday, not Mommy's," Bradley said.

"Yes, but your mommy gave birth to your sister. So really, it's her birthday, too." He knew that was too confusing for him, so he said, "Just nod and say 'good idea.'"

Bradley did just that.

"You guys look great," Hawk said as he stepped in close, peering through the lens of the camera. "Bones, how about putting Bradley down."

"Ready, B-boy?"

Bradley nodded, and Bones lowered his feet to the ground. Then he stepped away, and unease crawled over Sarah's face. That troubled look drew him right back. "How about if I hold Lila and you get a few pictures with Bradley?"

Bones took Lila to the grass and sat down with her, watching as Sarah moved behind Bradley, bringing him against her legs, and she bent to kiss the top of his head. She did that a lot, like she needed to love him up every chance she got. She crouched beside him, gazing into his eyes as Hawk took several pictures, moving as swiftly and silently as the wind. Bones could see he was capturing *everything*, and his chest felt full knowing Sarah would have these pictures to cherish forever.

"Bradley, why don't you take your mama onto the grass?" Hawk suggested.

Bradley took Sarah's hand and led her away from the arch as Hawk took pictures. Bradley plunked down in the grass, and Sarah sat beside him without a care about getting her dress dirty. Why did that speak so loudly to Bones? Lila crawled over to them, and Hawk captured one beautiful moment after the next, while Bones stood nearby, watching. Bradley picked up a leaf from the grass, and he handed it to Sarah. Within a few minutes, Sarah was so lost in enjoying her children, she sat with her legs tucked elegantly beside her, interacting with her children as if she'd forgotten about Hawk altogether.

Lila pulled herself up, clinging to the sleeve of Sarah's dress and smiling at her big brother. She glanced in Bones's direction, babbling, "Babababa..."

"Hey there, pretty little lady," Bones said.

"Bababa..." Lila's free hand opened and closed, as if she could draw Bones to her with the motion. "Baba!"

In the next second, Lila let go of Sarah's sleeve and took a step toward Bones, still babbling, grabby fingers reaching for him. It took another two steps before Bones—and Sarah, based on her reaction—realized what was happening, and then their eyes connected. Sarah gasped, tears instantly welling as her baby girl took another wobbly step forward.

"Are you getting this?" Bones asked in a hushed voice to Hawk. "Please tell me you're getting every damn step."

"Dude, I'm a pro. I don't miss anything," Hawk said, camera at his eye.

Bones went down on one knee, stretching his hands out toward Lila, afraid if he moved closer she'd topple to her bottom. "Come on, baby girl. You've got this."

Adrenaline coursed through his veins with her every step. Sarah wrapped her arm around Bradley, whispering in his ear, Bones assumed to keep him from scaring Lila. Lila wobbled forward, then back, and Bones froze. She plopped onto her bottom, eyes wide. They all cheered, rushing toward Sarah's magnificent little girl.

Hawk never stopped taking pictures.

Sarah picked up Lila, hugging and kissing her, all of them laughing and commending Lila at the same time. "What a smart girl you are. Good job, baby! You walked!" She lifted watery eyes to Bones, speaking a little softer as she said, "You walked to Bones."

"She walked to *you*, Bones!" Bradley chimed in.

"She sure did." *And it was incredible.* He'd never felt so much pride, and she wasn't even his child. He lifted Bradley into his arms and couldn't resist hugging the three of them.

As he gazed into Sarah's happy eyes, she said, "She walked to you. That was amazing."

"She let me in," he said truthfully. "If I'm lucky, her mama will, too."

Chapter Five

HOW WAS SARAH going to survive this day? First Bones acted like it was the most natural thing in the world to carry her son down the aisle. Then her daughter took her first steps—toward the man who put pictures of her family above his own brother's first wedding dance. Sarah had so many emotions zooming around inside her, she felt a little dizzy. She stole a glance at Bones, carrying Lila and telling her little girl how smart and strong she was and asking her what she was going to surprise them with next. She'd never met a man like him before. He made her want to shake him silly to wake him from his misguided affections and ask what the heck he was doing wasting his time with *her*. She was only going to get bigger, and in a few months she'd have another mouth to feed. One that would keep her up at night and would definitely leave behind even more stretch marks and probably ten extra pounds.

"Sarah!" Gemma called out, rushing toward them with Dixie at her heels. "I saw Lila walk! I came out to see where you guys were and holy cow! She *walked*! You must be so excited!"

"A little *too* excited," she said honestly.

Bones slid her a smoldering look. Either that or her hormones were playing tricks on her again.

"There's no such thing as *too* excited," he said in a seductive voice that made Gemma's eyes goes wide.

Nope. No hormonal tricks.

Dixie chuckled. "Geez, Bones. Is a baby walking some kind of aphrodisiac?"

"No, but look at that smile." Bones winked at Sarah. "*That's* one hell of a turn-on."

"*Ohmygosh,*" Sarah said softly, shifting her eyes to the ground.

Bradley tugged at Sarah's dress. "I'm thirsty."

"Why don't I take him in for some lemonade so you can visit with the girls," Bones offered.

"You don't have to do that." Sarah went for Bradley's hand, but he was already reaching for Bones. "At least give me Lila."

As Bones transferred Lila to her arms, he said, "Careful. She's wiggling like crazy. I think she's anxious to get her feet on the ground again." He touched the tip of Lila's nose and said, "Right, peanut?"

"Sounds like you've got baby fever," Gemma said.

"What's not to get excited about?" Bones cocked a brow. "Remember how we all went crazy when Lincoln started walking?"

"Uh-huh." Dixie rolled her eyes. Then she leaned closer to Gemma and lowered her voice as she said, "I didn't see him get *let's-do-the-dirty* with *you*."

Bones glowered at her. "Come on, B-boy, let's go hit the soda bar."

As he walked away, Dixie crossed her arms and set narrow eyes on Sarah. "Do not tell me it's not like *that* between you two. Did you *see* him? I know what's normal for my brother, and Bones is acting like he got shot in the ass by Cupid's arrow. *Bear* is the emotional, tap-babies-on-the-nose guy whose heart gets all wrapped up before he has a chance to think. *Bullet* barrels into situations following his gut instincts. But Bones has *always* been the guy who stands back, meticulously analyzing situations before making decisions, much less a move toward anything—unless someone's in imminent danger. Then he goes on instinct, and he'll obliterate everything in his path. He's as deadly as Bullet, but with lethal precision, striking as fast and viciously as a rattlesnake. But his careful nature, his need to analyze and understand every aspect of anything he touches, is what makes him such an expert in his field. He doesn't make mistakes or give off vibes that aren't exactly what he wants to portray."

Before she could ponder that nerve-racking assessment for too long, Dixie said, "The only thing he's ever jumped into with two feet was medical school…and *you*. So, babe, if it's not like that between you two, you better buckle up, because it's gonna be."

Red came outside and began ushering everyone into the tent. "Girls! Come on, you don't want to miss everything." She patted Lila's back and said, "I hear our little girl took her first steps and I missed it."

Our little girl. Warmed by Red's love for her daughter, she said, "I think Hawk took lots of pictures."

"Yes, but you know it's not the same as being right there when they get that shocked look in their eyes, like they can't believe they're walking," Red said as Dixie and Gemma took their seats. "And then the whole adorable wobbly thing they do…" She sighed and said, "I love that. Wayne—*Bones*—nearly drove me crazy as a baby. I thought he'd never take a single step."

Wayne. She'd seen his real name on his lab coat at the hospital, and it didn't take much imagination to figure out how he got his biker name.

"Why?" Sarah's gaze found the man who had nearly driven his mother crazy. He was sitting at a table talking to Bullet, looking incredibly handsome with his new appendage—*Bradley*—sitting proudly on his lap. Bradley's little arm circled Bones's neck, and his cheek rested on Bones's shoulder.

Red stepped closer and said, "Because while Brandon—*Bullet*—was aging me with recklessness, toddling all over creation, climbing the stairs like a little monkey, bulldozing into things, falling down the stairs on purpose, Wayne was watching, learning, biding his time until he had it *all* figured out."

Sarah couldn't stifle her giggle fast enough. "I can see him doing that."

"It's a wonder I have any red hair left at all. Thank goodness for Chicki and her mad dying skills." Red patted her hair. "Brandon was a little stinker. He would climb two or three stairs, then grin at me and let go of the railing, laughing as he tumbled down. It was no wonder Wayne waited until there was something *worth* chasing after."

"You'd think a big brother would be enough of a draw." She tried to picture Bones as a little boy. Was he everything Dixie said? Lethal when protecting others *and* careful? How could the two possibly go together?

"Lord knows it was for Bobby—*Bear*—and Dixie. But not my Wayne. He was in no hurry to fall down the stairs. It wasn't until Biggs brought a wounded kitten home that Wayne made a move. Biggs was sitting on the couch tending to its cuts, and the poor little thing was mewling. My heart nearly broke at its cries.

It went on and on, like it needed us to listen to every single complaint."

Red gazed at Bones and said, "I'll never forget the feeling in my chest when Wayne heard the cries from the playroom. He looked at me with such compassion in his little brown eyes. Then he pushed to his feet, using a plastic castle for leverage, and he marched right out to the living room. He fell once," she said with a smile. "But he stood right back up and toddled over to the couch like a pro. He spent every minute he could with that kitten even after it was healed up. You should ask him about it sometime."

"So Dixie was right? He really does analyze things before he makes a move?"

"*Overanalyze*, sweetheart." Red looped her arm through Sarah's. "Come on. Let's find your seat. My bet is that it's next to Wayne. And if it wasn't, I'm sure he switched the place cards so it is now."

Why wasn't anyone warning Bones against this attraction? How could they overlook a walking red flag?

Do I want them to?

"Mommy!" Bradley called out as they approached.

Bones's gaze darted to her, sending heat straight to her core as she followed Red to the table, feeling dizzy again. No, not dizzy exactly. Her stomach was all fluttery, and her skin felt cold and hot at the same time. No doubt because Bones looked like he wanted to devour her and everyone in the tent seemed to know it. She glanced up at the sparkling lights and the white and pink streamers strewn across the ceiling, wishing life came with a guidebook.

Red was right: Her place card was next to Bones's, and Bones had even moved a high chair to the other side of her seat.

She settled Lila into the high chair and moved Bradley to the seat between her and Bones, needing the buffer. Just because everyone else seemed comfortable with this situation didn't mean she was a jump-in-with-two-feet type of gal. She was barely a dip-her-toes-in-and-test-the-waters person. But at twenty-six, she was still a young woman, and she couldn't continue to ignore the truth or keep trying to write off the sizzling heat between them as pregnancy hormones. Bones awakened her body in a way that no other man ever had, and Bullet's dirty-doctor comment had created a whirlwind of curiosity she could no longer ignore.

Ugly thoughts snuck in. Thoughts that were so deeply ingrained, she wasn't sure she could ever escape them, though she so desperately wanted to. Sex had always equated to survival for Sarah, with a brief exception when she'd *thought* she was on the path to love. She gritted her teeth against the sting of painful memories, fighting to bury them down deep for the millionth time.

"Hey, beautiful," Bones said softly.

Her eyes clashed with his. He sat with one arm across the back of Bradley's chair, watching her in her moment of turmoil. She may not believe in happily ever afters and she definitely had trouble trusting, but she longed to be closer to him, to experience this loyal, thoughtful man on a more personal level. Emotionally and physically. Swallowing hard, feeling happy and sad, nervous and calm, petrified and curious. It was so overwhelming, she was sure everyone could sense it. But it was Bones who pushed his hand farther across the back of Bradley's chair until his fingertips brushed her arm, concern written in those dark eyes.

"You okay, darlin'? Want to go for a walk?"

A walk? No, she definitely wouldn't survive this night with Dr. Whiskey looking at her like he could heal all her wounds. She needed space to clear her head.

"No, thank you," she finally managed. "I'm just going up to the house to change Lila."

He pushed to his feet. "I'll walk you up."

"No," she said quickly. "I'm fine, really. I just need..." Grasping for an excuse, she decided to go with honesty, because at the moment she was just that pathetic. "To *breathe*, and you sort of make that impossible."

A slow grin spread across his lips.

"*Ohmygosh*," came out before she could stop it. "Could you please look the other way?"

"Not a chance, darlin'."

His arrogance came out smooth as velvet. *Ugh.* She pushed to her feet, needing to escape before he worked his magic on her. "Come on, Bradley. Let's go potty before dinner."

"I don't have to go," Bradley whined.

"I'll watch him," Bones offered, that panty-melting grin still in place.

Great. Another ovary-exploding dose of goodness. Just what I need.

THE FESTIVE AFTERNOON drifted into evening on a celebratory cloud of too much food and a hefty amount of cheer. Bones stood by the bar with his father and brothers. Bullet's eyes were riveted to his bride, cutting loose on the dance floor to "Girls Just Want to Have Fun" with Dixie, Penny, Isabel, and about a dozen other women. Bones found Sarah sitting beside Gemma, each with a baby on their lap. Truman sat on the floor beside Gemma's chair with Kennedy and Bradley on his lap. Bradley and Kennedy had played together all afternoon and now shared matching glassy-eyed looks of exhaustion. Hawk moved stealthily around the tent, capturing treasured moments. Sarah looked happy and untroubled, which was an amazing combination on such a beautiful woman, and he hoped Hawk had caught the look on film.

"Man, Cassie sure killed it with the catering." Bullet passed a shot to each of his brothers. "Here you go, old man," he said as he handed a shot to Biggs.

"I couldn't eat another bite," their father said, curling his fingers around his cane as he accepted the glass. The stroke had left him with slow speech, the left side of his mouth permanently weighed down, and worst of all, it had stolen the lifelong biker's ability to ride a motorcycle. But that didn't stop him from heading up the Dark Knights, as his father had done before him, or from wearing the club patches with pride. And it sure as hell didn't make him any less of a man.

Bones was proud of his father. He'd taught them how to fight, ride, and protect. Beneath that thick, unkempt gray beard and inked skin marred with deep grooves earned from miles ridden under the heat of the sun lay the spirit of a warrior. Biggs Whiskey would probably go out of this world the way he brought up his children—fighting for the lives of others.

"Did you get a look at the dessert table?" Bear asked. "I might have to steal some of those chocolate-covered strawberries for later." He waggled his brows, his gaze moving to Crystal, who was still dancing her pretty little heart out.

Bear had fallen hard for Crystal from practically the moment they'd met, but it had taken him more than eight months to finally get her to go out with him. Bones looked at Sarah, the woman who was unraveling his every thought. He had always considered himself a patient man, but Sarah was proving him wrong. Because, *damn*, he'd taken Bear's comment about the chocolate-covered strawberries and shredded it down, imagining Sarah lying naked in his bed, her long, golden hair strewn across his pillow as he licked chocolate from her beautiful breasts and rounded belly and then devoured the very heart of her until she cried out his name so many times she'd never forget it. And there was no way in hell he'd wait eight months for that to happen.

"Dude." Bullet nudged Bones, jerking him from his fantasy. "Where the hell did you go?"

"Someplace magnificent until you fucked it up." He gazed down at the drink in his hand. "What are we toasting?"

"Christ, Bones. You really did zone out," Biggs said. "We're toasting my boys, but first, if we don't say a toast to your mama and the women in your lives we'll be accused of drinking just for the hell of it. So here's to strong, loyal women. May they always want our ugly asses."

"Here, here," they said in unison as they clinked glasses, then downed their drinks.

The bartender was already passing out the next round.

Biggs stroked his beard, eyeing the three of them. He lifted his glass, his mustache twitching as one side of his lips lifted. "Two men down, one to go, *motherfuckers*. We done good."

They all laughed and drank their shots, but as quickly as that laughter hit, Bones's mind traveled back to the night he'd had dinner at Sarah's, to her brother's comment about their home life. The liquor in his stomach soured, and he set down his glass.

His father's hand clapped onto Bones's shoulder, and he said, "That little darlin's got hurt in her eyes. Tread carefully, son."

"I appreciate your advice, Pop. I've treaded carefully my whole life, and it's always served me well." Bones inhaled deeply. Sarah had done an excellent job of surrounding herself with other people and engaging them in conversation every time he approached. He was done waiting. If she couldn't breathe when he was around, he'd just have to be her oxygen. "Everything you've ever taught me has led to this moment. Now is *not* the time to tread carefully."

Biggs nodded, his eyes narrow. "Well, hell, boy. Then what're you standing here for?"

His father gave him a shove toward Sarah, but Bones had other plans. He'd heard enough of this girly music. It was time to turn up the heat—and the charm. He headed straight for the band and then he went to get his woman.

Gemma motioned in his direction, and Sarah lifted her face, looking adorably nervous and treacherously sexy.

"Ladies," he said, never taking his eyes off Sarah. Right on cue, the band began playing the tune he'd requested. He reached for Sarah's hand. "Dance with me, darlin'."

Her eyes darted nervously to Gemma, then to Lila, and then to Bradley, now sitting beside Truman. Bones was vaguely aware of Truman and Gemma watching them. He had a feeling nearly everyone in the tent was holding their breath to see if she'd accept.

"I can't," she said softly, holding Lila a little tighter. "I've got the kids."

"I'll watch them," Truman and Gemma said at the same time.

Sarah's cheeks flushed. "No. I can—"

Gemma reached for Lila, and Truman pulled Bradley onto his lap, leaving her no babies to hide behind.

Bones gently lifted her to her feet. "Come on, darlin'. This song is for you."

He led her to the dance floor. Sarah looked over her shoulder, watching her children as Bones swept her into his arms. Her pregnant belly brushed against him as he guided her arms around his neck. She glanced at the kids again.

"They're okay. I promise," he said as the band began singing about remembering the first time he'd seen her.

"I know. I just…"

"Focus on me, Sarah, nothing else. I'd never put your kids in danger. Just give yourself this moment." He saw unease in her eyes and said, "Give *us* this moment."

Her gaze surfed the room, and he realized it wasn't just her children she was worried about. He slid his arm around her waist, holding her tight, and headed out of the tent and into the yard.

She hurried to keep up with him. "Where are you going? I can't leave!"

"We're not leaving." Out of eyeshot from everyone else, he drew her close again, guided her arms around his neck for a second time, and said, "I want to dance with you, and if you're worried about what everyone else will think, then I'll dance out here with you."

"Why, Bones? Dancing with me is awkward." She glanced down at her belly between them.

He lifted her chin and gazed into her eyes. "Dancing with you is beautiful. *You're* beautiful, Sarah."

Her face crumpled into a mask of disbelief, and she shook

her head, but she was swaying gracefully, moving *with* him, not trying to get away despite what he saw in her expression.

"Don't do that," he said firmly. "Don't dismiss my words like they don't matter."

"I just…" She looked away for a moment. Then her eyes found his again, a little bit softer this time. "Do you have a pregnancy fetish or something?"

He chuckled. "Not that I'm aware of, and I'm a pretty observant guy."

"So I've noticed," she said with a small smile. "It feels weird to be out here, away from my kids, *dancing*."

"Dancing, or dancing with me?" He wanted to know all her thoughts, even if they weren't what he wanted to hear.

"Dancing at *all*, but dancing with you feels funny, too. *Nice*," she clarified with a spark of heat in her eyes. "But that's scary and crazy. Why me, when there's a tent full of gorgeous women right there?"

"Listen to the lyrics. It's a song by Maggie Rose called 'It's You,' and I swear, darlin', the words were written with us in mind." He watched her taking in the lyrics. They were so true. He'd never seen her coming, and he never wanted to see her leave.

"Bones…?" she said full of wonder.

"From the moment I first saw you, I had to see you again, and in the months since, that desire has intensified. I think about you and your children *all* the time." He looked down at her belly, and then he gazed into her eyes and said, "And that little miracle, too."

The breath rushed from her lungs. "You're doing it again. I can't breathe when you look at me like that."

"Then why fight it? You've spent two months getting to

know me. You know I'm not going to hurt you."

"I can't know that," she said vehemently. "Good people do bad things. You said so yourself."

His heart ached for what she must have been through to cause so much distrust. "That's true. But after thirty-plus years I can honestly say I've never done a single bad thing toward a woman. It's not in my makeup. I've done things I shouldn't have, like most people, but hurting you will *never* be one of those things. If you let me into your world, into your life, I promise you that I'll put my own life on the line before I let anyone hurt you or your children."

She choked out a breath.

"Let me prove it to you, Sarah. Let me take you on a real date. Get to know me better and decide for yourself."

"I can't go on a date. The kids—"

"I have a whole family who will gladly watch them. Scott said he would, too."

Her jaw dropped open. "You asked *Scott*?"

"He's your brother. In my world that means he looks out for you and deserves a heads-up." He spread his hand over her upper back, his fingers brushing the ends of her hair, and felt her heart beating rapidly.

The song ended, but they continued dancing. When the next song started he said, "Everyone is in our corner, darlin'. One date. One night to see if whatever this is between us is as real for you as it is for me."

"How do you know it's *anything* for me?"

Did she really think she hid her emotions that well? "You said you can't breathe when I look at you."

"*Ohmygosh*," she whispered. "I'm the lamest woman on earth."

"What does that make me? Because each and every time you look at me, I feel like I'm finally breathing for the very first time. And when you look at your children? Dear God, woman. That smile and the love in your eyes…? It makes all the bad in the world seem not quite so harsh. Go out with me, Sarah. Trust me enough for one date."

Her brows knitted. "Are you…? Dixie said you could be *lethal*."

"Dixie looks up to all her big brothers, but I promise she didn't mean it the way you're thinking. We were brought up to protect our own and those who are close to us. I'd take a bullet for anyone in that tent. I'd take a bullet for you."

"That's terrifying." Her hands slipped to his shoulders, holding on tighter, as if she didn't like the idea of something happening to him.

Cancer was *terrifying*. The thought of her leaving home at sixteen and her sister at thirteen was *terrifying*. Caring for a family without health insurance was *terrifying*. But he didn't say any of that to her. She had enough worries on her plate, and he felt her walls coming down. "No, darlin'. The thought of you turning me down for this date is terrifying. Having someone watching out for you is reassuring."

"You have all the answers. So tell me this. What did Bullet mean when he called you the *dirty doctor*? Because I'm not a biker groupie. I don't want to be tied up or spanked or to wear a leather collar."

"Is that what you think Dixie and Gemma are like? Or Crystal? Finlay?"

"No! I just meant…What did Bullet mean? I don't know what you're into. Obviously you have some weird sexual hang-ups, because you like *me*."

He clenched his jaw. "You need to stop doing that, please."

"What?"

"Putting yourself down. You're a gorgeous, intelligent, strong woman who puts her children ahead of herself, works hard, and still makes time to do things for others."

"Fine, but just because you think I'm pretty or smart doesn't mean *I* have to see myself that way. But I'll take *strong*," she said lightly. "And a mother is *supposed* to put her children first. Now, if you want to go out with me, then stop dancing around the answer and fess up, *dirty doctor*."

"I like your sass," he confessed. "My brothers have always been very open about their sexual conquests. For as long as I can remember, they'd joke about it. Until they fell in love and finally had a reason to stop. They wanted to protect their significant other's privacy. I've been private since day one. If I take a woman to bed, that's between me and her, not an act for someone else to get off on. I've never questioned them, but I assume they call me the dirty doctor because they have no idea what I'm into, and since I like leather and appreciate a woman in lace, maybe they think I'm into kink." He pulled her closer and said, "I'm a private guy, but don't worry, darlin'. If you want dirty, I can be as naughty as you like."

"No, I didn't mean…I like naughty, but…" She turned bright pink and huffed out a sigh. "Never mind. I can't believe I said *that*. I told you I was lame."

She tried to pull away, and he slid his hand down her bottom, angling their bodies so her side was pressed against him, bringing her ear close enough for him to whisper, "You're anything but lame." He pressed a kiss just below her earlobe, feeling her shiver in his arms. "How about that date?" He turned her face toward his, desperate to take his first taste of her. Her lips were so close, so tempting. If he leaned in… "Say yes, Sarah. Give something good a chance."

"I have baggage."

He wondered how she'd ever gotten pregnant with how hard she fought getting close. Disturbing ideas came to mind. He pushed them away to dissect later and said, "I have a knack for unpacking."

"I'm not kidding," she said with pleading eyes. "You've only seen my children, and they're my best features. I have *real* baggage that you can't see."

"I see *you*, Sarah, and your beautiful children. Whatever it took for you to be right here, right now, whatever made this moment possible *didn't* ruin you."

She looked away and said, "You have no idea."

"Then let me in. What's the worst that can happen?" Bones had known killers and drug dealers and women who had been raped and beaten. There was nothing he couldn't handle or help with.

"I could lose you as a friend." She gazed at the tent and said, "My children could lose you. We could lose *all* our friends, and this is the first place I've ever had any friends who were good people not because they wanted or needed something but because they just were. I'm afraid to lose that."

Her confession slayed him. "We're not going to let that happen, darlin'. How about we take things one step at a time? Say yes, Sarah. Let me show you how a lady should be treated."

She was quiet for a long moment. The band faded to white noise, leaving Bones to listen to the sound of his own thundering heart.

"I can't believe I'm saying this," she said tentatively, "but okay. One date, but I can't ride your motorcycle."

He chuckled, then feigned irritation. "*Damn.* What about skydiving?"

"Oh, sure. Why not?" She laughed sweetly. "We should go back in. I'm worried about leaving the kids for too long."

They talked through their schedules and settled on Thursday night for their date so Scott could watch the kids and put them to bed. He knew Sarah was still nervous, but as they headed inside, he draped an arm over her shoulder and said, "You know, some people around here might think I'm a catch."

"Ya think?" she said sarcastically.

"They'd be wrong, darlin'. In this equation, you're the catch."

"That's a pretty smooth line, but don't get too cozy. It's *one* date, and you'll probably end up regretting it."

"Like hell I will," he said more harshly than he meant to. If he did nothing else, he was going to break her of that self-deprecating habit. "We've got a date, which makes you *my girl*, and—"

"I had no idea you were so possessive," she said. "Maybe I need to rethink this date."

"No rethinking, and *nobody* talks smack about my girl. Including *you*."

She winced. "I'm sorry. I'll stop. I'm just nervous, and—"

As they neared the entrance to the tent, he drew her into his arms, catching her by surprise. In a split second that surprise turned to heat. He lowered his lips toward hers to quiet her worrying mind and satiate his thrumming desires.

"There you are!"

Dixie's voice startled Sarah, and she stumbled backward with a gasp before he had a chance to kiss her. Bones kept one arm around Sarah, glaring at his sister. "Great timing, Dix."

"Shit. Sorry. Wait. I thought…?" She looked at Sarah.

Sarah bit her lower lip and shrugged one shoulder.

"*Hallefuckinglujah!* About damn time." Dixie hiked a thumb over her shoulder, mischief flickering in her eyes. "I'll go back in and leave you alone."

"No!" Sarah said way too fast.

Bones arched a brow, but embarrassment was written all over her face. *Well, hell.* It looked like he'd have to tread even more carefully after all.

"Good, because you have got to see this." Dixie grabbed Sarah's wrist and hauled her into the tent. Sarah looked over her shoulder at Bones and mouthed, *Sorry!*

He thought he'd take them on a wild ride, but he had it all wrong. Sarah definitely held *his* reins in her hands.

He walked into the tent, mesmerized by her sappy expression as she looked at the dance floor. He followed her gaze, his insides melting at the sight of Biggs dancing with Lila in one arm, his cane in the other. The little angel had her fist buried in his beard, her head on his shoulder. By his side, Bradley and Kennedy danced with their arms around each other. Hawk stood discreetly off to the side, catching it all.

"Does she know?"

Bones turned at the sound of Bullet's voice. He hadn't even heard him approach. "Know what?"

"That you paid Hawk to take pictures of her and the kids all night."

Bones smiled to himself. "No, but we're going out Thursday night."

"The dirty doctor strikes again."

Bones put a hand on Bullet's shoulder and said, "About that. How about you calm that shit down around her, okay?"

Bullet chuckled.

"I'd hate to kick the living hell out of you before you have a chance to consummate your marriage."

Bullet looked across the dance floor at Finlay. Her hair was tousled, her lipstick worn off, and she had a sated expression on her flushed face. "Too late."

"What? Where? *How?*" Bones couldn't imagine sweet, proper Finlay sneaking off to have sex at her own wedding. Then again, it was obvious that her love for Bullet knew no limits.

"Dude, real men don't say shit." Bullet took a pull on his beer and lowered his voice to just above a whisper. "Fins told me if I told a soul that was all the action I'd get for a very long time."

"Never thought I'd see you pussy whipped."

"Never thought I'd like it so much." Bullet nudged him toward the bar. "Let's go celebrate. Sounds like we both got lucky tonight."

Chapter Six

THURSDAY AFTERNOON BONES sat in his office at the Peaceful Harbor Center of Hope, a premier East Coast cancer center, listening to his patient Wendy Stockard talk about her fourteen-year-old son Ollie's latest musical endeavor, his friends, grades, and just about everything other than herself or the aggressive form of breast cancer she was dealing with. The disease was so invasive, it had spread dramatically in the time between her biopsy and the date she was supposed to begin chemotherapy, and they'd had to act while there was still time. She'd had immediate surgery to remove her right breast, along with several lymph nodes in her armpits and neck. That was ten weeks ago. She began aggressive chemotherapy and radiation two weeks after surgery, and the entire ordeal was taking its toll. Bones met with her every week before her treatment to go over lab reports, adjust medications, and assess her mental state. Which was currently par for the course for Wendy, avoiding the topic of herself and the disease. Though this wasn't a case of denial. From the start she'd been determined to conquer the bastardly disease. Now he understood that, like Sarah, as a single mother she attacked everything this way, putting her son first and then dealing with her own issues. It had been a struggle for her to learn to put her health first, but she had come to understand that her well-being would feed her son's.

She touched her headscarf, an uncomfortable expression rolling into place. It broke his heart every time he saw the familiar embarrassment in his patients' eyes. He knew some patients had a hard time because they had come to see him initially with coiffed hair, flawless skin, and their lives under control. They thought their lack of hair, ashen skin, fatigue, and anything-but-in-control lives made them less attractive or appear weak, but the truth was, those were the signs of their strength. Bones was in awe of every person he treated and of every family member who had to deal with the hell that was cancer.

"Ollie wants to shave his head," she said with a small smile. "He has such thick, gorgeous hair. He got that from me, you know, not the man who fathered him."

He'd been waiting for her son to do it. He'd seen many loved ones take that step—showing the world their support and relieving a little of the feelings of helplessness that plagued them. "I'm surprised he's waited so long."

Ollie was as tough as his mother. Bones had been with them when Wendy told Ollie about her diagnosis. She hadn't wanted to do it alone, for fear of breaking down. Ollie had cried for only a minute before that sadness had morphed to anger, and weeks later, when Wendy was sick and weak from treatments, it had turned to pure rage. He'd run away, and Bones and his Dark Knights brothers had taken to the streets and tracked him down. Ollie had needed something other than his mother's disease to focus on. Something to give him a purpose and let him feel as though he was helping. They'd gotten him a job at the marina, where he earned enough money to bring his mother a little present now and then. He could have made the encouraging cards he left in her purse the mornings of her treatment, but knowing he'd worked toward them gave him a sense of pride.

He was a good kid. His world had been ripped out from under him, but he had a grip on things now, and his desire to shave his head proved how far he'd come. He was no longer running with fear; he was acting on it and supporting his mother in the only ways he knew how.

"It doesn't worry you?" she asked nervously. "Because I want him to be thinking about girls he wants to kiss and music he wants to create. I want him to gripe about doing homework and slam his bedroom door because his mother doesn't understand him."

Bones had become adept at distancing himself from his patients in order to keep his emotions out of his professional medical decisions, but at the end of the day, after those decisions had been made, thoughts of his patients and their families lingered.

"You want him to be a typical teenager," he said, "but I'm not sure there is such a thing. Every teenager has something they're dealing with. Ollie happens to be dealing with your illness."

"But he's just a boy," she pleaded.

"Don't let him hear you say that," Bones said with a smile, earning one in return. "He's almost fifteen. That's a strange time for guys. Their bodies and minds are maturing, but there's a place inside them that fears the changes as much as they crave them. As you told me the day I shared your diagnosis, you and Ollie are all each other have. He felt powerless, and now he's showing you that he can handle it. He wants to be in the trenches with you. I think he might be well served if you let him have the sense of *doing* something."

She sighed. "I guess you're right. Maybe I should be thankful that he asked my permission in the first place."

"That's one way to look at it." Bones clasped his hands and set them on his lap. "Now, how about you tell me how Ollie's *mom* is faring?"

She wrinkled her nose. "Do I have to?"

"Seems like a good idea. I hear your doctor is a pretty good listener."

"I'm still wondering how you're single."

Bones chuckled. If he had a dollar for every female patient who said something similar, he could buy a second boat. "Nice try at changing the subject."

"I really am wondering…*and* changing the subject." She sighed and sank back in the chair. "I'm tired, my body is hairless, and half the time I don't want to get out of bed."

"And do you stay in bed?"

She nodded. "Sometimes, but not because I want to give up. Single moms don't rest. We don't rely on others or wallow in our misery. We can't afford to. When I stay in bed it's because I don't have a choice."

He thought of Sarah and how hard she pushed herself for her family. "And the other times, when you're not in bed?"

"I'm either getting treatment or thanking the heavens above that I have these things to worry about and I'm not buried six feet under."

As hard as it was to hear, her blatant honesty was reassuring. She recognized the value of the treatments. They talked for a while longer, and when Wendy left, Bones found himself thinking of Sarah and her children again. There was no escaping the worries and what-ifs of single parenting. He knew Sarah had health insurance through the salon, and she had Scott to help her if something were to happen. *And she has me. If she wants me.*

She wants me, he mused. Even if she hadn't admitted it to herself yet.

It had been such a busy week, he hadn't had a chance to really talk with her. Sunday he'd gone on a ride with Bear and a bunch of their buddies, and Monday night they'd had *church*, which was what they called the meetings of the Dark Knights. He'd helped Scott Tuesday and Wednesday evenings with the basement, but Sarah hadn't gotten home from work until after eight, and then she'd been busy with the kids. They'd texted a few times since, but even through her texts he could tell she was nervous about their date.

He pulled out his phone and sent her a quick text. *Hey, beautiful. Three short hours until you go on the best date of your life.*

His office phone rang. He picked it up and said, "Dr. Whiskey."

"Wayne? Hey, man, it's Jon." Jon Butterscotch was an orthopedic oncologist who worked in his building, and he was a good friend. He drove a motorcycle, hung out at Whiskey Bro's, and was an avid extreme sports fanatic with a boisterous personality. But on the job, he was purely professional.

"How's it going?"

"Could be better. I need a consult for a seventeen-year-old girl with a brain tumor."

After discussing the patient and setting up a consultation, he read the text from Sarah that had come in while he was talking with Jon. *Are you sure you want to go out tonight?*

She'd asked if he was *sure* each time they'd spoken. It was time to quash the question once and for all. He grabbed his jacket and stalked out of his office.

"I'll be back in twenty minutes," he said to the receptionist on his way out the door. He climbed onto his bike, tugged on his helmet, and drove over to Chicki's salon. He parked by the curb and took off his helmet on the way inside.

"Hi, Bones. Do you have an appoint—" the receptionist began as he set his helmet on the desk on his way past, heading for Sarah.

Sarah was busy putting a cape around Jasmine Carbo's neck, oblivious to his approach. Jasmine watched him through the mirror. She'd known Bones forever. She and her twin brother owned a café in town.

"Hey, baby!" Chicki called from the back of the salon.

Bones waved, his eyes never wavering from the blond beauty before him.

Sarah started when he came to her side. "Bones? What are you doing here?" Her eyes flicked to the other hairdressers, who were curiously observing them.

"Sarah," he said evenly, gazing into her unsure eyes. He glanced at Jasmine and said, "Sorry to interrupt, Jazz. It seems Sarah and I have a bit of a communication gap. I just want to clear it up."

"Go right ahead," Jasmine said. "I've got *all* afternoon."

He took Sarah's hand in his and said, "Darlin', let me make something perfectly clear. I haven't changed my mind about our date, and I'm not going to no matter how many times you ask. So the next time you get the urge to send that particular text, remember this." He hauled her into his arms, taking her in a long, slow kiss, vaguely aware of the surprise sounding around them. In the space of a breath, he felt her shock give way to an inner struggle, and just as quickly she surrendered to their white-hot kiss, melting against him. He couldn't resist taking the kiss deeper for just a brief second, and *man*, what a blissful second that was.

As he drew away, Sarah wobbled. He ran his hands gently up her arms, steadying her. He knew he'd embarrassed her, but he'd had to, and hopefully he'd also taken away any lingering doubts, and given her something to think about until their date. Because *holy fuck*, he'd think of nothing else but kissing her again from that moment on.

"Wow," one of the hairdressers said.

"Whoa," Jasmine said. "How do I get a guy like you?"

Bones chuckled, still focused on Sarah. "Are we clear about our date tonight?"

"No!" Chicki called out. "I think you need to kiss her again."

"Mm-hm," Jasmine said, earning agreement from the other hairdressers. "We need an encore."

"No!" Sarah's eyes widened with shock, but there was no hiding the desire brimming in them. "We're, um...*clear.*"

"Great. I'll see you in a few hours, darlin'." He turned on his heel, grabbing his helmet on his way out the door, trailed by whispers and giggles. Once on the sidewalk, he saw Sarah was standing in the same place, touching her lips, as if she could still taste him—and *damn*, he couldn't wait to get another taste of her.

SARAH WAS A mess all afternoon. Bones Whiskey had a way of distracting her, but kissing him? That sent her into a tailspin. She already felt weird going on a date while she was pregnant, much less going out with the man Jasmine, and all the other women who had been in the salon when he'd planted his incredible lips on her, called the *catch of Peaceful Harbor*.

No pressure there or anything.

She wasn't sure how a pregnant woman should dress for a date with such a man, but on her way home she'd stopped at a maternity boutique Chicki had told her about and splurged on a pair of under-the-belly skinny jeans and the prettiest teal, pink, and black kimono she'd ever seen. On the plus side, it wasn't like she had to worry about sexy lingerie.

Ohmygosh. Don't even think about that.

She stood in front of the mirror assessing her outfit. She hadn't had a great body when she wasn't pregnant, a little thick around the middle, with nothing-to-write-home-about boobs and legs that were a little too thin. Nowadays she was lucky if she remembered to shave them. She ran her hand over her belly, wondering again why Bones would want to date her of all people. After two babies, with a third growing bigger inside her every day, her belly was a map of stretch marks, and when she wasn't pregnant, her breasts were like two half-deflated balloons. But she had to admit, the scoop-necked black shirt she wore beneath the kimono didn't look half bad, and her legs looked longer with a pair of wedge-heeled sandals. She put on her makeup, a spritz of perfume, and a black leather choker, because not only did the choker pull the whole outfit together, but she'd noticed Bones favoring his leather jacket and she thought he might like it.

What if Bones had something fancy planned? She wasn't a

fancy person, but he was a doctor. *Fancy* wasn't out of the realm of possibilities. Should she wear a dress? She didn't even really know what women her age wore on dates. She'd *never* been in that world. Not once in her life. Come to think of it, she'd never been on a proper date. Not even with the father of her children.

She heard Bradley's voice, though she couldn't make out what he'd said.

Oh God, what am I doing?

She should be with her children tonight, not out pretending to be a single woman with no responsibilities. What if the kids needed her? What if watching them was too much for Scott? She sat on the edge of the bed, feeling like she couldn't breathe.

A knock at her bedroom door made her jump. "Yeah?"

Scott peered into the bedroom, his casual expression morphing to worry. He rushed to her side with Lila on his hip. "What's wrong? What happened?"

"Nothing. I just..." She closed her eyes for a second, trying to catch her breath.

Scott put a hand on hers. "Are you sick?"

She shook her head and opened her eyes, meeting her brother's concerned gaze. "No, but do I look it?"

"No. You look great."

She exhaled loudly. "You have to help me cancel tonight. I've never even gone on a real date. I have no idea why I said yes. I can't do this." She wanted to, but at the same time, as she looked at her sweet baby girl playing with a rubber toy, she wanted to be right there with her, too.

"Can't, don't want to, or are afraid to?" Scott asked carefully. "Because if you can't or don't want to, I'll call Bones right now and say you can't go. But, Sarah, if you want to go, but you're scared, I think you should go out with him. I had a long talk with Bones at the wedding. He's genuinely interested in you, and I admit, at first I thought it was weird as sh"—he glanced at Lila, who was happily playing with her toy—"because you're pregnant and have a family, but you know what? After talking to him, I honestly believe he—"

"Don't say he sees past it, because…" She glanced at her stomach with a deadpan look.

"That's just it. He didn't even try to pretend he saw past anything. He embraced it. The guy really likes *you*, Sarah. And I realized that's not so weird after all. You're a cool chick, and you're a great mom. Sure, you're pregnant, but that doesn't change those things."

Though she hung on to his kind words, she still couldn't believe this was right, and she shook her head. "Great moms don't leave their children to go out on dates. Or maybe single moms do, but single pregnant moms? I feel like everyone's going to look at me weird. I'm looking at myself weird."

She jumped at the sound of a car door closing out front. Scott squeezed her hand, and then he peered out the window. "Were you expecting Dixie and Gemma?"

"No. What if something happened to Bones?" She hurried out of the bedroom.

Scott followed her out, chuckling. "You're going on this date, sis," he said as she whipped open the front door. "You definitely like the guy."

She didn't have time to reply as Dixie and Gemma both squealed with excitement and ran up to hug her.

"Hello, sexpot. You are one hot mama!" Dixie said.

"You look gorgeous," Gemma added.

"What are you doing here?" Sarah asked. "Is Bones okay?"

Dixie smirked. "If he's not, he will be when he gets a look at you." She shifted her gaze to Scott and said, "And damn, boy. You look hot with a baby in your arms."

Scott grinned. "Maybe I'll have to babysit more often."

"My children are not wingmen...*wingkids*," Sarah said firmly.

"Bones is fine," Gemma reassured her. "We came to help Scott with the kids and to make sure you were okay."

"She's not," Scott said.

Sarah glared at him, reeling from the idea that they'd shown up to help without her asking. She couldn't back out *now*. That made her happy and more nervous.

"We heard about what happened at the salon," Gemma said.

Dixie tickled Lila's belly. "Gotta give my brother props. You two are the talk of the town."

"Oh no," Sarah said under her breath as she followed them inside, feeling nauseous. *The talk of the town?*

"Gemma!" Bradley ran over and wrapped his arms around Gemma's legs. Then he blinked curiously up at Dixie and said, "Mom can't play right now. She's going out."

Dixie scooped him into her arms. "We came to play with you and your sister, silly goose."

"You did?" Bradley wiggled from her arms and dragged Dixie over to his toys. "We're playing farm. You can be the pig."

"I think we need to have a little talk about how to speak to women." Dixie winked at Sarah. "I'll straighten this boy out. Sarah, you'd better sit down. You look white as a sheet. Are you sure you're not sick?"

"Just really nervous," she said honestly.

Gemma took her hand. "Since I can't offer you a drink to take the edge off, why don't we go talk in private?"

Scott pointed down the hall. "Her bedroom's down there."

As she and Gemma went to her bedroom, Gemma said, "Scott looked as pale as you when we got here. But he sure looks better now, thanks to Dixie. She knows how to get a man's attention."

"He was doing a pretty good job of talking me off the ledge, but I don't think he's used to dealing with nervous women."

"Then he and Dixie will get along just fine. I swear nothing rattles her." Gemma sat on the edge of the bed and patted the mattress.

"I can't sit down. I'm too nervous." Sarah paced the small bedroom, unable to hold back her worries. "I'm not sure I should go on this date. I'm glad you guys are here, but still. They're *my* kids. I don't want to be the kind of mother who puts herself before her children. And look at me." She placed her hand on her belly. "I shouldn't be dating. I should be here, with Bradley and Lila—"

"Wishing you were with Bones?" Gemma pushed to her feet, stopping Sarah from pacing. "You're a single mother, and single mothers are allowed to have lives, Sarah."

"Single *pregnant* mothers? What's everyone in town going to say about me going out with Bones? They'll think I'm a gold digger or looking for a baby daddy or something."

"Wow, you *are* nervous. Did anyone at the salon look at you like that? Because from what I heard they were all excited *for* you. You might not know this, but Bones doesn't do things like that. I mean, *ever*."

"They cheered at the salon, but I figured that was just because, you know, I was standing there like a deer in the headlights, stunned." Sarah plunked down on the bed. "And don't tell me he doesn't do that. He sure seemed to know exactly what he was doing."

"That's just it. He knew *exactly* what he was doing. He doesn't even date women around here. He's really careful with his reputation. The fact that he kissed you like that in front of lots of gossipy eyes means he was sending a message. He wanted everyone to know how he felt. Most of all, *you*."

"That's supposed to make me less nervous? Look at him, Gemma. I'm not even in his league. He's not just hot. He's smart and funny and caring, and you've *seen* him with my kids. I swear there's nothing sexier…"

"Didn't I tell you that on Halloween? And if you want to talk about leagues, you're talking to the wrong girl. Leagues are things rich people make up to rationalize their snobbery." Gemma leaned her butt against the dresser and crossed her arms. "I grew up in a *very* privileged world. We had everything money could buy, and I hated it. *All* of it. To be honest, I wouldn't be friends with Bones if he were like that."

"I didn't mean he was snobby—"

"I know, but just listen, please. The thing about Tru and the Whiskeys is that they are the realest family I have ever met. They taught me the meaning of acceptance. They don't judge by where we came from or what we have or don't have. They only care about who we are now, and you are a magnificent mother and a beautiful, sweet woman. Bones sees that in you, and it shouldn't matter what anyone else thinks other than you. Do you *want* to go out with him?"

Sarah sighed, nodding. "It's scary, but I'm happy when we're together." She heard another car door close, and panic engulfed her. She grabbed Gemma's hand. "Are you sure I'm dressed okay? What if people look at me funny?"

"You're with Bones Whiskey. Do you really think *anyone* will look at you funny? He'll protect you with his life, and trust me when I say that Bones will shut down any sideways glances before you have time to think twice about them."

"Sarah?" Scott called from the living room.

Sarah hugged her. "Thank you. I'm not good at this kind of thing."

"None of us think we are, but our guys have proved us wrong. Come on, let's go *wow* your man."

Chapter Seven

"HE'S NOT MY—" Sarah stopped cold at the sight of Bones crouched by the front door with Bradley's arms around his neck and Lila toddling toward him babbling, "Bababa."

Lila had taken only a few steps since the wedding, but she was cruising like she'd been practicing for this moment all week.

"Mom porn at its best," Gemma whispered.

Bones caught Lila as she tumbled into him, and his hearty laugh made Sarah warm and fuzzy inside. He looked over, and his expression went from amused to dark and desirous.

For me.

So much for warm and fuzzy. She was suddenly hot and bothered, and by the grin spreading across his lips, he sensed it. *Deep breaths*, she told herself. *Say hello.* There was a disconnect between her brain and her body, because she just stood there, taking in his deliciousness and remembering the way he'd swept her into his arms and kissed her breathless.

"Hi, beautiful," he said, rising to his feet with a child in each arm. His leather jacket hugged his broad shoulders, and beneath, a dark dress shirt revealed a hint of ink on his chest.

Why did that make her pulse quicken?

"Doesn't your mama look pretty, B-boy?" Bones asked, eyes locked on Sarah.

Bradley nodded. "She always looks pretty."

Surely her heart couldn't take much more of this sweetness.

"Okay, you two oglers." Dixie reached for Lila, giving Scott a *get on the ball* look.

"Oh, right." Scott took Bradley from Bones, freeing him to pick up a bouquet of red roses Sarah hadn't noticed on the table by the door.

Ohgodohgodohgod. She could tell by Gemma and Dixie's stifled giggles that she was doing an awful job of hiding her elation. She'd never been given flowers before, and she'd wondered what it would feel like to mean enough to a man that he would do something so thoughtful. As Bones stepped closer, she wanted to memorize everything about this moment. The way her chest tingled and happiness bubbled up inside her made her even more nervous.

"Hi, darlin'." He put a hand on Sarah's hip and pressed a kiss to her cheek, lingering for a beat longer than she'd expected, just as he had earlier.

Even if they never stepped foot out the door, these few minutes were right up there as some of the best of her life, right alongside the first time she'd held her babies and the first time she'd seen them walk and heard them say *Mama*.

"These are for you," he said as he handed her the bouquet.

"They're gorgeous. Thank you."

"Want me to put them in a vase for you?" Gemma asked.

"Sure, thanks." She stood stock-still as Gemma took the flowers, and Bones's smile grew wider. She realized she hadn't moved since she'd seen him by the door. Forcing her brain to function, she said, "Let me just kiss the kids, and then we can go."

Sarah crouched beside Bradley, who was busy playing with Dixie, and said, "I'm going to go out for a little while. Be good for Uncle Scott, Dixie, and Gemma, okay?" He nodded, barely paying her any attention. She gave him a kiss goodbye, feeling a little less guilty about leaving. She tickled Lila's belly, earning sweet little-girl giggles, and then she kissed her and said, "I love you, sweet girl." Looking at Scott, she said, "Are you sure you'll be okay?"

"I have reinforcements. Go," he urged. "And don't give us a second thought. It's just like when you go to work, except they'll be tucked in and fast asleep when you get home, so don't hurry back."

"Thank you, all of you." She put her phone in her purse, and when she reached for her coat, Bones took it and held it up for her to put on.

"Thanks, you guys," Bones said. "Call us if you need to for anything at all, and we'll come right back."

She knew she couldn't return without him, but still, hearing him say *we'll come right back* made her warm and fuzzy again.

When the door closed behind them, with the brisk evening air on her face and Bones's hand on her back, the thrill of their first date hit Sarah anew. His arm drifted up and around her shoulder, holding her closer.

"Thanks for agreeing to go out with me. You look amazing."

She stifled her knee-jerk reaction to deny his compliment and said, "Thanks. So do you."

He unlocked the door of his sleek black sports car, and she slid onto the leather seat. "Oh, this is nice. What is it?"

"Nothing special. Just a car."

He closed her door, and she watched him walk around to the driver's side. As he climbed in, she admired the sleek interior and noticed a Porsche insignia and *Panamera* on the center console.

Holy fudge. She didn't know there were Porsches with four doors.

Gemma was wrong. There were definitely leagues, and she was so far out of hers she'd need a crane to haul her pregnant heinie back to it.

As he drove out of her development she asked, "Where are we going?"

"I thought we'd have dinner, get to know each other a little better."

She waited for him to say more, like *where* they were going, and when he didn't offer any clues, she got even more nervous. Needing to fill the silence, she said, "How was your day at work?"

He slid her a slightly confused, and very hot, grin. "I don't think anyone's asked me that for years."

"Really? Your job is so demanding. I imagine it's hugely emotional. If nobody asks, how do you get out from under it?"

He focused on the road as he drove through town, his brows knitting. "I deal, you know."

"I don't know, but I'd like to," she said honestly. "I don't know anything about being a doctor, but I've always been intrigued at how doctors can see patient after patient and keep them straight. I know you have charts, but at least with the doctors at the women's clinic, they're in and out so quickly, I think we all must blur together. But I guess it doesn't much matter, because there's no guarantee we'll see the same doctor each time anyway. It's a little uncomfortable. Do your patients see just you, or do they see other doctors in your practice?"

"Depending on their situation, they might see a team of doctors, but if I'm overseeing treatments, I see them at every appointment." Tension tightened his features. "You don't have a private obstetrician?"

"No."

He was quiet for a moment before saying, "I have a good buddy who's an ob-gyn, Damon Rhys, and if you prefer a woman, his partner, Stephanie Blair, also has a great reputation."

She knew private doctors were more expensive than the clinic, but she appreciated his offer, so she said, "Thanks. I'll have to see if they take my insurance. What's the name of the practice?" He gave her the name as they neared Whiskey Bro's and said, "When we park, I'll text you his number."

"Are we going to Whiskey Bro's?" Finlay handled the food for the bar, and Sarah knew she wouldn't have to worry about allergens.

"I thought we'd have a few drinks before…Oh wait…" He made a teasing *tsk* sound. "You can't drink. *Damn.*" He shook his head as they drove past the bar, feigning disappointment. "First I have to bring four wheels instead of two, and now I have to skip my nightly brews?"

She knew he was teasing, but before she could come up with a sassy retort, he reached across the console, taking her hand in his. Then he lifted it to his lips and pressed a kiss there, making her heart sing.

When he turned off the main road onto a narrow lane near Bullet and Finlay's street, he pulled over to the shoulder and put the car in park, giving her his full attention.

"I don't know what type of guys you're used to going out

with, but I'm relatively intelligent. I know what it means to be pregnant and to worry about food allergies. And I know that even if you're not worried right now, in about half an hour, regardless of whether you're having a good time or not—and trust me, you will be—you'll probably start worrying about your kids."

Feeling suddenly shy because of her transparency, she lowered her gaze.

He lifted her chin and said, "You're safe with me, darlin'. And if you want to call and check on your kids, or sit in your backyard for our date so you don't feel so far from them, that's okay with me. I just want to spend time with you."

She didn't know what to say to that. Apparently he didn't need a response, because he turned his attention back to the narrow lane before them, and they drove in comfortable silence for a long while. Eventually they came to three forks in the road. Bones turned down the one farthest to the right, and a few minutes later the woods gave way to a beautiful view of a small marina.

"Where are we?" she asked as he parked.

"Harborview Marina. It serves the houses in my development. It's empty this time of year. Almost everyone's got their boats put away for the winter."

He climbed out of the car and came around to help her out. She took in the moon reflecting on the inky water and the boats rocking gently in the marina. Bones tucked her beneath his arm again. She wasn't sure why he'd gone from a hand on her back to holding her closer, but as they walked toward the docks, a breeze swept over them, and she was thankful for his warmth.

"You said you were from Florida. Did you spend much time on the water?" he asked as they stepped onto a dock and he guided her toward the last boat.

"Not really. Life was a bit crazy back then." She saw concern rising in his eyes and tried to dissuade him from asking more questions. "You know how it is when you live by the water. You take it for granted."

"That's a shame. The water brings me a sense of peace. Give me one second." He climbed onto the luxurious boat, which had a massive indoor area with several large windows across the front and more on the sides. There was a deck on top of that area with an awning above. The back of the boat had lots of comfortable-looking cushioned benches. She was pretty sure this would be considered a yacht. It was beautiful, like something out of a travel magazine.

He lowered a ramp to the dock, and then he walked with her onto the boat with one arm around her back.

"Is this *yours*?" she asked.

"It is. Sarah, meet *Edison*. *Eddy*," he said to the boat, "be good to my girl."

"Are we going sailing?" she asked nervously. "I've never been, and I don't know if I'll get seasick."

"Don't worry, darlin'. We aren't taking the boat out. I didn't think you'd want to be that far from the kids in case they needed you."

She followed him to the seating area, and he lifted one of the cushions, revealing a secret compartment. He withdrew several blankets and said, "I'm sorry, but I need just a few minutes to get us set up. Do you want to sit down and relax? Can I get you some lemonade? Iced tea? Hot tea?"

"Hot tea on a boat? That sounds elegant."

"Hot tea it is."

She sat down, and he draped a blanket over her legs. "I'm

not too cold, but thank you. You sure you don't want some help?"

"No. I've got it. You sit there and relax."

He disappeared into the cabin, and a few seconds later strings of tiny amber lights bloomed to life along the boat railings and up the mast, making the evening even more romantic. Country music began playing softly from speakers near the entrance to the cabin, and then Bones appeared with an old-fashioned-looking lantern, which he lit and set on the table. He disappeared into the cabin again, returning a minute later with a tall, silver contraption. He fussed with it, and a moment later it glowed orange, and she realized it was a space heater. He'd thought of everything. He ducked inside again, longer this time, and when he returned he set the table for two and then popped back into the cabin for another minute and brought her a mug of tea and a plate of sliced lemon, honey, and packets of sugar and sugar substitute.

"You have quite a system," she said, wondering if he did this for all his dates.

"I wish I had a system," he said with a shake of his head. "I've never cooked dinner for anyone before. It's usually just me and the sea, or family, of course. I bought the space heater *today*, and Scott helped me set up the lights. I'm winging it, Sarah, and I'm sure it looks that way. I wanted everything to be perfect for you." He held up one finger and said, "I only need another minute or two. I guess if I were smarter, I'd have had the meal catered, so I wasn't running back and forth, but I didn't want to chance it with your allergies."

Back into the cabin he went, leaving her slack-jawed. He'd *cooked* for her and *bought* a space heater just for tonight? All her basal instincts wanted to pick apart his thoughtfulness and figure out what he expected in return. But when he came out of the cabin carrying a silver tray with three dishes on it and his eyes found hers, she saw in them everything she needed to know. He wasn't looking at her like he wanted to take anything from her. No, she sensed just the opposite, that he wanted to *give*. To spend time together, just as he'd said.

He set the food on the table and sat down beside her. "I hope this is okay. Creamy Tuscan chicken with sundried tomatoes and cilantro and lime sweet potatoes. I got the recipes from Finlay before they left on their honeymoon. She assured me that it was gluten free, dairy free, soy free, egg free, tree nut and peanut free."

She felt herself tearing up.

"Oh no, I blew it, didn't I? Are you allergic to something here? Do you have allergies other than to food? I should have asked. I can put this away and we can go to a restaurant." He pushed to his feet, but she touched his arm and shook her head, bringing him back down beside her.

"No, you didn't blow it, Bones. It's beyond perfect." Pregnancy hormones always made her more emotional, but she had a feeling even without them she'd be teary eyed. "I'm sorry. Other than when Finlay brought meals right after the accident, nobody has ever cooked for me, much less done anything like this." Even her parents hadn't gone to any lengths to feed her things she'd enjoy. She'd go weeks eating only jam sandwiches on gluten-free bread and taco meat without shells.

"That's a shame, because a woman like you deserves to be treated special."

SARAH TRIED SO hard to mask her feelings, she actually drew more awareness to the depths of which he'd touched her. As much as Bones hated to see and acknowledge it, there was also something much darker lingering in those gorgeous eyes. Unhappiness perhaps. Bones had always had a sixth sense about despair in others. It helped him in the medical field and in the dating world, telling him which women were potential trouble before he got involved. But with Sarah, it felt different. His feelings for her over the past couple of months had grown too deep to heed the red flags she'd tried to warn him about.

"I think you have a second calling as a chef if this whole doctor gig doesn't work out for you," she said as they ate. "This is delicious."

"Oh yeah? I'll let them know at the women's shelter where I volunteer. I bet they could use another cook."

"I didn't know there was a women's shelter here." She took a bite of the sweet potatoes and closed her eyes. "Mm. I *love* sweet potatoes."

He stabbed a piece of sweet potato from his plate and held it up for her. Her adorably shy smile tweaked his heart as she leaned in to eat it.

"The shelter is in Parkvale, about thirty minutes outside of town, and run by Eva Yeun, the wife of a Dark Knight. It's in a pretty rough area, but they provide housing and counseling for women and children who have suffered abuse or are in danger of being abused. I volunteer when I can, usually once or twice a month, to examine the residents and children, but oftentimes they need someone to listen more than they need medical attention."

Sarah gripped her fork tighter and shifted uncomfortably, putting a little more space between them. "They don't mind a man doing the exams?"

"Finding volunteers can be difficult, which is why an oncologist is doing general exams and not a family practice doctor. I can't say that all of the women are open to being examined, but I do what I can."

She nodded, fidgeting with a seam on her jeans. "You sort of avoided my question earlier about what your days are like as a physician. I get it if you don't want to talk about it…"

The quick subject change, and her discomfort, did not go unnoticed, but Bones didn't push. "It's not that I don't like talking about my day. Nobody ever asks. I'm glad you did, but I guess I've learned to compartmentalize my work, the Dark Knights business, and everything else in my life. My family says I'm the king of distancing myself from people and situations, and they're probably right." He'd learned how to do it after losing a childhood friend who had been the impetus for his going to medical school. A familiar pang of longing washed through him. "I've done it for a very long time, but I don't seem to have the same inclination when it comes to you."

A sweet smile appeared for only a moment before turning serious again, and she said, "I know all about distancing yourself from people and situations, and I'm honestly interested in hearing about your day. I want to get to know you better. The *real* you, not just the person you want everyone to see. I mean, I really like who you are, but we spend so many hours being *something*—a doctor, a hairdresser, a mom, a bartender, *whatever*—it shapes us into who we are in other parts of our lives. But oncology is such a scary field. Even the word *cancer* makes the pit of my stomach hurt, and you deal with it every day. I guess what I'm saying is, if you want to talk, I'm a pretty good listener."

Bones had gone out with a lot of women over the years, and never once had any taken such an interest in those aspects. He loved that Sarah wanted to know more about him and about the more important parts of his life, but he wondered again about her background. What or who had shaped her to be such an amazing mother and empathetic person, when from what he'd gathered, her parents hadn't been either?

He knew she'd clam up if he asked, so he said, "I'd like to share what it's like with you. The truth is, as sad as cancer is in general, my days revolve around *hope*. When a person receives a cancer diagnosis, they suddenly go from *living* their life to *fighting* for it. Nobody is prepared for it. It's not something we teach our children, like being wary of strangers or how to interview for a job. It's like being dropped onto an iceberg, where the landscape they've always navigated is suddenly foreign. Even patients with strong support systems can feel like they're battling the disease alone. In addition to doing everything I can medically for my patients, I try to give them what they need sometimes more than medication. I *listen*, and I don't overbook my schedule for that reason. I never know if a couple will have an hour's worth of questions, a single parent will need to talk about his or her children, or an elderly patient will wax nostalgic and simply *need* to tell a story. I give them the best care I can and the most time I am able."

"That's why you offered to refer me to Dr. Rhys. Because you care so deeply, you think every doctor should."

He knew most did, but he also knew many who slighted their patients, jamming in as many as they could to make more money. "You're having a baby. Your doctor is not just looking at your most private area, which I would imagine is uncomfortable enough, but they're caring for your most precious gift. I guess I feel like your emotional state is just as important as your physical. Connecting with a doctor during multiple visits allows him to assess that on a more personal level, picking up on nuances a doctor who doesn't know you might miss."

"I see what you mean. Being a doctor is so different from what your other family members do. Did you always know you wanted to be one?"

"Not always," he said honestly. "To understand me, you have to understand all the pieces of my life. I'm not sure how much you know about the Dark Knights beyond the fact that we're a club, not a gang, and we help people in need and protect the community."

"I've seen that firsthand," she said with a smile. "I don't know if any of us would be alive if not for Bullet's bravery. He literally ran into a burning car and saved all of us and then stayed with me at the hospital. That's...well, you know how unbelievable that is. I would be knee deep in debt if not for you guys. I've never met anyone like you or your family and friends. It's so far from my life, it feels like a dream."

"Well, that's how we were raised in and out of the club. My great-grandfather founded the Dark Knights as well as our family businesses. He was a hard-ass biker, and he brought his sons up to be as well. That's why Biggs, my father, takes total responsibility for everyone around him, including the residents of this town. He raised us the same way. From a young age we were taught to help and protect—*everyone*."

"So that's why you became a doctor? You wanted to help and protect? That makes sense."

"It makes sense, but it wasn't the reason I became a doctor." He'd never told a soul about Thomas, but he wanted to tell Sarah the truth, and if he ever expected to find out about the shadows behind her eyes, he had to expose his own. "When I was in seventh grade, a boy named Thomas moved to town. He was wicked smart. The kind of smart that blows your mind, but he was this skinny, meek kid who wore glasses and kept to himself. The only way you knew he was smart was by listening to his answers in class. He never acted like he was better than anyone else. One day after school, I saw a kid giving him a hard time, and I stood up for Thomas. The bully was a real jerk, and I ended up giving him a black eye. He was just a punk who skipped school more than he showed up. But I hung around Thomas after that, knowing that guy would try to find a time when Thomas was alone just to show he was the top dog. Well, Thomas was afraid of me at first, trying to avoid me, because I had fought the other kid. But I was relentless," he said, remembering those early days vividly and fondly. "I can still see Thomas looking over his shoulder as he walked home from school, telling me I didn't have to watch out for him."

"Aw, the poor kid was probably embarrassed."

"Better to be embarrassed than to have a broken nose. Eventually, he gave up telling me to go away and we became friends. Really good friends. We'd go down to the docks at the big marina where his dad used to keep his boat, and we'd hang out for hours. The summer before ninth grade, Thomas got sick." He swallowed against the emotions clogging his throat and said, "At first they thought it was just a virus. He had headaches and was tired a lot. But then he developed other symptoms, numbness in his legs, blurred vision."

Sarah put her hand over his. "He had cancer?"

Bones nodded. "Brain tumor. They found it too late. I spent as much time as I could with him, whether he was in the hospital getting treatments or at home. I saw the way he looked at those doctors, hoping for a miracle. He never got his miracle. After he died, I wanted to give him miracles. I wanted to give every kid, every parent, every damn person touched by cancer miracles."

Tension spiked across his shoulders with the memories, and he looked away to avoid letting Sarah see his pain. "I used to call him *Edison* because he was so smart. You know, like Thomas Edison? He called me *bonehead*, because the guy I decked was twice my size and he thought I was stupid for going after him. After he died, I felt like school was moving too slowly. I wanted to get on with things, go to medical school, and make a difference. That's why I graduated at sixteen. When I told my dad I wanted to go to medical school, I also told him I'd chosen my biker name. *Bones.*"

"Because of what Thomas called you?" Sarah tried to blink away her tears, but her heart was too big, and they tumbled down her cheeks. "I'm sorry you lost your friend. That must have been horrible. But I bet he's smiling down on you as you give other people miracles."

He touched her cheek, brushing her tears away with his thumb. Her eyes darkened, but there was trepidation there, too. "Do I scare you, Sarah?"

She shook her head. "The way I feel about you scares me."

That made him smile. He slid his hand to the nape of her neck, drawing her closer.

"Why?"

"Because I have kids, and I can't afford to put them at risk by making a mistake."

He touched his forehead to hers, breathing her in. "Why would we be a mistake?"

"Because I'm usually really good at distancing myself from

others, but being with you…"

She shook her head, and he drew back, searching for some hint of what was going on in her mind. "Are you afraid I'll hurt them in some way?"

She shook her head again.

"That I'll hurt *you*?"

She was quiet for a long moment before saying, "Not purposefully."

"Oh, my sweet Sarah," he whispered, pain slicing through him. "What have you been through that's made you so scared?"

Fresh tears slid down her cheeks. "If you knew all my secrets, you wouldn't want anything to do with me."

"You're wrong, Sarah. Give me a chance and you'll see the truth."

She swiped at her tears and turned away. "I'm sorry. Here you've given me the best night of my life, and I've turned into a sniveling mess."

He drew her into his arms, gazing deeply into her eyes, and he touched his lips to her damp cheeks, tasting her salty tears. "You're not a mess. We all have pasts. I've done things I'm not proud of."

"Yeah, right. The guy who was raised to help and protect? What have you done? *Jaywalked?*"

"Yes. But other things, too. I stole a car once."

"I can't even imagine that," she said with a smile that faded so fast it made him ache. "We're from two different worlds."

"Are we? Because I grew up with *nothing* but family. We didn't have much money. My parents were leather-wearing, motorcycle-driving badasses who got sideways looks when we traveled outside of Peaceful Harbor. I grew up with rough men coming over to our house at all hours, my father leaving with them to go pound the shit out of some guy who had raped a woman and drag his ass to the police, or to stand watch over some poor abused woman's house to keep her safe. As a boy, there was always scary stuff going on, things I wasn't supposed to notice or talk about."

"That does sound scary."

"That kind of thing has a huge impact on a kid," he said. "Part of me wanted to be just like my father, and another part feared it because although Biggs has physical deficits from his stroke, he's *still* the kind of man who'll toss his cane aside and step in front of a moving train to save someone else. As a kid I wasn't sure I could pull off being that fearless, and following in Bullet's footsteps? The man's a beast. Living up to the expectations of a man who would stop at nothing to protect a stranger makes you dig deeper than you ever knew was possible. I'd put my life on the line for most anyone, but getting to that point? For a kid whose mind went through a methodical process before making even the littlest decisions, it took more than a leap of faith to wrap my head around what it *really* meant to be a Whiskey."

"I can't even imagine. Your father would really go after bad guys to save strangers?"

"We all would. I'm not the squeaky-clean guy you think I am, but I'm not a deviant who would ever hurt you or your children. You don't have to trust me right now, Sarah, but I've never told a soul about Thomas until tonight. My family knows, and those who have lived here long enough to remember him know we were friends. But his family has long since moved away. I trust you, and I want to open up to you. I hope one day you'll do the same."

She inhaled a ragged breath, lowering her gaze to her belly.

"Part of me wants just this one night without revealing my past. One night with you looking at me like no one ever has before, so I can pretend to be a normal single woman for just a short time."

He knew he'd never stop looking at her like that, no matter what she shared with him. "One night will never be enough."

He cradled her beautiful face in his hands, their connection drawing him closer. Her eyes were so dark and alluring, he was powerless to resist lowering his lips to hers. Her lips were soft and sweet, and she opened for him a little tentatively at first, but as he took the kiss deeper, she gave in to their passion, meeting every stroke of his tongue with an eager one of her own. He threaded his fingers into her hair, and holy hell, he'd been wanting to do that for so long, his entire body pressed forward, craving more.

"*Fuck*, Sarah," he ground out against her lips. "Please don't be afraid of me."

He reclaimed her mouth, sliding his tongue over hers, along her teeth and the roof of her mouth, everywhere he could reach. He wanted to possess every inch of her, to wrap her in his arms and *show* her he'd protect her. The kiss went on and on, with no beginning and he sure as hell didn't want it to end. But he needed more of her. He kissed the edge of her mouth and down her neck. She turned, giving him better access, and *man* he loved that.

"That's it, darlin'. Show me what you like."

"You," she panted out. "I like you."

He sealed his mouth over her neck in a series of slow, openmouthed kisses, cradling her face with one hand, *feeling* her sexy little whimpers, pleas, and gasps. Each one made his body thrum with heat. As he kissed and nibbled his way up to her ear, she turned her face, bringing his thumb against her lips. She dragged her tongue up the length of it, and he swore he felt it on his cock. A growling sound escaped before he could stop it, and she shuddered in his arms.

"I have wanted to kiss you like this for weeks." He licked the shell of her ear and whispered, "I love your sexy mouth."

She slicked her tongue along his thumb again, and he couldn't resist pushing it between her lips. She closed her mouth around it, shocking the hell out of him and spurring him on to feast on her neck. Her tongue swirled around his thumb, and then she sucked *hard*, drawing a groan right out of him. He curled two fingers into the collars of her shirts, tugging them to the side, and lowered his mouth to her bare shoulder. Her skin was warm and smelled like lilacs. So fucking good he wanted to disappear into her. When she arched forward, he dipped lower, kissing the swell of her breasts. His hand moved along her thigh, beneath her shirt and up her side, feeling the roundness of her belly and the underside of her breast. He caressed her breast, and her nipple rose to a tempting peak against his palm.

She gasped a tiny, stilted breath.

The difference between hunger and hesitation hit him like a truck.

He slid a hand to the nape of her neck, gazing deeply into her eyes. Her silent warnings came through loud and clear—*Be careful with me. I want this, but I'm scared.* Taking her fears to heart, he put his mouth beside her ear and said, "Don't worry, darlin'. I'm in no rush."

"But I want to kiss you," she pleaded, desire and hesitation still battling in her eyes.

He pressed his hand to her cheek, kissing her lightly, giving her a chance to back off, but she intensified their kisses. She was so eager, and so vulnerable, everything she did made him fall harder for her. He drew back again, needing to take a pulse on where her head was, and brushed his thumb over her lips. She inhaled another sexy gasp, this one void of any hesitation. He followed the same path with his tongue, and she pressed forward, meeting his mouth hungrily as he took her in another penetrating kiss. Her mouth was hot and sweet, and her body was sensual and sexy. *Heavenly.* She writhed against him, belly and breasts to chest and abs. He clutched her ass, hauling her closer without breaking their connection.

He'd fantasized about kissing her for so long, thought about how her hands would feel on his body, her mouth on his flesh. But nothing had prepared him for the sweetness that was Sarah Beckley. She kissed the same way she protected her children, vehement and loving at once, and it was the sexiest make-out session he'd ever experienced.

She wanted one night without questions, one night to feel *normal.* She was so far *beyond* normal, there wasn't a woman alive who could measure up to her, and Bones vowed to make her not only see it, but *believe* it.

Chapter Eight

WHEN THEIR LIPS finally parted, Sarah turned away and fixed her shirt, avoiding his gaze. Bones reached for her, and she stiffened.

He smoothed his hand down her back and said, "Sarah, there's no reason to be embarrassed."

"That's easy for you to say. You didn't just suck on a man's thumb on a first date."

He gathered her hair over one shoulder, trying to see her face, but she kept turning away from him. "Here, darlin', let me fix that." He lifted her hand and sucked her thumb into his mouth.

She yanked it away with a sexy laugh. "It's different for guys. It's expected. I'm not the kind of woman who does that, and I don't want to be that person in your eyes. I just got swept away in the moment."

"First of all, you're right about perceptions, and that's got to suck from a woman's perspective. But not all guys are like that. I haven't seen you as anything other than a strong, guarded woman and mother who also happens to be sexy and beautiful. What we did doesn't change that. If anything, I feel closer to you because you let me in."

She faced him then, her cautious eyes sailing over his face. Could she see that he was being blatantly honest? Did she want to see it, or was she too scared? Or worse, had he somehow misread the situation?

"Did you feel pressure to be close to me? Because if you did, I—"

"No," she interrupted. "It's not that. I wanted to kiss you. I wanted to do *more* than kiss you. I'm just…I told you I have baggage. I'm better at being friends than I am at this, and I'm not even very good at being friends. I'm always waiting for the smiles people wear, the kindness they share, to peel off like shed skin, revealing monsters I don't want my children to see."

He gritted his teeth against the anger simmering inside him for whatever she'd gone through that had left her so scarred. He flattened his palms to his thighs to keep them from curling into fists. "Because of the situation you grew up in? Or the father—or fathers—of your children?"

She pressed her lips together, her arms circling her belly, as if to protect her unborn child from hearing what she had to say. Then she lifted her chin, squared her shoulders, and said, "Both."

The word devastated him like a bullet to the chest. "Sarah…?"

"My father was abusive to me and Scott, emotionally and physically, but luckily, not sexually." She didn't look away, didn't flinch or slow down, as if she were talking about someone else. "By the grace of God, he didn't touch Josie. But for whatever reason, Scott and I were targets. When I look back now, I wonder why I never told a teacher or the police. *Anyone.* But when you're in the thick of it, all you think about is surviving from one minute to the next. Walking on eggshells. Trying to figure out what you did wrong every time you got hit or yelled at. I'd see kids at school, girls holding hands with boys, kissing in the halls, passing notes, and I'd wonder what that must be like. Why weren't their parents calling them sluts? Or were they? Did they have bruises on their bodies, too?"

His heart broke, and his anger mounted with every word she said. He moved closer, taking her hand in his, and held on tight, wishing he could have been there to protect her.

"I used to hide in the bushes and write stories about a girl my age and how she'd fall in love with a boy and run away. They were just silly stories, but they were *my* stories of hope. They gave me a place to disappear into my imagined world, where a boy would want to hold my hand, carry my books. Where my parents would read to me or smile and tell me I did a good job instead of saying I was a tramp or a whore for doing nothing more than getting my period."

She looked away with a nostalgic glimmer in her eyes that blew Bones away. How strong did she have to be to survive such an upbringing? To *create* a shred of hope and to become the woman she was today?

Her expression darkened, and she said, "As Scott got bigger, he fought back. What Scott didn't mention the other night at dinner was that my father beat him up really bad the night he left. I'll never forget. I thought they were going to kill each other. Scott got him good, too, but my father's a big man, and even if he was almost six feet tall, Scott was only a teenager. Josie and I were a mess, crying and screaming, begging them to stop. My mother was hollering at us, slapping me as I tried to pull my father off Scott. Josie huddled in a corner. God, she was so small at thirteen, I remember thinking if they ever hit her, she'd break."

She swallowed hard, fighting tears. Bones reached for her, but she pulled away.

"Please don't," she pleaded. "Just let me finish, or I'll never get it out."

It took every ounce of restraint not to haul her into his arms. He nodded, jaw tight, hands fisted.

"I tried to break up the fight," she said softly. "But my father went after me, so Scott told me to take Josie downstairs. That's where our bedrooms were. A few minutes later Scott flew down the stairs and into his room, panting and bloody. He grabbed a duffel bag, which he must have packed earlier. He told me and Josie not to go upstairs no matter what until the next day. I guess he'd been planning on leaving for a while, because he had a fake ID, and he gave me a bank card and said to guard it with my life. He'd had a friend open a bank account for me. He said he'd get a job and send money to that account so my parents wouldn't know. I wanted to go with him, but my father threatened to have Scott arrested and thrown in juvie."

"Jesus, Sarah. What about your mother?"

She shook her head. "She's a waste of a human life. She was just as bad. She'd slap me and Scott around, call me awful names—*slut, bitch, whore*. I'd never even kissed a boy. I used to wonder if Scott and I were adopted or something, but…" She shook her head. "I know Bradley told you she was dead. I told him they were, but I have no idea if they are or not. I don't ever want them near my children." She inhaled shakily and said, "Things got better for a while after Scott left, and I thought maybe my parents had realized they'd run him off and were trying to change their ways. But then I came home one day and found my father in my room. He'd torn it apart and he was holding one of my notebooks. The others were shredded all over the floor. My mom and Josie were gone. That was the day I got the worst beating of my life. When my mom and Josie didn't come back that night, I thought my mom had come to her senses and tried to save Josie. I knew she'd never save me. The next morning I packed what I could in my backpack, like I was going to school. My father worked at restaurants. He was a cook, but he also worked as a janitor for a company, so he was always working weird hours. He was still asleep that morning when I left. I went straight to the bank, cleared out the account, which had about four hundred dollars in it. I don't know how Scott got the money so fast. He still won't tell me. I took half of it and left the other half for Josie with a note telling her I'd come back as soon as I had a place to live. We had a secret place we left notes for each other, in a crack in the foundation of the house out back behind the heat pump. I knew I had to get away while I could, so I went to the main drag and hitchhiked."

It was all Bones could do to let her speak without unleashing his anger.

"I must have had a guardian angel that day, because a girl named Susan picked me up on her way out of town. She'd hooked up with some guy at the military base and was heading home to Orlando. She was nineteen and worked at a salon. She let me stay with her, and after a week, when my bruises weren't as noticeable, she got me a job as a shampoo girl. They paid me under the table in cash. I was going crazy worrying about Josie, so the next week when Susan had time off, she took me back and we waited for Josie after school, but she never came out. I saw a girl Josie knew, and she said she saw Josie leave in a car with some guy two days earlier and she hadn't seen her since. She thought the car was blue, but it could have been gray; she wasn't sure. Susan and I went back to the house, and I snuck around to check our hiding place. Josie had left me a note that said she was afraid to wait any longer. She found a way out and she took it."

Bones felt sick with rage. He wanted to hunt down her parents and slaughter them. "She was thirteen? Did you find out who she left with?"

Sarah shook her head. "Susan and I drove around all night, but…" She shrugged. "I thought I lost her forever, and I didn't know how to get in touch with Scott. I had no idea who his friend was who set up the bank account, and I just felt lost and scared—"

"But you had Susan; that's something."

"Not really. She helped me look for Josie over the next couple of weeks as time allowed, but then she got scared that she'd get in trouble. She drove me to a homeless shelter the next night, but I was worried they'd send me back to my parents. I guess she felt bad, so she gave me two hundred dollars and her driver's license and dropped me off at the bus station. I bought a train ticket to Baltimore. I got another job at a salon as a shampoo girl, and I was sleeping out back in the bushes by the salon. One night I woke up to a guy grabbing at me, so I took off and finally went to a shelter. I had Susan's ID, so I used her name there just in case. I had no idea how the shelters worked with minors, and I wasn't taking any chances. After a few weeks, I met a girl named Reagan at the shelter, and we hit it off, and we rented a room together. Eventually I met Lewis Warsaw, the father of my children. I went to cosmetology school, and a few years later he shed his skin, too."

Bones ground out a curse and drew her into his arms. This time she came willingly, allowing him to shift their bodies so he could hold her closer. He lifted her legs over one of his, holding her against his chest, and pressed a kiss to her forehead, wanting to seek vengeance and protect her in equal measure. "Nobody will *ever* hurt you again. And before you tell me you don't need saving, you're right. You've proven that several times, but it doesn't hurt to have backup."

"IS THAT HOW you convinced Thomas to let you hang around? As *backup*?" Sarah's lame attempt at humor didn't work. Bones looked like he wanted to kill someone, and he didn't even know the half of it. She wanted to tell him the rest of her story, but talking about it had thrown her right back into that awful house again. She was exhausted, and even with his arms around her, her insides were all knotted up.

"I stuck to him like glue," Bones said. "Just like I have since I met you." He hugged her tighter, making her smile despite the ugliness she'd just revealed.

"You are pretty sticky," she said, breathing a little easier. "I'm okay, Bones. I survived, and eventually with some help from Reagan's brother and his friend Reggie Steele, a private investigator, I was able to reunite with Scott. And then, with Reggie's help, we were able to track down Josie."

"That's good, Sarah."

"Sort of. She was bartending about forty-five minutes away. We had to call and leave messages at her work, because we didn't have her number or a stable address. Reggie looked, but I guess she moves around a lot. She was less than receptive to our calls, but we kept trying. The area where she worked was pretty scary, so Scott and I decided to try to start over as a family here, with the hopes of eventually reuniting with her. The night of the accident I called the bar where she worked from the hospital, and she must have heard how upset I was because she didn't hang up on me. But when she came to see us that night, she wasn't the same person I remembered. None of us were. She was so hateful and angry. I don't know why she feels that way toward us, but we've all been through so much. I guess I understand being angry at the world. She only stayed at the hospital for a few minutes and she hasn't returned our calls since. I'm just glad she's alive, and I have hope that maybe someday she'll want some sort of relationship."

"Have you driven there to see her?"

She nodded. "Once, right after Scott got out of the hospital. She no longer works at the bar, and they didn't know where she was living or working."

"Did they have a cell number for her?" Bones asked.

"I know it seems weird in today's world, but they said she didn't have one. I've had nothing, Bones. I know what it's like to wonder where your next meal will come from. Believe it or not, cell phones really are luxuries."

"I understand. Would you mind if I tried to track her down?"

"I don't think she wants to be found. She knows we live here, and she hasn't reached out."

Bones didn't push for an answer about Josie, which was good, because she wasn't sure if he should try to track her down or not. She knew what it meant to want to leave a life behind, and if in Josie's mind she needed to leave Sarah and Scott behind, as much as it hurt, maybe she should let her.

"Thank you for trusting me enough to share your past with me," he said as he draped a blanket around her. "I'm sorry for everything you went through. I wish I could have been there to protect all of you, but I'm here now. I know we should get back soon, but I just want a few minutes to hold you."

She didn't try to be her own hero, or prove she didn't need him, because in that moment, even though she missed her children, this was exactly what she needed. *He* was exactly what she needed. As he held her, expecting nothing in return, the tension inside her eased, and the soothing sounds of the water lapping at the boat came into focus. The amber lights twinkled against the dark sky, and she closed her eyes, sinking into his comfort.

Her baby kicked, and she guided his hands lower on her belly and placed hers over them. She felt another kick.

"Oh, man. That's incredible, darlin'. This baby is strong like its mama."

"I don't think I'll ever get used to the feeling." She was talking about the baby's kicks *and* Bones's comfort.

"The miracle of life is a beautiful thing." His big hand moved over her belly. "Hey, I have an idea. What are you doing Saturday?"

"I have to be at work at three. Why?"

"My buddy Nick Braden owns a horse ranch in Pleasant Hill. His dog had puppies a few weeks ago, and he's got pygmy goats and chickens. It might be fun to take the kids before it gets too cold."

She glanced over her shoulder. He still looked a little tortured from the information she'd shared, but beneath the shadows was the compassion and pure maleness that made butterflies take flight inside her. Would he shed his skin one day, too?

Will I ever stop waiting for the other shoe to drop?

"Are you asking me on a *kid* date?" she asked lightly.

"I took you and your kids out before I asked you on a real date. Remember the fundraiser?"

It was a day she'd never forget. Not only because he'd stuck to her like glue then, too, but because of how the community had come together to help her family.

"Come to think of it," he said with a sly grin, "I picked you guys up, hung out with you, bandaged up Bradley's scraped knee, changed diapers. I think that counts as a kid date. And I had lunch with you and Bradley the first week we met, remember? In the hospital?"

She'd never forget that day, either. He'd come in to check on her and the kids several times even though he wasn't their doctor. Initially, he'd said he'd come in because Bullet had wanted to make sure they were okay. But she'd wondered why he'd kept coming back. It was in those first few days when her family was in the hospital that she'd first felt a connection more substantial than as an acquaintance to him. He'd sit down for fifteen or twenty minutes and talk, asking as many questions about how she was feeling as he did about her family's healing.

"You mean when you came in and I was eating the food Finlay brought?" she asked, though she knew that's exactly what he meant. He hadn't eaten, but he'd stayed while she did.

"Yes. You were sitting on the edge of Bradley's bed, wearing a pretty pale blue blouse and white pants. Your hair was piled on top of your head in a messy bun, like you hadn't slept in days, and I knew you hadn't been sleeping because you were so worried about your babies and your brother. I wanted to make sure you were at least eating. You were feeding Bradley."

"You told me to make sure Mama got some, too," she remembered fondly.

After her children were released from the hospital, he'd stopped by the house with bags of groceries and little surprises for the kids. He'd stuck around, making small talk, slowly becoming such a big part of their life, her kids looked forward to seeing him. She did, too, but until this very second, she hadn't even admitted that to herself. He'd taken care of her in ways that no one else ever had. How could she have chalked that up to him just being a kind friend or a curious doctor? She was beginning to realize how skewed her views were, and she wondered if having her guard up for so many years had made her oblivious to even more acts of kindness.

"That's right," he said. "That should count as a kid date, too. And Bradley *was* my riding partner at the Halloween parade. *Kid date.* We also met Bear and Crystal for dinner with the kids and Scott a couple of weeks ago at Woody's Burgers. Another kid date. I think we've been going on kid dates for a while now."

Oh boy, he's kind of right. Plus, tonight was a more intimate, and more revealing, evening than she'd ever shared with anyone. And yes, her desires had taken over, and that was a little embarrassing afterward—and very exciting during—but there was so much more than that between them.

She knew the risks of becoming too attached, and she also knew that no matter how much she fought it, how much she *denied* it, where Bones was concerned, her heart was already at risk. But she didn't want to monopolize his time or become a burden. "Don't you usually go riding with Bear and your friends on the weekends?"

"Sometimes, but a man has got to have priorities." He brushed his thumb over her cheek and said, "Say *yes*, Sarah. Keep letting me in."

God, he was looking at her *that* way again, like hearing her agree was all he'd ever wanted. A thrill of delight chased over her skin, bringing rise to goose bumps. She was afraid to believe this could be real between them, but every time she looked into his eyes, it felt too real to deny.

"Okay," she said, reveling in the way happiness lit up his eyes.

She had never had many blessings to count, but right then, being in his arms and thinking about the way his family had embraced hers, she felt like a glutton. "I've never been particularly lucky, but my babies are my miracles. Reuniting with Scott was a miracle. Bullet finding us after the accident and everything that followed was a miracle. And for a girl like me, who wasn't sure she'd survive to be seventeen, being here with you feels like a miracle, too."

"It's not a miracle, darlin'. It's destiny." He kissed her softly and then said, "And one day, hopefully Josie will come back and she'll be on your list of miracles, too."

Chapter Nine

"YOU'VE GOT AN extra bounce in your step this morning," Scott said to Sarah when she carried Lila into the kitchen at the crack of dawn the next morning. He was leaning against the counter in sweats and a white T-shirt, holding a coffee mug in one hand. His hair was damp from the shower. "I guess your date went well?"

"Mm-hm. Very well," she said, trying not to sound like a schoolgirl with a crush, which was difficult considering she hadn't been able to stop thinking about Bones since he'd kissed her good night last night. Their kisses had gone on and on, even better than the daydreams she'd had as a young girl when she'd watched the magical moments of others and then written about her own. She set Lila in the high chair and put a handful of Cheerios on the tray. "I hear you were sneaky and helped with the lights on his boat."

She still couldn't believe Bones *had* a boat.

Scott sipped his coffee, watching her with a curious expression. "He's a pretty romantic guy."

"You can say that again." She gave Lila some juice and began mixing ingredients for blueberry pancakes. *Romantic, thoughtful, a mind-blowing kisser, and more…* "Thank you again for watching the kids. You wore Bradley out. He's still out like a light."

"I had some help. The girls and I took them for a walk." He made her a cup of coffee, eyeing the pancakes. "I have physical therapy in forty minutes. Think you can squeeze in a few extras for me?"

"Always." She poured batter into the pan.

Scott pressed a kiss to Lila's head. "Morning, peach." She held her hand out, offering him a palmful of sticky cereal. He chuckled. "No, thank you. You eat that. I'll wait for your mama's delicious pancakes."

"I don't know about *delicious*, but then again, I can't remember what anything other than allergen-free foods taste like."

"You're not missing out on much," he said as she cut up a pancake for Lila and then handed Scott a plate for himself. He touched her hand, which he did when he wanted to slow her down. "Did you tell Bones the truth?"

After he'd blurted out information she'd rather have told Bones herself, she'd asked Scott not to talk about their past until she had a chance to tell Bones what their lives had been like. "Most of it." She turned back to the stove to flip her pancakes. She hadn't even told Scott everything she'd been through. Some ghosts were better left buried.

"Sarah, nobody is going to judge you because we had shitty parents."

She knew that wasn't true. She sat down beside Lila with her coffee and pancakes. "I guess you don't remember how I was never allowed to go to birthday parties or playdates. Or how eventually kids stopped asking. Other families might not have wanted to get involved, and they turned a blind eye, but I don't believe for a second that they didn't judge us. Or at least me."

He speared a piece of pancake with his fork and pointed it at her. "They were ignorant. Bones isn't."

"I know. I told him about Mom and Dad. I told him about how we all left." She took a bite and watched her daughter shove a tiny fistful of pancake into her mouth. She couldn't imagine ever feeling anything but love for her children. "Do you remember how old we were when things went bad? Was there *ever* a happier time? I always wondered if maybe there was an incident, something that changed how they treated us."

"Dad was always a prick, and Mom was always a bitch. It's a wonder we both didn't turn out to be more effed up." He finished his pancakes and sat back. "What I want to know is how Josie ended up worse off than either of us."

Scott had gone through so much after the accident, they hadn't talked about Josie's odd visit in any great detail. Sarah had wanted to lately, but it was like jumping into a volcano of awful possibilities. "Did you ever find out where she went after she left? Or who she left with?"

"No. We were lucky to track her down at all. I looked for both of you for so long, but I had no idea what state you were in, much less what city. I was relying on word of mouth because, you know, I couldn't afford a PI back then. You used that girl's license, so now I know how you went invisible. I assume Josie did the same thing. Paid under the table, living in shelters, making her way by whatever means she could. I've said this before, and I'll probably say it until the day I die. I wish I'd never left you two that night."

She gazed at him across the table, pain and love swallowing her up. "I've thought the same thing about my leaving Josie. But one thing I've learned is that wishing something didn't happen won't make it go away. You helped both of us with the money you put in the account. And you know Dad would have had you arrested if you'd come back or if you'd tried to take us with you. I have no doubt that he would have done the same to me if I had taken Josie."

"Yeah, but now we know there were other options. We could have gone to social services or the police."

Sarah finished her pancakes and put her dishes in the sink. Then she wet a washcloth and cleaned Lila's hands. "That's true, but even if someone had told us to do that, would you have done it? Because I know for a fact I wouldn't have. I'd have been too scared that they wouldn't believe us and then we'd suffer even more."

She lifted Lila from the high chair and set her down by her toy bucket near the glass doors, so she could clean up from breakfast. Scott began washing the dishes as she cleaned Lila's tray.

"Did you tell him about Lewis?" Scott asked.

"Not specifics, but he knows he exists and that things weren't good. I'm a lot to take in, Scott. I know you don't think so, but I've got two kids, another on the way, a past that should scare off anyone in their right mind, and I have trust and intimacy issues. As much as I like and trust Bones, which I do, it's scary for me to believe he doesn't have some kind of fake persona, because that's all I know."

He gave her a pitying look that quickly turned to disbelieving. "It's not *all* you know. I've never been fake a day in my life."

"You know what I mean. I'm trying to stop thinking that way, at least about Bones and his family. But when something has shadowed so much of your life, it's hard to go against the grain."

"Try harder, Sarah. I trust the guy completely, or he wouldn't be anywhere near you or your kids." He went back to washing the dishes. "Dixie asked if the kids ever see their father."

An icy chill skated down Sarah's spine. "Over my dead body."

"Let's not go there." He handed her a towel to dry the pan he'd washed.

"Do you think Josie will ever come around?"

He shrugged. "From what you said, she was a mess."

"I know. I've been wanting to ask you something." Every time she'd asked him about his personal life, he'd blown her off, but after last night, she wanted answers. "Why did you give up your job on the rigs and let me move in with you? I know you said you wanted to move here because of Josie, but you never hesitated to start over. Until last night, I never wondered why that was. I just accepted it. I figured we both wanted to rebuild what family we could. You know, two broken people trying to make ends meet. But when Dixie was flirting with you, I realized you're more than my brother, Scott, and you're not broken like I am. You're open about what we went through, and you don't seem to have as many issues letting people into your life. You're a good-looking, smart guy who had a great job. Why on earth would you give it all up for a job at a marina, and why are you still alone, Scott?"

Lila squealed, drawing their attention. She'd pulled herself up against the patio door, watching a squirrel eating from the feeder. When they'd first moved in, Lila had been enamored by the squirrels in the backyard. They'd hung a squirrel feeder in the tree closest to the house, and now she watched them nearly every morning.

"That's a *squirrel*, Lila," Sarah said, even though she knew there was no way her little girl could say that complicated word. She waited for Scott to answer, but he was silent for so long, she had a feeling he wasn't going to.

Bradley toddled into the kitchen, rubbing sleep from his eyes, and leaned against Sarah's legs.

She lifted him into her arms and kissed his cheek. "Good morning, sleepyhead."

"Can I have pancakes?" Bradley asked with a yawn.

Scott set the pan on the stove again with an amused expression. "I'm not alone. I've got a squirrel-loving niece and a pancake-eating nephew. Life is good, sis. I've got no complaints." He dropped a kiss on Bradley's head and said, "How late do you work tonight?"

She wondered if her son and daughter had saved Scott from whatever he didn't want to talk about and took some comfort in that thought. "I've got an early shift," she answered, wondering if Bones would be helping Scott with the basement tonight. She quickly chided herself for becoming so needy overnight. The man had a life, and so did she. "Nine to five. I was thinking we could grill out tonight. Bradley loves chicken kabobs."

Bradley confirmed with a nod.

"Kabobs it is. I've got to swing by the store to pick up paint for the basement and stop by the carpet store to finalize the installation for next week, but I should be home by six or so." He raised his brows like he was waiting for her to say something.

"What…?"

"Just trying to decide if I made a mistake or not," he said too casually.

She set Bradley down. "Go play, honey. It'll take me a minute to make the pancakes." Bradley joined Lila by the toys. She grabbed the mixing bowl and said, "What did you do?"

"Yesterday I told Bones I didn't need his help with the basement tonight in case your date didn't go well."

"Oh," she said, trying to hide her disappointment.

"I can text him." Scott reached into his back pocket.

"No. It's fine. I want to finish the curtains tonight anyway. Besides, we have a date tomorrow. We're taking the kids to his friend's farm to see the animals before I go to work."

"Nice. Kid dates are the equivalent to meeting your parents."

She rolled her eyes. "Don't you have physical therapy to go to? Or are you going to stand around here making me nervous all morning?"

"It's kind of fun to see you all"—he pursed his lips and then spoke in a high-pitched voice as he said, "I'm not secretly wishing Bones were here."

She shoved him toward the living room, laughing. "Go. *Please.* I forgot how pesty a big brother could be."

After Scott left, she fed Bradley and got the kids ready to go to Babs's house. *Nana Babs*, she corrected herself. Not for the first time, she wondered about her own grandparents. She couldn't remember ever meeting them. Her parents had never mentioned them. They'd simply acted like they didn't exist. She'd always wondered if that was because they were nice, normal people who wouldn't approve of how they were treating Sarah and Scott, or if they were as bad as her parents had been. She pushed those thoughts away, glad her children had nice women who cared for them and treated them like family.

As she gathered her purse and keys, she realized she didn't

worry about Babs, Red, or Chicki shedding their skin, and she wondered what that said about her. Did she want a mother figure bad enough to accept what she was having such trouble accepting in Bones?

She locked the door behind them and stepped off the porch.

"Look, Mommy! Presents!" Bradley ran toward the car, on top of which were gift bags, two pink and one blue. He jumped up, trying to reach them. "Hurry!"

"Hold your horses, buddy." *Mommy needs to pick up her jaw from the ground.*

She didn't have to see the cards to know they were from Bones. She picked up the blue bag, which had a little white tag hanging from the handle that read, *To B-boy, Love, Bones* in careful script. Her heart squeezed when she peeked inside and saw two farm animal books.

"Is it for me?" Bradley asked.

"Yes. It's from Bones." She hadn't yet told him about their date tomorrow, just in case something came up and Bones had to cancel. But she should know better. The man really did stick like glue.

"Books!" Bradley plopped down on the grass and began leafing through one of the books, chattering about each of the animals, and it dawned on her that Bones had seen Bradley playing with his toy animals so often, maybe Saturday wasn't just a last-minute thought after all.

Lila squealed, reaching for the bags. "Mamama!"

"There's one for you, too, Lila boo." She reached into the smaller of the two pink bags and handed Lila one of the cloth books it held. They were also farm animal books, and she was touched that Bones had thought to get Lila's in cloth, since she was teething on everything these days.

She got the kids settled into their car seats and then retrieved the last pink bag and read the tag. *For you, darlin'. Let's never let your dreams die. Love, B.*

She sat in the driver's seat and peered into the bag. Her heart thumped harder at the sight of several notebooks. She took them out one by one and admired them. The first was white with *She believed she could so she did* written in pink across the front. The second notebook was light green and white, with blue lettering that read *Let your dreams be bigger than your fears.* The third was a regular red spiral notebook like she'd used in school. There were three big, uneven stars of varying sizes above the words *Sarah's Stories of Hope* written in gold marker. Beneath that, written smaller and in black was, *We're going to make them all come true. Xox, B.*

Her chest constricted as she spied gold and black Sharpies in the bottom of the bag, along with a pack of fancy black pens. She wanted to cry and laugh at once. Out of everything she'd told him last night, he'd held on to the one piece that had been the most important to her.

"Go, Mommy. I want to show Nana Babs my books," Bradley urged.

"Okay, honey." She set the gifts on the passenger seat and vowed not to let the darkness and hurt Lewis had caused overshadow the beauty of Bones.

LATER THAT AFTERNOON, Sarah sat in the courtyard behind the salon with her notebooks and pens, eating lunch and thinking about the stories she used to write. She'd been just a young girl escaping her awful life by disappearing into little-girl fantasies. Now the thought of writing stories for herself seemed silly because she knew the truth. As a girl she'd caught only moments, *glimpses* of people's lives. As an adult she knew glimpses were like pictures posted on social media—carefully posed and chosen. They were propaganda. Just like her young-girl stories. Back then it had been Sarah doing the selecting of captured images, as if she were stranded on an island and collecting scraps for a raft. She'd looked away from boys talking smack and fights between young couples, choosing to remember only the most stable, hopeful images.

She was no longer in an unsafe house. Her babies were safe, she'd reunited with at least one sibling, she had friends, and she and Bones were getting closer every day. Her life was incredibly happy at the moment. What more could she possibly hope for?

As she put pen to paper, images of her father tearing her notebooks to shreds, red-faced, veins plumped up like snakes on his neck and arms as he'd yelled at her, made her hand tremble, her breathing still. She set the pen down as a realization dawned on her.

There was only one thing she really wanted. One thing she craved more than anything else in the world. But how did a person write a story about something as intangible as *peace of mind*?

BONES STOOD IN the middle of Got Toys?, the biggest toy store in Peaceful Harbor, with his motorcycle helmet under one arm, studying an article on his phone about the effect of toys on children and trying to ignore Dixie's tapping foot.

"This isn't that hard," she snapped, shifting her helmet to

her other arm and jutting out her hip. "Just grab a stuffed animal and a noisy rattle."

Bones shook his head. "The right toys enhance cognitive development."

She peered over his shoulder at his phone. "Are you seriously reading about that right now? Shouldn't you have geeked out before this?"

He shoved his phone in his pocket and strode back toward the entrance, leaving Dixie to try to catch up.

"Where are you going?" she called after him.

"We need a cart."

"A cart?" Dixie hurried next to him. "What are you buying her, a playhouse?"

Bones stopped walking and pulled out his phone. "The kind for a yard or for dolls?"

"Are you shitting me?" She grabbed his arm and hauled him toward the front of the store as he navigated to an article about playhouses. "She's *one*. Do not buy her a playhouse."

"It looks like that's better for three- and four-year-olds." He pocketed his phone again and set his helmet in a basket. "We need blocks, balls, stacking cups, musical toys, dolls, stuffed animals, and action figures."

"Anything else, Santa Whiskey?"

He glared at her as she put her helmet beside his with a chuckle.

"She's a *girl*. You know that, right?" she asked as he pushed the cart toward the ball aisle.

Ignoring her smart-ass comment, he chose a big rubber ball, another the size of a grapefruit, and a smaller one made out of cloth. "Come on, the stuffed animals are two rows over." As he pushed the cart, he said, "When she pretends to give her friends a bath, or feeds them, she's practicing the things that will help her make sense of the world."

"And of course every little girl needs action-figure friends, because they might end up with a Special Forces bestie in preschool."

"It's a good thing you don't have children." He picked up two stuffed animals, then glanced at the aisle directory. "Ah, *strollers*. She needs one for her dolly."

"*Dolly?*" Dixie snort-laughed. "You are pussy whipped."

"Nice mouth on my baby sister. And no, I'm not. Sarah isn't like that. She's the least demanding and most caring, selfless woman I know. I'm not pussy whipped, Dix. I'm…"

"Falling for her," Dixie suggested.

Falling? Hell, he'd fallen off the edge of a cliff the day he met her. "Something like that."

He picked out a pink toy stroller, and as they headed for the doll aisle he stopped to pick up a doctor kit.

"Now she needs medical supplies?"

"It's for B."

"Bullet?" Dixie said absently, eyeing a bearded guy who was scoping out bicycles at the end of the aisle.

"You think Bullet needs a toy doctor kit?" Bones yanked her in the opposite direction, grabbing the cart on the way.

"*Ow!* I meant *Bradley*. Sorry."

"Put your eyes back in their sockets." When they reached the next aisle he released her.

"News flash, Bones. If I want to look at a hot guy, I'm going to do it."

"News flash, Dix. Not on my watch. Nothing good comes from that."

"What do you want me to do? Put on a frilly dress and wait

for a guy to ask my daddy for my hand?"

"Sounds about right to me." He laughed and headed for the block aisle.

"Or maybe I'll just crash my bike in another town and see who comes by to rescue me. Maybe I'll get lucky and meet someone's brother who'll go *gaga* over me."

"Is that before or after you tell them they're doing everything wrong?"

Chapter Ten

BONES DROVE DOWN the long, lazy driveway toward Nick Braden's ranch Saturday morning, wondering if there was any sound better than the laughter of children. He had experienced many great moments in his life. The day when his parents got the all clear about his father's stroke and times when his family was together and he could feel love all around him. But if he had to pick one day, one single moment of complete happiness, he was currently in the thick of it—surrounded by gorgeous maple trees kissing the sky with vibrant red and orange leaves, his girl's hand in his, and the two children who had stolen his heart giggling in the back seat as horses frolicked in the nearby pasture.

He parked in front of one of the cream-colored barns and spotted Nick in the distance, coming up from another barn. A cowboy hat sat low on his brow as he lifted a hand in greeting.

"Horsies, Mommy!" Bradley yelled. "I smell them!"

Lila squealed, arms flailing and legs kicking in excitement. "Moos!"

"No, Lila," Bradley corrected her. "They're *horses*, not cows."

Lila giggled. "Moos!"

Bones squeezed Sarah's hand, bringing her eyes to his as Bradley corrected his sister again. He'd never seen a woman look so beautiful in a simple long-sleeved white shirt, a thick cardigan, and jeans. Sarah had tied a pink sash just above her baby bump. Her boots had seen better days, but they looked like a million bucks on her.

"How do you stand it day after day?" he asked with a smile.

"I'm sorry. I know they're noisy."

"No, darlin'. They're *incredible*, and so are you." He pressed a kiss to the back of her hand and said, "Don't look so shocked. You know just how amazing your children are." He knew the look of disbelief was probably because of what he'd said about her and not her children, but he wasn't going to give it credence. She looked radiant, and he hoped that soon she'd trust him enough not to doubt his words.

He climbed from the car and walked around to Sarah's door as Nick approached.

"How's it going?" Nick pulled him into a quick, manly embrace.

"Couldn't be better." Bones opened Sarah's door and helped her out. "Sarah, this is my buddy Nick Braden. Nick, my girlfriend, Sarah." Another flicker of shock appeared in her expression. *Get used to it, darlin'.* He went to help Bradley out of his car seat.

Nick tipped his hat. "Nice to meet you, sweetheart."

"Nice to meet you, too. Thank you for letting us come out today," she said.

"My pleasure," Nick said. "Kids and animals go together like peanut butter and jelly."

"Or in our case, Wowbutter and jelly," Bones said, earning

another hint of surprise from Sarah. "Nick, *this* is Bradley. You've got to watch him. He's been studying farm animals, and his knowledge puts me to shame."

Bradley tipped his face up toward Nick, squinting into the sun, and said, "Are you a real cowboy?"

Bones grabbed his backpack, in which he'd stowed all of the paraphernalia Sarah usually brought in her baby bag. The backpack was easier to sling over both shoulders if need be. He picked up Lila and joined the others, catching the tail end of Nick's answer.

"Lila! He's a *real* cowboy!" Bradley gushed, earning excited sounds and hand clapping from his baby sister.

"I think we might have to keep her away from ranches when she's a teenager." Bones pressed a kiss to Lila's cheek.

"The little one's got good taste," Nick said. "She could end up with a doctor." He shuddered dramatically, making Sarah laugh.

Nick gave Bradley a quick, kid-friendly safety lesson about the animals, and Bradley listened like a pro, nodding and repeating the important points to Lila. It was just about the cutest thing Bones had ever seen.

"What do you say, partner?" Nick said to Bradley. "Think you're ready to say hello to the horses? I have some that are just your size."

Bradley nodded and took Nick's outstretched hand.

"Should we get the stroller?" Sarah asked.

"No. I've got her," Bones said as they followed Nick and Bradley around the barn to another pasture. He took Sarah's hand, enjoying her shy smile, and said, "But if you get tired, just say the word and we'll sit down and rest."

"Don't be silly," she said. "I'm like the Pregnant Woman of

Steel. I'm faster than a speeding three-year-old, able to step over Lego buildings in a single bound."

Bones chuckled. "Then what's your kryptonite?"

She smiled up at him, heat emanating from her eyes as she said, "You are."

Man, he loved that. He leaned in for a kiss, then thought better of it with the kids around. A kiss on her hand or a quick peck on the cheek was one thing. But something told him even a child would feel his emotions toward her if he kissed her on the lips now. Instead, he whispered, "Careful using your heat vision in front of the kids. You don't want me to combust."

She laughed and quickly covered her mouth. "Sorry, but does that line *ever* work?"

"Apparently not," he mumbled.

"It's a *little* horse!" Bradley hollered, pulling them from their secrets and sending Lila into a wiggling, squealing bundle of excitement.

"Moo!" Lila called out, pushing to get out of Bones's arms. "Moo!"

"*Horse*," Bradley said, as if his sister should know this by now.

"It'll take her some time to learn, B-boy." Bones set Lila on her feet, holding tightly to her hand as they approached the fenced area where a miniature horse was grazing.

"Look how sweet it is," Sarah said. "Go slow, Bradley. Remember what Nick told you."

Bradley squinted up at Nick. "Hand up?"

"Palm up," Nick said, showing him the proper way to hold out his hand. "Let her smell your hand and get used to you."

Bones crouched beside the kids, one arm around each child's waist in case the horse acted out.

"She's the tamest old girl I've got," Nick reassured him. "She grew up around kids, and we've never had an incident. Littler ones than Lila have petted her."

Good to know, but I'm not taking any chances.

Bradley let the horse sniff his hand, then pulled it back quickly, giggling. "It *tickles*!"

Lila squealed, reaching for the horse's nose as Bradley did it again. The horse nudged Bradley's palm, and they both stumbled backward, giggling. Bones pulled Lila against his side to keep her from plopping onto her bottom.

"Gentle," Sarah reminded them, moving to Bradley's other side. She pulled her phone from her back pocket and took a few pictures.

"Try it, Mommy!" Bradley urged.

Nick held his hand out. "Why don't I take a few pictures of your family?"

"Thank you." Sarah gave him the phone and put her hand out toward the horse, who pushed her lips along it. "She's so soft. What's her name?"

"Snickers," Nick said. "But I call her Charmer, because she can charm the heck out of the crankiest people."

Sarah glanced at Bones. "Seems you two have something in common."

Bones winked, keeping his arm around Lila as she toddled forward. "Slow, sweetie. Careful."

Lila poked a finger toward Snickers, and the horse touched it with her nose. Lila squealed, her little legs backpedaling as her giggles consumed her. She immediately did it again, and more squeals and giggles rang out.

SARAH COULD WATCH Bones with her children all day long. He was as patient as he was sexy, and he was beyond attentive, asking if she needed a drink, to rest, or to use the ladies' room. She wasn't used to being looked after, and she was surprised at how much she enjoyed knowing he cared enough about her and her children to do so.

Nick took them to play with the pygmy goats, which were the perfect size for Bradley to chase around and feed from his hand. Lila toddled after them, falling on her bottom so many times, eventually she just sat there letting the goats come to her. Bradley asked so many questions, Nick told him he should write them down so he could create an answer sheet, which sent her inquisitive little boy into a litany of other questions. Starting with, *What's an answer sheet?*

Nick was the perfect host, teaching the kids and never rushing them along. He took them to see baby chicks, and by the time they were finally ready to see the puppies, the kids were filthy, hungry, and tired.

"Why don't we wash up, give the kids a break to eat lunch, and then see the p-u-p-p-i-e-s," Bones suggested.

She wondered how he knew to spell it out rather than deal with begging from Bradley. "Sounds perfect."

After washing up, Nick got called away to check on a horse. Bones, Sarah, and the kids sat beneath a big oak tree to eat the lunch they'd packed. Bradley ate and chatted about the animals, but Lila sat in the cradle of Bones's lap, nibbling on only a few crackers. Bones urged her to drink some juice, but after a tiny sip, she refused.

"Come on, sweet girl," Bones coaxed. "How about one bite of fruit?"

Lila shook her head, pushing his hand away.

"It's just the excitement of the day," Sarah reassured him.

"I *love* this day," Bradley said between bites. "Lila falled a lot, but I didn't."

"That's because your sister is still learning to walk," Bones said as Lila cuddled against his chest. He brushed his hand gently down her back. "It takes all of her energy to keep up with her big brother."

Bradley seemed to think about that as he took another bite. "I teached her how to walk."

Bones tousled his hair. "You sure did. She watches everything you do. You know, Dixie's my little sister."

"Dixie's big," Bradley pointed out.

"You're right, but she's still my *younger* sister, like Lila is to you, and she wanted to keep up with her big brothers. She'd follow us everywhere, chase us around the yard."

"Did she fall on her butt?" Bradley asked.

Bones smiled and said, "She did, but you know what falling down did to her?"

"Gave her an *ouchie*?" he asked.

"Maybe, but it also made her stronger, more determined to keep up. So, you keep learning and growing, and the more you accomplish, the more Lila will, too. Because she's going to want to be just as cool as her older brother."

A glimmer of pride shone in Bradley's eyes. "I'm cool?"

"The coolest," Bones said. "And Lila will be, too."

Sarah's insides turned to mush. "You're pretty cool, too, Dr. Whiskey."

He touched her hand, but his gaze dropped to Lila and he brushed a kiss to the top of her head.

Bradley popped up to his feet. "I'm done! Can we see more animals now?"

Lila sat up straighter, then slumped against Bones again.

Bones touched her cheek. “She’s a bit warm.”

Sarah began collecting their trash. “Probably from running around so much.”

Bones didn’t look convinced as he pressed a kiss to her forehead.

They made their way over to the barn to see the puppies. As they approached, the pungent scent of leather and horses drifted out the open doors. Sarah had never seen such a big, beautiful two-story barn. The entire barn was painted cream, though around the stalls it was dusty and stained. Two gorgeous horses, one tan, the other dark, peered curiously out of their stalls.

“All fed?” Nick asked as he came out of a room on the other side of the barn. The tan horse nickered, bobbing its head as Nick approached. The horse pressed its head against his sternum, and Nick planted a kiss on its forehead.

“Most of us,” Bones said, glancing at Lila, who was almost asleep on his shoulder.

An old pug waddled out of the room from which Nick had come, making grunting noises.

Lila lifted her head, then settled against his shoulder again.

“Come on, Pugsly.” Nick crouched to love up the dog.

“Can I pet it?” Bradley asked.

“Sure can, but be extra gentle,” Nick warned. “Pugsly is old, and he’s blind in one eye.”

“Da.” Lila reached out, opening and closing her hand.

Bones knelt beside Bradley. “That’s right, baby. *Dog.*”

“He can’t see?” Bradley got down on his hands and knees beside Nick and peered at the dog’s face.

Nick smoothed his hand down the dog’s back. “He can see, just not so well.”

"Close one eye, B-boy." Bones waited until Bradley closed his eye, then said, "That's how Pugsly sees."

Lila began closing and opening her eyes, moving her face in front of his. "Babababa."

"I think you're *Ba*," Sarah said, in awe over her little girl trying to say Bones.

The pride in Bones's eyes couldn't be missed. Neither could the smirk on his lips when he said, "Better than most things I'm called."

"I hear ya, man." Nick pushed to his feet.

"Is Pugsly the father of the litter?" Sarah asked.

Nick shook his head. "Good old Pugs is lucky he can still chase a few butterflies. My neighbor's Australian shepherd got too frisky with my golden retriever. Now I've got six pups to care for. Who wants to see *puppies*?"

"Me!" Bradley sprang to his feet, snatched Nick's hand, and went with him toward the other end of the barn.

"*Ba*, huh?" Bones draped an arm around Sarah, and Lila rested her head on his shoulder.

"It kind of made me all warm and tingly inside," she admitted.

A slow grin spread across his lips.

Sarah poked him in the side. "Don't get all cocky. It was probably just the baby moving around. You might be hot and you might be sweeter than sugar to my kids, but you're still a man. And in my experience, that never ends well for me."

He glanced at Lila, whose eyes were closed, and then he glanced at Bradley, who was skipping happily along next to Nick. His eyes went dark and lustful as he said, "Wanna bet?"

Before she could respond, he pressed his lips to hers. His tongue slid deliciously over hers in a quick and thoroughly *thrilling* kiss, leaving her breathless. With a cocky expression that made her body heat up even more, he nudged her forward, as if he hadn't just taken advantage of the thirty seconds they had without the scrutiny of little eyes.

"That was sneaky," she whispered.

"It was smart. We're just getting started, darlin'. How about you stop anticipating an *end* and start counting on my not disappointing you?"

That sounded good to her. If only she could figure out how to do it.

She heard Bradley giggling and puppies yapping before they stepped into the room.

Bradley was sitting in the middle of the floor surrounded by five, adorably fluffy puppies. He giggled as they crawled all over him, yapping and licking, tugging on his T-shirt with their tiny teeth. Nick sat beside him, snagging the pups when they got too nippy. A beautiful golden retriever lay in the corner of the room, watching the chaos unfold.

"No bite," Bradley said between giggles. A puppy climbed up his chest and licked his cheek. "Tickles!"

Lila woke with a whimper, and then her eyes widened with glee.

"Look at the puppies, Lila boo," Sarah exclaimed.

Bones knelt and tried to reposition Lila on his knee so she could see the puppies better, but she lifted her legs against his chest, clinging to him.

"It's okay, sweetheart. I won't let them hurt you." Bones tried again, but Lila cried. He rose to his feet, pressing his lips to her forehead. "She's pretty warm, Sarah. I don't think this is exhaustion."

Sarah stepped around two puppies tumbling at her feet and

pressed her hand to Lila's forehead. She was definitely too warm. Lila buried her face in Bones's neck, crying louder.

"We should go," Bones said. "One more minute, B-boy, and then we need to get your sister home."

"No!" Bradley rolled onto his stomach, letting the puppies climb over his back.

Sarah crouched beside him and felt Bradley's head, relieved that he wasn't warm, too. After letting him play for a minute, she said, "Lila's not feeling well, Bradley. Thank Nick and let's go."

"The baby's sick?" Nick picked up a puppy in each hand and set them into a gated area. "Come on, buddy," he said to Bradley. "Maybe you can come back another day."

"No!" Bradley sat on his butt and grabbed a puppy. "I want to play!"

"We did play, but Lila's got a fever," she said more sternly. "We have to go *now*, Bradley."

Tears sprang from his eyes. "I don't want to leave!" Using his heels for leverage and clinging to a puppy, he scooted backward. "I'm staying. Let her leave!"

Nick got busy corralling puppies, and Sarah went to pick up Bradley.

Bones put his arm between them. "Take the baby. You shouldn't carry him."

He tried to peel Lila off, but she clung to him for dear life, screeching at the top of her lungs, which sent Bradley into a crying, kicking tantrum.

"Bradley, that's enough," Sarah said sharply, both embarrassed by her child and brokenhearted for him. She grabbed his hand and hauled him to his feet. "Your sister is sick. We have to go."

Bradley tugged in the opposite direction, screaming and crying hysterically, causing Lila to cry even harder. Nick said something about giving them privacy and left them alone to deal with her out-of-control children.

Bones looked from Bradley to Lila with an overwhelmed expression.

This was it. The end.

Why had she even thought she had a chance with him? Kids were fun when they were sweet and compliant, but what man in his right mind would want to be in the thick of it with children who were not his own?

Bradley plopped down on his bottom, with Sarah clinging to his hand as he kicked and cried. It was all she could do to look at Bones and say, "Welcome to the darker side of my life."

Bones gritted his teeth. His eyes narrowed, as if he were mentally preparing to settle world peace—or maybe tell her off. A few seconds later that look became clear determination. He shifted Lila to one arm as she bawled her little eyes out, arms strung so tight around his neck his skin was red. Then he crouched beside Bradley, speaking calm as the day was long—and she had a feeling it was going to be a *very* long day.

"B-boy, I know you're disappointed. I'm sure Lila is, too. But your baby sister is sick, and we need to take care of her, which means getting her home so we can help her feel better."

Bradley cried louder. "I want to stay!"

Bones scooped up her angry, out-of-control boy, tucked him against his side, and said, "Let's go, darlin'."

She hurried to keep up with his fast pace.

"You got this, *Daddy Whiskey*?" Nick asked as they passed him near the horses.

Oh boy. If today doesn't send him running for the hills, nothing will.

Bones didn't slow down as he said, "Damn right I do. Thanks, man. I'll call you."

When they stepped into the afternoon sun and made their way toward the car, the kids' hysterics settled to whimpers and hitching gulps.

"Give me one of them," Sarah pleaded. "I'm used to this."

Bones nodded toward Lila without missing a step and said, "This one takes after me. She's stuck like glue." Then he lifted his chin in Bradley's direction and said, "And this one needs to be stuck like glue. How about you reach into my pocket and pull out the keys?"

Even amid the craziness, his eyes darkened, and that coy grin that made her heart flutter appeared.

He stopped walking when they reached the car and said, "Might want to get a move on, darlin', before their alarms go off again."

The desirous look in his eyes clashed with the scene that was finally calming down. Didn't anything make him lose his cool? She carefully reached into his pocket, feeling for the keys.

"A little lower," he urged, and she pushed her fingers deeper. "To the left. Don't be shy," he whispered sinfully.

She gave him her best deadpan look, feeling her cheeks burn. She couldn't believe he wasn't running the other way. "You're so bad." She pushed her fingers deeper into his pocket. "I can't—"

"You have no idea how *good* bad can be." His gaze turned hungrier despite the children in his arms, and he said, "The keys are in the backpack."

She scoffed and yanked her hand from his pocket, unable to stop a half-laugh, half-shocked sound from escaping. "You are *unbelievable.*"

"Someday, darlin', you'll have *no* doubts about me." He leaned over as if to kiss her and stopped short, as he'd done earlier.

She knew he'd hesitated because of the kids again. She was thankful for him letting her make the decision about when and if they saw them kissing. With her frazzled nerves on fire and hoping harder than life itself that she wasn't making a mistake, she went up on her toes and said, "I have a feeling you enjoy trying to convince me." Then she pressed a kiss to his lips—just as Lila lifted her head and threw up all over his chest.

Chapter Eleven

"SCOTT'S AT THE marina today. I need to call the salon and have them reschedule my clients," Sarah said as she and Bones carried the kids into the house. "I can't let Babs watch Lila when she's sick. I don't want to chance her picking something up and passing it on to Kennedy and Lincoln." Babs babysat them, too.

"I'll stay with the kids while you're at work." He didn't want to leave them, anyway. Not while Lila was sick and after Bradley had such a hard time leaving the ranch. Both kids had fallen asleep within minutes of leaving Nick's ranch. Bones had stopped on the way home to get baby Tylenol and Pedialyte and had woken up Lila long enough for her to get the Tylenol and a few sips of Pedialyte down. She was starting to cool off, but Bones knew how quickly kids could take a turn for the worse.

"No way," Sarah whispered as she laid Lila in the crib and tucked Bradley into bed. She grabbed his hand, leading him down the hall and into the bathroom. Then she wet a washcloth and started scrubbing the puke stain from his shirt. "I appreciate the offer, but this isn't your responsibility. You've been hollered at, cried at, and barfed on. You have gone above and beyond the call of duty as my boy—" She closed her mouth, surprise rising in her eyes.

"Boyfriend?" He touched her hand to stop her from scrubbing the stain. "Finally, you see it, too. This is *exactly* what boyfriends do. Over the past several weeks I've watched you come to grips with letting other people watch your kids. You went from standing guard over them and calling to check on them several times while you were gone to trusting that they were being cared for properly. This is just another step in the ladder of trust. I want to help. Take the step, Sarah."

"They're my kids. I'm used to this. I can handle it."

"I know you can, but you don't have to. You're not alone anymore, Sarah. I know you trust me to take good care of them. If you didn't, you wouldn't have allowed Bradley to ride in my sidecar at the parade."

"Of course I trust you."

"Then what is it? Are you afraid I'll want something in return? That I'll expect sex? Because I don't and I won't. You know I want you, and I know you want me, but not in return for a favor or because it's expected."

"I know you aren't like that," she said.

"I believe you, but we both know you're waiting for me to reveal some awful side of myself that simply doesn't exist."

She took a step back, sighing heavily. "God, I hate my past. I don't think you'll turn into a monster, and I do trust you. It's just hard for me to accept that you—or anyone—can be so nice. You've shown me over and over that I can let my guard down, just as your family and nearly everyone else in this town has. But when I start to let it down, I remember…"

"Remember what, Sarah? Your father? Your ex? I'm not them, and I'll never, *ever*, raise a hand to you."

She made a pained sound, like she hated being in her own head. "I know that, or at least I want to believe it. But watching my kids when Lila is sick? You'll be pulling your hair out by tonight, and then we'll be over before we even have a chance to get started. I'll never be the carefree woman you should be with, Bones. I'm a package deal."

"I adore you and your *packages*. These last two months have shown me how good and right we are together."

"We've barely begun dating, and there's so much you don't know about me."

"We have nothing but time for me to learn. And by the way, for a brilliant woman, you have a very short memory." He tugged off his dirty shirt and quickly washed his chest where Lila had thrown up on him.

As he gathered Sarah in his arms, her eyes skimmed down the tattoos on his chest to his nipple piercings.

"Oh." Her eyes darkened and flicked up to his. "Do you have more?"

He gathered her in his arms and said, "Tattoos, yes, piercings, no, and I cannot wait for you to play with them, but we need to talk about your concerns first. Didn't we already establish that we've been going on semi-dates for weeks now?"

"Yes, but that doesn't mean I can take advantage of you."

"Darlin', that's *exactly* what it means in *every* way, shape, and form. In fact, I can't *wait* for you to take advantage of me."

"You know what I mean." She ran her fingertips up the back of his neck. "I love how you go from talking about kids to talking dirty. Doesn't anything rattle you?"

"Yes, but not this. Taking care of your kids is the top priority." He kissed her neck tenderly. "But you're gorgeous, funny, smart, and the *only* woman I want to have my hands on.

Talking about the children will never take away from how I feel about you."

Her eyes darkened, and she swallowed hard, but it wasn't embarrassment he saw. It was pure, unbridled desire.

"Are you telling me that you aren't thinking about kissing me right now?" he whispered against her lips, and her eyes fluttered closed.

"No," she said softly.

He ran his hands down her back and palmed her ass, earning a throaty moan. "Or touching me?"

Her lips parted, but no words came as he continued kissing her neck and running his hands over her sweet curves. She leaned into him, craning her neck so he could kiss it again. He kissed and licked, and when her fingernails dug into his flesh, he stopped.

"Don't stop," she whispered, heightening his arousal.

He sealed his lips over her neck and sucked, earning more pleasure-filled sounds.

"Does motherhood negate desire?"

"Not when I'm with you," she said desperately.

He tugged her shirt from her shoulder and sank his teeth into her warm flesh, giving it a good, hard suck.

Her eyes sparked with heat, and she said, "Do that again."

Hell yeah, baby. He sealed his mouth over her neck, kissing and sucking until she was rocking against him, panting needily. He rained kisses along her chest, telling himself not to go too fast or push too far. He reclaimed her mouth, more demanding, searching and probing, wanting to inhabit *all* of her. One arm circled her waist, and his other hand drifted to her ass. She moaned into the kiss, and that sexy sound sent bolts of heat straight to his cock. Kissing Sarah was exquisite, holding back from taking more was torture.

"*Bones*," she said with so much raw passion he could drown in it. "How do you do this to me?"

"Do what?" he asked between kisses.

"*Oh God.* Never mind. I can't think. Just kiss me again."

Their mouths crashed together, teeth clanking, tongues tangling. He kissed her deeper, greedily taking as much as she was willing to give. She was right there with him, moaning and digging her fingers into the back of his neck. He wedged his knee between her legs and clutched her ass, trapping his hard length against her thigh. She pushed closer, her belly pressing into him as they groped and ground against each other.

Fuuuck.

She tore her mouth away and said, "You make me want to touch you—and be touched by you." She guided his mouth to her neck again and ran her hands over his piercings, sending lightning to his cock. "Kiss me there. I love when you kiss me there."

"Darlin', you have no idea what you have over me."

He nipped and sucked, grazing his teeth along her neck, earning one sinful noise after another as she rode his thigh, shattering his last shred of control. He backed her up against the wall. Kissing her passionately, he closed the bathroom door with his foot. She played with his piercings. He wanted to strip her bare and love every inch of her, but now wasn't the time. Not when the kids could wake up and she had to go to work. Not before he'd earned every ounce of her trust.

"Want to lick them?" he asked in a husky voice full of restraint that he barely recognized.

"Yes." Her cheeks flushed as she lowered her mouth to his nipple ring. She licked carefully at first. Slowly dragging her tongue around the piercing, then over it, sucking harder. She held on to his back and began riding his thigh again as she sucked and tugged on the piercing. She was a fucking dream come true. She kissed a path across his chest, over his tattoos, and sealed her mouth over his other piercing, a barbell, tugging with her teeth, then sucking hard.

"*Fuck…*" he ground out, and grabbed her face, slayed by the hunger in her eyes. "You destroy me, Sarah."

He crushed his mouth to hers, kissing her with hard thrusts of his tongue, the way he wanted to make love to her. She moaned and pawed at him as she pushed his hands beneath her shirt. He trapped her lower lip between his teeth and gave it a tug. Then, holding her gaze, he grabbed the end of the pink sash tied beneath her breasts. He held it for a long moment, silently seeking her approval. Her nod was like a gift, and he tugged it free, kissing her as he slipped his hands under her shirt, caressing her soft skin as he lifted it up over her belly. He drew back, taking in her beautiful curves. Her jeans rode lower than her belly, and she quickly splayed her hands just above the soft band.

He laced his fingers with hers and said, "Don't hide from me, beautiful."

"Stretch marks aren't pretty," she said.

"Every part of you is stunning. I'm going to make you see and appreciate how beautiful you are, so you'll never want to cover up from me again."

He sealed his promise with a kiss, then dropped down to one knee, lavishing kisses all over her belly. When he reached the places she tried to cover up, he traced each slim stretch mark with tender kisses and slicks of his tongue.

"Beautiful," he said.

She pushed her fingers into his hair, holding so tight it stung. It felt fucking fantastic. Her eyes were closed, her lips slightly parted, glistening from their kisses. She was stunning, and she murmured sounds of appreciation with each press of his lips as he loved every inch of her belly, from the soft material of her jeans, along the rounded sides, and all the way up to the crest below her breasts. He lifted her shirt higher, revealing her full breasts straining against pretty white lace. He took a moment to appreciate the trust she was giving him, and then he framed her face with his hands, taking her in a slow, intoxicating kiss.

When their lips parted, her eyes fluttered open and she whispered, “Please don’t stop.”

He unhooked the front clasp on her bra, freeing her gorgeous breasts, and dragged his tongue around her nipple. Nervousness rolled off her as strongly as the heat between them. He lifted his face, searching hers to make sure they were on the same page.

“Feels so good,” she said breathlessly.

He lowered his mouth over one taut peak, sucking and teasing in equal measure. She clutched his arms like she needed him to remain erect. A stream of erotic sounds left her lungs as he cradled her breasts, loving both slowly and sensually. Her skin was warm, her scent potently feminine, and when she arched and murmured, her sweetness drove him out of his frigging mind. He needed to pleasure her, to feel her come apart for him, and he wanted to strip down her jeans, bury his mouth between her legs, and make her come like an avalanche, but that would have to wait. She wasn’t ready to open herself up to him like that. She needed worshipping, to know he was in this for the long haul, and he would enjoy every second of it.

He continued teasing her with light flicks of his tongue, followed by deep, hard sucks, making her breathe harder, and then hardly at all. He squeezed her other nipple between his finger and thumb. She moaned, arching off the wall, and he wedged his thigh between her legs again, creating the friction he knew she needed. She bit down on her lower lip, and her eyes slammed shut. She was so fucking beautiful, it took all of his control not to take more, to at least slip his hand inside her jeans and into her tight heat. But that, too, would have to wait. Instead, he feasted on her mouth, then breasts, neck, and belly, until she was arching and moaning. Her hand slid off his arm and she palmed his cock, squeezing so tight, so *perfect*, he got carried away and bit down. She cried out in raw, unbridled pleasure, and he slanted his mouth over hers, capturing her sounds as her body quivered and quaked—and then he continued kissing her long after her fireworks ended.

The alarm on her phone sounded, jerking them from their reverie, and she scrambled to pull it from her back pocket before it woke the children. She silenced the alarm, flashing the beautiful smile that always did him in.

"I can't believe we've been in here that long," she said, wide-eyed and flushed as he rehooked her bra and helped her fix her shirt.

He drew her into his arms and said, "Good lovin' takes time."

"I can't believe you made me…" she said bashfully. "Without touching me down there."

"I'm going to make you…so many ways, darlin', you'll come from across the room when you see me."

Her cheeks turned impossibly redder. "A little arrogant, aren't you?" She wound her arms around his neck and pressed her lips to his.

"It's not arrogance. It's what I know will be true. Our connection is that strong. You may not be ready to admit it, but I am. Once we come together, you'll never want to leave my bed."

She didn't respond to that, but the hunger in her eyes, followed by a shadow he wished he didn't see, told him everything he needed to know.

"When you're ready," he said reassuringly. "And no, I don't say that to all women."

"How did you know…?"

"Because you've been hurt, and every time you let me in, I learn more about you. One day you'll see that the man before you, *your* man, has no skin to shed."

"You make it hard to hold back."

"If I said I didn't mean to, I'd be lying."

She glanced at her phone and sighed. "I'm going to be late if I don't go. You're a master of distraction. It's too late to call out from work now. My first client will be there soon."

He pressed his lips to hers, and then he bent and kissed her belly. "No worries. I've got the kids."

"Are you sure you don't mind watching them?" She sniffed the air. Then she lifted her arm and sniffed her sleeve. "I smell a little farm fresh. I think I'd better take a quick shower and rinse off." She reached into the shower and turned on the water. "What if Lila needs me when she wakes up?"

Feigning concern, he said, "Gee, if only there were a device that would allow me to speak to you if we can't manage."

"Has anyone ever told you you're a pain?"

"I think I like it better when you call me *hot*. I'll take good care of the kids while you're at work." He slapped her ass and said, "Now get ready. I've got to go read Dr. Spock or watch a baby show or something, because if I get my hands on your naked body, you're going to smell like a lot more than hay."

BONES COULDN'T REMEMBER the last time he'd been alone in a woman's house. Not that he was alone now, but he *was* the only adult in the house, and he still felt Sarah's presence everywhere—in the curtains she'd made for the back door, which had pictures of little squirrels all over them, in Bradley's drawings hanging on the side of the refrigerator, and even in the colorful plastic letters stuck to the front of it. He glanced around the cozy living room, littered with toys, blankets, stuffed animals, and other child paraphernalia. He went to the bookshelves, noticing a few romance novels by authors he recognized from the book aisle at the grocery store. *You might not be writing your hopeful stories, but at least you haven't closed off your heart from the idea of romance.* A plethora of parenting books, self-help books, and not surprisingly, dozens of children's books filled the shelves. He scanned the spines of the adult books. The number of books geared toward overcoming fear, becoming emotionally stronger, and teaching a child how to love and be loved brought an ache to his chest.

He pulled out one of the parenting books and flipped through the frayed, dog-eared pages. He wasn't surprised to find passages underlined and notes written in the margins. He inspected a few of the other books, finding the same evidence of having been studied.

He chose a few of the titles to look through while Sarah was at work and set them on the coffee table. His phone vibrated with a text, and he didn't have to look to know it was from Sarah.

Are they still asleep?

He sent a quick response as he walked to the bedroom. *Shouldn't you be making someone beautiful?*

He took a picture of Lila, fast asleep and snuggling her hedgehog. She was suckling, though her mouth was void of a thumb. He fought the urge to pick her up, wanting desperately to take away the sickness that flushed her cheeks, and turned toward the bed.

Sarah's response rolled in as he noticed how small Bradley looked in the big bed. Bones smiled to himself thinking of how hard Bradley had fought to remain on the farm. His gut instinct had been to tell Bradley he was the big brother and that he needed to protect his baby sister, the way he'd been taught. But it seemed like too big a responsibility to put on such a little guy, and that thought was accompanied by a large dose of guilt.

He took a picture of her sleeping boy and quietly left the room as he read Sarah's message. *She's getting her hair washed. Are they okay? I feel so guilty leaving when Lila's sick, and even worse leaving you with them. I'm sorry.*

He texted her the pictures of the children despite knowing the pictures might momentarily ease her worries, but nothing could dismiss them altogether. He texted, *We're all fine. Turn off your mommy brain and turn on your hairdresser brain. I promise we're good.*

Her response was immediate. *They're such angels when they're sleeping. Thank you. I'll make it up to you.*

He started to type a sexy innuendo, then ground out a curse as he deleted it. He didn't want her to think he expected anything in return for watching the kids. Instead he typed, *No need to make up for anything, but I'll happily accept whatever you're offering.* After sending the message, he couldn't stop thinking about their bathroom tryst. He hadn't even touched her below the waist and he was hard thinking about making out with her. A smile crept across his lips, and he sent another text, hoping to give her a little rush, too.

PS: I can still taste you…

His phone vibrated seconds later. *How am I supposed to think about cutting hair with THAT on my mind?* She added an emoji with wide eyes, flushed cheeks, and a straight line for a mouth.

"Darlin', you are too cute," he said softly. He sent her an emoji licking its lips and one with hearts in its eyes. Then he scratched an itch on his chest and remembered he was shirtless. He needed clean clothes and a shower. He called Bear.

"Hey, Bones. What's up?"

"You busy?"

"Not *naked*, if that's what you mean. What do you need?"

Bones heard the smirk in his voice. "Can you swing by my place to pick up clean clothes for me and drop them off at Sarah's?" He explained that he was watching the kids while Sarah was at work. "You should probably grab a few T-shirts in case Lila pukes again. Actually, can you hang out here while I shower, too? You know what? Never mind. I should probably ask Tru."

"What? Why?" Bear sounded offended.

"Lila's sick, man. You've never taken care of a sick kid."

"Dude, you're *showering*, not going for a three-hour ride. I'll be there in half an hour. Try not to panic before then."

Bear arrived with a duffel bag and shoved it into Bones's hand as he came through the door. "How's the Daddy Daycare going?"

"They're still sleeping. Thanks for coming over." He unzipped the duffel and rifled through the clothes. There were several T-shirts, a few pairs of jeans, sweatpants, boxer briefs, socks. "What'd you do, clear out my drawers?"

"You've got a puking baby. Trust me, you'll need them. Crystal was puking yesterday. There must be something going around. Now, get your ass in the shower so I can get back to my girl."

"Thanks, man." Bones went to shower.

The steam heightened the scent of Sarah's lilac bodywash, reminding him of how good she felt and of all the sensual sounds she'd made. It was only a short leap to imagine her naked in the shower with him, her mouth on his piercings, then lower. *Aaand* now he was hard again. He turned up the cold water. Now he was cold and hard. He gritted his teeth, forced himself to think of Bear hanging out in the living room waiting for him.

Mission accomplished.

Ten minutes later he was clean, dressed, and thanking Bear. "I really appreciate you sticking around."

"You're really overprotective, you know that? How do you think Sarah showers?"

"Naked," he said to shut him up.

Bear chuckled.

"I have no idea how she does any of what she does," Bones admitted. "She makes it all look easy. But hey, she trusts me with the two most important things in her life. I don't want to screw it up."

Bear scoffed. "Dude, you've never screwed up a damn thing in your life."

"Sure I have." The ability to disassociate came in handy in more ways than one. Not only hadn't he been there to help when his father had a stroke, but although he was an equal partner in both family businesses, he had never gotten his hands dirty in either one. He pitched in capital when they wanted to expand or needed to renovate, but he'd gone straight from medical school to practicing medicine. There was a certain amount of guilt that went along with not being in the trenches with his family—and it was only about half as much guilt as what he carried over Thomas's death.

"You got in your fair share of trouble when you were young and bullheaded, like we all did," Bear said. "But you don't screw up. I bet you've already figured out which websites you should look at to make sure you change Lila's diaper right or to read the right bedtime story."

A low laugh rumbled up from Bones's chest. "You're an idiot."

"I'll take that to mean I'm *right.* You riding with us tomorrow? We're heading out to Capshaw Island." Capshaw Island was a small fishing town a little more than an hour away, best known for wild horses that had inhabited the island for hundreds of years.

Thinking about Sarah he said, "Not this time. Thanks."

The edge of Bear's mouth tipped up. He raked a hand through his thick dark hair, a twinkle of mischief shimmering in his eyes. "Hoping to get a little Mommy action?"

"Dude, watch it."

"What? You think it's a secret you two are into each other?"

"No, but come on. *Mommy action?*"

"She's hot—there no doubt about that—but she's also a mother and pregnant with some other dude's baby. You sure you want to go there?"

Bones gritted his teeth. He didn't give a fuck about what anyone else thought. "I've never been more certain of anything in my life."

"I figured as much, but you know, you're used to only seeing a chick here or there. This is instafamily all the way."

The hair on the back of Bones's neck stood on end. He stared directly into Bear's eyes and said, "You saying I like to shirk responsibility? Do you see any other guy here right now? No. *I'm* here, man. And I'm not going anywhere."

"Whoa, dude." Bear stepped back, holding his hands up. "What just bit your balls?"

Bones turned away, rubbing a knot in the back of his neck. He hadn't meant to go off on Bear, but sometimes guilt ate away at him. "Sorry."

"No, really, what was *that* all about?"

Bones faced him again. "Misplaced anger. I wasn't there when you needed me when Dad had his stroke. I thought you were giving me shit about it."

"Are you fucking kidding me?" Bear took a few steps away, an incredulous laugh falling from his lips. "Dude, you asked me if I wanted you to come back. I said stay at school. Done deal. The only reason I asked about Sarah is that you're the guy who researches the hell out of everything before making decisions. Remember when you wanted to buy a new bike? Man, it took you almost nine months *comparing* all the models. You just about drove me crazy. I design and fix bikes for a living, and you couldn't take my opinion as gold? And how about when you bought each of your other vehicles? *Months*, man. A fucking car and a truck, and you're acting like you're breaking into Fort Knox. You had no couch in your house for half a year after you moved in. All I'm saying is you're not a quick decision maker. And with Sarah, you were in from day one. Whether you knew it or not, the rest of us did. You didn't know a lick of information about her. You saw her and *bam. Done.* Everyone expects that from me, but not from you."

Bones clenched his jaw. He wasn't about to deny the truth or make excuses for his feelings.

"I just want you to be careful," Bear said, a little kinder. "I like Sarah a lot, and her kids are great. But you're my blood, and in my book, that comes first. You give your all to whatever you set your mind to. That's who you are down to your very soul. When you die, you're going to have researched and planned it to the very second."

Bones chuckled.

"You laugh, but trust me, bro. If anyone can do it, it'll be you. I don't want you to be the one who is giving it all he's got and planning a life that could be taken away at any second. What do we even know about the father of her kids? Huh? What if he comes back for them?"

"We know he's a fucking asshole and if he dares show his face around here, he'll have me to deal with."

Bear picked up a parenting book from the coffee table and waved it at Bones. "No. He'll have *us* to deal with."

The Whiskey way.

He tossed the book on the table and said, "Are we cool, or do you want to kick my ass? Because"—he grabbed his own ass and smirked—"I don't need bruises before I go home and show my sexy-as-fuck wife how much I missed her."

"We're cool. Thanks for coming over." He offered a hand, and when Bear took it, he pulled him into an embrace. "I appreciate you having my back."

"For real, man. I'm behind you one hundred percent. But I gotta ask. Is it true what they say about pregnancy hormones?"

"Bear," Bones warned.

"What? I hear preggos never leggo—"

Bones smacked him upside the head. "Go home, Bear."

"Careful, or the baby will be born with a dent in its head."

Bones swatted at him, and Bear ducked, laughing as he headed for the door.

"Okay, okay, I'm going." He pulled open the door and turned a shit-eating grin to Bones. "Hey, since she's pregnant, does that mean you get to eat her out for twice as long?"

Bones landed a punch on Bear's arm and chased him out the door, stopping halfway to the driveway. "You went too far, man. *Too far.*"

Bear climbed on his motorcycle and hollered, "Love you, bro. And don't think I don't know the only reason you aren't hammering me is that you wouldn't be able to hear the kids while you did it."

"Damn right. Now, get out of here and give Crystal a hug for me."

"Keep my girl out of your fantasies, or I will crush your skull." Bear pulled on his helmet and drove away.

"Idiot," Bones mumbled as he walked back to the house.

Damn, that motorcycle might wake the kids.

The thought stopped him in his tracks. *Hell yeah, I'm all in.*

Chapter Twelve

RED BLEW THROUGH the front door of the salon just as Chicki was locking up for the night. She strutted across the floor in her black boots and leather jacket and set serious eyes on Sarah. "Please tell me you have a nanny cam."

Sarah's pulse spiked. "Why? What happened?" She grabbed her phone to check for a text from Bones. She hadn't heard from him for almost two hours.

Red touched her hand, a smile warming her green eyes. "Nothing bad, sweetheart. I just never thought I'd hear my most levelheaded son so frazzled."

"Oh no." Sarah's shoulders slumped. "I knew my kids would be too much." She had even called Scott earlier to ask him if he could relieve Bones if she got an SOS call, but before she could ask, Scott told her he was going to a party with Quincy and not to expect him home until late, if at all.

"No, honey. They're just enough," Red reassured her. "You found my son's Achilles' heel. He called me earlier about Lila, and I swear you'd think the boy had never been around a sick child or been to medical school." She lowered her voice an octave and said, "'Mom, how do I know if she's sleeping too long? She's still warm. Should I give her a cool bath?' Wayne navigates life and death on a daily basis, but when it comes to your babies"—Red made a *whoosh*ing sound and pushed her hand backward over her head—"he forgets everything."

Sarah breathed a sigh of relief, and of *surprise* that Bones had called his mother. "Was Lila worse? I haven't heard from him since about seven o'clock."

"Oh, honey. Lila's fine, and Bones had his hands full when we talked. While we were on the phone, Bradley carried blankets to the stairs and wanted to slide down."

"Oh my gosh," Sarah muttered. "He always tries to do that while I'm preoccupied. He knows he's not allowed to."

Red winced. "Yeah, Bones sort of learned that a little too late. It wasn't until Bradley went down the third time and squealed, 'Mommy never lets me do this!' that he realized his mistake."

"He *let* him do it?" *Bradley should be nice and hyped up by the time I get home.*

"Oh, don't worry," Red said. "He set up pillows at the bottom of the steps and caught him every time."

Sarah grabbed her purse. "I'd better go rescue Bones. The poor guy had no idea what he was getting into. I hope he has his running shoes," she said as she headed for the front door.

"Why?" Red asked.

"Because running for the hills will be hard in biker boots."

She left the salon and drove home mentally preparing a litany of apologies for Bones.

When she got home, she listened by the front door but couldn't hear a thing. Preparing for the worst, she quietly opened the door and stepped inside. Toys and children's books were scattered all over the floor, along with a few clean diapers and an open baby wipes container. Two sippy cups and a bowl of crackers sat on the coffee table alongside Bones's phone. She heard the washer going and peered into the kitchen, not surprised to find dirty dishes in the sink.

She didn't care about the mess or the dishes, but she knew this was a bad idea, and all these signs of *overload* for a single man proved it.

She swallowed hard before heading down the hall, preparing herself for the anger that was sure to come after a frustrating night with a sick baby and a rambunctious three-year-old. Why had she agreed to let Bones watch them?

She glanced downstairs, spotting a pile of blankets at the bottom and wondering what else her little rascal had convinced Bones to let him do.

Sending a silent plea to the universe and hoping Bones wouldn't totally hate her, she peered nervously into the bedroom. Bones lay on the bed in sweatpants and a white T-shirt with Lila draped over his chest fast asleep, one tiny hand on his cheek, the other cuddling her hedgehog. Bradley lay sleeping across Bones's legs. Bones had one thick arm wrapped around Lila, and the other held one of her parenting books as he read. Her chest constricted as he lowered the book to the mattress and put one finger over his lips. Lord help her, because her heart thudded even harder with the loving look in his eyes as he lowered that hand to Bradley's hair and ran his fingers through it. Was it possible to freeze a moment? To take a snapshot and relive it a million times over?

"I was afraid to move," he whispered with a warm smile.

Struggling against the emotions clogging her throat, she set her purse on the dresser and went to transfer Lila to her crib. As she reached for Lila, Bones touched her hand. "Maybe you shouldn't move her. She was warm again after her nap. I had my buddy Jonas, a pediatrician, come over and check her out. He thinks it's just a virus, but she needs to sleep, and every time I put her in the crib she cries."

"You had a doctor make a house call? She just has a fever…"

Thump, thump, thump. She was sure he could hear the sound of her falling for him, too.

"Can't be too careful." He pulled her down so close she could smell apple juice on his breath, which also made her all warm and squishy inside.

He tugged a little harder, bringing her lips to his in a tender kiss—and then he kissed her longer, turning that warm squishiness into white-hot desire.

"Go do whatever you need to," he whispered. "Except the dishes and cleaning the living room. I'll do that in the morning. Then come back." He patted the space beside him. "We'll be here waiting."

"You're…*staying*?"

His smile faded. "Unless you want me to leave?"

"No," she said quickly, unable to believe her ears. "I just thought…" *You'd be done with us.*

He. Wasn't. Running.

She tried to wrap her head around the situation and the man who was turning her beliefs upside down one moment at a time.

"What is it, darlin'?"

A trickle of worry wormed its way into her mind, urging her to take a step back. She glanced down at her sleeping babies, Bones's strong arms now draped protectively around both of them. He wanted to stay and care for the babies, not stay and try to get in her pants. What ulterior motive could he possibly have, beyond being a sadist who wanted to drive himself insane with a crying baby at three in the morning?

As if he'd read her mind, he reached for her hand again, brushing his thumb over the back of it in slow circles that made her crave his hands on her again as he said, "I'm here because I want to be here with you *and* with them. I know it's hard, but try looking forward with me, not over your shoulder for your past to become your present."

She nodded, choking back another rush of emotions. He understood her so well, she didn't even have to say a word.

"It's your call, Sarah. I can leave, or you can take a leap of faith and trust me to catch you on the other side."

There was only one way to answer a request like that.

After getting ready for bed, with her pulse racing and her mind not far behind, she crawled in beside the three of them.

Bones tucked her against his side and pressed his lips to her temple. "Thank you for trusting me."

"Just promise me that if you start to feel trapped or overwhelmed you'll end things before they get scary. I don't want my babies to know *scary*."

He kissed her again and closed his eyes. He remained silent for so long that if it weren't for the brush of his thumb along her shoulder, she'd think he'd fallen asleep. And then his warm breath whispered over her skin as he said, "If I have it my way, they never will."

SARAH AWOKE THE next morning from a shift in the mattress and found Bones quietly stepping from the bed with Lila in his arms. Bradley lay sprawled across the blankets between them. She'd been up half the night trying to calm herself down. It had been a long time since she'd had a man in her bed, and she definitely wasn't used to having one who was perfectly content to hold her babies instead of pawing her. Her ex had never allowed the babies to be in bed with them. He'd insisted she not even nurse them, and here was Bones, loving them up like they were an extension of himself. Guilt niggled at her. She had hoped to tell him more about her past last night, and now she worried about how he would react *after* taking this step, which felt bigger and more intimate than any sexual act ever could.

"I'll get her." Sarah moved toward the edge of the bed.

"I've got her." Bones turned, looking impossibly handsome with his dark hair sticking up all over, thick scruff peppering his jaw, and her precious baby draped on his chest like she belonged there.

She noticed the bump of his piercing through his shirt. How had she missed it before? Embarrassingly, she'd spent the other half of the night trying not to think about how he'd reacted to her mouth on his nipples, tugging at his piercings. She'd been shocked to see those little shiny pieces of jewelry on his hard body, but the sight of them had heightened her arousal. His reactions had made her even hotter. The piercings told her so much about him. She'd known strippers who had nipple rings, and they'd told her all the benefits. Knowing Bones wasn't afraid of a little pain for pleasure would be scary if he were anyone else. But he'd shown her how careful he was, not just with her and her children, but with his life in general. She sensed this was his erotic little secret—and she liked being a part of it. Her mind wandered back to the feel of his thick, hard shaft against her thigh and palm. Even through his jeans she could feel his girth. A streak of heat coursed through her.

She must have looked like she was fantasizing, because Bones cleared his throat and arched a brow. A knowing look hovered in his eyes as he pointed lower than his chest—where she was still staring—to a big wet spot on his shirt, sending Sarah's stomach into a nosedive.

"Oh gosh. I'm sorry!" *As if it weren't enough for you to be thrown up on, now you've been peed on, too?* Familiar panic spread through her as she bolted to her feet, praying he wouldn't get gruff in front of the kids. Or worse, *toward* them, the way Lewis did.

"Lie down and rest, darlin'. It's just a little pee. I'll get her cleaned up and changed." He kissed Lila's forehead, and her baby girl whimpered. "She's a little cooler, but I want to get some Pedialyte into her system." He pretended to inspect his arm and said, "No scales yet. I think we're safe."

He winked and turned toward the dresser, leaving Sarah stunned as he rifled around in Lila's drawer.

"Mommy?" Bradley rolled over, rubbing sleep from his eyes. He blinked up at Bones, his eyes rolling over his tall, broad body. "Ew! Lila peed on you!" he said loudly, startling Lila into a wail that practically echoed off the walls.

Bones tried to calm Lila down, bouncing her and talking soothingly as he caressed her back.

"I gotta go potty!" Bradley bolted from the bed and ran toward the hallway, sending Lila into another crying fit.

"Sorry!" Sarah hurried after Bradley.

Before she made it out the bedroom door, Bones grabbed her hand, drawing her closer. Her mommy brain was still frantically chasing Bradley down the hall, needing to make sure he didn't miss the potty. But in the next second, Dr. Whiskey's lips covered hers in a long, sensual kiss, calming the mommy side of her despite her baby girl's whimpers, stoking the womanly desires she'd been trying to tamp down all night. She knew Lila was safe, even if unhappy at the moment, and really, what was a little pee on a toilet seat? Sarah's knees wobbled, and her nipples hardened to burning, needy points. When their lips finally parted, there was no room in her lust-addled brain for stressing over anything.

Lila clung to the collar of Bones's shirt as he pressed a kiss to Lila's forehead. "Sorry, baby girl. Your sweet mama just needed a good-morning kiss to remind her there's nothing we can't handle."

He slowly and purposefully brushed his fingers down Sarah's cheek as he said, "Good morning, beautiful."

Before she could reel in her spinning thoughts enough to respond, Bradley dashed into the bedroom and dove onto the bed, immediately bouncing on his butt like the Energizer Bunny.

"Let's get them cleaned up and settled," Bones said with another sexy smile. "Then I'll make breakfast while you get ready for the day."

"You must be crazy if you still want to stick around." She was only half kidding.

He pressed his lips to hers in a quick kiss and said, "Like Krazy Glue, baby. Now, let's get moving before this one lets loose from the other end."

Chapter Thirteen

LILA'S FEVER BROKE Sunday afternoon, and by Monday morning she was back to her smiling self, which was a good thing, because Bones worried over her like a new mother. It was Thursday afternoon, and Sarah was at Whiskey Bro's with the girls, planning the birthday party for Lila and Bones. Sarah slid her hand over her baby bump, thinking of the way Bones had shown up each night to help Scott put the finishing touches on the basement—pulling up on his motorcycle, looking tough in his leather jacket, jeans that hugged him in all the best places, and those black boots that made him even taller than he was, with a helmet under his arm. She got hot and bothered just watching his confident swagger, but when that coy smile lifted his lips—the lips she was already addicted to—it was impossible for her not to fantasize about the rest of him. Luckily, it seemed Bones thought of her just as often, because he stuck around each night long after they finished working in the basement, helping her put the kids to bed, encouraging her to write—she still hadn't found the inspiration to start, although she carried a notebook in her purse at all times just in case—and then reminding her in the most delicious ways that she wasn't only a mother but also a *woman*. As much as she liked living with Scott, she was starting to feel like those teenagers she remembered from school who snuck into empty classrooms to make out. Only there were no such spaces in her house, which meant she and Bones were relegated to remaining clothed in case Scott came into the room. And there was no easy way to dry hump with her baby bump between them. She went to bed every night hot, bothered, and *needy*. If she didn't get alone time with him soon, she was going to lose her freaking mind.

"Hello..." Dixie waved her hand in front of Sarah's face, snapping her from her horny ruminations and bringing her attention back to their conversation. "Wow, you've got the look in your eyes that Bullet has when he's staring at Finlay, and Bones isn't even in the room."

Finlay and Bullet had just returned from their honeymoon. The girls had spent the first twenty minutes of their lunch date poring over their honeymoon pictures. They'd gone to Elpitha Island, just off the coast of North Carolina. The island had no cars, and the girls roared at pictures of Bullet riding a ten-speed bicycle. Tinkerbell was in nearly every picture with them, and in each and every one, Bullet and Finlay were holding hands, kissing, or touching in some way. Sarah's mind had tiptoed into dangerous territory, wondering what it might be like to have that type of alone time with Bones—if she weren't pregnant. Would they be all over each other? *Would we ever leave the bedroom?*

Finlay glanced over her shoulder at Bullet, standing behind the bar talking with Jed.

Bullet looked over and lifted his chin. "Need me, lollipop?"

"Always," Finlay said sweetly, then turned back to the girls and said, "I think Sarah has a bad case of Whiskey fever."

Dixie rolled her eyes. "That's not even a *thing*."

Crystal, Gemma, and Finlay gave her disbelieving looks and said in unison, "Oh, yes, it is."

"I don't have Whiskey fever," Sarah insisted. "It's pregnancy hormones."

"Mm-hm." With a flick of her chin, Crystal sent her jet-black hair away from her face, revealing her mischief-filled blue cycs. "And when's the last time you fed those pregnancy hormones?"

"You don't want to know," Sarah mumbled, thinking back to the night she'd gotten pregnant and the horrific night that followed a few weeks later. If she were honest with herself, she couldn't remember ever having *fed* her emotions *or* her hormones except with Bones. Maybe at first it was like that with Lewis, but it had never been the feverish, bone-deep desires and emotions she felt with Bones. She'd never known a relationship could be as warm and wonderful as it was sensual and thrilling.

Isabel's eyes widened. "That long? Have you moved into your new bedroom yet, because, you know…?"

She'd spent several nights thinking about what *you know* might be like when they had privacy. "The basement carpeting was just installed. Scott's home now meeting the furniture delivery guys, and my bedroom should be all set up by tonight." For now the kids would share their current bedroom, Sarah would take Scott's room, and Scott would move downstairs. Once the baby was born, it would sleep in her room so he or she didn't wake the other kids.

"Are you excited?" Gemma asked.

Isabel pushed her short dark hair behind her ear and said, "I sure would be. I can't imagine sharing a bedroom with kids all the time. I mean, how do you flick the bean when you get the urge?"

"Izzy!" Finlay scolded, her cheeks pinking up as badly as Sarah was sure her own were.

"Oh my gosh, you guys…" Until Bones had come along, she hadn't flicked her bean since before she'd met Lewis. But she swore every breath Bones took had a direct line to her very lonely *bean*. Thank goodness for the privacy of showers. But she wasn't about to say that in the presence of Isabel and Dixie, who were as open about sex as Finlay was about adoring Bullet.

"What?" Isabel said with a laugh. "You're married to a guy who asked you if you wanted to take a ride on the Bullet Train and *this* embarrasses you?"

"Shh!" Finlay covered her face, making everyone laugh.

Gemma rolled her eyes and said, "Seriously, Sarah. Are you excited to finally have your own room?"

Sarah was as excited as she was nervous about their new accommodations. Mostly because of the possibilities of…*you know*. Although she wasn't quite sure how she'd navigate that with Scott around or how she felt about Scott knowing about her sex life, because he'd know exactly why Bones was staying over. "It's going to be strange after sleeping in the same room as the kids for so long."

"No, it's going to feel amazing, because then you and Bones will have a place to *bone*," Crystal said with a wink.

"Can we please not talk about my brother boning anyone?" Dixie leaned back in her chair, crossing her long legs and kicking her high-heeled foot up and down.

"Yes, *please*," Sarah begged, glad for the reprieve from embarrassment. She was one hundred percent certain that if—*when*, because she really wanted to—she and Bones did have sex, it wouldn't be *boning*.

"Sure," Gemma said. "How's this? Sarah, you and Bones will have a place to retire behind closed doors for a sweet evening of sharing secrets."

"And *boning*," Crystal added with a smirk.

Dixie swatted her.

"You're just jealous because you're having a dry spell," Isabel teased.

All the girls looked at Dixie.

"You try hooking up with a bunch of burly buttheads watching over you," Dixie said.

"So bang Scott," Crystal said. "He's gorgeous, and you're always hanging out with him anyway."

Sarah cringed. "Stop. Not that I mind the idea of Dixie and Scott, but it would be weird for either of us to...*you know*...with both of us living there. It would be so *obvious*."

"I'm not going to bang Scott," Dixie said so loud Bullet looked over and said, "Damn right you're not."

Dixie flipped him off.

"Scott's a grown man," Isabel said, turning the conversation back to Sarah. "He gets laid like everyone else. He *knows* you and Bones need intimate time alone, and I'm sure he won't care. It's not like he's going to listen at the door."

"*Ohmygod.* That's a thought I didn't need." Sarah slumped a little lower in her seat.

Scott had told her more than once that he really liked Bones. He'd even gone so far as to say he *approved of him* for his little sister. They'd had a good laugh about the *little* part when Scott had patted her belly. She knew he'd respect their privacy. The truth was, even though she dreamed about making love with Bones and fantasized about doing all sorts of naughty things to his hard body, and him to hers, she was extremely nervous about it. It was one thing to want someone and quite another to try to figure out how to make love with a burgeoning baby bump. She didn't imagine it would be very sexy. Not to mention the fact that she'd never truly *made love* with anyone in her life. What if everything she did was *off*?

"Seriously, you and Bones *need* alone time," Crystal said adamantly. "Bear said Bones was all twitchy at the club meeting Monday night."

Bones had texted her a few times from the meeting, checking on the kids, telling her he missed her and that he wished he was there with them instead of at the meeting. Everything he did pushed the worries that had plagued her farther away.

"He was probably exhausted from sleeping with my children Saturday night and from them laying all over him Sunday afternoon," she said. "Lila fell asleep on his chest when he was reading on the couch, and he refused to put her in the crib. He was afraid she'd wake up and not go back to sleep. He worries so much about her, and I swear he checked Bradley's temperature—casually kissing his forehead, as if I didn't know what he was doing—at least a dozen times over the weekend."

Gemma sighed. "Isn't that the best? You can't fault a guy for loving children."

"Especially when they're not his. He turns me into a swoony mess when he's sweet with them like that," Sarah admitted, but she kept silent about what else it did to her. She'd wanted to rip his clothes off, but the best they could do was duck into the laundry room while the kids watched television for a few minutes of making out and heavy petting. Goose bumps rose on her arms just thinking about his hard heat pressing into her thigh and how badly she'd wanted it in her hands, her mouth, her *body*.

"Scott did great babysitting. Can't he watch them overnight?" Gemma asked.

"He can, but I hate putting that responsibility on him, and I've never left them overnight."

"Never?" Gemma asked.

Sarah shook her head. "Our lives were never conducive to date nights or anything like that. I had never even been on a real date before the night Bones took me out."

The girls went wide-eyed with astonishment.

"When are you and Bones going out again?" Crystal asked.

"He's volunteering at the Parkvale Women's Shelter Saturday evening, and he asked me out for afterward. I'd really like to volunteer with him, but Scott's got something going on and I haven't asked Babs if she can babysit yet."

"Forget Babs," Finlay said. "We'll watch them overnight. Bullet and I want to start a family soon. What better way to prepare than to babysit?"

"Really?" Sarah asked. "I can't put you guys out like that. You're fresh off your honeymoon, and the kids are major sexy-stuff blockers."

"Have you seen my man with Gemma's kids?" Finlay said. "Children are about the only thing he likes more than sex."

"TMI," Dixie chimed in, earning an eye roll from Finlay.

"Bear and I can help," Crystal said. "We can stay overnight."

"I'm working," Isabel said. "Otherwise I'd offer to help."

"Tru and I can come over with the kids for a little while so Bradley and Kennedy can play," Gemma offered.

"Wait a second," Dixie interrupted. "There's no way any of you are going to fit sleeping on a couch with either of your ginormous men. *I'll* stay overnight with the kids. Gemma can bring her kids over to play," she said to Gemma. "And the rest of y'all can come hang out, but you don't have to sleep over."

"I appreciate all of this, but it feels funny," Sarah said. "Like I'm planning to jump his bones or something."

"Well, yeah," Crystal said with a laugh. "That's the point, isn't it?"

"Sometimes you have to *plan.*" Gemma touched Sarah's hand and said, "*Especially* with little ones around."

Laughter burst from Finlay's lips, and she covered her mouth, her gaze darting around the table. "Sorry," she said from behind her hand. "I just realized Dixie is the one complaining about knowing what you want to do with her brother and *she's* the one who's babysitting."

"They're *sharing secrets*, remember?" Dixie snapped.

"Text Bones," Finlay said excitedly. "Tell him you're on for Saturday night. He's going to be *so* pumped!"

Sarah nervously sent him a message. *Dixie is going to watch the kids Saturday so I can go out with you, but I'd like to also go with you to volunteer at the shelter if you don't mind.* She decided to leave out the part about Dixie offering to stay overnight, because come hell or high water, she *was* going to share her *real* secrets with Bones Saturday night, and she wasn't sure he'd want to continue seeing her afterward. At least this way if they broke up she could wallow in sadness alone for a few hours before being Mommy again.

After ironing out details so Sarah and Bones could *share secrets*, Finlay guided the conversation back to the reason they were there, planning the birthday party for Bones and Lila. While the girls discussed balloons, cakes, and games, Sarah thought about her impending date with Bones. Her heart hurt even thinking about the possibility that he might not want to see her anymore after she told him the rest of her story, but every time she tried to tell him—and there had been many times—she'd given in to wanting just one more hour, one more night, with him. She'd played the procrastination game long enough. The guilt was eating away at her.

It was time to come clean, even if it meant losing him.

Chapter Fourteen

BONES HAD BEEN volunteering at the Parkvale Women's Shelter for years, and although it was on the outskirts of a seedy area, he'd never been nervous about going there. The brick building was beside a gas station on a side street and looked more like a two-story apartment complex than a shelter. It was monitored twenty-four seven, and police made regular rounds in the area. There hadn't been any incidents at the shelter for a very long time, and there shouldn't be any reason that the hair on the back of his neck stood on end as he parked behind the building with Sarah sitting by his side.

Except there was.

Sarah had fidgeted nervously with the edge of her thick gray sweater for the past thirty minutes. He had asked several times if she'd changed her mind, but she insisted she wanted to volunteer at the shelter, even if just to talk with some of the residents.

He helped her from the car and drew her into his arms, remembering how scared she'd been to go to a shelter all those years ago, when her friend had driven her to a bus station instead.

"Sarah, we don't have to do this. If it brings back too many bad memories, we can get in the car and go home right now."

She lifted her chin, and a lock of hair tumbled in front of her face. When he brushed it away, the look in her eyes made his heart ache. There was fear, yes, but there was also sadness, and beneath it all the strength that had allowed her to survive so much of her life shone through.

"I'm okay," she said. "I want to do this even if I'm nervous. The women in the shelter need to see that there's hope, and I can help them see that. I'm living proof that where they are right now doesn't have to be all there is for them."

She amazed him in so many ways, not just because she'd somehow learned how to be an incredible, loving mother when she hadn't had a positive role model, which was a feat in and of itself, but the way she took every responsibility to heart—including this one, which wasn't hers to own. Her unyielding efforts to conquer her past and help others made her seem even more powerful than the strongest men he knew.

He kissed her tenderly and said, "Where have you been all my life, Sarah Beckley? I wish we'd met years ago."

She lowered her eyes, and then she smiled up at him and said, "Considering that I'm only twenty-six and you're thirty...?"

"Something," he answered with a chuckle.

"Considering you were twenty*something* when I left home, I think maybe fate did have a plan after all; otherwise you'd have seen me as jailbait back then, and that would have been that. We might never have gotten to where we are now." She looked up at the building and said, "At least I'm not crossing this bridge alone. I've got you by my side, which is more than I've ever had when I've walked into a shelter in the past. So, let's go see who we can help."

With one arm around her, he scanned their surroundings as they headed toward the front of the building. It wasn't a safehouse, although Bones had visited plenty of those. The Dark Knights were involved in keeping Peaceful Harbor safe and free from abuse and bullying, and they'd intervened on many occasions and arranged for women and children's safe departure from their homes.

"I'm glad you're here," he said when they reached the building. "When I first started working with shelters, I thought I'd be met with a sense of desperation, embarrassment, self-loathing, and other undeserved emotions. While that was true, I found that *hope* outshone them all. It took a little longer for some of the women and children to embrace it, but I'm always a little awed by the power of it."

She looked at him curiously. "I've never thought about it that way, but you're right. I'm glad I'm here, too."

He held the door open for Sarah, and she stiffened. Then she reached for his hand and held on tight, taking in the nondescript entrance as they ascended the stairs to the shelter entrance on the second floor.

He punched in his code, and the unlocking mechanism sounded. Sarah held his hand a little tighter.

Inside, Eva Yeun's daughter, Sunny, came around the reception desk to greet them. "Hi, Bones. I'm glad you made it." She hugged Bones. His big body dwarfed five-foot, slight-as-a-bird Sunny. "And you must be Sarah. Bones told me he was bringing his very special lady friend." She pushed her silky black hair over her shoulder, nudged her round spectacles to the bridge of her nose, and opened her arms to Sarah. "I'm a hugger, but I know not everyone is. Your choice."

Sarah leaned in, a little uncomfortably, and hugged her. "Hi. Thanks for letting me come today. I'm not sure how I can help, but I'm a really good listener."

"That's what most of our residents need," Sunny said as she hurried around the desk and picked up a stack of folders. "But first let me get Bones ready for his evening. There are a number of women and kids for you to see. I'm particularly worried about one little boy. He's four, and he looks a little pale, but his mother refused to take him to the urgent care center. She had another little one with her, but he looked healthier. I put her folder on top."

Many of the women refused care, but when it came to their children they were usually more open to it. "I'll see them first. The mom's skittish?" Bones asked.

"More like a fierce lioness, sure everyone's out to take her kids away. Tread carefully. She guards the den with claws and fangs."

Bones nodded and turned to Sarah. "If you need me, just let Sunny know."

"I'll be fine," Sarah reassured him.

Something in the way she said it told him she'd made some type of internal leap and had taken control of her fears. He leaned in for a kiss and said, "Thanks, darlin'."

"Could you two be any cuter?" Sunny pushed Bones toward the hallway that led to the office where he did exams. "My mom is back there waiting for you. She'll usher everyone in and hand them swoon rags when they come out to wipe the drool."

Bones rolled his eyes and made his way down the hall.

SUNNY LEANED CLOSE to Sarah and lowered her voice. "Like he doesn't know that even women who have been through hell notice hot, kind guys. Come on, I'll show you around and introduce you to some of our residents. When is your baby due?"

"Mid-February. Do you have any children?" Sarah asked as they walked down another hall.

"No. I have a history of not being very respectful to myself, and I'm working on that before I think about bringing little humans into the world. Bones has helped me a lot." She must have seen the curiosity in Sarah's expression because she stopped walking and said, "I don't know if he told you or not, but my father is a Dark Knight, which means I grew up with enough *brothers*—each of the Dark Knights fathers and sons—for twelve girls. It's annoying as hell, but there's safety in knowing a bunch of guys have your back. Unless you're me, in which case you rebel against everything they've tried to teach you and end up dating heavy-handed assholes." She sighed and said, "I swear, from the time I was sixteen until I was twenty I was a hellion. I moved here after high school so I wouldn't be in Peaceful Harbor and got into so much trouble, it's a wonder I'm still alive."

Every now and then Sarah still felt a pang of longing for the childhood she'd missed out on, which should have included things like teenage boyfriends and rebellions, but then there were times like this, when she knew the grass wasn't always greener…

"How did Bones help you?"

"Everyone else *commanded* and *demanded*," Sunny explained. "But Bones never did. He found me at a party one night, and he didn't drag me out or tell me I was a rebellious jerk who was going to get myself raped or killed. He just sat with me at the party, listened to me bitch, and at the end of the night he drove me to my apartment. He did that every night for a couple weeks, and one day my neighbor asked why I made my boyfriend sleep outside. He wasn't my boyfriend obviously. I had no idea, but Bones had been standing guard outside my place every night. I only found out afterward that when the guys I'd hang out with showed up, he sent them away. He got into quite a scuffle with a few, from what I understand."

She thought of Halloween night and the way Bones had stuck around outside until Scott came home. He'd never mentioned it to her, had never sought accolades or even a thank-you. It was enough for him just to know she was safe. "And that was enough for you to want to change?"

Sarah turned that question back on herself, and yes, his thoughtfulness had been enough for her to start opening up to him.

Sunny shook her head, her dark eyes filling with sadness. "It was enough for me to slow down and wonder why he was doing it. He didn't owe my family anything. He had nothing to gain except fatigue. When I asked him, he said, 'You tell me.' It was the first time anyone had posed such a question, and it made me think. Why *would* anyone want to help me? That question ate away at me. And the next night when I went to a party, Bones was there leaning against his motorcycle waiting for me. The hottest bachelor in Peaceful Harbor spent his evenings trying to get me to want more for myself. I blew him off for a few more days, and then one night he was waiting, leaning against his bike again, legs crossed at the ankle, and he said, 'I can do this all year long.' My whole life had been selfish, but suddenly it hit me. Here was this guy, willing to help people, and there I was, a girl with more support than I could ever want, throwing it all away. How many people didn't have that? How many other girls could Bones save if he hadn't been trying to get through to me?"

There weren't many men like Bones in the world, and Sarah hoped to heaven that after tonight he'd still want to be with her. "I would have given anything to have had someone like him in my life when I was younger. It might have saved me from doing things I'm not proud of."

"Bones says as long as we're honest with ourselves, shame has no place in our lives. He's not a preachy guy, but that's a little subtle gift he's shared with our residents. I think it helps to forgive ourselves. That was part of my problem. I was too embarrassed to go back to the harbor and face all the people who had tried to help me. What Bones said, and what he did, helped me to step in here, beside my mom, and help others, and eventually, to face the people who had tried so hard to help me." Sunny nodded toward the entrance to a recreation room and said, "Ready to make a difference?"

"More than you could know."

She followed Sunny into the bright, open room. A blond woman sat on the floor by the television with two young boys building a tower with blocks. Sarah watched them for a moment, wondering if that was the woman whose claws and fangs came out to protect her children. She looked like any young mother, and neither of her boys looked particularly pale. The fact that Sarah could have been in that same position if she hadn't found Scott didn't escape her. How many times had she wished she'd taken her chances and gone to the shelter near her hometown just in case Josie had shown up there?

She shifted her eyes away in a futile attempt to ignore the

black hole Josie had left behind. A pale-skinned heavyset girl with frizzy auburn hair sat on the couch reading a magazine, and across the room two women about Sarah's age huddled close together talking in hushed whispers. Sarah almost missed the young woman sitting by herself on a love seat, her legs tucked beneath her, a purple hoodie covering her head. She looked like she wanted to curl up small enough to become invisible. Sarah knew that feeling all too well.

She paused, second-guessing her decision. Why would these women even want to talk to her? What did *she* have to offer them? Was hope enough?

"That's Tracey," Sunny said softly. "She's new here, and she has no one. I think she'd appreciate talking with you." She touched Sarah's elbow and whispered, "Let's give it a try."

She couldn't back out now. As they approached, she realized Tracey was reading a book that rested in her lap.

"Tracey?" Sunny said. "This is Sarah. She's visiting today, and I thought you two could get to know each other."

Tracey lifted her face, revealing a dark bruise on her swollen right cheek. She had wary dark eyes, the kind that screamed she'd seen too much and wanted to forget all of it. She studied Sarah for a moment, eyeing her belly. Sarah absently put her hand over it.

Tracey shifted her gaze away. "Whatever."

I shouldn't have come. They don't want to hear how lucky I've gotten. It's like throwing it in their faces.

"Okay, I'll leave you two be." Sunny winked at Sarah and left the room.

For a moment Sarah stood frozen in place, unsure of what to do. Her head told her to turn tail and follow Sunny out. But the idea of Bones knowing she'd chickened out brought forth her voice. "Um…I'm not very good at this type of thing," she said, more nervous now because Tracey wasn't even looking at her. "Do you mind if I sit down?"

Tracey shook her head, and Sarah sank down to the sofa, suddenly thrown back to being sixteen years old again, scared and alone. Tracey was obviously older than she'd been. Sarah guessed her to be about twenty-three or -four. Tracey shifted on the cushion and winced. Sarah didn't have to ask if she had other bruises. Her father had been an expert at grabbing her arm near her shoulder, where sleeves would cover the bruises, and beating her across her hamstrings or upper thighs, stomach, or back. Panic spread through her like a gust of never-ending wind, stealing her breath as more memories peppered her. She could still feel herself trembling as she stood on the side of the road with her thumb out, imagining her father rolling up, ready to do her in. She remembered the force of her father's hands with every hit, the horridness of her mother demeaning her relentlessly. The way the cold sounds of the city streets echoed in her ears when Susan had brought her to the shelter and how she'd run back to Susan's car, begging her not to leave her there.

She gasped for air, falling back against the sofa, and crossed her arms over her belly in an effort to shield her unborn baby from the harsh memories, but there was no escaping the fear inside her.

"Are you okay?" Tracey asked.

"I'm not sure," Sarah managed. "I came here to try to help women who were going through what I did, but…this is *hard*."

"No kidding. Take a few deep breaths so you don't go into labor or pass out."

That made Sarah smile. "Thanks."

"There's a cute doctor here today. He's really nice, too.

Maybe I should get him."

She moved to stand, and Sarah put her hand on her arm. "No. I'm fine." She was already breathing a little easier. "I came here with that doctor. He's a friend. But really, I'm okay. It was just a momentary flashback to a time I'd rather not remember."

Tracey flopped back onto the cushion and said, "My whole *life* is a series of times I'd rather not remember." She reached up and touched her swollen cheek.

"Did a guy do that to you?"

She nodded.

"I've been hurt, too," Sarah said, surprised at how easily that came after what she'd just experienced. "*A lot.* For many years. But each time I escaped, I told myself to be strong, day and night, until I heard it in my sleep."

"Not the doctor…?"

Sarah shook her head. "I can't even imagine him hurting anyone. He's a good man. The kind of man I always hoped existed but never believed really could."

"Guys change," Tracey said, looking down at her lap again.

"Yes, some of them do. I've been down that road, too, and it almost kept me from seeing the good in B—Dr. Whiskey. I'm sure you've heard this many times, but just because you are here in this moment doesn't mean it is your destiny." As she said the words, she felt the empowering truth of them. "I know how easy it is when you're in that dark place, surrounded by venom and ugliness, to forget there's a whole world outside the walls in which you live. A world of nice people, opportunities. A world where hitting or belittling isn't accepted. But I'm living proof that we can create a new life, our own futures, if we believe and try hard enough."

Tracey clutched her book with a death grip. "It sure doesn't feel that way."

"I know. I'm living a better life, and I still fear that it's all going to fall apart. But that just gives even more power to my parents and my ex-boyfriend."

The woman sitting on the love seat looked over.

Angry tears filled Sarah's eyes, and she didn't even try to hide them as she said, "I don't want to live in fear anymore when everyone around me is giving me reasons to trust them. I won't give those assholes that power."

They talked for a long while, and eventually the other women in the room—Ebony, the woman who had been on the couch when she'd first arrived, and Camille, the mother of the two boys—joined them. They put the cushions on the floor and sat close together, keeping their voices low, because that's what you do when you're talking about awful things you'd rather not say.

By the time Bones came looking for Sarah, three other women who had been examined by him had joined them, and they'd all shared their horror stories.

All the women looked up from their perches on the floor, some of them whispering behind their hands. Sarah felt her cheeks flush. She hadn't shared any intimate details, but she'd told them she was dating Bones—a fact that she was still trying to wrap her head around. Especially after spending time there, with women who had experienced the same nightmares she had. It felt good to get it out. As much as Sarah hated to admit it, there was a certain amount of comfort in talking with other women who had been through similar circumstances. But it also drove home the realization that she *had* come a long way.

"Dr. Whiskey?" Tracey said with a mischievous glimmer in her eyes, which Sarah was glad to see.

"Yes, Tracey?" he asked as he crouched beside Sarah, sliding his big hand down her back.

"I was going to make a smart-aleck remark about cloning you, but what I really want to say is, I hope you continue to be good to Sarah and her kids." Tracey pulled her hood off, revealing a cute dark pixie cut that made her look even younger than her twenty-four years.

His devilish dark eyes found Sarah's, sending heat skittering through her as he said, "That's the plan."

"Need some more time, darlin'?" Bones asked.

"*Darlin'*," Ebony whispered. "Be still my heart." She patted her hand over her heart, making them all laugh—and making Sarah blush.

"I'm ready," Sarah said, accepting his hand to help her to her feet.

As they returned the cushions to the couches, Sarah felt like she was leaving good friends behind. She had intimate things in common with these women, and though it didn't take away the shame she felt for things she'd done, talking with them had cleared the rain from the windshield of her mind. She was still nervous about revealing more of her past to Bones, but there was clarity and strength in knowing she wasn't alone in how far she'd fallen and the things she'd done to survive. She'd come here to help these women. She hadn't realized how much they could help her.

"Will you come back?" Tracey asked.

"Yes." Sarah mentally ran through her upcoming schedule. "How about next Wednesday afternoon?" They all agreed to meet there next Wednesday afternoon, and Sarah wrote down her number and handed it to Tracey. "You guys can all use it. I work odd hours, but I'd love to chat."

"If I had Dr. Whiskey as my man," Ebony said, "I'd have better things to do than talk with the likes of us."

Bones hiked a thumb over his shoulder and said, "I think that's my cue to wait by the doors."

The women hugged, promising to stay strong and see each other next week. Ebony asked if Sarah could do something with her hair, and Sarah said she'd bring her supplies and a few hairstyle magazines. Then she went in search of Bones and found him in the lobby talking with Sunny.

"Sorry I took so long," Sarah said as he reached for her, drawing her into his warm embrace.

"Don't be sorry," Sunny said. "It sounds like you made a few friends, and this guy just said his night is dedicated to a hot date with you."

Sarah liked the sound of that, although as they headed out to the car she became nervous about telling Bones all the things that seemed easier to talk about with the girls in the shelter.

A breeze rustled the leaves of the trees along the sidewalk. He slung an arm around her shoulder and said, "Glad you came?"

"Very." She thought about her new friends and the abuse they'd suffered. She wanted to give them all happily ever afters. "Was Camille the mom Sunny had mentioned being all *claws and fangs*? Because her boys didn't look sick to me, and she was really sweet."

"No. That woman took off before I could see her." Bones held her tighter, walking quickly toward his car.

"What'll happen to her son?"

Bones shrugged. "I wish I knew. Sunny's going to call me if she shows up and agrees to have him examined."

"Good." She couldn't imagine not wanting her children

cared for properly.

"Scott gave me a list of your favorite foods, and I found a restaurant that assured me they can prepare them completely allergen-free."

She snuggled closer and said, "The things you do for me..."

"Darlin', there's nothing I wouldn't do for you."

As he opened the passenger door, she wrestled with telling him the truth. If they went out to a romantic restaurant she might play the *one more night* game. Heck, just knowing he'd planned such a special night made her want one more night without her past interrupting the beauty of what they had.

She slid into the seat and he helped her with her seat belt, then kissed her tenderly. "How can I miss you so much after just a few hours of being apart?"

Oh God. Just one more night sounds really good.

He closed the door, and she watched him stride around the car and climb in. The first thing he did was reach for her hand and give it a squeeze.

It wouldn't be fair to either of them if she let this go for even one more day. He deserved to know the truth, and if it meant he ended things with her, better now than after they made love. It would hurt like hell now, but once she opened herself up in *that* way? Once they made love? Not only would she be handing over complete trust in him for the man he was now, but also in the man he would be in the future. She would be trusting him not to shed his skin.

That sent a shiver of panic up her spine, but it washed away with one glance at him. She didn't see darkness with Bones. She saw glorious light that had already enveloped them. She knew the passion of his kisses and touches was only the surface of the man he kept under wraps. When they made love, it just might be a life-changing experience, and losing him after that would be harder than anything she'd ever survived.

Tonight, she decided as he started the car. Tonight she would reveal the part of herself that might ruin them.

"I'm proud of you for going in there," he said as he drove out of the parking lot. "I know it must have been nerve-racking at first."

Not as nerve-racking as what's yet to come.

"It was, but I'm really glad I went, and as much as I love that you went to the trouble of finding a restaurant that can deal with my allergies, do you think we can get dinner to go? I was hoping we could be alone tonight."

Heat flamed in his eyes.

"To talk," she said too quickly. With hope in her heart she added, "And maybe other things."

Chapter Fifteen

AS SOON AS they were in the car, Sarah texted Dixie to check on the kids, and then she took one of the notebooks Bones had given her out of her purse and began writing, leaving him to wonder what she wanted to talk about. Had the shelter been too difficult for her after all?

"You're writing again," he said.

"Mm-hm. The women I met inspired me."

"In a good way?"

"Mm-hm."

She was quiet the rest of the way home as she wrote. Every once in a while she'd close her eyes for a moment, then put pen to paper again. Bones stole glances, enjoying the determined set of her brow, the way she wrinkled her nose, pressing harder with the pen and then smiling and writing with faster, lighter strokes. Whatever had happened in there had definitely struck a chord—or *several.* They stopped by the restaurant to pick up dinner, and only then did he realize that maybe she said she wanted to talk because it was easier to say that than to say she wanted to jump his bones.

Now, there's a thought.

When he returned to the car with their dinner, she looked up with a troubled expression and said, “I just realized I probably sounded ungrateful about dinner, and it was rude of me to write instead of paying more attention to you. I’m so nervous. I’m sorry if you preferred to eat at the restaurant.”

He reached across the console for her hand and kissed the back of it. “Don’t be sorry for wanting time alone with me.”

He drove through town as she wrote, and as he turned down the narrow lane toward his house, Sarah tucked the notebook back into her purse and looked around as if she’d been too lost in her writing to recognize where they were. He took the left at the fork in the road that led toward his house, where they’d turned right to go to the marina the other night. A few minutes later, the woods gave way to his long driveway and a view of his house, sitting high up on a bluff.

Sarah gazed silently out the window as he drove up the driveway, and when the edge of the bluff came into focus, the endless sea spilled out before them. Moonlight danced on the rippling water, and Sarah said, “I didn’t know you lived on the water. This is gorgeous, and so private. If I lived here, I’d spend all my time staring and daydreaming.”

He’d known the minute he’d seen the spacious home with the wide wraparound porch and stone front that it was where he was meant to live.

The motion-sensor lights came on outside the multicar garage where he kept his bike and truck, and the third bay door opened. Bones let the car idle in the driveway for a moment, not wanting to deprive Sarah of the view. He parked the car, and as he helped her out, he realized he’d been sure of three things in his life—that this house was meant for him, that he was meant to be a doctor, and that he and Sarah belonged together.

He grabbed the bags from the restaurant and then they headed inside. "What do you daydream about?" he asked.

"I don't know. When I was younger I dreamed about finding a better life. But now..." She shrugged and took her shoes off by the door. She slid her socked toes along the dark hardwood that ran throughout the first floor and said, "I like your house. Bradley would probably make this into a sock-skating rink."

He winced as he set the bags on the counter, remembering her boy's stair rides. "I am sorry for letting him slide down the stairs." The main living space had vaulted ceilings, with the living room, dining room, and kitchen bleeding into one another. It *would* make an awesome sock-skating ring. But as much as he loved his home and it had always felt right being there, ever since he'd met Sarah and her children, it had felt like something was missing.

"That's okay. Nobody got hurt, and I'm probably too overprotective sometimes. I want to be the best mother I can, and while I trust you to catch him at the bottom of the stairs, I don't really trust myself to catch him in my current condition."

"Then it's best that he not do it at all," he said as she walked into the dining room.

She ran her fingers over the edge of the dining room table. "Are you sure you live alone? It looks like you're going to host all of Peaceful Harbor or feed an army." She began counting the chairs around the table. "But maybe you're just ready for Thanksgiving?"

"There are twelve chairs, and the table extends to seat twenty," he explained. "My parents have always hosted holidays at their house because they have the room. When I furnished the house, I realized our family has grown to include Tru and Gemma and their kids; Quincy; Crystal and her brother, Jed; Finlay, and her sister, Penny; and of course Izzy is Finlay's best friend and has become like a sister to us, so we can't leave her out." He smiled and said, "It's a good thing I went big, because now we have the lovely Beckleys joining us for Thanksgiving, too."

"You're amazing. You're one guy and you plan for everyone else."

"*Family*, darlin'." They walked into the living room, and he said, "At the end of the day, family is what it's all about."

"That's what I want to instill in my children. Kindness, love, and the importance of being there for one another." Her gaze trailed up the stairs to the loft that ran the length of the house. "Your house belongs in a magazine."

"It's nice, but the only thing that makes it magazine worthy is seeing *you* in it."

She wandered through the living room, checking out the fireplace and bookshelves. "Smooth, Dr. Whiskey. What's upstairs?"

"Three more bedrooms, and I speak the truth, *Ms. Beckley*."

"Ms. Beckley makes me feel old, whereas Dr. Whiskey is sexy. So, tell me, *Dr. Whiskey*, are there bedrooms down here, too?"

Damn, he loved the way she snuck sexiness into the conversation. He wondered if she even realized she was doing it. "A guest bedroom and my office are back there." He pointed to the hallway adjacent to the sofa.

She ran her fingers along the back of the couch, walking slowly from one end to the other. "You like leather."

"I do." He wrapped his arms around her from behind and

kissed her neck. "After you have the baby, I'll buy you a leather jacket and leather pants so you can ride my bike with me."

She craned her neck to the side, giving him better access. "You think you'll still like me after I pop out this little one? Fair warning, that means more puke, dirty diapers, and for me, sleepless nights and probably even more stretch marks."

He nibbled on her ear. "Mm. Sounds perfect."

"You're a sick man," she said with a sweet laugh. "I've never ridden a motorcycle. You'll have to teach me."

"I'll teach you how to ride." He turned her in his arms, sliding his hand down her back to her ass. She had a great ass, a delicious neck, and an enchanting mind that blew him away. "But maybe we should start with something simpler."

"Like…?" Her eyes darkened as he held her tighter against him.

He'd been careful with Sarah, taking things slow, but lately when they kissed, when they touched, she was as aggressive as he was. Tonight he wasn't going to hold back. He hadn't been with another woman since they met, and he was wound as tight as a rocket ready for takeoff. He dipped his head beside her ear and whispered, "Like riding your man."

She stilled, staring wordlessly into his eyes. Silence stretched between them for so long, he wondered if he'd completely misread her. He opened his mouth to apologize, and she put her finger over his lips, shushing him.

"I think we should eat and talk and then see if you still feel the same way afterward."

He slipped her finger into his mouth and swirled his tongue around it, loving the way her eyes darkened and her lips parted. He pulled her finger from his mouth and pressed a kiss to her palm. "Anything you want, darlin'. But nothing will change how much I want you."

"Can you give me that in writing?" she asked as they made their way into the kitchen. "In *blood*, please?"

"I don't sign in blood. But my word is worth its weight in orgasms." He tugged her back into his arms, earning a smile.

"Be serious."

"I am serious." He kissed her then, slowly and longingly, until she went soft in his arms. "Let's eat and talk. After you're done stripping for me as an apology for not believing my feelings are real, I can devour you for dessert."

She froze, eyes wide, mouth closed.

He brushed his lips over her cheek and said, "Don't worry, sweetheart. You don't owe me anything." When the tension in her body didn't ease, he said more seriously, "I was kidding. I want to hear what you have to say, but the desire to love every inch of your gorgeous body, to cherish you the way you deserve to be worshipped, will still be there after we talk even if we don't act on it."

She pressed her hand over her heart and said, "Now that there's *zero* chance of me thinking straight…"

"Come on, let's get dinner. Maybe if you're well fed you'll find your rational brain." He reached into the bag and then realized what he'd said. "Actually, you finding your rational brain won't work in my favor, will it?"

"If you keep looking at me like I'm Little Red Pregnant Sexpot and you're the Big Bad Wily Wolf, we'll skip talking, go straight to naughty stuff, and then we'll have to start all over on our next date."

He waggled his brows.

"No," she said adamantly. "We have to talk."

"That sounds ominous," he said as they dished their dinner

onto plates—roasted vegetables, salmon, rice, and whipped sweet potatoes.

"Just…let's eat. This smells amazing," she said appreciatively, but it was shadowed by the weight of whatever she wanted to talk about.

"So do you." He winked and pulled a bottle of iced tea out of his fridge. "Gluten free. Okay?"

"Sounds great, thank you."

He patted her ass and kissed her again, before pouring them each a glass of tea. "Do you want to eat at the table or out on the veranda? I've got a fireplace, blankets, and—"

He reached for her, but she slipped away, carrying the plates and walking quickly toward the back door. "*Outside.* Forget the fire. I need *air. Cold,* cold air."

Bones followed her out. He lowered the bamboo blinds on the sides of the veranda, leaving the view of the water unimpeded while blocking the wind. He dimmed the recessed lights and said, "Sure you don't want a fire? It'll only take a few minutes."

"First, I'm certain, because every time you look at me I get hot all over. And second, you're making me feel spoiled, going to all this trouble."

He draped a blanket over the extra chair and sat beside her at the table. "It might feel like being spoiled because you've never been adored. It'll be my pleasure to teach you the difference."

"I've never been taken care of like this," she said a little uncomfortably.

She pushed her food around on the plate, which made him wonder if he'd totally misread her. He took her fork and set it beside her plate, then scooted his chair closer and took her hands in his, gaining her full attention. "Sarah, I'm sorry if I misread you earlier. I thought *talk* was code for *fool around*."

"I do want to fool around," she said a little too quickly.

He cocked a brow, knowing there was more. "Maybe so, but did something happen at the shelter that you want to talk about?"

"Not really *at* the shelter." Her face became inescapably troubled. "At first," she said softly, "I had a bit of a panic attack when I tried to talk to Tracey. But I got over that pretty quickly." She curled her fingers around his.

"You should have asked Sunny to get me. I hate that you went through that alone. What brought it on, being at the shelter?"

"I think so, just bad memories. I wasn't expecting it, so my reaction surprised me, but then I realized I wasn't around people who wouldn't understand what I'd gone through. And I wasn't alone in that shelter, facing my own awful life, like I was all those years ago. That made it easier to get out from under the panic. Tracey and the other women had gone through just as much as I had, and talking with them helped me to be able to talk to you about what I need to."

Her beautiful eyes took a slow stroll over his face. "A few months ago, I didn't know people like you and your family and friends existed. I knew there were good people in the world, like Susan, Reagan, and a few more, but they're not like you. Trusting is hard for me, as you know, so I hope you will forgive me for not telling you everything the other night."

"Sarah, you don't know everything about me and my family yet. It could take years to get there, and that's okay. We have plenty of time."

"But what I have to say might not be okay. And I can't take years to tell you because the guilt of not telling you is eating away at me."

"You can tell me anything," he reassured her.

"I want to believe you. I'm just not sure where to start—at the things I'm most ashamed of, or the parts that led me here, which I'm also ashamed of."

He had no words to soothe the pain in her voice, so he did the one thing he knew he needed and hoped it would help her, too. He wrapped his arm around her and held her, breathing her in as she clung to him.

"Can I just stay right here and never tell you the truth?" she whispered.

"Sure, darlin'." He held her for a long time before drawing back and gazing deeply into her eyes. "You need to do what feels right to you, because your babies need your attention, and there's no room for guilt or shame when raising children."

"'As long as we're honest with ourselves, shame has no place in our lives,'" she said, eyes trained on her lap as if she'd said it to herself.

"Sunny shared my thoughts?"

"She did, and she was so nice and easy to talk to. I really like her." Her gaze flicked out at the water, around the room, to the table, looking everywhere except at him.

He placed his hand over hers and said, "There's no pressure to tell me anything. Being honest with yourself doesn't mean exposing your secrets to others."

"But…" She finally looked at him. "If you met a guy who was reminding you of all the hopes and dreams you had as a young girl and made them seem possible, the dreams that helped you survive a horrible time, wouldn't you want to be honest with him?"

Bones got a little choked up knowing he did that for her

and tried to lighten her worries. "If I met a guy who did those things, I'd have to rethink my entire world. But the fact is, I met a woman who is doing that to me on a daily basis. A woman whose children feel like an extension of myself. So yes, I'm trying to work up the courage to be completely honest with you, too."

"You haven't been honest with me?" she asked carefully.

"I haven't lied, but we all have things that have been buried deep for so long, it's difficult to separate the decayed memories from the truth."

"I WISH MY memories would decay until they disappeared completely," Sarah said, trying to ignore the mounting apprehension making her hands sweat. It was unfair that she'd had awful parents, that her brother had had to leave, and that she and Josie had lost touch. So much of her life felt unfair, and she finally had a chance at something real and wonderful, but she had to spill her shitty life on this, too. How much ugliness must she wade through to prove herself worthy of happiness?

"People shouldn't grow up with only bad memories," she finally said, frustrated with everything—the oppression of her secrets, the unfairness of life, and the reality that Bones might walk away from her, ending the only good relationship she'd ever had. "The truth is..." Her tone was a little too angry, and she forced herself to rein it in. "Until we moved here, most of my memories were pretty awful. I told you about working in a salon and eventually meeting Lewis, but what I didn't tell you was that living on a shampoo girl's salary was impossible or that Reagan had worked as a dancer at a nightclub and she suggested

I join her." Shame formed a cold knot in her stomach.

"A dancer..." he repeated, jaw tight. He sat up a little straighter, putting a fraction of space between them.

Although she tried not to react, her heart sank, but she forced herself to go on. "I fought it at first, but after almost two years of eating only one or two meals a day because I had no money for groceries, I gave it a try. It seemed like an easy gig, you know? A few hours a night, however often I wanted to work. I earned more in one night than I did all week as a shampoo girl. Although I kept that job too, because when I started dancing, I realized I needed to save every penny to pay for cosmetology school so one day I wouldn't have to keep dancing. And honestly, it made me feel like I wasn't such a loser to have something normal and acceptable in my life. I could pretend during the day that I wasn't"—*stripping* sounded too awful to say out loud—"taking off my clothes at night."

Her voice wavered, but she needed to go on or she'd never get it all out. "I'm so ashamed of what I did, Bones. My parents called me all sorts of things growing up—*slut, whore, worthless tramp*—and what did I do?" Tears spilled from her eyes. "I went out and proved them right. I took off my clothes for money because I had no idea what else to do to keep a roof over my head—"

Sobs stole her voice, and she turned away, curling into herself as shame and sadness racked her body. She heard him moving and opened her eyes. He was kneeling in front of her. Through the blur of tears, she saw anguish in his eyes. He leaned forward and pressed a kiss to the crest of her belly before cradling her face and touching his warm lips to hers.

"It's okay, darlin'."

"I'm sorry," she cried, tears tumbling down her cheeks.

"No, sweetheart. Don't apologize for doing what was necessary to survive." He brushed her tears away with his thumbs. "You were so young, you should have been *fragile*, but you went into this big world alone and kicked its ass."

"But I'm so ashamed," she said between sobs. "I didn't even know how to dance, much less strip. I had never even kissed a boy, and trying to act sexy did *not* come easily for me. I'm not sure I *ever* got it right. If it weren't for Reagan I probably would have been fired. And not that it makes a difference but, although I was topless, I wore a G-string. And those awful high heels? I had blisters that didn't heal for weeks, and at first I even stumbled onstage. I must have looked ridiculous."

He brushed away more tears. "I bet that innocence earned you even bigger tips."

Taken off guard by his levity, she smiled.

"Seriously, though," he said steadily. "Did anyone hurt you? That can be a rough crowd."

She shook her head. She'd been hurt plenty, but not while stripping. "They were strict about the no-touching policy. Apparently touching can be considered prostitution, or at least that's what they said. I never slept around or anything like that, in case you're wondering."

"I'm not wondering."

She looked at him disbelievingly.

"If this was what you were worried about, don't be. If anything, it makes me realize you're even stronger than I imagined."

"I'm not strong, Bones, and there's more." More tears came as she thought about how weak she'd been. She hated feeling like every step forward brought her two steps back.

"Lay it on me," he said with a hint of irritation in his voice, "because I think you're wrong. Nothing you could ever say would make me believe you were weak."

"Trust me, I'm not wrong. When you hear about my life with Lewis, you'll understand how weak I really was." Panic swept through her as it had earlier. She inhaled several deep breaths, blowing them out slowly, reminding herself that talking about Lewis wasn't going to draw Lewis to her.

Bones leaned closer, but she held out her hand, stopping him. "I'm okay. It's just bad memories. Let me get it out."

He took her hand, watching her intently. "I'm not letting go. In fact…" He rose to his feet, bringing her up beside him, and strode to the couch. Then he sat down, plunked her onto his lap, and wrapped his arms around her. "Okay, darlin'. Whenever you're ready. Tell me about life with the asshole who I already want to slaughter."

Another wave of emotions flooded her. She was used to scaling rocky *uphill* roads, but Bones brought an onslaught of positive emotions even more powerful than the roughness she'd lived with for so long.

"I met him at the club," she said shakily. "He was a regular customer. He'd show up a few times a week, then disappear for a week or two, then come in again. He was nice to me, and he tipped well, flirted all the time. He used to hang around and talk with me after work. I was young. I had no real experience with guys, and I made the mistake of telling him that, which I know now he used to his advantage."

He held her tighter, eyes narrowing.

"I'm not a victim, Bones. I was just stupid, and he was—"

"Preying on a young, frightened girl," he ground out between clenched teeth.

She sighed. "Okay, that's fair." And true, even if she didn't want to come across as a victim. She knew what victims looked like, and later in their relationship, she became much more of a victim. "But it didn't feel that way at the time. It felt like he was paying attention to me, not the stripping, not anything other than *me*."

Her throat thickened, and he pressed a kiss to her arm. "I was looking at him through rose-colored glasses, seeing only what I wanted to see. He was a good-looking guy, and he wasn't gawking at all the other girls—he looked at *me*. That felt huge back then, even though I realize how pathetic it sounds now. I was only twenty, but in the world of dating, I was probably more like seventeen. The flirting went on for a few weeks. One night he asked me to go back to his place, and he said all the right things to make me feel special. Now I know they were stupid lines, but not as stupid as the ones I usually heard at work, which were poorly veiled offers of cash for sex. He was smarter than that. He played on my emotions, telling me he wanted to show me what it was like to be with a man who knew how to treat a woman." She shifted on his lap. "You're holding me too tight."

"Sorry," he said sharply, visibly trying to regain control. "I'm sorry, Sarah," he said in a gentler tone. "This is hard to listen to. But I need to know what you've gone through."

"So you know how badly to pummel him?" She arched a brow, needing a break in the tension.

He threaded his fingers into her hair and drew her in for a tender kiss. Then he brushed his lips along her cheek and said, "So I know how passionately I need to love you to wash away the memories of him."

Lord. How would she survive this man's goodness?

"And how hard to pound his ass," he ground out. "Go on,

darlin'. I need to hear this."

She leaned into him, borrowing his strength. "Anyway, he wasn't too rough that night, and the next time it was better, and things kind of went on like that for a while. He'd come to the club, give me all of his attention, and sometimes we'd go to his place after my shift. He told me he'd grown up with just his father, and he'd inherited his house when his father died. And his father had been an alcoholic and mean when he was drunk. Lewis said he never wanted to be like him, so I thought we had something in common. It didn't matter that my parents weren't drinkers; abuse was abuse, right?"

He nodded, teeth clenched.

"He was a pharmaceutical sales rep. I had no idea what that was when I met him. It seemed like a whole different *glamorous* world. He traveled a lot, which explained the weeks away. And the way he threw money around at the club, it seemed like he was doing well. I told him I'd saved money for cosmetology school, and he suggested that I move in with him. He said he didn't want me to strip anymore and that I could go to school. I had saved a *lot* of money, but you know what the funny thing was? No matter how much money was in the bank—and I had more than I could dream of—I never felt like I was on solid ground. I always felt like I needed to save more, *just in case*."

"That's understandable after all you'd gone through."

"I guess," she said. "I thought his invitation meant that he cared about me, but not long after I moved in I realized that wasn't the case. Or maybe he did at first on some level, but he never treated me like you do, or even like you treated me before we started going out. Until the night on your boat, I'd never been on a real date."

He cleared his throat, and she knew he was trying to push

past his anger, because every muscle in his body was taut. "What was your life like with him?"

She thought about that for a moment before answering. "It was so many things, it's hard to describe. At first it was all so new, his attention, having a real house to live in instead of a rundown room. I enrolled in school the next semester, and it was exciting. I had this new life, and we weren't in love, but he made me feel worth spending time with. I was so enamored with it all, I didn't see the signs that were right in front of me. Maybe I didn't care because what I had was so much more than I had ever had before. I had no basis of comparison for our relationship, and suddenly a guy didn't want me to strip, he was supportive of my going to school, and he even helped me buy a used car. I had enough money to buy it outright, but he pitched in a few hundred dollars."

"Big spender," Bones said sarcastically.

"When you're used to fighting for every penny, a five-dollar bill feels bigger than life."

"I know," he relented. "I'm sorry."

"It's okay. I thought he wanted more with me. *A life.* He traveled a lot, so I got busy building a life. I went through school, and then I got pregnant with Bradley, and that's when I started noticing just how often he came home late or didn't come home at all. We lived in his childhood home, which he'd inherited when his father died. At first I thought it was great living so far outside the city. A fresh start and all that. But then I became *lonely*, which wasn't something I'd experienced before. I'd never known what it was like to live with a man or have a man trying to win me over, and once I did, and I was out of school, working and playing house, I missed it. He said I was just being needy and I had no frame of reference, so..." She shrugged.

"That's not needy, Sarah," he said adamantly. "I hope you know that now. When you're in a relationship with someone, you should be able to take certain things for granted, like the fact that they'll put you before everything else. That they'll come home at night. Family first. *Always.*"

Tears burned in her eyes again. "I think that's the Whiskey way, but in my world, you guys are unique."

"You're in my world now, and you can take me for granted." He embraced her and said, "What happened after Bradley was born?"

"Lewis didn't want me to work, so I stayed home, which was what I'd wanted, too. I wanted to be with my baby. But then things changed. I was exhausted, and Lewis hated dirty diapers, the messes babies made, the crying. Most of the time I slept on a cot in Bradley's room because he was colicky and Lewis would get upset if he was woken up. When Bradley started sleeping through the night, things seemed okay again. And then I got pregnant with Lila, and he came home even less. After Lila was born, I was busy with two babies, and I knew our relationship wasn't good, but I had a roof over my head and children to care for. I thought I had my priorities straight. Keep them healthy, safe, and loved. If *I* was unhappy with Lewis, it didn't matter. I'd chosen my lot in life, but they were dealt it."

Bones caressed her hand and said, "Please don't ever doubt that you're an amazing mother."

"I don't know about *amazing*, but I know I'm a good mother. My children are my heart and soul, and there is nothing—*nothing*—I won't do for them." Images of the nights leading up to her leaving rushed back to her, and she struggled to push them away.

"That was when the real nightmare started. Lewis and his friend got into a car accident. They were both drunk. Lewis wasn't driving, but he'd gotten banged up pretty badly, broken ribs, a crushed cheekbone, and a fractured foot. He got hooked on pain meds and lost his job. Things escalated from there. I'd never taken drugs, or even drank, so I had no idea he was using. I thought he was angry all the time because of his injuries and the babies, but it went on for months. I was sleeping in the kids' room again, because he got so upset when Lila woke up. I found out too late that he'd blown through every penny of his savings and then taken my debit card and cleaned out my account, too. One day he said a friend was picking up my car because it was making a noise and he was going to fix it. Well, it turned out he sold my car for drug money. I was stuck with no money, no car, two babies, and a drug-addicted boyfriend."

"Jesus, Sarah," he said through gritted teeth. "Is that when you left?"

"How could I? We lived forty miles outside town, I had no friends to come get me, no money for a cab, and there were no buses. But it got worse. One day this woman showed up at the house with a suitcase full of his clothes. She called me all sorts of names, and that's when I realized he'd been spending time with other women. *Duh*, right? It should have dawned on me sooner, but I don't think I wanted to see it. After he came home from wherever he got his drugs, I waited until the kids were in bed, and I confronted him about her. We fought, and he swore he hadn't seen her since Bradley was born. I didn't believe him, and things escalated. He threw me against a wall, and forced himself on me, supposedly showing me he wasn't lying." She put her hand over her belly.

Bones made a sound somewhere between a growl and a

groan. He put both hands on her belly and then he kissed it. When his eyes met hers, his restraint was evident. "I'm going to kill him."

She shook her head, tears sliding down her cheeks. "He's not worth it."

"He's not getting anywhere near your children, Sarah. Not *ever*. Please tell me that's when you left."

She shook her head, remembering the weeks in between. "I couldn't. I didn't have a penny. It was eight weeks later when I was finally able to leave. He'd had a party, and when everyone passed out, I took their drug money, the keys from one of the guy's cars, and I left with nothing more than the clothes on my back, my babies, and a handful of diapers."

She swiped at her tears, but they just kept coming. "It was, like, three in the morning. I drove to the salon where Reagan had worked and waited until they opened. She was gone, so I went to the place where we danced, but it had been so many years, she was gone from there, too. The manager took pity on me and made some calls. He found out she was dancing at another club about an hour away. I found her and she let me stay with her and her brother. I didn't even know she had a brother. He helped me ditch the car, and as I told you, he connected me with Reggie Steele, the PI who tracked down Scott and then figured out where Josie was working. I didn't know I was pregnant until three weeks after I left. I was spotting but never really got my period, so I went to a clinic."

"Jesus, *fuck*." His fists clenched and his chest puffed out. "Baby, your life is never going to be like that again. Not *ever*. That's a promise. Whether you stay with me or not, I'll never allow anyone to hurt you again."

"You make me want to believe in *us*, but you're not thinking this through. Or you've forgotten the first part that I told you about. The *stripping*." She looked down at his strong hands wrapped tightly around her, and it broke her heart to say, "You're a highly respected doctor, someone the whole community looks up to. What will they think if they find out you're dating a girl who used to be a stripper? It wasn't just for a month or two. I did it for a few years. It wasn't a blip on my radar, or an accident I didn't see coming, and I was in *Baltimore*. That's not that far from here, and our clientele was pretty upscale, so you never know…"

"I should give a damn what someone else thinks *why*, exactly?" he said in a low voice taut with anger.

"Because it could affect your job, your relationships."

He drew in a deep breath, as if he were trying to tamp down the anger revealed in his flaring nostrils. "People come to me for my expertise as a physician. If they're asinine enough to forgo the best damn oncologist in the area because you did what you had to in order to survive, *fuck them*. There's not a person on this earth I'd allow to talk shit about you. You never have to worry about that."

"Bones—"

"*No*, Sarah. I'm not adamant about many things, but this isn't something you should spend another second worrying about. I don't give a *fuck* what anyone thinks. I care about you and the kids. In all my years, I've never felt what I feel for you. From the first time we met, I've been drawn to everything about you, and in the weeks since, those feelings have deepened tenfold. I'm done trying to hide my feelings. I don't care if you stood naked on a street corner. The person you are is the woman I'm falling for, and whatever it took for you to get here is ours to accept. Not yours, not the kids. *Ours*."

Tears spilled down her cheeks, and he framed her face with his big, warm, safe hands and brushed them away. Everything he did was as fiercely protective as it was tender. She didn't want to push away her feelings or be careful with him, even though her past dictated otherwise. She finally felt like her heart and her head were walking hand in hand, and *God*, she wanted to follow them.

"My children are getting attached to you, and I…" Fear tried to wrap its greedy claws around her neck, choking her voice, but she pried them off and kicked those suckers to the side. "I am, too, Bones. So, are you *sure* you want this—me, my baggage—in your life?"

"More than you could ever imagine, and your past is not baggage. It's part of you, and even if some of it isn't pretty, I accept it, Sarah. So please don't ever ask me that again. But accepting me means accepting the Dark Knights. Do you have any idea what it means to be with a Dark Knight? To eventually ride on my bike with me? If you remain my girl, Sarah, no one will want to face my wrath or the power of the brotherhood. You and your children will be treated with utmost respect and protected, but it comes at a cost. I have to attend club meetings. They're family, which means if one of them needs something, or if there's a problem and we're called in, I'll drop everything and do *whatever* is necessary. I've told you about that."

"Bones…" was all she could manage.

He brushed her hair away from her face and said, "I want you, darlin'. The question is, do you want *me* in your life?"

"Yes," came out vehemently.

His entire body seemed to exhale and pull her closer at once as he drew her mouth to his. Weeks of wondering, dreaming, *wanting* finally came together, sending a shock wave from her head all the way to the ends of her toes. She could barely think, but as his mouth devoured hers, she felt infused with vitality. His hands pushed into her hair, angling and holding her exactly where he wanted her. Her entire being tingled and hummed. His arms were strong and safe. His big hands moved possessively over her body, pushing into her, slowing to caress and squeeze—her thigh, her hip, her ribs, as if he needed to claim all of her. Lost in the heady anticipation of where they both knew they were headed, she realized she was moaning, groping his arms and chest like a hungry tigress. She wasn't even the least bit embarrassed. She finally felt free in a way she never had, and she wanted to explore all of him. His mouth, his body, and even more of his *heart.*

"Sarah—"

His rough whisper washed over her, the need in it making her crave him even more. How was that possible? His hot, demanding lips moved over her cheek and jaw, to her ear, where he licked and kissed until every inch of her was on fire.

"I want you in my bed, where I can love all of you, but if you're not ready—"

She couldn't crawl off his lap fast enough. They groped and kissed, stumbling through the house and up to his bedroom, which was dark, save for moonlight spilling in through the windows. His mouth blazed down her neck. As her eyes fluttered open and closed, she took in flashes of steel-gray walls, a bank of floor-to-ceiling windows, dark, manly furniture, and an enormous bed. Her nerves sprang to the surface as he lifted the edge of her sweater, his dark eyes catching on hers seconds before he lifted it off and tossed it to a chair.

"I got checked for diseases three times and I'm clean," came out fast. She was too nervous to slow down, and the words kept tumbling out. "The doctor said it was ninety-nine percent accurate three months after exposure. Not that I was exposed to anything that I know of, in case you're wondering. And Lewis is the only man I've had unprotected sex with."

He slid his arm around her waist, pulling her closer and holding her gaze. "I'm clean too, Sarah. I know how much your children mean to you, and I knew you'd get yourself checked out, for the sake of your unborn baby and to be sure you'd be around for Bradley and Lila. And, Sarah, he might have been your first, but I hope to be your last."

Her heart swelled to near bursting at what he'd said, but maybe even more so at what he knew. How could he possibly know she'd been terrified to get the tests done and that her children had been the driving force for her to face even the scariest of outcomes?

He reclaimed her mouth, kissing her deeply and slowly and so incredibly passionately, he righted all the upended pieces of her. When he drew back, gazed into her eyes, and ran his fingers through her hair, the whole world seemed to disappear, until there was only the two of them.

"I don't want to rush." He kissed the edge of her mouth. "I want you to feel how special you are to me."

He rained kisses down her neck, slowing to love the spots he knew drove her crazy. Then that wicked mouth moved across her shoulder, kissing and nipping, whispering sweet things as he went. Anticipation mounted inside her, pulsing like thunder as his mouth moved lower, along the crest of her breast. He dragged his tongue above the edge of her bra. Her eyes closed and her legs weakened. Just when she was ready to beg for more, he unhooked the clasp and dropped her bra to the floor.

"So fucking beautiful," he said huskily as he lowered his

mouth to her breast.

Her mind was ten steps ahead of his mouth. Knowing he could send her over the edge with just this made every tantalizing suck that much more excruciating. She buried her hands in his hair, holding tight as he tweaked and licked, kissed and sucked, sending her right up to the edge of oblivion.

"*Bones, Bones, Bones—*" she pleaded.

He rose and captured her mouth with his, kissing her devouringly until she could barely breathe again. He guided her hands to his shoulders, and then he dropped lower and slipped off her shoes and socks. She was so nervous, so aroused, she shook as he kissed her belly. He curled his fingers around the soft waist of her jeans and hooked them into her panties. His thick knuckles pressed against her as he pulled them down and helped her step out of them. He ran his hands up her legs, kissing as he went, loving her from ankle to the crest of her thighs, making her wet and even needier. His mouth moved over her inner thighs, then crawled up her belly. As he loved his way up her body, sensations came from everywhere—his hot lips, his wet mouth, and his strong hands. He slowed to tease and taste all of the places that made her sex swell and clench and her insides twist into hot, greedy knots of desire.

By the time his lips found hers, her legs felt like jelly. She had a burning need, an aching desire to feel him inside her. He led her to the bed with a smoldering kiss. As he tore the blankets back and propped pillows by the headboard, he watched her intensely, full of not only lust and greed, but something so much deeper she felt it in her bones. For a second she wondered about positions and awkwardness, but as if he'd read her mind, he guided her to the mattress, helping her recline against the pillows. Then he reached behind him and tugged off his sweater, revealing his broad chest, chiseled abs, and the piercings that sent rivers of heat through her veins. He tossed his sweater aside, and as he unbuckled his belt, she drank in his brawn and his beauty. Across the right side of his chest was the Dark Knights emblem, a skull with darkness for eyes, coiled and pointed brows, and fanged teeth. Above the haunting figure was the word *family*. His shoulders were tantalizing canvases of words and images she didn't have time to process as he stripped out of his pants, boots, and socks and stood before her in a pair of dark boxer briefs straining over his formidable erection.

Then those hit the floor, too, leaving her salivating at Bones Whiskey and all his naked glory. He crawled onto the mattress with a wolfish grin, and then his mouth hit hers, and that grin turned to tantalizing persuasion. He propped himself up with one hand, his other blazing a path up and down her thigh, each stroke earning a manly, sexy groan. He eased their kisses to a series of torturously soft and teasing touches before his sinful mouth moved lower. With a mouth like his, he'd wear her out before they even got around to intercourse. Every second pulsed with electricity as he kissed his way down the crest of her belly, toward the place she needed him most.

No. The place she needed him *second most.*

She held her children in her heart, which meant her heart would always need him most.

She closed her eyes, fisting her hands in the sheets as his thick fingers spread her thighs, and she felt his breath between her legs. He pressed featherlight kisses to her inner thighs. She held her breath with every touch, gritting her teeth against the urge to beg as he dragged his tongue so close to her greedy center, she thought she'd lose her mind. His tongue slicked slowly and sensually along her center, and he moaned.

"So sweet, darlin'."

It was a good thing she was lying down, because the hunger in his voice would have dropped her to her knees. He clutched her thighs, nudging them wider, sending spears of heat racing down her limbs as his mouth came over her center. He didn't rush, didn't feast. He *savored.* Her hips rocked in time to his efforts, soaking in every masterful lick. He quickened his pace, taking her to the brink of madness. She dug her heels into the mattress. Her head fell back and she sucked in air between clenched teeth as savoring went out the window and he full-on *feasted.* She rocked and moaned. He pushed his hands beneath her ass, lifting her higher, holding her as he did magnificent things with his tongue. Then he dipped his fingers inside her, causing her entire body to clench and quiver.

"Oh *God,*" she panted out. Sex had always been a little painful and rough. She'd always felt empty before, during, and after. She never knew touch could feel so sensual and loving. *So freaking amazing.*

Her legs began to tremble, and he moved faster, reading every hitch of her breath, every gasp and shudder, learning—and expertly playing with—all her most sensitive spots. She breathed faster as his fingers moved in and out of her slick heat, and he teased her clit with his tongue. When he added pressure, her eyes slammed shut and a million fireworks exploded behind her closed lids. She cried out his name as rivers of pleasure raged through her. Just when the thrill began to abate, he quickened again. Every slick of his tongue made her legs tense, her breathing faster.

"*Theretherethere,*" she begged.

Using teeth, tongue, hands, and mouth, he sent her soaring again and loved her through the very last quiver of her climax.

Only then did he rise up and ravenously claim her mouth, swallowing her murmurs and moans. His mouth was heaven, his skin hot, his body hard. So very *hard*. She reached between them and took hold of his erection, earning a wicked growl that spurred her on. Heat rippled beneath her skin, awakening dormant desires she never knew existed. Being with Bones was like crawling beneath a thick blanket in the dead of winter, warm, safe, and so enticing, she wanted to give herself over to him completely.

She tore her mouth away and said, "My turn."

"Jesus," he ground out. "How can two words make my head spin?"

She pushed at his chest, feeling bold and insatiable. He lay down on his back, reaching for her. "You don't have to—"

"Shh." She filled with a sense of overwhelming rightness as she crawled beside him, and as embarrassing as it should be, she wanted to share it with him. "I have never *wanted* to do this before. I have never in my life *wanted* a man the way women want their men in movies, until I met you. It took me all this time to trust my feelings enough to act on them. So please don't give me an out." As she lay beside him, her head by his cock, her belly by his chest, she said, "Stop being careful with me tonight and tell me how much you want my mouth on you."

His eyes glowed with a savage inner fire. "Darlin', I want your plump, gorgeous lips wrapped around my cock as much as I want to fuck you with my tongue again."

"Geez." She sighed. "You're really good at this. Now I can't think."

He chuckled as she wrapped her hand tightly around his cock, pulling another greedy noise from his lungs. *Oh*, how she loved that! He pressed his lips to her thigh as she lowered her mouth over his shaft, getting it nice and wet. Every slide of her tongue made him kiss her harder and had him emitting more of those sexy noises and growls that made her insides tingle and burn.

So she did it *a lot*.

She stroked and sucked, lost in his fresh, manly scent, the feel of his hard heat in her mouth and hand, the wetness of his lips as he trailed kisses along the underside of her belly and the crest of her thighs. When he slid his fingers between her legs, she stilled, his cock still deep in her mouth as she enjoyed the pleasures slithering through her core. He clutched her ass, and she began moving in time with his efforts, with long, slow sucks, until it was *him* who stilled, *him* who was barely breathing, empowering her to love him as *she* wanted to.

He pushed his hand along her arm and said, "I need you, baby."

She didn't hesitate as she crawled over him, aligning his thick shaft to her entrance, and sank down, reveling in every blessed inch as he filled her completely. He reached for her as she leaned down for a kiss, and with one hand around her waist, he shimmied up against the pillows so she didn't have to bend so far. He was such a thoughtful lover, it heightened her pleasure and her affection. He clutched her hips, thrusting as she rocked, kissing her like he'd never get enough of her. Every slide of their tongues, every inch she took, brought them closer together, but it was his sweet murmurs and whispers of tenderness—*You feel so good. We're made for each other. Are you okay? Let me know if I move too hard or too deep*—that nearly brought her to tears.

He swept her carefully beneath him, took a moment to settle a pillow behind her head and shoulders, and then he sank into her. *Deep.* She gasped as shocks of lightning sparked through her veins.

"Too much?" he said, panic in his voice.

"No. Too *good.*" It was the single most intense and exquisite feeling she'd ever experienced.

"I want to make love to you until I feel every beat of your heart," he said in a voice laden with emotion, "and until every breath you take joins with mine."

"Bones..." No words could describe the immensity of her feelings.

His lips came coaxingly down over hers, and they began to move. His hips rolled and thrust in a careful, mind-numbing rhythm. His kisses were potent and thorough, taking as much as he gave. He was so aware of her belly, lifting and angling himself, mindful of not putting too much pressure there. There was no rushing to the finish line, no grimacing or harsh moments like she'd experienced with Lewis. Bones was all power, but at the same time, every move, every touch, and every kiss was finessed and *enjoyed.* They made love like that for so long, she felt everything changing, like they were really becoming one being, heart and soul, transporting her to a safer, freer place. The newness of that awakening coalesced with the feel of his thick heat inside her and the love flowing through her, driving her wild. Fire bloomed in her belly and sizzled through her veins. Her nails dug into his back, clawing in pursuit of *more.* He must have sensed the change, because a husky growl left his lips, and then he took charge, lifting and angling, giving her exactly what she wanted where she needed it. He clutched her ass and sucked the base of her neck, sending waves of ecstasy crashing over her. She bucked and writhed, clawing for purchase, drowning in their magic. Just when she caught her breath, he took her right up to the clouds again, her body shuddering and shaking so hard she panted for air. His mouth swooped down over hers, giving her the air she needed and the love she craved.

As she floated down from the peak, her body limp but still hungry for more, he cradled her beneath him, devouring her mouth, his hips pistoning with laser precision, catapulting her into another intense climax. And then he buried his face in her neck as he surrendered to his own powerful release. Her name sailed from his lips over and over like the sounds of secrets—important and meaningful.

Their secrets.

Sounds she'd never forget.

THEY LAY NOSE to nose as their world came back into focus, and Bones filled with a sense of unexpected completeness. He kissed the tip of Sarah's nose, her cheek, and finally, as he tried to wrap his head around the emotions swamping him, he kissed her beautiful lips.

She put her hand on his cheek and closed her eyes with a sweet *hum*.

He knew he'd never get enough of that sound. It was the sound of his girl's happiness. There were so many things he wanted to say to her, but she was so sleepy and relaxed, he decided they could wait, and he soothed his hand down her back as she drifted off to sleep.

This was where she belonged, with him, safe and loved. Listening to the even cadence of her breathing, he thought about the things Bear had said to him. *You give your all to whatever you set your mind to. That's who you are down to your very soul. When you die, you're going to have researched and planned it to the very second.* His brother was right about how he approached things, but there was no researching or planning for this. No weighing pros and cons, because they didn't matter. The only thing that mattered was that whatever obstacles might lay ahead, his heart belonged to Sarah and her children and he would protect them with his life.

After a while, he knew he had to wake her. They couldn't leave the kids overnight. He kissed her again, and then he whispered, "Sweet darlin'."

"Mm." She nuzzled closer.

No part of him wanted to wake her, much less take her home and come back to the bed that would smell like her, the house that would feel too empty without her. But the kids needed her more than he did, so he kissed her again and said, "I need to take you home, sweetheart."

Her eyes fluttered open, and her beautiful blond brows slanted. "You're done with me?"

"Hardly." He planted a kiss between her brows.

"I want more time with you." She pushed her leg between his, hooking her heel to the back of his calf. "Dixie said she could spend the night..."

Her voice trailed off, as if the meaning of Dixie spending the night, the idea of not being there in the morning with the children, just became clear. He hadn't realized Dixie had offered to spend the night, and he wondered why Dixie—and Sarah—hadn't mentioned it to him.

As he opened his mouth to ask, he remembered how nervous Sarah had been about telling him that about her past, giving him his answer. Thinking about that jackass made his blood boil. Bones vowed to make sure that asshole paid for everything he'd done to her—and he'd take such good care of her children, even that fuckhead's DNA couldn't ruin them.

But right now Sarah didn't need an angry boyfriend. She needed to see that he was the opposite of everything she'd known, so he buried those harsh feelings down deep and focused on his sweet love in his arms.

"I know you," he said. "You need to wake up near your kids, and they need to see you in the morning."

"You don't mind?"

"That's debatable." He shifted her onto her back and moved over her. "Do you mean do I mind letting you out of my bed?" He pressed a kiss to her shoulder. "Because the answer is definitely *yes*." He moved lower, teasing her nipple and earning a long, low moan. "But do I mind letting you out so we can both be assured your babies are safe? Not even a little."

"You say all the right things." She shifted her hips, aligning his cock to her entrance. "You must have read a book about aphrodisiacs for moms."

He chuckled. "I'm falling for a mother, and it comes with the territory. And this particular mom needs extra lovin' before she leaves my bed."

Chapter Sixteen

SARAH GOT UP before the sun and began writing more of the love story for Tracey she'd started when they'd left the shelter. She desperately hoped the women she'd met would find men who were as good-natured as Bones. Someone who would teach them that love doesn't have to hurt. Saying good night to him last night had been harder than ever before. No matter how much she tried not to, she'd approached their relationship as if it might be temporary, but he'd proven otherwise, and she'd had to fight the urge to ask him to stay. Now it was almost seven thirty, and the kids had been up for half an hour. Neither one had any interest in breakfast. They were too busy playing with their farm animals. Bradley set them up, and then Lila would knock them over. Even after being away from Lewis for several months, she still worried that Bradley might have picked up traits from him. She often held her breath when Lila did something that might cause Bradley to lose his temper. But she was amazed at her little boy's patience, and she thanked her lucky stars that he didn't show intolerance the way Lewis had.

As she nursed a cup of decaf tea, her pen moved swiftly over the notebook, creating a life for Tracey. One where she came home to a quiet apartment and didn't fear making too much noise or rattling someone's concentration. A life where she could wear pretty dresses and sleeveless shirts and not have to cover bruises. A life where she was happy and loved. As Sarah crafted the tale, she filled with a sense of longing for her sister. She worried she might never have another chance at reuniting with her and wondered why Josie hated her and Scott so much that she could leave and never look back.

She buried that hurt down deep so it wouldn't impact her children.

"Mamama." Lila pulled herself up on the edge of the couch with a goofy grin.

Sarah set the notebook on the table and ran her fingers over her daughter's fine hair. She wondered if her own hair had been like that as a baby. Bradley had been born with a mop of hair, so different at birth from her daughter's nearly bald head.

"Are you getting hungry, Lila boo?"

The roar of a motorcycle approached, and Sarah's heart leapt. She had said goodbye to Bones four or five hours ago, and still excitement trampled through her like they'd been apart for months.

"Baba!" Lila turned too quickly and plopped down on her bottom. She pushed up on all fours, speed crawling toward the window. "Bababa."

Bradley ran to the window in his Batman pajamas. "It's Bones!"

Seeing her children as excited as she was felt incredible. Knowing they felt that way because of a man who was *worthy* of their sweet little hearts? That was a crazy, beautiful, *miraculous* feeling.

Sarah pushed to her feet as Bradley raced to the door and

tried his hardest to unlock the dead bolt.

"Hold on, baby. Let me get the locks." She unlocked the door with Lila hanging on to her leg and Bradley's hands on the doorknob. Sheesh. It was like the Easter Bunny himself had arrived.

She hoisted Lila onto her hip and helped Bradley open the door, glad she'd showered before the kids had woken up. Her heart tumbled at the sight of Bones draped in soft black leather, a gray sweater, and worn jeans that looked like old favorites. In one hand he carried a grocery bag and his shiny black helmet, which made his sexy suggestion come rushing back. *Maybe we should start with something simpler. Like riding your man.* As if he had read her mind, a slow grin slid across his handsome face, illuminating the inky darkness of his eyes.

"Bones!" Bradley shot out the door in his bare feet.

Without missing a step, Bones scooped him up, and Bradley's arms locked around his neck in a hug so sweet and pure Sarah not only felt her heart melting, but she saw the same reaction in Bones's embrace and in the press of his lips on her little boy's temple. She heard it in his voice when he said, "Morning, B-boy. How's my favorite buddy?" and she felt it when those inky eyes turned soft and found hers again.

This was dangerous.

This was beautiful.

This. Is. Real.

"Babababa." Lila reached grabby hands toward Bones.

"Hey, beautiful girls." He set the bag and his helmet beside the door, and Lila snagged his sweater as he reached for her. She squealed excitedly, and her little legs kicked as he lifted her into his arms. Lila's fingers shot into his mouth, earning a throaty laugh. He kissed those wiggly fingers and then he leaned in for a kiss from Sarah. "Hey, sweet mama. How's my girl this morning?"

In a state of euphoria. "Even better now. I wasn't expecting you. I thought you were going riding with your brothers today."

"I thought I'd have breakfast with you guys first," he said as she closed the door behind him. "I printed out a recipe for gluten-free, dairy-free, nut-free, and egg-free banana-apple-cinnamon muffins and picked up all the ingredients. I hope that's all right."

"Let me see…" She tapped her chin, gazing up at the ceiling, unable to suppress her joy as she said, "A handsome biker shows up unannounced and wants to cook breakfast with me?"

"Babababa!" Lila babbled, bouncing in Bones's arms.

"I agree, peanut. Let's start breakfast while Mama decides." He winked at Sarah and headed into the kitchen. "You going to help me cook, B-boy?"

Sarah grabbed the bag, watching her little man nod emphatically, as hooked on her big man as she was.

Fifteen minutes later, the counters looked like a bakery, with packages of sorghum flour, baking soda, cinnamon, sea salt, apples, organic turbinado sugar, olive oil, vanilla extract, flaxseed, and tiny pieces of Bones's heart in every thoughtful purchase. Bradley sat on the counter among the mess, mashing bananas with a fork, while Lila sat in her high chair, her sticky fingers covered in mashed banana, because Bones insisted that if Bradley was allowed to help mash bananas, so was Lila.

"Excellent," he said to Bradley. "Smash those big pieces."

"Like this?" Bradley banged the fork on a pile of banana pieces, sending one flying to the floor.

Sarah stilled.

"That was perfect…*if* we were trying to make flying bananas," Bones said with a laugh. Then he proceeded to hold Bradley's hand and show him a better technique with so much patience, the air left Sarah's lungs in a dreamy sigh.

Old habits die hard.

"What's going on up here?" Scott asked as he limped into the kitchen, shirtless, his hair askew, wearing a pair of sweatpants.

"We're making muffins!" Bradley announced.

"Ca!" Lila grabbed a handful of banana and offered it to Scott.

Scott put a hand on her head and said, "Nah. I'm good."

"There's coffee." Sarah handed him a mug.

"Thanks." He filled his cup and took a sip. "I didn't mean to interrupt the happy-little-family thing you have going on."

"Sorry if we woke you," Bones said. "It's my fault."

She didn't even try to argue. He'd win anyway, and the truth was, they'd all been excited to see him, so yeah, it was kind of his fault in a good way.

"Want to help?" Bradley asked Scott. "What's next, Bones?"

"Apple grating for Uncle Scott." Bones handed Scott an apple. Then he turned to Bradley and said, "While you, Lila, and I measure the sugar and olive oil, maybe Mama can do the flaxseed and vanilla."

"I think I can handle that." She went to work, soaking in all the goodness around her. "Did you have an okay time with Dixie last night?"

"Oh yeah," Scott said with a seductive lilt to his voice.

Bones glowered at him.

"I mean, she was good with the kids," Scott added quickly. "She's a cool person. Tough, funny, and wicked ho—"

That warning glare appeared again, and Sarah stifled a

laugh.

"Wicked *smart*," Scott said, turning back to the apples. "What would you do if I did that to *you*?"

"What?" Bones asked all too innocently.

"Looked at you like I'd"—he glanced at the kids—"be unhappy if you got too close to my sister."

Bones's scoffed. "Wild horses, baby. That's what it'd take to keep me away."

"Hm." Scott grinned. "Good to know."

Yes, it is.

Scott and Bones joked around as they measured, mixed, and poured. After they finished preparing the batter, Bradley helped spoon the mix into the muffin pan. When Lila squealed, Bones let her help, too. She got more batter on Bones than she did in the pan, but he took it all in stride.

"I didn't know you were dating Mrs. Doubtfire," Scott said as Bones stripped Lila's shirt off.

"That's *Dr. Doubtfire* to you, thank you very much."

Scott headed out of the kitchen and said, "As long as I don't find you wearing a skirt."

Bones hoisted Lila into his arms and said, "Double bath so they're done by the time the muffins are ready?"

"I can do it," Sarah said.

Bones winked and said, "Come on, B. Let's see how quickly we can get the two of you cleaned up."

Bradley sprinted down the hall, and in one swift move, Bones's hand slid around Sarah's waist, tugging her in for a delicious kiss.

"Gotta steal the moment," he said, and held her hand as they headed down the hall. He leaned closer and whispered, "I missed having you in my bed this morning."

Heat and happiness zipped through her.

As they bathed the kids, Bradley told Bones all about their new sleeping arrangements. "Now I have a big-boy bed, and Lila has a baby bed, and Mommy has a mommy bed."

"And how do you like your new bed?" Bones asked.

"I love it!" He grabbed a rubber duck from Lila's hands, causing her to shriek.

"How about if you *ask* Lila for a turn with that?" Bones suggested.

Bradley eyed the toy, and then he looked at his bawling sister. Bones soothed one hand down Lila's back, watching Bradley carefully. It was all Sarah could do to let this play out instead of telling Bradley to give it back, or trade for another toy, but she was curious to see how Bones handled it.

"It's hard to be a big brother," he commiserated, one hand soothing down Lila's back as he spoke to Bradley. "If you're good to your sister, she'll look up to you her whole life and play with you, learn from you. But if you steal toys and make her cry, well, she might not want to do those things."

Bradley looked forlornly at the toy.

"What do you say?" Bones urged. "Want to teach Lila how to share by showing her how to ask for a turn?"

Please, please, please don't have a meltdown.

Bradley nodded and reluctantly handed the toy back to Lila. Lila clutched it to her chest, her tears abating.

"Atta boy." Bones tousled Bradley's hair.

Sarah finally breathed.

"Can I have a turn?" Bradley said as fast as he could, and then he ripped the duck from Lila's hands, causing her to scream and fight for it.

"So much for diplomacy," Bones said. He took the toy from

Bradley, which caused him to cry, too, and he handed it back to Lila. Then, in a gentle but firm voice, like he'd been handling cranky kids forever, he said, "When you're ready to *ask*—not *take*—we'll try again."

He continued bathing Bradley through his wails, seemingly unaffected by his pleas for justice, as Sarah bathed Lila. Bradley cried as they dried them off, and Bones didn't snap. He simply said, "When you're ready to do the right thing—to *ask* and not *take*—we'll try again."

On the way into the bedroom, Sarah called down to Scott, "Shower's free."

Lila clung to the rubber duck, and Bradley whimpered as Sarah and Bones dressed them.

When they headed back into the kitchen, Bradley stood in front of Lila, who was sitting down with the duck, and he said, "Can I have a turn?"

Lila turned away with the duck tucked against her chest.

"It's Bradley's turn, peanut," Bones said, and he took the duck from her, handing it to Bradley.

Lila screamed and dove for it.

Bones scooped her up, turning an utterly *lost* look to Sarah. "What now?"

"Hedgehog!" She ran and got the stuffed toy while he tried to quiet her screaming girl. She shoved the hedgehog into Lila's hands, and within seconds her wailing stopped and her mouth did that little noiseless frowny thing.

Bones exhaled loudly, brow furrowed as he set Lila in her high chair. "I tried."

"You were amazing. You just need to learn about trading and distractions."

"That works?" he asked.

"Sometimes. They're kids. Nothing works all the time. They have drive-Mommy-crazy buttons inside them that only they have access to, and when that's switched to the right position, *nothing* works." She turned to Bradley, who was walking the rubber duck across the glass door. "Come on, honey. Let's try the muffins we made."

He dropped the duck and scrambled into his chair.

"Hey." Bones retrieved the duck. "I thought he wanted the duck."

"He only wanted it because he couldn't have it," she said, trying not to laugh.

Scott came into the kitchen showered and dressed. "World War III over?"

"I've got a lot to learn." Bones looked thoughtfully at the kids.

"Don't we all?" Scott clapped a hand on Bones's shoulder. "It's all good, man. At least you know how to cook."

After feasting on scrumptious muffins and apple slices, Scott headed off to meet Quincy and Jed in town, and the kids played with their toys in the living room while Sarah and Bones cleaned the kitchen.

Bones motioned over the half wall as he wiped down the counter. Sarah looked up from the dishes she was washing and saw Bradley pulling Bones's helmet over his head. It was so big it rode on his shoulders. Sarah started to tell him not to touch it, but Bones touched her arm and shook his head, mouthing, *It's fine.*

Bradley picked up a diaper and opened it. Then he placed it on Lila's head and said, "That's your motorcycle helmet."

Bones and Sarah both laughed.

"I hope it's okay that I came by," he said quietly. "I should have called, but I was halfway here when I realized that."

"It's more than okay."

He threw out the paper towels he'd used and gathered her hair over one shoulder, pressing a tender kiss to her neck. "Our first Thanksgiving together is just a few days away."

"This will be the first Thanksgiving I haven't been terrified of what might happen next."

He wound his arms around her middle from behind and said, "I wish I could erase all the bad things you've experienced, but since I don't have that power, I'm going to do everything I can to give you and the kids so many happy memories, the others will seem like a story you once heard instead of ghosts whispering from the closet."

She closed her eyes, leaning back against his chest as he spread his hand over her belly and spoke just above a whisper. "Were you okay last night? I didn't hurt you, did I?"

She shook her head, a little embarrassed by how aggressive she'd been.

He turned her in his arms, his loving eyes washing over her face. "I wasn't kidding, Sarah. I missed you this morning. These last few months have brought new meaning to my life, but these last few weeks and last night? They've changed me in here." He put his hand over his heart, and then he touched his forehead to hers and closed his eyes without saying another word.

He didn't have to.

He'd already said it all.

Chapter Seventeen

MONDAY ROARED IN with unrelenting winds, cold, driving rain, and bursts of thunder and lightning, and Bones had been on a dead run the entire day. Sarah had to be at work at three o'clock. Car seats could be pesky, and if the kids were having a hard morning, he knew they'd all be drenched by the time she finally got everyone situated. He had hoped the storm would abate, and when it hadn't by two o'clock, he called Biggs, the one person he knew had the time to and wouldn't mind helping her out. Now, as he answered his cell phone, he glanced out his office window at the gray, angry sky and cursed Mother Nature for unleashing her wrath on Peaceful Harbor.

"You fucked up," Biggs said.

"Shit. Did I get the time wrong?" Bones asked, kicking himself.

"No, son. You're hovering over a woman who's got her shit together. I got there at two fifteen, just like you asked me to. Bradley and Lila were already in the car, and Sarah was climbing into the driver's seat with one of those big-ass golf umbrellas over the open door. She was bone dry and smiling until I told her why I was there."

"Aw, fuck."

"Didn't I teach you anything? Never underestimate a capable woman. Those kids were happy as clams with their little rain boots and rain jackets, all buckled up in their car seats."

Bones leaned against the sill with a wide-ass grin. "*You* taught us to take care of our women even when they don't want it."

His father's husky laugh came through the phone.

"Seriously? I'm up shit's creek and you're laughing at me?"

"I'm laughing because you've been bit in the ass by the love bug, and it wouldn't matter what I said to you. You're going to do all the wrong shit, thinking it's right, you bullheaded bastard."

More laughter rang out, making Bones smile despite screwing up, because if Biggs was one thing, it was honest as the road was long.

When Biggs finally stopped enjoying Bones's stupidity, he said, "It'll serve you well, son. And she wasn't pissed. The tears I saw in those pretty eyes were happy. She got *out* of the car beneath that huge umbrella and hugged me."

"What? Then how did I fuck up?"

"Because I got the hug, you jackass." Biggs chuckled. "She thanked me for coming by and for raising such a thoughtful son. Then she got back in the car and drove away with that sappy look women get when they're too happy to see straight. She's a good egg, Bones."

"Yeah," he agreed. "She sure is. I better get off the phone and text her before my next patient comes in. Thanks, Pop. Love you."

"Love you, too. See you tonight at church."

After he ended the call, Bones texted Sarah. *Sorry to send*

Biggs to help with the kids. Told you I have a lot to learn.

Her response came a few minutes later. *So do I. We can learn together.*

Damn, he was a lucky guy.

Later that afternoon, he sat with his patient Wendy Stockard, who, surprisingly, didn't pussyfoot around her feelings or buy time with Ollie's latest adventures. Instead, she plunked herself down in front of him, looking agitated and angry. Mood swings were fairly normal in his practice, and that wasn't too concerning. But what had her riled up also had him on edge.

"I know stress is bad for me, but I can't get out from under this. I'm doing everything I can to make sure Ollie will be cared for if…if I don't beat this. But my attorney said Calvin will get custody of Ollie. It doesn't matter that we're divorced or that I was given full custody, because Calvin wasn't a bad father. It's not like he abused him or anything. He's just too busy with his *girlfriends* to be a parent." Wendy's hands trembled. "But his name is on the birth certificate, and there is no doubt that he is Ollie's father, so…"

Wendy had never spoken about her ex-husband before, but again, this didn't surprise him. Unless an ex was involved in his patient's life, they rarely brought them up. She was doing all the right things to make sure her son would be cared for if the worst-case scenario came to fruition. He fucking hoped it didn't, and he was doing everything within his power to keep that from happening.

"You've never mentioned him before. Is he part of Ollie's life? Would Ollie want that?" Bones asked. It wasn't his job to fix these types of situations, but maybe he could try to ease her worries enough for her to be stronger for her treatment.

"He hasn't seen him in several years, but apparently that

doesn't matter. All that matters is that he's Ollie's father. And I don't know if Ollie would want it, but I doubt it."

She looked up at the ceiling, her finger curling around the arms of the chair as tears filled her eyes. Bones remained quiet, allowing her space to regain control of her emotions. As she took a few deep breaths, his mind traveled to Sarah, and he wondered if Lewis was listed on her children's birth certificates. Would he be listed on the birth certificate of her unborn child? The muscles in his neck tightened at the thought.

Wendy sat up straighter and drew her narrow shoulders back, reminding him of Sarah when she strengthened her resolve.

"My sister said she'd fight for custody if I don't make it," Wendy said a little shakily. "But goddamn it, Dr. Whiskey, I *have* to make it. He's my child. *My* responsibility."

"He's your heart and soul," he said absently, then caught himself and cleared his throat.

"Exactly. I know you can't promise me anything, but just tell me again that you are doing everything you can. I need to hear that. I need to hear that a lot."

Bones came around the desk and sat beside her. He looked into her pleading eyes and said, "Yours and Ollie's battle is my battle. I promise you that I am, and will continue to do, everything within my power to help you beat this."

She nodded, teary eyed, and eked out, "Thank you."

Now came the hard part. "Can your sister help you with this to take some of the pressure off? Can she meet with your attorney, figure out a game plan so you can focus on treatments?"

"It's not her battle," Wendy said adamantly.

"No, it's not. And I'm sure you're used to handling everything, no matter how big. But just like it was okay to ask friends to help with driving Ollie and making meals when you had surgery, it's okay to get help with the emotionally draining parts of your life that need to be ironed out. I'm not suggesting that you let her make decisions for you. I'm simply suggesting that you consider allowing whoever is closest to you to help shoulder the burden of outside influences so you can focus on your health."

He thought of Sarah and knew if she were in Wendy's position she'd never step back, even if it drained every ounce of her energy. As a physician, he'd refer Wendy to the right specialists to handle her emotional state. He'd get her through her treatments and hope she was strong enough for everything her body needed to beat this monster. But separate from his medical persona, as a human being he wanted to take away her—every patient's—anguish. To talk to the damn attorneys, to plead her and Ollie's case. But that was a line he couldn't cross. That was a line meant for a boyfriend, husband, or family member.

He might not be able to be all things for his patients, but he sure as hell could be for Sarah.

A FEW HOURS later, Bones sat beside Bullet in the Dark Knights clubhouse, stewing over the idea of Sarah's ex having any rights to her children. Crystal wasn't feeling well tonight, and Bear had stayed home with her, but his brother's concerns had been playing loud and clear in his mind all afternoon. *What do we even know about the father of her kids? Huh? What if he comes back for them?* Bones considered himself a pretty fair man, and he didn't believe in separating parents from children, but that man was no parent. A father took care of his family, cherished, taught, and protected them above all else. Hell, a father would give his life for his children without a second thought. Bones ground his teeth together. That man—Lewis—was a slug, a bully, and a fucking *rapist*.

And he was only the tip of the iceberg.

Sarah also deserved justice where her cretin parents were concerned.

He glanced up at his father, who was seated at the head table, discussing club business. Before his father's stroke, Biggs had run the bar. If a customer got too drunk to drive, instead of calling the customer a cab, Biggs would have Red drag Bones and Bullet out of bed to drive the drunk home. It took two of them, one to drive the customer's vehicle and one to follow in their own. If someone was being treated unjustly when they were out shopping, or at a restaurant, they'd been taught to step in. To do the right thing, often what others were too scared to do. It had always been and would forever be the Whiskey way. Biggs had always been as intimidating as fuck, tougher than any man Bones had ever known. He knew his father was capable of killing a man with his bare hands, and he also knew he'd do it only if the situation called for it. Not out of vengeance. No, vengeance required only a good ass kicking and dragging the sucker to the police if they'd broken the law. When Bones was younger, he'd had trouble with that line of thinking. He hadn't understood how vengeance could ever be a good thing. It had been one of his biggest struggles in feeling like he fit into his family when what he saw as the right thing differed from what the rest of them did. But when Thomas passed away, Bones had *wanted* vengeance. He'd wanted to kill someone for stealing his friend. But there had been no one to kill, no one to blame. So he'd turned that blame on himself. He knew he didn't deserve it, but it had to land somewhere or it would destroy him in other ways. He channeled that negative energy to push past the difficulties of medical school and become the best damn doctor he could.

But he'd grown up since then. He'd seen the worst, learned that some people needed to be put into their place. Now, as he thought about the way Lewis had treated Sarah and the children, his hands balled into fists, his chest expanded, and he saw red.

He wanted vengeance.

He wanted to torture the motherfuckers—all of them: Lewis and Sarah's parents. Neither an ass kicking nor jail seemed a harsh enough punishment for what had been done to the woman and children who already owned a piece of him. But taking a human life wasn't something Bones could do *after the fact*. Before Sarah, he wasn't sure he was capable of it at all. As a doctor he'd taken an oath to act morally and ethically. Hell, even the biker code was to help others, not harm them. But those lines got blurred when catching an asshole in an outright egregious act. Bones had taken down enough men, had sent them to the hospital for raising a hand to women or children and not heeding his warnings to back off. Had he walked in on Lewis or Sarah's parents treating her like shit, they would probably have already taken their last breaths. But he needed to find other ways to deal with this. Ways that would ensure they couldn't come anywhere near Sarah and the kids *and* remove Lewis's parental rights.

Bones looked across the room at Charlie "Court" Sharpe, a family law attorney. Before the meeting Bones had researched how to terminate parental rights. He had no idea if Lewis was listed as the father on the children's birth certificates, but even if he wasn't, he could prove paternity and try to stake claim to the children. Bones needed expert advice and a concrete plan in place before he took another step. He hoped Court could provide that.

Bullet nudged him and leaned closer, speaking in a low voice. "What's got your cock in a knot?" He seemed lighter, happier since he'd returned from his honeymoon, but the fierceness in his eyes flashed unencumbered. Bullet was always ready to tear someone's head off. Happy or not.

"I need to talk to Court." Bones glanced at Biggs. He was winding down the meeting, confirming dates for an upcoming anti-bullying rally and wishing everyone a happy Thanksgiving. He felt the heat of Bullet's stare and found his older brother studying him.

Bullet's eyes narrowed. "What's the problem?"

"I don't know yet." He needed answers from Sarah, but she was at Bullet's house tonight with the girls, going over menus for Thanksgiving, and he wasn't going to try to talk about this over the phone. It would have to wait until the kids were asleep.

"What don't you know?" Bullet pushed.

Biggs rose to his feet and grabbed his cane, signaling the end to the meeting and sparking a cacophony of conversations. Men headed for the kitchen, gathered around pool tables and dart boards, and milled about catching up with each other, creating a sea of Dark Knights patches. *Brotherhood.* If Bones revealed what had happened to Sarah, there'd be thirty-plus brothers hunting down Lewis and her parents before the end of the night. He wasn't about to let that happen. Taking down those assholes or putting them in prison wouldn't give Sarah—or him—the peace of mind they needed. This required what he was best at, planning, strategizing, and then making sure he succeeded on *all* fronts.

Bones stood, and Bullet pushed to his feet beside him, beer in hand. Bones stared into his brother's dark eyes. "I've got this, B." It struck him that he'd called Bradley the same endearment since the first day they'd met. Had he subconsciously known even then that he'd end up being this much a part of his life?

"So do I," Bullet said. "Whatever it is."

"Not this time, B. I need to handle this on my own. At least until I have things under control and understand what needs to happen." He clapped a hand on Bullet's shoulder and said, "I appreciate it, though."

Bullet's jaw clenched, making his beard twitch. "This about Sarah?"

Bones gave a single curt nod. He knew Bullet was only trying to help, but he wasn't in the mood to have his path blocked. He had a plan and wanted to get the hell on with it.

"You go after someone, I go after him. Got it?" Bullet's eyes turned stone-cold black.

Bones took a step away without answering, and Bullet grabbed his arm. Bones glared at him. "I've got this, B. If the time comes when I need help, you'll be the first to know. Now take your hand off me before I break your fucking fingers." He yanked his arm free and headed for Court, who was playing pool with his brother, Tex.

Court was a barrel-chested guy who spent as much time in the gym as he did on his bike. His hair was buzzed to a sheen of black, his beard and mustache shaved just as close. His T-shirt strained against bulbous pecs and biceps. In his leathers he looked intimidating, but like Bones, from nine to five he was all dress shirts, slacks, and professionalism.

"Bones, how's it going, man?" Court said as he lined up his shot.

"I'll know after I talk to you. I need some legal advice."

"Give him a minute to make a shitty shot." Tex smirked. He had a serious side, but most of the time he was cocky as hell. His hair was thick and finger combed, his beard scruffy, and he had colorful tattoo sleeves, the polar opposite of both Court and their youngest brother, Ramsey "Razor" Sharpe, a professional baseball player.

"You still working at Rough Riders?" Bones asked. His buddy Sam Braden owned Rough Riders, an adventure company located on the river. Now that he was thinking about it, he imagined taking Sarah and the kids there in a few years, teaching Bradley and Lila how to row a boat. Soon there would be an infant in the mix, but maybe next summer they could have a picnic by the river and he could show the kids then. That thought led him right back to the reason he needed to talk to Court.

"Yeah," Tex answered. "Come down sometime. We do fall adventures."

"I'm pretty busy, but maybe in the spring or summer. Thanks."

"Talking *here* okay?" Court motioned around them. "Or should I give up my stick?"

Bones hadn't thought about that. Now he felt like a dick for interrupting his friends' game, but he definitely didn't want to talk there. Not with Bullet watching his every move. "Finish your game. I'll catch up with you afterward."

"No, man." Court tapped Hawk on the shoulder. "Hey, cameraman. Mind finishing my game?"

Hawk shifted an arrogant grin in Tex's direction. "Not

unless your brother's going to whine when I kick his ass."

"Go for it." Tex took a swig of his beer.

"Bones, I've got those pics for you," Hawk said. "Want to stop by next week and look through them?"

"Yeah. Tuesday night after work okay?"

"Perfect." Hawk leaned on his cue as Tex lined up his shot.

Bones and Court each snagged a bottle of beer on their way out back. Bones inhaled the cool night air, glad to be out from under Bullet's radar.

"I take it this isn't club related?" Court asked.

"Personal, and I'd appreciate it if you kept it between us."

"Always, Wayne."

It was rare to hear his given name at the clubhouse, but he and Court had met professionally before Bones had brought him into the club several years ago.

Bones explained Sarah's situation and shared what she'd gone through with Lewis and with her parents, leaving out the details about her stripping.

"Damn, Wayne. That's an ugly situation. I'm sorry you two are dealing with it. Unfortunately, there's a statute of limitations that varies from state to state on child abuse. In most cases it's seven or eight years after they turn eighteen. I'll look into Florida law, but I think you'll be hard-pressed to do anything with her parents in that regard. Although she can certainly get a restraining order to keep them away. But you know how that works. It's a piece of paper."

"Her parents haven't been in her life since she left home at sixteen. I'm less worried about them than I am about the father of her children, although I'd like to see her parents' asses in jail."

"We both would. As far as this other guy goes, the easiest tactic is to have him voluntarily terminate his parental rights. If he's as strung out as you made him sound, he might be happy to do it. Terminating rights means no child support. Not that it sounds like he could provide any. But there's a flipside to that coin. He could want something in exchange and hold the kids over Sarah's head, but if he raped her and if you threaten to turn him in, there's a chance he'd let that go. But you know proving a rape that happened months ago, without a police report, will unfortunately be a nightmare for Sarah. I'm not saying give up, but she needs proof. Evidence of some kind to get a conviction. I don't suppose you have an eyewitness that'd come forward?"

Bones's gut twisted. "There was just her and the kids. Thankfully, they didn't see it."

"That could get ugly, and even if he doesn't want the kids, they could get dragged into it. It'll be hell for everyone."

He ground out a curse. "Sarah's a pillar of strength, but I'd never put her or the kids through that."

"Talk to Sarah, get this asshole's name, address, and any other contact info she can give you. I'll draft termination-of-parental-rights papers. But you need a witness, and the papers have to be notarized. After that they'll be reviewed by the court. If he consents, I'll handle court for you and plead your case."

"Thanks, man." Bones began making a mental list of the things he needed to do, at the top of which was talking with Sarah.

Chapter Eighteen

SARAH'S PHONE VIBRATED with a text from Bones a few minutes before she heard his car pull up out front Monday night. She stepped onto the porch as he ran up the walkway, bringing with him a gust of sweet rainy air and even sweeter *man*. He crushed her to him and pressed his beautiful lips to hers. She slid her hands along his neck and up into his damp hair. She'd thought about him all day. Her hunger for him no longer worried her. Her life had been dictated by necessity for so many years, she was thrilled to finally be in control. And tonight, when she was planning the joint birthday party for Bones and Lila and Thanksgiving menus with the girls, listening to them rave about their men, everything had become crystal clear. There was no difference between her and Gemma or Finlay or any of the other girls. Yes, she had a shitty past, and yes, she'd stripped to make ends meet, but at her core, she'd been a woman trying to survive. And now she had a chance at not just surviving, but living a full life with a man she adored, and who, despite everything, was equally attracted to her.

She was *done* hesitating.

"Hey, gorgeous," he said seductively. "Let's get you out of

this weather. Are the kids asleep?"

"Yes," she said softly. "And Scott is hanging out with Jed at the bar, so we have a few hours alone."

Passion simmered in his eyes as he peeled off his wet jacket and hung it by the door. "I wanted to talk with you about something."

She grabbed him by the collar and tugged him toward her. "After."

"Christ, darlin'." He took her hand and pressed her palm to his hardening cock. "That look in your eyes gets me every time."

Just the feel of his arousal was enough to make her wet.

His mouth descended over hers, hot and demanding, as they stumbled toward her new bedroom. His hands moved greedily over her body, and he made those sexy *male* noises that had her whimpering with anticipation.

In her bedroom, he broke away long enough to quietly shut the door. "Baby monitor?"

She pointed to the monitor on the nightstand. Oh yeah, she'd planned this all right, and from the look in his eyes as he tugged off his boots and socks, he appreciated it.

"You smell like heaven," he said as he lifted her sweater over her head and tossed it onto her dresser.

The second she'd gotten the text from Scott saying he was going to be out for a while, she'd taken a quick shower, and since Bones liked to get up close and personal with every inch of her, she'd put perfume everywhere—her neck, inside her elbows, the backs of her knees…

Her bra sailed to the floor, followed by his shirt and their pants, until they were gloriously naked. She crawled onto the bed, and he followed her, grabbing her hips from behind. His lips touched the space between her shoulder blades, sending shivers of heat rippling along her skin. He kissed his way down her spine, and she closed her eyes, loving every slick of his tongue as he moved down her body, over her bottom, caressing and kissing. His scruff tickled, his tongue tantalized, and when his hand pushed between her legs, teasing and tasting as he explored places she'd never been touched, it didn't take long for her climax to crash over her. Her insides pulsed and quivered endlessly, but he didn't relent, keeping her in a heightened state of ecstasy for so long, she shattered into a million sizzling, pulsing pieces.

As his appreciative sounds came back into focus, it seemed impossible that everything around her hadn't shattered right along with her.

"You're so sexy, baby," he rasped against her bottom.

He pressed a kiss there, still fucking her with his fingers, every inward thrust taking her higher. "I want you to come on my mouth."

"Oh *God—*" Her arms and legs turned to jelly.

"No?"

"Yes! So much *yes.*"

He flipped onto his back and guided her hips until she straddled his mouth. *Good Lord*, the man knew just what to do with that talented tongue. She rocked in time to his efforts, feeling the pull of another orgasm. Blood rushed through her ears, pounded through her veins. He fondled her breasts and squeezed her nipples, sending sharp *zing*s ricocheting inside her. He sucked and fucked, tweaked and teased, until her whole body felt like one raw nerve. And then he did something exquisite with his mouth, and she bit down to keep from crying out as her climax consumed her.

Before she came down from the peak, he guided her hips lower, shimmying up to devour her breasts as he pulled her down onto his shaft, thrusting hard, taking her up, up, *up* again—and holding her there, at the edge of a cliff. He was a master at heightening her arousal, at making her crave and ache, until she felt as though she'd sell her soul for release. But he'd never want that. He didn't command or belittle; he coaxed and cherished, giving her exactly what she needed, at the perfect time.

"Grab the headboard," he said in a growly voice as he guided her trembling hands. "That's it. Now lift up so just the head of my cock is inside you."

His dirty talk nearly did her in. And *oh my!* She followed his directions, and he thrust in and out, slowly, masterfully, sending her right up to the stars.

He rose, bracketing her face with his strong hands, like he never wanted to let go, kissing her as she rode the waves of pleasure. One hand moved between her legs. His fingers wreaked havoc with her most sensitive nerves, working her over with a fast, precise rhythm as his shaft filled her. He filled her everywhere—in her heart, her mind, and her body. When she surrendered to their passion, lights exploded behind her closed lids, and he swallowed her every plea.

"Keep holding on, gorgeous," he coaxed as he withdrew from between her legs and moved behind her.

There was no way she could let go of the headboard. She was trembling all over, her nerves were on fire, her heart was practically beating out of her chest, and she freaking loved every second of it. She was still trying to grasp the idea that sex could be hot *and* loving and that her pregnant body was capable of feeling this toe-curling good. She'd half believed that she'd mentally made their lovemaking into more than it really was Saturday night, but *holy fudge*, Bones was *amazing*.

His lips touched her spine again, and his strong arms circled her. "I'll go slow in case it's uncomfortable."

She closed her eyes as he entered her one slow inch at a time, making every sensation excruciatingly intense. She felt the deep slide of his cock and the warm press of his hips, and then he took them both to paradise.

Afterward, he pressed his loving lips to her back, and then he rested his cheek there, hugging her for a long moment. "Missed you today. All of you." His hand moved over her belly.

"Mm. I missed you, too."

"Let go of the headboard, baby. I've got you."

She did, and he lowered them both to their sides, spooning her, his cock still nestled between her legs. He kissed her cheek, her neck, whispering sweetly, "You okay, darlin'?"

He was so intense and tender at the same time, emotions clogged her throat. It was all she could do to say, "Mm-hm."

A few minutes later, he put a little space between them and used his palm to massage her lower back. How did he know exactly what she needed? He kissed her shoulder, and she melted under his touch. She knew she shouldn't allow herself to play in the sandbox of a hopeful future, but she couldn't help it. She wanted to stay right there, wrapped up in him, feeling the happiness that even thinking about him brought. She wanted to see her children's eyes light up when he walked in the door a month from now, a year…

She thought about when she'd seen him running through the rain and about his father coming to help her with the kids today. And she remembered he'd wanted to talk with her before she'd seduced him.

"What did you want to talk to me about?" she asked.

He kissed the back of her neck, pulling her close again. "It's not exactly post-amazing-sex talk."

"Is it eating-popcorn-and-cuddling-on-the-couch talk?"

He chuckled. "Hungry?"

"You gave me quite a workout."

They took turns tiptoeing out to the bathroom, and Bones lovingly helped her dress amid stolen kisses and sinful promises of illicit love for another time. He hugged her as the popcorn popped, and she couldn't think of a more perfect moment than being in the quiet house, her babies safely tucked in their beds and her man's arms around her.

"I never knew it could be like this," she said softly, her arms around his neck.

"*It* meaning sex?"

She lifted her chin, gazing into his gorgeous eyes. "*It* meaning life. Sex, kissing, touching, talking. I spent so long living on edge, being afraid. I'm finally able to slow down and relax. Instead of fearing what comes next, I'm looking forward to it. I look forward to going to work, to talking with Chicki and my coworkers. To evenings like tonight with the girls, planning a birthday party for you and Lila and being part of your family's Thanksgiving." She went up on her toes and pressed a kiss to his neck. "And nights like this, with you. I'm afraid to be this happy, and at the same time, I don't want to miss a second of it."

His smiling lips came down over hers, and then he said, "You'll never have to miss it or be fearful again. That's what I want to talk with you about."

They took the popcorn into the living room and sat on the sofa. Bones glanced at her notebook on the coffee table and said, "You're writing a lot lately. Is that a good sign?"

"Yes, I think so, but it feels off. I started writing a story for Tracey, trying to give her a happily ever after. But we're not twelve years old. We know what the world is really like, and I don't think a fictional story is what she needs. I'm going to keep writing because I enjoy it, but I'm not going to share it with her."

He slid an arm around her shoulders, drawing her closer. "You're starting to clear the darkness from your life. Give it time and I'm sure you'll find your muse."

She nibbled on popcorn, thinking about that. "I hope so. I enjoy writing. Maybe one day I'll write stories for Lila and Bradley."

"Tru writes fairy tales for Kennedy and Lincoln. He's been doing it since they came into his life. Maybe you two should collaborate."

"Look at you, building a business for me. Writing is too personal for me to write with someone else. It just feels good, probably like riding your bike does for you. By the way, thanks for sending your dad over today. I'm used to taking care of the kids, but it was the sweetest gesture."

He touched his lips to hers, and his eyes grew serious. "I would have come myself, but I was slammed all day. That's what I wanted to talk to you about. I saw a patient, a single mother, and she brought up her ex-husband's rights to her son. It made me think about the kids and this little peanut."

She probably shouldn't put too much hope in the fact that he said *the kids* instead of *your kids*. But when he touched her stomach with a thoughtful expression, her emotions whirled.

"Sarah, have you been in contact with Lewis at all since you left?"

"No, and I want to keep it that way." She sat back, her reverie broken. "I don't want him near my kids. He'll ruin them."

"I know, darlin'. That's why I'm asking."

"Well, the answer is *no*, and I hope I never have to."

He pulled her closer again and said, "I know this is uncomfortable to talk about, but he's their father. He can come back at any time and try to see them. I don't want you, or them, to have to deal with that."

"Stop," she said angrily, and climbed off the couch. "Why are you doing this? We had such a perfect night." Just talking about him made her skin crawl. She wrapped her arms around herself.

"Because we can't ignore the possibilities. We need to talk about this. He has rights."

She pushed to her feet and paced. "He gave up those rights the minute he took drugs, and if that wasn't enough, he put the nail in the coffin when he forced himself on me."

Bones went to her, but she shrugged him away. "I don't want him in your life," he said emphatically. "I want to prevent him from trying to come back to see the kids. We can try to get him to consent to giving up his parental rights. Then you'll never have to look over your shoulder again."

She shook her head, her heart racing. "I can't talk about this." She put a hand on her chest. "It's making me anxious just thinking about it."

"Then let me do it for you. Let me track him down and get him to sign the papers."

"No," she snapped. "You don't understand." How could he? "We're good. Me and my kids and you and me. I don't want to open that door *ever* again. He's never looked for me. Why would he in the future?"

"What if he gets clean and realizes his mistakes? It happens."

She held up her hand, needing him to stop. "Don't do that. Even if he gets clean, he still *raped* me."

"Do you think I want this?"

The anger in his voice surprised her.

"Do you think I want to talk about this? To bring up something that I know hurts you? I want to kill that motherfucker with my own hands. But I can't do that because it would leave you and the kids alone."

He raked a hand through his hair and turned away. She watched his shoulders rise with every long inhalation, the tension in his shoulders easing with each exhalation. When he faced her again, his expression was softer.

He reached for her, touching his fingers to hers, and said, "I'm falling in love with you, Sarah."

He paused long enough for his words to sink in, filling her with warmth and happiness. "You are?"

"I am," he said with a secret, surrendering smile, as if he had no choice in the matter, and that was A-OK with him. "I think of you and the kids all the time. I feel empty when we're not together. I want you in my arms, in my bed. I want the kids with me. With *us*. I want to protect all of you and to teach the kids to share and stand up for themselves. I know three months is fast, and we've been more than friends for only a few weeks, but it's been building since day one. I don't need you to say it back. I just need you to know how I feel."

She curled her fingers around his. Her heart swelled and ached with happiness, and at the same time, with hurt for what he was asking her to do.

"The thought of him coming anywhere near you makes me

blind with rage," he said evenly. "I can't ignore something that could bring harm to you and the kids. I want—*need*—to eradicate that threat, Sarah. I want the guy in prison, but without evidence of what he did to you, it'd be a nightmare for you and possibly for the kids, too. All I'm asking is that you think about it. If not because I'm asking you, then for the kids. So when Bradley is eight or ten or fifteen, he won't have to deal with that guy. So Lila will never have to face the man who did horrible things to you. So *you* won't have to."

She sank down to the couch, tears welling in her eyes. "You're falling in love with me, but you're asking the impossible."

He knelt in front of her and put his hands around her, then kissed her belly. "I'm falling in love with all of you, and I'm asking that we try to clear a path of safety for your future. I'll do it. You don't even need to be involved."

"I can't." Tears slipped from her eyes. "What if he refuses and wants to see the kids?"

"What if he agrees and signs the paper? He hasn't come looking for you yet."

She tried to imagine Lewis agreeing, but that meant imagining his face, and panic burned in her chest, flooding the rest of her into a shaking, bawling mess.

Bones gathered her against him, soothing his hand down her back, and said, "I'm sorry. Maybe it's too soon."

"It'll always be too soon," she choked out. "I can't take a chance of bringing him back into our lives."

"I'd never let that happen."

She shook her head. "I'm sorry. I just can't let you risk it."

Chapter Nineteen

THE NEXT TWO days Sarah felt like she was being chased by a ghost. It was Wednesday afternoon, and she was at the shelter, cutting Ebony's hair and thinking about her conversation with Bones. She'd managed not to think about Lewis coming back into her life by *refusing* to let her mind visit that awful darkness. But ever since Bones brought up the idea of getting him to terminate his parental rights, she couldn't stop thinking about it. She'd asked Scott his opinion, and apparently he'd been harboring worries about the same thing. Like Bones, Scott thought Lewis was a ticking time bomb. But since she'd told Scott early on that she didn't want to talk about Lewis, Scott hadn't pushed.

But Bones had.

Because he's falling in love with me.

Warmth flooded her. She'd never been in love. She'd only ever been in a state of *hopeful, deep like* with Lewis. And over time, instead of falling deeper into him, as she had with Bones, she'd become removed. She'd gone from hopeful, to being happy there was a roof over her head, to being terrified.

"You're not going to give me one of those boy haircuts like

Tracey, are you?" Ebony asked with a wink. When they'd first met, she was all hard edges and rough talk. By the time Sarah had left on Saturday, Ebony had softened up, and today she was even less guarded.

Sarah pushed her thoughts aside and snipped another lock of Ebony's hair.

"Only if you're lucky." Tracey looked up from her perch on the arm of the couch, where she was reading a book Sarah had loaned her about starting over after domestic abuse. Her bruises had faded to a yellowish green.

"I love Tracey's cut, but don't worry," Sarah reassured her. "You said I could cut it to just below your ears, and that's as far as I'll go."

"That's what he said." Ebony smirked. "Then he's all *hello, back door!*"

That brought a litany of jokes and comments. Thank goodness Camille's children were playing across the room out of earshot. Sarah's mind traveled back to Monday night, only this time she revisited the deliciousness she and Bones had shared in her bedroom. After growing up with parents who made her feel shameful for even being female, and being manhandled by her ex, she'd wondered if she had a chance at *ever* having a normal sex life. Now she wondered what *normal* was, *if* there was any such thing. Because while the girls talked about putting that particular area under lock and key, she didn't think there was any part of her body she'd *want* to make off-limits to Bones.

Did that mean she was healing?

Did it make her normal?

A whisper of worry tiptoed through her. *Or does it make me trampy?*

Her answer came in the form of Bones's loving voice whispering through her mind. *I want to make love to you until I feel every beat of your heart and until every breath you take joins with mine.* No, she wasn't a tramp. She was a woman who was falling for a good, trustworthy man.

She finished cutting Ebony's hair and said, "Can I blow it dry?"

"I never blow-dry my hair. It just gets frizzier." Ebony ran her fingers through her newly shorn locks. "It feels so light."

"I thinned it out a little. I brought a diffuser and some product that will help reduce the frizz and enhance your natural curls. I can show you how to use them."

"Do it," Camille encouraged. "My sister uses a diffuser, and her hair always looks great." She pointed to her own beautiful, straight blond hair and said, "Nothing can make my hair hold a curl, but her hair is like Sarah's, thick and wavy."

"Okay, I'll be your Barbie doll," Ebony agreed. "*But* you're not dressing me up in any of that girlie shit." She tugged her T-shirt over her belly rolls. "I don't need to be like Meghan Trainor, strutting my stuff in tight jeans and short skirts. No *siree*. That just brings man trouble."

"Just because we had bad men doesn't mean they're all bad," Camille said. "Look at Dr. Hottie."

Tracey nudged Sarah. "That's your Whiskey man. We've renamed him, and we're all a little jealous."

"Oh my gosh. I've never been the target of jealousy before. It feels weird," Sarah admitted as she plugged in her hair dryer and attached the diffuser. "I never imagined being with a man like him."

"Hot?" Camille asked.

"*Yes*, but no," Sarah said. "Thoughtful and kind. A guy who thinks about me and my children before anything else. How about if you call him Dr. *Dreamy*? Because when I think of him, it's not his looks that come to mind first. He makes me feel all melty, and I swear when he's with my kids, there are no words to describe that feeling."

Camille gazed across the room at her children. "I'd give anything for a man who put my children first. My husband treated them like they didn't matter. He only cared that I was his to own, humiliate, and belittle."

Sarah and the others exchanged a wary glance. While Camille had told them she'd been hurt by her husband, she had been tight-lipped about just what kind of abuse she'd suffered. Now that she was opening up, Sarah could see that the other girls were just as worried as she was about how far he'd gone.

"Did he ever hurt you physically?" Sarah asked carefully as she applied product to Ebony's hair.

"Sometimes…"

"I'm sorry," Sarah said. When Camille didn't say more, Sarah grasped for a change in subject, but Camille spoke before she could get a word out.

"But not like Tracey, where he left bruises I couldn't cover up." Camille worried her hands in her lap, her blond hair curtaining her face. "He'd force me against a wall, squeezing my ribs so hard they'd bruise, or grab my wrist and hold it up behind my back so far I thought my arm would pop out of its socket. But mostly he controlled me with threats of violence." She lifted her face with shame in her eyes and said, "When he threatened to hurt David, my oldest, is when I finally got up the courage to leave."

Sarah wiped her hands and then hugged Camille. "I'm so sorry you went through that. It's crazy the power abusers have over us. But you got out, and your kids are safe. That's a start in the right direction."

"The power they *had* over us," Camille said. "Never again."

They all agreed.

While they talked about safer subjects, like where they were looking for jobs and what they did in their past lives—meaning before they fell into the hands of their abusers—Sarah dried and styled Ebony's hair: she parted it, pulling a few locks of bangs straight, then sweeping them over her left eye, and using the diffuser to curl the rest.

"Wow, Ebony!" Camille's blue eyes widened. "You look gorgeous."

Ebony reached up and touched her hair. She was sitting on the couch. "Really? You sure I don't look like a guy?"

"You couldn't look like a guy if you tried," Sarah said, and they all followed Ebony into the bathroom.

Ebony assessed herself in the mirror, leaning closer to get a better look, touching the straight bangs, then the curly sides, her eyes lighting up, and a smile followed. "Can you teach me to do this?"

"Absolutely. It's not difficult." Sarah retrieved the blow dryer and diffuser and showed her how to hold it to create curls and how to use the brush to straighten her bangs.

"I can't get over this. I have *great* hair," Ebony said with awe, making them all laugh.

"You have great *everything*," Sarah said. "You have the cutest dimple in your chin, and your eyes really *pop* now that you're not hiding behind your hair."

Ebony blushed and continued admiring herself in the mirror, but the longer she looked, the less she smiled. "I started dating my ex-boyfriend when I was twenty, and I have always been overweight. As things got worse between us, he called me thunder thighs and fat face. I took it because…*look* at me."

"Your ex was a shit," Tracey said harshly. "He's the reason you're here, so there's your silver lining. Now you've met us, and we won't let you hook up with shitty men ever again."

"You're beautiful, Ebony," Sarah said, her heart breaking. She remembered when Bones had said *I see you, Sarah, and your beautiful children. Whatever it took for you to be right here, right now, whatever made this moment possible didn't ruin you.* He had made her feel whole and normal, and because it was Bones and he had a way of making her feel things she'd never thought possible, he'd also made her feel beautiful. She wanted that for these friends, so she said, "I see *you*, Ebony, and when people see you, when they see Camille and Tracey, they won't see any of you through the eyes of an abuser. They'll see the beautiful, kind women you are. What we went through didn't ruin us."

Ebony wiped damp eyes, and Sarah put her arms around her, and then Camille and Tracey joined in for a group hug.

"We're done with assholes," Camille said. "All of us."

"I can't breathe," Ebony squeaked out, and they all took a step back. "Y'all are the best friends I've ever had, and I barely know you."

Thinking of Bones and his family, Sarah said, "Sometimes it's not the length of time you've known someone that matters. It's what they see and appreciate in you that others never have."

"Spoken like a woman with love in her eyes," Sunny said from outside the bathroom, startling them. She was carrying Joshua, Camille's youngest. "Bones called the front desk because you weren't answering your phone. He said to tell you he's not checking up on you and he knows you can handle picking up the kids, but he's at his mother's and he'll bring them to your place if you want him to."

Babs had canceled watching the kids at the last minute because of an appointment she'd forgotten about, but she'd asked Red to fill in for her. Red had been thrilled to care for, as she'd called them, her *surrogate grandbabies*. That had done inexplicable things to Sarah's emotions. She'd never imagined her children having grandparents, and now they were loved by Chicki, Babs, and Red, and the way Biggs had danced with Lila at the wedding told her they had touched him, too.

Ebony arched a brow. "His name is *Bones*? Dr. Dreamy just got even more interesting."

"Well, you know what they say," Tracey chimed in. "The hardest thing in the body is *bone*."

Sarah blushed, and Sunny said, "His biker name is Bones, not *Boner*."

"I like how he said he knows Sarah can handle picking up the kids," Camille said, taking Joshua from Sunny. As Sunny walked away, Camille said, "It's like he understands women like us need every bit of empowerment we can get."

"It's not that." Sarah told them about Bones asking his father to help her with the kids in the storm. "Like I haven't spent the last *year* mastering the ability to carry two babies, an umbrella, and everything else under the sun?"

"I still think it's amazing that he *listened* and understood," Camille said. "That's really important." She kissed her little boy's cheek. "I'm going to take him to the playroom."

Sarah thought about Bones as she put away her hair supplies. He was a great listener, and he was patient and understanding. She didn't know what she'd done to deserve this type of happiness, but the closer they became, the more she thought it had less to do with deserving or earning and more to do with something less tangible. Their connection was so strong, so deep, she had begun to believe they might have eventually found each other under any circumstances.

She gathered her things to leave and said, "I'm leaving the hair products for you."

"They should put *you* in the blessing bags," Ebony said.

"Blessing bags?" Sarah asked.

"When you come to the shelter, they give you a blessing bag. It's full of all the necessities—toiletries, socks, water, first aid kit, gloves, washcloths. All sorts of things," Tracey explained.

"Well, I won't fit in a blessing bag, but I can volunteer to do hair," Sarah offered. She liked the idea of helping women see themselves differently from the way they had before coming to the shelter. *A fresh start.*

"Good idea. Will you come back next week? Not to do hair, but just to hang out with us?" Tracey asked.

"Yes. Our own girls' club. I like it," Sarah said. "Ebony, if you have any styling trouble, call me. I'll try to walk you through it, but you should be fine."

"I'm never going to wash my hair," Ebony said as they walked Sarah out. "I'll sleep sitting up like a statue."

"You do that and your hair will look like a grease ball after a week," Tracey teased. "Hey, that's a good way to deflect men."

Sarah spotted Camille on the couch in the playroom watching her boys and thought again about what Bones had asked her to do about Lewis. "I'll be right back. I want to say goodbye to Camille." She went into the playroom and sat beside Camille, placing her bag on the floor by her feet. "I didn't want to leave without saying goodbye."

"I'm glad. I love what you did with Ebony's hair."

"Thanks. Me too." There was no easy way to ask what she

wanted to, so she just went for it. "I wanted to ask you something about your husband. You don't have to answer if it's too personal."

"You already know all my bad stuff," Camille said.

"I know, but…I'm just wondering if you're doing anything to keep him away from the boys. Legally, I mean."

Camille's eyes remained trained on her children. "I have a restraining order, but I want something more permanent. I don't have the money for an attorney, but when I do, keeping him away from them forever will be my first priority. Why? Are you afraid your kids' father is looking for you?"

"No." She put her hand on her belly and said, "I'm just trying to decide if I should do something so he never has that option."

"That depends on what you think is best for your kids. For me, that's keeping him as far away from them as possible."

Sarah thought about that as she picked up her bag. Was she being shortsighted by refusing to try to get Lewis to sign papers relinquishing his parental rights? Bones hadn't mentioned anything about the cost of doing it. She needed to find out about that, but she still wasn't ready to chance it backfiring.

She hugged Camille, promised to come by next week, and then she gave each of the boys a kiss on the top of the head. Ebony and Tracey flanked her in the hall, deep in conversation about Thanksgiving dinner, reminding Sarah she'd agreed to bring dessert to the Whiskeys' Thanksgiving dinner.

Sunny buzzed someone in as she said, "See you next week, Sarah?"

Sarah looked up and lost her breath at the sight of her sister coming through the door, looking gaunt holding the hand of a lanky little boy with longish, thick brown hair.

"Josie" fell from Sarah's lips.

Before Sarah knew what was happening, Josie dragged her little boy out the door and ran down the steps.

"Josie!" Sarah dropped her bag and ran after them. Her friends called after her, but she wasn't about to stop. Not when her sister was blowing through the doors to the building and running across the lawn.

Sarah held her belly up from underneath as she chased them. "Wait! Josie! Please!"

Josie's little boy looked over his shoulder, slowing her down. "Mommy, who is that?"

"Nobody. Keep going," Josie snapped.

The little boy stumbled, and Josie stopped to help him, giving Sarah time to gain on her. Josie moved in front of the boy, forming a barrier between Sarah and her son. "Stop right there, Sarah."

Sarah stopped a few feet away. "Why are you running from me?"

"Mommy!" The little boy peered around her legs with terror in his eyes.

"Stay there, Hail." Josie set a warning glare on Sarah.

Sarah held her hand up, using the other to lean on her thigh for support as she tried to catch her breath. "I just want to talk. I don't understand why you won't see me."

"I don't understand why *you* won't leave me alone." Josie set her jaw, like she had as a little girl when she was mad.

Sarah tried to piece together the angry young woman before her with the best friend she'd grown up with. The girl who had never suffered at the hands of her parents the way Sarah and Scott had but had endured their wrath the way secondhand smoke caused cancer.

"Because I love you," Sarah pleaded. "You're my family. Scott and I can help you. We have a house in a safe neighborhood, near good schools, and—"

"Hail is the only family I need." Her chin trembled, and Sarah took a step forward, needing to bridge the gap between them. Josie took a step backward, forcing her little boy to do the same. "I can't do this. Not now. Go back to your perfect life and leave us alone."

"Josie…?" Tears spilled from Sarah's eyes as Josie took her son's hand and walked away. "Wait!" Sarah pleaded. "Go back to the shelter. It's safe there. I'll get my stuff and then I'll leave you alone."

Josie stilled, her back to Sarah, and Sarah knew she was at least listening.

"Please go back, Josie. They're good people. Your son will be safe there. I promise to stay away." The pain that promise brought was excruciating.

Josie drew her shoulders back, and Sarah prayed she'd listen. But Josie didn't walk toward the shelter. She stormed away in the opposite direction.

"Josie, please!" Sarah called after as she disappeared around the corner.

BONES CARRIED LILA up the porch steps as Bradley relayed stories about their afternoon with Red. "She said I can call her Nana Red. I like that."

"I like that too, buddy." *A whole hell of a lot*, he thought as he knocked on the door.

Scott answered with a troubled expression. "Hey, guys.

Come on in."

Bones looked over Scott's shoulder at Sarah, who ducked into the kitchen, but not before he noticed her pink nose and watery eyes. His nerves went on high alert as he stepped inside. "What happened?"

"Ca!" Lila reached for Scott.

Focused on Sarah, Bones handed her over. Sarah had texted him an hour ago thanking him for offering to pick the kids up. He'd stuck around talking with his parents and had left their house later than he'd anticipated. He hoped that wasn't why she was upset.

"She saw Josie," Scott answered. "It didn't go well."

Christ. She never gets a break. Bones tousled Bradley's hair and said, "Hey, B-boy, why don't you play with Uncle Scott for a minute while I help Mom with dinner?"

"Okay." He headed for the toys, and Bones went to Sarah.

She stood at the counter putting rotini pasta and bite-sized pieces of meatballs into bowls. Her hair curtained her face, but her sadness filled the room.

"Hey, darlin'." He put his arm around her waist and said, "I heard you had a tough afternoon."

"I'm okay," she said in a strained voice.

He brushed her hair over her shoulder so he could see her face, aching at the grief gazing back at him. He embraced her. "Scott said you ran into Josie. I'm so sorry it didn't go well."

She nodded against his chest.

"Do you want to talk about it?"

She shrugged.

"Why don't you take a minute to relax. I'll feed the kids, and then we can talk," he offered.

She pushed away. "No. I can feed them. I need to. Life

doesn't stop because I'm sad."

Bradley bounded into the kitchen. "Mommy, look what—" His giddy voice silenced, and he frowned. "Why are you sad?"

Scott appeared behind him with Lila in his arms and mouthed, *Sorry.*

Sarah forced a smile. "I'm not sad. I just had something in my eye. Come sit down and eat."

Scott put Lila in her high chair as Bradley climbed into his chair.

"An eyelash like I had that time?" Bradley placed his toy pig beside his plate and said, "That's ouchie."

"Yes, an eyelash." Sarah set a bowl in front of him.

Bones grabbed a bib from the drawer and put it on Lila as she babbled, "Bababa."

"Who's Josie?" Bradley asked.

Sarah looked like she'd been gutted. "She's..."

"*Josie and the Pussycats*," Scott said. "It's a show your mom and I watched as kids." He turned his attention to Sarah and said, "How about if you guys go for a walk while I hang out with my niece and nephew." Making a game of it, he leaned closer to Bradley and said, "We can do secret stuff while Mom's gone."

"Secrets are bad," Bradley said around a mouthful of pasta.

"Okay, well, then I'll teach you how to make a train out of your pasta."

Bradley nodded, eyes wide with glee.

"What do you say, darlin'?" Bones asked Sarah quietly, hoping like hell she'd take her brother up on his offer. "Are you up for a walk?"

She nodded.

Sarah bundled up against the brisk evening air, and Bones

kept her tucked against his side as they walked silently to the end of the street.

"Josie was coming into the shelter as I was leaving," she said as they turned the corner. "She ran from me, Bones. She sprinted away with her son, like I was an enemy. I didn't even know she had a child. But she does. A beautiful boy named Hail. *Hail*," she said with a soft laugh. "When we were young we said if we ever had children we'd name them after nature. To us that signified strength and freedom. Hail, Rain… We had all sorts of ideas. Nothing can stop hail from pummeling or rain from falling."

"Why did you go with Bradley and Lila?"

"Because I didn't want any reminders of my past. I didn't want them to *need* those names. I wanted them to have normal lives." She remembered the moment she'd made that decision and the power that had come with it. "Why does she hate me and Scott so much? It kills me that she's so angry, and she's in trouble. She has to be. Why else would she have gone to the shelter?"

"I don't know, but why don't I call Sunny and see if she's been there before? Now that she knows what Josie looks like, she might recognize her."

"Would you? I promised her I wouldn't go back to the shelter so she would have a safe place to go. I told Tracey and the girls, and they understood. They were so supportive. They promised to help Josie if she showed up. I can't take the thought of Josie and her son on the streets…"

Tears tumbled down her cheeks, and Bones drew her into an embrace. "It's going to be okay, Sarah. She just needs time."

"She said I have a *perfect* life. She has no idea what I've been through."

"Then we'll tell her when the time is right." She drew back, and he kissed away her tears. "When she's ready to hear it."

"What if she never is?"

"We won't let that happen. She's your family. We'll do whatever it takes so she knows she's not alone."

"Can you call Sunny now? Please? I've been so worried. I just want to know she and her son are safe."

Bones made thc call and then relayed what he'd learned. "Sunny said they didn't come back, but she'd call if they showed up. She also said she thinks Josie's might have been there before, but she didn't stay. She just came in to check it out and left."

Sarah crumbled against him. "Why did this happen? Why couldn't she have found happiness? It's like we're cursed. I knew when she came to the hospital she wasn't in a good place, but I hoped and prayed I'd overreacted."

"We don't know what she's been through, but I promise you, Sarah, she's not alone in this, and neither are you. We will do everything we can to find and help her."

"Part of me wants to tell you to go fall in love with Josie, to make her feel safe like you make me feel. But I'm too selfish for that."

"The fact that you'd even think that way tells me how truly unselfish you are." He pressed his lips to her and said, "I'll do everything I can to make Josie feel safe and loved, but my heart is already spoken for."

A half smile lifted her lips. "Will you stay with me tonight? Hold me?"

"I thought you'd never ask." He pressed his lips to hers, tasting her salty tears. "I'm going to put out a call for the Knights to look for Josie."

"They'll scare her if they roll up on their motorcycles."

He kissed her again, slow and sweet, and when she melted against him, he kissed her longer. When their lips finally parted, he said, "Did that scare you?"

"Not at all."

"See? Not all bikers are scary. Trust me, darlin'. I wouldn't chance scaring your sister or her child."

On their way back to the house Bones called Bullet and explained the situation. "You know the drill," he said. "She's got a little one underfoot, so tell the guys to take it easy. No fear, B. She's a runner. I'd go myself, but I want to be with Sarah. She's had a rough time of it."

"You got it, bro," Bullet said. "I'll call as soon as we have news. Until then, tell your girl we've got her back."

AFTER AN EVENING of playtime, bubble baths, and bedtime stories, Sarah took a warm shower to try to relax, and Bones talked with Scott. "Any idea what's going on with Josie?"

Scott looked like he'd aged five years in the past few hours. "No. I wish I did. She was never harmed by our parents, as far as I know. I can't think of a single reason for her to be this way toward us."

"Guilt, maybe? For not being one of the children your parents went after?"

Scott shrugged. "Like I said, I wish I knew. All I know is I've got enough guilt on my back for all of us. I never should have left them. I should have killed that bastard and taken whatever punishment they doled out. Then both my sisters could have lived better lives."

"Dude, that's a lot of responsibility to put on a kid. You know about Quincy and Tru's background, don't you?"

He shook his head. "Just that Tru found Kennedy and Lincoln in a crack house when their mother OD'd."

"Their mother was a drug addict of the worst kind. When Quincy was thirteen, a dealer raped her, and he killed the guy. Tru showed up and took the fall for the murder. He spent years in prison for a crime he didn't commit. He'd thought he was saving Quincy, but then Quincy became an addict. He's clean now, but it was a mess."

"Damn, I had no idea." Scott shook his head.

"There are no perfect ways out of bad situations. You did the right thing. You got out, and you sent money to help your sisters. You can't let guilt eat away at you. If you'd killed your old man, your mother would have had you arrested. And it doesn't sound like she was any better than your father. When you dump anger on top of whatever was driving your mother to treat you guys that way, your sisters would have been stuck in an even worse situation. Thank God you did the smart thing."

"Thanks, man," Scott said. "Let's hope we get lucky and find Josie before she and her son end up in even worse circumstances. It's a weird thing to be separated from someone for so many years and then suddenly you're all adults and your little sisters have children and you realize how strong the little girls you knew grew up to be."

"You're all strong, Scott."

He pushed to his feet. "I can't just sit here. I need to go look for Josie. I appreciate the Knights looking for her, too. I don't know what we did to deserve you guys coming into our lives, but I appreciate everything you've done."

"No worries. You mind if I stick around tonight?"

"Not in the least. Until you came into Sarah's life, I'd never seen her happy for more than a few minutes here and there with the kids. She's lived through hell. She deserves a taste of heaven." He grabbed his cane from the corner of the room and said, "Hit me up if you hear anything."

"Will do. Be careful."

Hours later, Scott still wasn't back. Bones sat on the couch reading with Sarah's head in his lap, running his fingers through her hair as she drifted in and out of sleep. His cell phone vibrated, and as he reached for it Sarah jolted upright.

"Is it about Josie?"

He read the text from Bullet. *Found her in a shithole. Finlay convinced her to go to the shelter. She's safe. We tried to get her to come to our place, but Fin says I look too scary. WTF?* As he was reading, a text popped up from Sunny and another from Bear. He read Sunny's message. *She's here with her son. I'll take good care of them, but she told me not to let Sarah in to see her. Sorry.* He quickly scanned Bear's message, which relayed the same information, and said, "She's safe. She's at the shelter."

"Oh, thank goodness." Happy tears slipped down her cheeks. "Sorry. Pregnancy hormones make me cry over everything."

He put his arms around her and said, "Those aren't pregnancy-hormone tears. They're happy-that-your-sister-is-safe tears. They're emotionally-and-physically-spent tears." He kissed the tip of her nose and said, "Finlay convinced her to go to the shelter. She tried to get her to go home with her and Bullet, but I guess that was asking for a little too much trust for a single mother."

"Finlay and Bullet found them? Maybe that's a good sign since Bullet is the one who saved me and my family. Look where we ended up."

He didn't need to break her heart by telling her what Josie had asked of Sunny. Instead he said, "I think she needs space, babe. Let her settle in at the shelter so she doesn't run scared again. Once she realizes she can trust you and Scott, hopefully she'll come around."

"Like I had to learn to trust you," Sarah said.

"Something like that." He pressed his lips to hers and then helped her to her feet. "Come on, beautiful girl, let's get you out of those clothes and into bed."

She let out a sleepy laugh as they walked to the bedroom. "Dr. Whiskey, are you going to try to take advantage of my precarious emotional state?"

He closed the bedroom door and went to her. "I'd never take advantage of you." He lifted her sweater over her head and said, "But I am going to rub your back." He trailed kisses along her shoulders and down her spine. "And your legs and feet."

He carefully removed the rest of her clothes, kissing each bit of skin as it was revealed. Then he took her hand and led her to the bed. He pulled down the blankets and helped her lie down. He stood at the edge of the bed, began kneading the arch of her foot, and said, "And any other parts of your body that need special attention."

She sighed, relaxing into the mattress as he rubbed each foot. Then he worked his way up her legs, massaging and kissing in equal measure. He helped her onto her side and began massaging her shoulders, taking his time as he eased every muscle from there to the tips of her hamstrings and every beautiful inch in between.

"You know what would make this exquisite massage even better?" she asked in a husky voice.

"I can think of a few things."

He kissed her shoulder and she turned dark, seductive eyes toward him and whispered, "If the masseuse were naked."

"Your wish is my command." He stepped from the bed and stripped off his clothes. Her heated stare and the way she licked her lips as he took off his briefs made him hard as steel. But it was more than lust filling his chest. He wondered if it was possible to love her more than he did right at that second.

"Show me where you hurt and I'll rub the ache away."

She reached for him, her beautiful eyes full of emotion, and said, "My outside parts feel better, and knowing Josie and her son are safe makes my heart happy. But I have other inside parts that need a little attention."

Chapter Twenty

BONES'S HOUSE HAD been buzzing with activity and had smelled like family, love, and happiness when Bones, Sarah, and the children had arrived and found half his family inside. Bones had told Sarah that he and his brothers shared house keys in case of an emergency. She had tucked that knowledge into her Things I Love About Bones and His Family mental file. Now, as she waited the last two minutes for the oven timer to ding, she glanced into the living room. She'd worried about dressing right for her first holiday with Bones's family, and he hadn't been much help with his response. *You look gorgeous in everything—and particularly when you're naked.* She'd gone casual with a red blouse and jeans, and she fit right in. The guys wore their vests and jeans, and the women looked nice and comfortable, but not dressy. The holiday was just an excuse to celebrate what mattered most to the Whiskeys—family—as was evident in the pink and blue balloons and streamers decorating the entire first floor of the house. Truman had made a birthday banner for Bones and Lila, and he'd drawn a picture of Bones from the waist up with Lila in his arms. She had a pink bow in her hair and a smile meant for her *Ba*.

She glanced at Bones standing with Bullet by their father, who was sitting on the couch with Bradley on his lap. Bradley wore his vest and boots to match Bones, and at the moment he also wore an adoring, carefree smile. Lila sat in a splash of sunlight on the floor beside Tinkerbell, playing house with Lincoln and Kennedy. It was still a little strange, seeing so much love for her children, but she wasn't complaining. Isabel and Penny chatted nearby, watching over them. Sarah wondered if Isabel and Penny were aware that Quincy and Jed had their blue eyes locked on *them* from a few feet away, where they stood talking with Scott, Bear, and Truman. Jed's dirty-blond hair hung over his eyes but was cropped short on the sides, while Quincy's brown hair was longer all over. They were cocky guys, and she wondered why they didn't just ask the girls out.

Scott lifted his chin, catching her eye with a look of unmistakable longing. Josie's absence seemed more tangible around such a big family. She wondered what Josie was doing tonight. Bones had called Sunny before they'd left the house this morning and had asked her to let him know if Josie took off. Knowing she and her son were safe helped, but it didn't fill the void that could only be remedied by reuniting with her sister.

The buzzer on the oven sounded, and Sarah pulled the baked sweet potato casserole from the oven, earning appreciative sounds from the girls in the kitchen. Gemma and Dixie were busy setting the table, while Crystal cut the corn bread and set it on a pretty tray and Finlay put garnishes on the other side dishes. She made cranberry sauce, mushroom stuffing, roasted Brussels sprouts, and a vegetable medley look like they belonged in a fancy restaurant.

"That smells delish," Gemma said as she grabbed a handful of forks.

"This has become my favorite dish," Sarah said. "It has all sorts of goodies inside: pineapples, apple chunks, cinnamon, marshmallows, and brown sugar. Bones found it online the other day. I made a big batch and have been eating it with lunch every day. I'm sure I'll be scolded for my weight when I go for my doctor visit next week. I can't stop eating it." Thanks to Finlay, she had a plethora of foods she could eat without worrying. And since Bones had taken an interest in helping to find recipes, they'd collected quite a few more.

"You're a tiny little thing," Red said as she cleared a place on the counter for the dish. "And you never seem to look tired, even with two little ones to chase after."

"Thank you." She didn't look tired because Bones had let her sleep in today. He'd gotten up with the kids, fed them breakfast, and had even taken them on a walk to the park a few blocks away. Sarah hadn't woken up until they'd come home at nearly *ten* o'clock. She never slept in, but the last few days had worn her out. Between thinking about Lewis's parental rights and seeing Josie, she hadn't realized how fried she'd been.

"Bones said you were going to see Drs. Rhys and Blair?" Red said, bringing her mind back to their conversation. "They're good people."

"Yes. I'm seeing Dr. Blair. It'll be nice to see the same doctor each time I go."

"Damon Rhys's grandfather delivered every one of my babies," Red said. As usual, she was dressed in black, and yet somehow she radiated light. "I was sure that boy would go on to play pro sports. Guess he proved me wrong. You'll like Stephanie Blair. She's a sharp woman, and she tells it like it is."

"I'm seeing Dr. Rhys next week," Crystal said as she grabbed plates from the cabinet. Then she said, "Shit."

Red and Sarah exchanged a curious glance.

"Shit, like maybe there's more than turkey in the *oven*?" Red asked as Gemma and Dixie came into the kitchen. "Or shit, like I just hurt my finger on the plates?"

Crystal turned with an *oops I spilled the beans* expression, clutching a stack of plates to her chest.

"Crystal!" Gemma squealed and threw her arms around her. "Congratulations!"

"Shh!" Crystal urged as the rest of them converged on her. She set the plates on the counter and peeked into the living room.

"You're pregnant?" Dixie asked in a loud whisper. "Does Bear know?"

Crystal nodded. "But we haven't had a blood test. We did a home pregnancy test and it turned positive wicked fast, but still. Bear wanted to wait until the blood test was done before announcing it, just in case something goes wrong."

"Just in case my ass." Red hugged her. "Since when did my overzealous boy become so careful?"

"Since he fell in love," Dixie answered. "All your sons lose their minds when they fall in love, Bones included. The man bought so many toys the other day, we had to hire a truck just to get them here. I'm the only sane one of the bunch these days."

Sarah glanced at Bones, who now had Bradley on his shoulders so he could reach the string of a runaway balloon. Didn't he know that he was enough for them? No toys needed.

"We celebrate together," Red said to Crystal. "And if anything goes wrong, we mourn together."

"Now you're going to make me cry." Crystal opened her arms and waved them all in for a group hug.

"It's those pregnancy hormones," Red said as she put her arms around all the girls.

"You told them, didn't you?" Bear's voice startled them apart, but his big smile told Sarah he didn't mind sharing the news after all.

Crystal bit her lower lip, shrugging one shoulder. "Kinda, sorta, *yes.*"

He hauled her into his arms and gave her a loud kiss. "It's all good. I was struggling to hold it in when I saw you at the center of the crazy-girls hug, and I knew I was in the clear." He turned toward the living room and raised his beer bottle. "We think we're having a baby!"

"A baby!" Kennedy jumped up and down clapping. "Uncle Be*ah* is having a baby!"

Laughter and a whirlwind of activity followed as Biggs and the rest of the crew from the living room piled into the kitchen to shower Crystal and Bear with congratulations.

Bones wrapped his arms around Sarah and said for her ears only, "I can't wait to do that."

"Hug Crystal?" she asked.

"No." He gazed into her eyes and said, "Maybe one day that'll be us."

"Us…?" Holy moly, what was he saying?

"Unless you're done having babies after this little one?" He touched her belly. "That's cool, too."

"Um…" *Am I? Is this really happening?*

"Let's eat!" Biggs announced.

Bones put a hand on her back, guiding her toward the table, which was good, because she couldn't think straight with all the commotion and Bones looking at her like she was not only his girlfriend, but his *future.*

Dinner was delicious and loud, with endless sibling teasing and talk about Crystal's pregnancy. Lila and Bradley were right there in the thick of it all. Bradley chimed in with comments about being a big brother.

"I have a new big-boy bed," Bradley announced.

"I have a big-girl bed," Kennedy said louder. "But Linc is a baby. He sleeps in a crib."

"So does Lila," Bradley said. "But Mommy sleeps in a *big-girl-boy* bed."

Silence fell over the table, amused eyes turning to Sarah and Bones.

"I'll bite," Bear said. "What's a big-girl-boy bed? Sounds fun."

"It's a bed where a girl and boy sleep together, like Bones and Mommy." Bradley looked at Sarah, who was sure her cheeks would burn right off, and said, "Right, Mommy?"

"Outed by a three-year-old," Bullet said under his breath. "Gotta love it."

Bradley turned his adorable wide eyes to Red and said, "Do you and Papa Biggs sleep in a big-girl-boy bed? If you do, can I come over and sleep in it with you one day? I won't wiggle too much."

"Bradley, adults don't share beds with kids," Sarah said, wondering if it were possible to snap her fingers and delete this from everyone's memory banks.

"But you did," Bradley said innocently.

"And so did we, for many years," Red answered. "Bobby, who you know as Bear, used to climb into our bed and cuddle before joining his big brothers, Brandon and Wayne—Bullet and Bones—on the floor, wrestling like wild banshees. But my boys are all grown up. I could use some little-boy cuddles sometimes. That is, if your mama doesn't mind."

"She doesn't!" Bradley exclaimed. "I'm the best cuddler. She says so all the time."

As Bradley and Red made plans, Bullet looked across the table at Sarah and said, "So, what's it like to date the *good one*?"

Sarah looked at Bones. "What does that mean?"

"Most families have one kid who always does the right thing," Bullet explained. "Bones was that kid."

She sat up a little straighter, ready to stand up for her man—although standing up for him by outing him for doing something bad was weird, she felt oddly proud to have the knowledge to do it. "Just for the record, I love that he's a good person. There's nothing wrong with being good. But if you're implying that *good* means not tough, you're wrong. My bad-boy boyfriend s-t-o-l-e a car once."

"No way," Penny said. "I can't even imagine that."

"I can. Bones is a badass," Quincy said.

"Bad *boy*." Isabel said as Kennedy said, "Quincy said a bad word!"

Jed laughed. "Nice job, Quince."

Bullet's lips quirked, amusement filling his dark eyes as he looked at Sarah and said, "Is that what Bones told you?"

"Yes, he did." She looked at Bones and said, "Right?"

Bones closed his eyes, shaking his head.

"You didn't?" she asked. "But you said…"

"No, darlin'. I did."

"*Oh no.*" She lowered her voice to a whisper and asked, "Was it a secret?"

He shook his head. "No. They all know."

Now she was confused. Why was he acting so weird?

"Bones did s-t-e-a-l a vehicle, which was a bad thing to do,"

Dixie said. "But the reason he took it made it pretty forgivable."

"What does that mean?" Sarah asked.

"It was the summer I told you about, when Thomas was sick," Bones explained. "Near the end, all he wanted was to spend the night on his dad's boat. I snuck out late at night for a week straight and taught myself to drive my old man's car. Then one night when everyone was asleep, I took the car, snuck Thomas out of the hospital, and brought him to his father's boat. I loaded him up with blankets, and we lay there like we'd pulled off the greatest heist ever."

"You did," Bullet said, sounding a little choked up. "You gave that boy what he wanted. You made his last days the best they could be."

Tears welled in Sarah's eyes.

"Darn pregnancy hormones," Crystal said, wiping her tears with a napkin.

"What's my excuse?" Dixie asked, wiping her own eyes.

"You're human," Scott answered.

"You know what that makes him?" Sarah was talking to Bullet but looking into the eyes of her big-hearted, bad-boy good-boy boyfriend.

"A damn good man," Bullet answered.

Sarah, still looking at Bones, said, "You took the words right out of my mouth."

"Why is everyone crying?" Kennedy asked. "Should I be sad, too?"

"No, baby," Gemma said. "They're happy tears."

That led to a long discussion between Bradley and Kennedy about things that made them happy, which brought Sarah's mind back to Josie.

Bones put his hand on her thigh beneath the table and

leaned closer, whispering, "How are you holding up? Is it too noisy for you?"

The commotion never stopped, which was fun, exciting, and all around *wonderful.* She wasn't going to let her longing ruin anyone else's night. "No. I love it."

"And I love you." He leaned in with a sweet kiss. "Thinking about Josie?"

She nodded. "But I don't want to talk about that. Did I tell you that we didn't celebrate Thanksgiving when we were growing up?" She glanced at Scott, who was busy talking with Jed. "Our parents said it was just another day of the year. I always wondered what it would be like to celebrate, and this was better than I could have dreamed."

His eyes turned serious, and as if he'd read her thoughts, he said, "Mark my words. Next year Josie and her children will be with us."

"I hope you're right." *And I love you even more for saying that.*

"We're also going to make sure the kids have the best holidays—every single one of them—so they learn the meaning of holidays."

"Yes, we will," Biggs said from the head of the table, his eyes on them. "All these kids will know the meaning of holidays."

"And just what is the meaning of this holiday, Pop?" Bear asked.

Biggs stroked his beard, his dark gaze moving slowly around the table, finally landing on Bear again with a slow, uneven grin. "Son, if you don't know, then you haven't earned the right to be a father yet. And it's just that. A *right.*"

Bear scoffed and put a hand on Crystal's belly.

"I was kidding you, old man," Bear said. "Technically

speaking, we're commemorating the harvest festival celebrated by the Pilgrims, but realistically, it's a great excuse to get together with these mangy men, beautiful women, and adorable babies and remember all the things in life we're thankful for."

"I'm thankful for Uncle Boney and Lila!" Kennedy announced.

"Why is that, princess?" Truman asked.

"Because it's their birthday and Aunt Finlay made my *favowite* cake!" Kennedy turned toward Finlay and said, "I'm thankful for you and Uncle Bullet, too, and Tink and..." She went around the table naming everyone, proving what a sweet girl she was. "And I even like the *agerlin-fwee* dinner!"

"Allergen-free, honey," Gemma corrected her. "And I like it, too."

Scott said, "Thank you for a delicious dinner."

"And for making things I could eat," Sarah added.

"Have you always been allergic to so many things?" Crystal asked.

"I honestly don't know when it started or how it progressed," Sarah said. "Scott, do you remember?"

Scott shook his head. "You had peanut butter when you were little and we ended up in the emergency room. I remember Dad complaining about the cost of the visit, and when we got home he threw out a bunch of stuff that the doctor said you could also be allergic to. But I can't remember exactly when that was."

"Scott, are you allergic to anything?" Jed asked.

"Nope."

"They must have tested Sarah in the hospital," Bones said. "But most kids outgrow food allergies, especially some of what you're allergic to—dairy, eggs—whereas other food allergies, like nuts, tend to persist."

"Have you been tested as an adult?" Penny asked. "Imagine if you're not actually allergic to dairy. You'd be able to eat ice cream." Her eyes lit up and she said, "If you do get tested and you *can* have dairy, come down to the shop and I'll create a special sundae just for you. The Sinfully Delicious Sarah Sundae!"

"I'm not sure I want other dudes eating that," Bones said, earning chuckles around the table.

"Bones," Sarah whispered.

"Seriously, babe," Bones said. "Let them get their own sinfully delicious girl. You're mine."

How could she argue with that?

"But Penny's got a point," he said. "We should talk to an allergist. They can't test you while you're pregnant, but it's worth looking into, even if you have to wait until the baby's born. Maybe you've outgrown some of your allergies."

"I'm so used to eating this way, I'm not sure I'd know how to cook any differently."

"Fin and I can show you," Isabel offered.

"It would make things easier *and* less expensive," Sarah said. "But what if nothing has changed? Then I've wasted the money on the tests."

"I think your doctor-boyfriend can swing the hundred bucks," Bear quipped.

Bones glared at him, then turned a softer look to Sarah. "It could change your life, and if not, then at least we'll know."

"This seems to be the year of change for me," Sarah relented. "Why not?"

A YEAR OF change was exactly what it was turning out to be for everyone, and Bones had no complaints. He and the rest of the guys joked around as everyone cleared the table and he and Bullet did the dishes. Afterward, he headed upstairs with Bullet and Bear to get the presents he'd bought for the kids.

"What the hell did you buy?" Bear asked as he loaded his arms with presents.

"A better question would be, what *didn't* he buy?" Bullet said. "What's that Pack 'n Play for?"

"Lila. We're staying here tonight."

Bear smirked. "You bought all this crap and you couldn't afford a real crib?"

"Of course I can, you ass. I just didn't think Sarah was ready for me to push that hard." The truth was, he'd wanted to buy a crib, but Dixie had pointed that out about Sarah and had stopped him from doing it.

"Probably smart," Bear said. "But I don't know how all this Daddy Warbucks stuff is going to go over."

Bones glared at him. "What'd you guys get them?"

"A few toys," Bear said. "Not the whole store."

"I couldn't just buy for Lila. Bradley, Kennedy, and Lincoln would feel left out." Bones grabbed the gift he'd gotten Sarah and met Bullet's confused eyes. "What?"

"Now *we're* going to look bad," Bullet grumbled. "Fin said it teaches kids the wrong things if you give them presents on other kids' birthdays."

Bones looked down at the gifts. "Shit. Really?" They both looked at Bear. "What'd you do?"

"Dude, I have no idea. Crystal went shopping with Gemma. I have no idea what she bought or who it was for."

"Goddamn it." Bones went into the hall and looked down

from the loft. Sarah sat on the couch with Lila standing at her feet, waving her stuffed hedgehog. Bradley was lying beside Tinkerbell on the floor, scratching her belly. He pulled out his phone and took a picture. A snapshot of his happiness.

"Hey, Ma," Bones called down. Red, Gemma, and Sarah all looked up. "Sorry. Red, we need you for a sec."

"This should be interesting." Red handed Gemma her wineglass and headed upstairs. "What can't my big, brawny boys handle on their own?"

Bones nodded toward the bedroom, where Bullet and Bear had their arms full of presents.

Red stifled a laugh. "Y'all look scared. What'd you do or break?"

"One of us might have screwed up," Bones said. "I bought presents for all four of the kids."

Bullet cleared his throat and said, "I only bought presents for Lila."

"And you?" she asked Bear.

"I have no idea what we bought," he said sheepishly.

"What did you do with us?" Bones asked. "Did we all get gifts on each other's birthdays when we were little?"

Red flashed the kind of smile that said she loved them even though they were all clueless. "Y'all shared your gifts. There was no need to buy four of everything. Whenever one of you got something, you wanted to share it with the others, and if you didn't, then Bullet glared at you until you gave in."

Bear and Bullet looked just as confused as Bones felt. "So…?"

She patted Bones's cheek and said, "Your heart is overflowing, and it's showing in everything you do. There's nothing wrong with that. But in this case, less might be more. Kids can get overwhelmed when given too much."

"Not to mention spoiled," Bear said quietly.

Bones glared at him. "They can also feel like they aren't important if you don't care enough to do the shopping."

"You saying I fucked up?" Bear put down the gifts and stuck out his chest.

"I'm saying these kids are family, and you don't leave it up to your wife to pick out the gifts. You do it together."

Bullet nodded in confirmation. "He's right, dude."

"Excuse the fuck out of me. I was a little busy with this." Bear whipped an envelope out of his pocket and shoved it in Bones's hand.

"What's this?" He opened the envelope and withdrew a computerized drawing of something he'd never seen. It had the front of a motorcycle and the back end of a sports car with sides and a roof around three rear seats.

"It's a family motor-trike-car," Bear said as Bullet and Red leaned in to see. "I haven't picked out a name yet, but I figured it was only a matter of time before Bradley and Lila were begging for rides. And I know you. No matter how much you love your bike, you're not putting those kids on your lap for a ride. This will have five-point harnesses in the back. I know you need five seats, but I can't do it."

Overwhelmed, Bones took a moment before saying, "You designed this for me?"

"Yeah. It'll take a long time to bring it to life, but that's why I didn't go shopping. I've been spending my extra time trying to figure out what to get the guy who has everything."

"Christ, Bear. I'm sorry, man." He pulled him into an embrace. "This is the coolest thing I've ever seen. I'll fund it. No need for you to do all that."

"Bobby…" Red hugged him. "You're so thoughtful."

"He's fucking *awesome*," Bullet snapped. "Makes me look like a cheapskate. Our gift to Bones is watching the kids so he and Sarah can fuck like—"

"Brandon!" Red snapped.

The guys chuckled.

"Sorry," Bullet grumbled. "But we still don't have an answer about the four kids getting presents. There's no *Bullet* down there, and Lila's only a year old. She doesn't know about sharing."

Thinking of the bath-time duck war, Bones said, "I have an idea. We need to teach them to share, but from what I've learned, sometimes you need to distract or trade. They need gifts to trade, right? So we each give the four kids a gift. I've got enough to go around. I'll save the rest for Christmas."

"But what if that doesn't teach them to share? Fin may not like this," Bullet said.

"Before we hand over the presents, we tell them they have to share," Bear suggested. "And that if they want to play with someone else's toy, they have to offer a trade. And no fighting."

They all agreed and clapped each other on the back.

"Seems like you didn't need me at all," Red said as she left the room.

They stowed the extra gifts in the closet and headed downstairs, each armed with four gifts except Bones, who also carried Sarah's.

After a round of "Happy Birthday" and a lesson in sharing, the kids tore through their presents. The next hour was a cacophony of joy as they played with each other's toys.

Bradley shot up to his feet and ran to the backpack they'd brought from Sarah's house, which was lying beside the couch.

He dug around in it and ran over to the couch where Bones and Sarah were sitting.

"Happy birthday, Bones!" Bradley scrambled into his lap and handed Bones a crushed, rolled-up paper. "We made it for you."

"You made me a birthday present?" He glanced at Sarah and mouthed, *Thank you.*

Bradley nodded as Bones unrolled the paper. On it were Bradley's and Lila's handprints in red paint and lots of colorful scribbles, along with four stick figures. Each of the stick figures had long bodies, short arms and legs, and three fingers on each hand. One had scribbles of yellow for hair and a big, almost-round belly.

"That's you, me, Lila, and Mommy." Bradley pointed to the belly. "And that's the baby." Bones was drawn much taller than the others, and Lila was barely as tall as Bradley's waist. *Bones* was written in crooked letters across the top of the paper with a backward S.

"I've never seen a more beautiful drawing. I love it. Thank you," he said, meeting Sarah's proud gaze. "Tomorrow we'll buy a frame and hang it on the wall."

"Yay!" Bradley scrambled off the couch and ran back to the toys.

Sarah leaned closer and whispered, "You don't have to hang it up. He won't notice."

"Oh, we're hanging it up, because *I'll* notice." He reached around the side of the couch for the gift he'd gotten her and set it in her lap. "Is Lila's sweet mama ready for her birthday gift?"

"It's not my birthday," she said with surprise.

"You gave birth to that beautiful girl. That makes it your birthday, too."

"You spoil me," she said. "I have one for you, too, but I wanted to give it to you next Friday, on your actual birthday."

"Sounds perfect. I took off half a day off. I thought we'd pick out a Christmas tree."

"Now, *that* sounds perfect," she said and began opening her present.

Bradley ran over and helped her tear off the paper. "You got a present, too?"

"What's going on over here?" Penny asked, and everyone gathered around as Sarah and Bradley opened her gift. Quincy draped an arm over Penny's shoulder, but she shrugged it off.

"Bones is spoiling me." Sarah lifted the box top, and everyone crowded in for a better look.

She withdrew the photo book Hawk had made using the pictures he'd taken at the wedding. The picture on the cover was of Sarah sitting beneath the floral altar with Lila in her lap and Bradley on his knees, holding her hand. Both of them were looking at Lila, who was gazing over Bradley's shoulder. Bones knew Lila had been looking at him. He remembered every single one of the fifty shots in the book.

Sarah ran her fingers over the lettering above the picture, which read OUR BEAUTIFUL LIFE. She looked at Bones with teary eyes, but she didn't say a word. Her lower lip trembled, and he knew she was trying hard to hold it together.

He squeezed her hand and said, "I know."

"That's the sweetest picture," Gemma said.

"I want one of these when we have kids," Finlay said, cuddling against Bullet's massive body.

Bullet put his arm around her and said, "Anything you want, lollipop."

Sarah took her time admiring each picture, then glancing up

at Bones as everyone made appreciative comments. About halfway through the book she said, "Where are the pictures of you?"

"Keep going," he said, glad she wanted to include him.

The girls *ooh*ed and *aah*ed, telling Sarah how beautiful she and the children were as she flipped from one page to the next, her eyes catching his every few seconds. But all Bones could think about was how he wanted to see her in white, walking down the aisle toward him.

"Hawk wants to use the pictures in a spread in a parenting magazine."

Sarah's eyes widened.

"Really?" Dixie asked. "That's awesome."

Everyone talked at once, congratulating Sarah, but he noticed Sarah was inexplicably silent. He leaned closer and said, "What do you think?"

She looked at the book in her lap, then at him again, and said, "I love that he wants to, but if you wouldn't mind, I'd rather not be in a magazine with the kids. It might bring parts of my past into our lives."

Fuck. He'd been so excited for her, he hadn't thought about the article leading that asshole directly to her. He hated that Lewis could steal this opportunity from her.

"It'd be a shame to skip it," Red said. "This is something your family could have for generations."

"I know," Sarah said apologetically. "It's complicated, but I think it's for the best if we lie low."

"Whatever you need, darlin'," Bones said, and the others murmured in agreement.

Sarah continued looking through the pages, and when she reached the last one, a picture of the four of them standing beneath the altar, she ran her fingers over it with a thoughtful expression.

"Dude, you're a romantic," Truman said. "And here I thought you were all about science and textbooks."

"Maybe I was," Bones said. "But not anymore."

"Look at that, Biggs," Red said quietly. "Don't they make a sweet family?"

A tear trickled from Sarah's eye, and Crystal said, "Damn pregnancy hormones."

Everyone laughed except Sarah. She managed a shaky smile, leaning closer to Bones, and said, "This is...You are..." She wound her arms around his neck and said, "I love it." She stayed there, her breath warming his neck for a long, silent moment before whispering, "And I love you."

Chapter Twenty-One

SARAH KNEW HOW much could change in an hour, much less a day or a week. She shouldn't be surprised that in the eight days since Thanksgiving, her life had seamlessly joined Bones's. She lay in his bed Friday morning, his body spooning hers, his birthday gift in the nightstand drawer, and her babies sleeping just down the hall. As she had most days since seeing Josie, she tried to push away the guilt of being happy when Josie was so very unhappy. She'd seen Tracey, Ebony, and Camille Saturday, when she'd invited them over for lunch. They'd said Josie kept to herself at the shelter. Yesterday Sarah had called the shelter and asked Sunny to see if Josie would talk to her, but as she'd expected, Josie wasn't budging. As much as she wanted to go to the shelter and try again in person, she'd made a promise, and it was more important that Josie and her son were safe than for Sarah to have a chance to understand why Josie wanted nothing to do with her.

"Morning, beautiful." Bones pressed a kiss to her shoulder. Then he rubbed her belly, as he did every morning, and said, "Morning, peanut."

"The peanut is dancing on my bladder, but I didn't want to

wake you up."

"She's feisty, huh?"

Bones was sure this baby was a girl, but Sarah thought it was a boy, because she was carrying it the same way she'd carried Bradley.

He kissed her belly and said, "She's going to rule the world one day."

"*He's* going to be a football player and be nice to *all* the girls, not just the cheerleaders," she said, scooching to the edge of the bed. She felt the heat of his gaze all the way to the bathroom.

When she returned to the bedroom, Bones was lying with his hands clasped behind his head, grinning like a Cheshire cat.

She crawled under the covers beside him and said, "Happy birthday. You look like you already peeked at your birthday present."

"I thought last night *was* my birthday present."

A shudder ran through her with the memory of making love, and as usual, a hint of embarrassment at how bold she'd been dusted her thoughts. But Bones was such a sensual, thoughtful lover, he made her feel sexy and bold, which made her want to explore with him. He encouraged without pushing, led without demanding. She'd splurged on a cute nightie, and after the kids were asleep and Bones was in the shower, she'd lit candles and turned on soft music. He'd come out of the bathroom wearing only a towel, and by the time he'd reached the bed, he was naked, hard, and hungry for her.

He ran his fingers through the ends of her hair and said, "I love how you get a little shy when I say things like that."

"It's hard not to be in the light of day. I talked so naughty last night."

His eyes turned coal black. "I love when you talk naughty and when you play with my nipple piercing with your *teeth*."

"Stop," she said breathily. Just thinking about her mouth on his nipple and the way a little tug of the barbell drove him wild got her wet. "You have to get ready for work, and you'll get me all flustered."

He shifted her onto his lap and said, "I love you flustered."

He brushed his lips over her neck, teasing her with light licks. "Bones," she whispered. He sealed his mouth there, sucking as his hips rose and he began rubbing his enticingly hard shaft against her.

"Bones, you'll be late, and Bradley might catch us."

He groaned. "Late I'm okay with. Little eyes, not so much."

She opened the drawer of the nightstand and took out his birthday gift. They'd decided not to celebrate his and Lila's birthdays again so as not to confuse the kids. She was glad she'd waited to give Bones his present, though. It was nice to do it while they were alone. She pressed the gift to her chest and said, "I'm not very good at gifts."

"You're excellent at gifts." He ran his hand up her thigh.

She rolled her eyes. "I mean real gifts."

"That was as real as it gets, darlin'."

"Okay, well, maybe so. I hope you like it."

"I already love it." He kissed her, and then he unwrapped the brown leather journal she'd bought him. His eyes flicked to hers as he opened it, and then he read the first page aloud. "The Adventures of Thomas aka Edison and Wayne aka Bones." He looked at her again with a curious smile. "Oh, sweet darlin', what have you done?"

Thanksgiving night, after they'd made love, as they'd lain tangled together, he'd told her about how guilty he'd felt after

Thomas died. How Thomas had gotten pneumonia in the days after they'd snuck out, and he'd never forgiven himself. He said that he knew Thomas's days had been numbered anyway, but he'd sounded so sad, she'd wanted to replace those thoughts with better ones, the same way he'd helped her with her memories. She'd planned on giving him the leather journal, and over the next few days, she'd added this story.

"I know it's a little silly, and I'm not a very good writer, but I wanted you to have a happy ending with Thomas, and this was the only way I could do it."

He embraced her and said, "God, I love you. I feel like I've been waiting my whole life to meet you."

Don't cry. Don't cry. Don't cry.

She'd kept from crying for so many years—at first to remain strong for herself and later to be strong for her children—she had a feeling the tears had been multiplying inside of her forever, and she finally felt comfortable and safe enough to let them fall.

She shifted off his lap, and he put an arm around her, keeping her plastered to his side as he read the story. She'd written a happy tale about an adventure at sea, where Bones and Thomas sailed to far-off lands and explored like little boys do. They collected rocks, captured lizards (named them and then set them free), slept under the stars, and talked to all the strangers they passed on dry land, sharing their adventures. They called each other by their nicknames, and when they sailed back to Peaceful Harbor they left thousands of people whose lives they'd touched in their wake. They knew the legend of Edison and Bones would live on forever. When they got back to the harbor, they lit a bonfire on the beach, did a secret handshake, and said their goodbyes. Thomas floated up to a big boat in the sky, and every day he sprinkled a little miracle dust over Bones, so every miracle he performed had a little piece of Thomas in it.

When he finished reading, he pulled her onto his lap again, embracing her, with his head resting on her chest. He didn't say a word, but just as things had been at their closest moments, he didn't have to. His loving embrace, and the goodness that was Bones Whiskey, was louder than words could ever be.

LATER THAT AFTERNOON, they bundled up against the cold November air and went to a local Christmas tree farm. Bradley zoomed around the trees, pretending to be king of the forest, while Lila toddled after him at a turtle's pace. When she got too far behind, she plopped down on her bottom and either chased him on all fours, or gave up in favor of something she found in the grass to play with. Bones must have taken a hundred pictures and stolen even more kisses.

"Did you have Christmas trees in your house as a kid?" Bones asked as he cut down a tree.

"Yes, but they were usually cut down from the woods so my father didn't have to pay for them." She had made a point of decorating a tree for her children each holiday, but because her relationship with Lewis had deteriorated, it was never a happy time. And like everything with Bones, *this* was different. This was another celebration of family. Of *her* family.

Our family?

"Presents?" he asked.

"Mm-hm," she said, mulling over how much they already felt like a real family. "A few. It was the one time of year my parents tried to pretend we weren't miserable. I remember feeling like I held my breath all year, and that was the one day I could breathe."

As the tree toppled to the ground, he said, "I'm glad they made the effort."

"Me too. But I was always waiting for that shoe to drop."

Bones put the saw down and wrapped his arms around her. "There will be no more shoes dropping." He put his mouth beside her ear, and in the rich, seductive voice that made her insides turn to liquid heat, he said, "Unless we're alone and those shoes are followed by every stitch of your clothing and leads to my mouth on your sweet, sexy body."

He always gave her the best distractions.

By the time they cut down trees for each of their houses, since they were staying at both, the kids were pink cheeked and exhausted. They napped on the way to her house and remained asleep as Bones put up the Christmas tree. Scott was working, so they decided to wait until tomorrow to decorate their tree.

After the kids got up, they went to Bones's house and set up the tree there. Bones had two boxes of ornaments. One box contained what looked like an assortment of ornaments he used every year, including one wrapped in tissue paper, which turned out to be an ornament Kennedy had made for him. It was a picture of Kennedy with her arm around Tinkerbell. She'd glued fabric trim on a cardboard frame and written *To Uncle Boney, Love Kennedy* on the back.

"We should make those with the kids for our trees," Bones said as he strung colored lights around the tree.

He opened the second box, revealing about a dozen child-safe ornaments made from plastic and rubber, with oversized plastic hangers that were perfect for clumsy little fingers. Sarah and Bones hung the breakable ornaments up high, allowing the kids to hang theirs wherever they wanted, with help of course. The kids hung ornaments all along the bottom with just a few higher, leaving gaping holes in their decorations.

Sarah had never seen a more beautiful tree.

They turned off the overhead lights and plugged in the tree lights. Bradley and Lila clapped.

"We did that!" Bradley hollered, pride brimming in his eyes.

"We sure did, buddy," Bones said as he scooped Lila into his arms. "Let's get a picture."

He knelt in front of the tree. With Lila sitting on his lap, Sarah kneeling beside him, and Bradley standing in front of them, Bones held out the camera and said, "Say 'fuzzy pickle.'"

Bradley looked away as Bones took the picture, so he took another. Lila sneezed, messing up that shot. After several tries, they ended up laughing and making funny faces as they took pictures. Even Lila wrinkled her nose, but mostly she just giggled. It was a perfect depiction of their day, and one Sarah would never forget.

After dinner, they gave the kids baths, and Bones made a fire in the fireplace as Sarah made popcorn. They pulled out the sofa bed in the living room and cuddled under blankets to watch *Cars*. The kids were so worn out, they fell asleep after only a few minutes. Lying with her babies asleep between them, the lights of the tree glittering around them and the warmth of the fire casting dancing shadows across the floor, Sarah thought she should be the happiest woman on earth. But her mind traveled back to Josie, filling her with the sense of being suspended between two worlds, wanting to be part of both of them and knowing she might never be part of one.

"Hey," Bones whispered. "Hawk called when you were making popcorn. I know you're worried about doing it, but before I tell him no, I thought I should ask again. Are you sure you don't want to do the spread in the magazine?"

"I really want to, for the kids' sake, but I can't. What if my background comes out? The dancing? Lewis?" She saw disappointment *and* understanding in his eyes, both of which hurt, because she knew he wasn't disappointed *in* her. He was disappointed *for* her. "And it might give Josie the wrong impression. She already thinks I have a perfect life."

"You could take care of Lewis by getting those papers signed, and you know, maybe it'll prove to be inspirational for Josie, once she knows you and all you've been through. You did what you had to do to survive, and it allowed you to be where you are right now. Where *we* are right now."

"I know, but everything I went through is embarrassing."

"I understand." He looked down at the kids, who were fast asleep, and said, "If you're really worried someone might recognize you, wouldn't you rather the kids heard it from you than a stranger? You might broach the subject with them when they're old enough. They'd be proud of how strong you were."

"I didn't think about that. I'm kind of going on the hope that it'll never come up."

"And maybe it won't," he said supportively. "But do you really want to live a veiled life with your kids? I'm not saying tell them you stripped, but when they're older, they'll go through hard times. All kids do. It might be better that they know you did, too, and how you handled it, what you learned from it. They'll never be in the position of being alone like you were. Even if something happens to me, the friends you've made are friends for life. I hope you know that. And there are lessons the kids can learn from what you've been through. Lessons about how to love, being resilient, and believing in yourself."

Everything he said resonated as true, but agreeing and actually taking those steps were very far apart. "It's so hard to know what's right."

"Have you talked to a therapist? I know a few good ones who might be able to help you think things through."

"Maybe at some point I'll do that."

"Someone who's not romantically involved with you might see things differently than I do, and that might help. Maybe you can talk about Josie, too. I know you need to mend things with her to be happy. I see the distant look in your eyes when things are really good. I might be reading you wrong, but that's happened more often since you saw her. We won't give up, but we have to accept that it might take months, or longer, before Josie is willing to talk. As hard as it is, maybe we need to find a way to accept that whatever comes of it will have to be on her terms, when she's ready."

"I know I have to. I'm trying, and it's a little easier than it was a week ago, but it still feels like a black hole inside me that nothing else will ever completely fill."

"I know, darlin'. I wish I could fix it."

"It's not fair to you or the kids that thoughts of Lewis or Josie pry me away the way they do."

"We can handle it," Bones said. "There's nothing we can't get through together."

She believed that with her whole heart. But how could he know that when she was the one keeping herself tangled up in this web of fear and he was the one offering her an out, at least with Lewis.

Lewis. The rat bastard who could come back at any time and demand to be involved in the kids' lives. The drug-addicted asshole who had done horrible things to her. Why was he still controlling her?

She glanced at her babies and knew what she had to do as clearly as she'd known the right thing had been to walk out of her parents' house and never go back. "If I agree to try to get Lewis to sign those papers, how would we do that?"

"I'll go see him, talk to him, *show him* the right thing to do."

The fierceness in his voice told her he'd do whatever it took, but she knew Lewis. Or at least she knew the man he'd been when she'd finally left. He was unstable and ornery.

"He won't talk to you," she said shakily. "I'm sure of it."

"I won't leave until he does."

"No, Bones. That would only make it worse. He can't sign papers under duress; they won't hold up in court. Even I know that." She'd googled terminating parental rights, and she knew the papers needed to be notarized and that if it wasn't voluntary the courts might not even approve it. Even if it was voluntary, there was a chance the courts would deny it. But she had a feeling with the rape and drugs, they had a solid enough case to protect her children. "It has to be me."

"No way. You're not going anywhere near him." His jaw clenched so tight, she thought he might hurt himself.

"He'll never do it for you, and he might not do it for me, but it's the best chance I have."

"No, Sarah," he said in a vehement whisper.

"Bones, you were right," she said just as firmly. "He can come back at any time, and I'm sick of being stuck and worrying about worse-case scenarios. I've already lived through them. I don't want to be shackled by them forever. It's bad enough that I have to accept the possibility that I might have already lost my sister. I'm not losing my kids to *him*." As she said the words, they became even more important. She needed to do this, as much for herself as for the children.

She needed to stand up to Lewis.

"I'm doing it, Bones. For once in my life, I refuse to run away. So let's do whatever's necessary to get the papers ready, and then we'll go together. You can even bring your brothers if you want to."

His eyes narrowed. "I don't need to bring *anyone* else to keep you safe. If he goes near you, he's a dead man."

Chapter Twenty-Two

OVER THE NEXT week, Bones and Sarah had the papers drawn up for Lewis to sign, and Sarah tried to wrap her head around the fact that they were *really* going to confront Lewis. She'd talked to Tracey about it, and Tracey had called her brave *and* stupid. Sarah agreed, but she chose to cling to the *brave* part. Scott wanted to come with them, but on some undefinable level, he was a reminder of how Sarah had failed Josie. Maybe it was the fact that it had always been the three of them together when they were growing up. She couldn't put her finger on it and it didn't lessen her relationship with Scott, but when she thought about her childhood, she felt weaker, and today she needed strength. Today she needed to be *impenetrable*.

As they drove down the rural Baltimore roads, she eyed the folder with the termination papers on the seat. The plan was to have him sign them at the bank that was ten minutes away. They'd already spoken to a manager, and there was a notary ready and waiting. Her heart pounded harder with each passing landmark—the red mailbox at the end of the street, the road that led to an abandoned farmhouse, and the woods that lined the long road that led to Lewis's house—and she knew she'd made the right choice. Bones made her feel strong, and being in his massive black truck with the emblem of the Dark Knights on the back made her feel even tougher.

Today I am the Pregnant Woman of Steel.

She glanced at Bones. He was always tough, but nothing could have prepared her for the formidable man sitting beside her. An aura of darkness surrounded him, as if a hurricane of rage was trapped beneath all that black leather and denim. His dark eyes were narrow and supremely focused on the road before them, but she knew him well enough to realize he was strategizing, playing out every possible outcome in that brilliant mind of his. His large hands gripped the steering wheel so tight his biceps pushed against his black leather sleeves. He seemed more powerful than life itself. *An unstoppable force.* Even more commanding than last night, when he'd been pacing like a caged animal, memorizing the layout of Lewis's house, asking about weapons he kept, what he was like when he wasn't high and when he was blitzed out of his mind. He asked about his friends, habits, and a litany of other questions he'd already asked her. But she knew that was all part of his making certain he had his bases covered—and hers, by asking for the umpteenth time if she was sure she wanted to do this.

She wasn't backing down.

Even if she felt like her heart was hammering so hard it would fly out of her chest.

As they passed the dense woods leading up to his property, she said, "It's after all these bushes and just before the big tree."

Bones reached for her hand, squeezing it as he said, "If you change your mind—"

"I won't. I need to do this," she snapped.

He turned down the driveway, still holding her hand, and

took his foot off the gas, slowing as he scanned the grounds. The grass was all but dead and littered with dried leaves. The trees looked like angry skeletons, dark and withered, with spiky branches and moss growing up the trunks. Sarah wrapped her arms around her belly as the dingy yellow rambler came into view, and bad memories slammed into her. Panic flooded her chest, but she forced herself to breathe through it.

He couldn't hurt her. Not anymore.

Her instinct was to look away from the house that had enticed her with hope and slaughtered her with hurt, but she forced herself to look at it, to *remember.* The first time she'd seen his house, she'd been so elated by Lewis's attention, she'd failed to notice the most obvious things, like dead bushes beneath the front windows and the darkly tinged areas where there once were shutters. She'd asked Lewis if they could replace them, but like everything else, his promises went unkept.

The house looked like it was in a state of dying, just as she'd been. She stared at it, willing herself to finally face *all* of it—her stupidity as a young girl and her bravery on the day she'd left. She remembered the smell of drugs, sweat, and desolation the last night, the night of the party. The fear that had swamped her when Lewis had opened the bedroom door where she was hiding out with the babies. The anger that had brewed hot as fire as she'd collected her children, cash, and keys, the night she'd left and stood out front tempted to burn down the house with him and his monsters inside it. Would they have woken up and come after her, or would it have ended her nightmare forever?

It didn't matter, because she wasn't capable of that kind of evil.

"Three cars. They his?"

Bones's voice jerked Sarah from her thoughts, and she noticed three old cars parked out front. The back window of one was patched with cardboard and duct tape. The other two were indistinct.

"I don't recognize them," she said. Her voice sounded shaky and unfamiliar.

Bones parked behind the vehicles and set those serious eyes on her. They softened a tad as he reached over and caressed her cheek. She closed her eyes for a second, soaking in his love. When she opened them again, Bones lowered his hand to her belly, and his face grew serious.

"You said he doesn't have guns in the house, right?"

"No," she said, and then she realized it had been months since she'd left. "At least he didn't when I lived there. He never needed them. He lorded the kids over my head."

His features hardened. "I will *never* let him near you. Do you hear me, Sarah? No matter what he does, I'm your shield, your firepower. It doesn't matter who or how many guys are in that house. I will take them all down to protect you. But you need to promise me something."

She swallowed hard, unable to nod for the fear gripping her.

"I'm leaving the keys in the ignition. If you get scared or things get out of hand, I want you to get in the truck and drive away. Do you hear me?"

"I'm not leaving you."

"I'll be fine. Those secrets I haven't told you about? They're about this kind of stuff. Getting assholes to do what's right, protecting women and children. I'm a Dark Knight. I've been trained for this shit since I was a kid, and I've put it to use more times than I care to admit."

He pressed his lips to hers in a kiss so tender she wondered if she'd dreamed it after his vehement declaration.

"I've never lost a battle, darlin'. I'm not about to lose the war."

Oh. Shit.

Bones got out of the truck, and the voice in her head screamed, *Fuck this! Go home and hope you never have to see his ugly face again.* She mulled over how to back out, and she knew Bones would support her decision.

He opened the door with a warning in his eyes. "You should drive away. Let me deal with this and come get me when it's over. I'll text you."

"Fuck that." She climbed from the truck, having no idea where her strength was coming from, and said, "That asshole *raped* me. He threatened my *children*. I'm going to tell him exactly what I think of him, and he damn well better sign those papers."

DAMN. MY GIRL'S got fire inside her. Bones was so fucking proud of Sarah, but her rapist was behind that door, and neither of them knew what would happen when their eyes met.

He pushed that pride aside to lavish on her later, when she was safely away from this hellhole, and said, "Stay behind me. I love you, and I believe in you, but I want you a safe distance from him, got it?"

Sarah nodded, eyes wide, some of the courage draining from her face.

Fuck. He hated this shit when he did it for strangers. Doing it for Sarah made him want to break the fucking door down and maul the bastard. But that wouldn't get the papers signed.

As he approached the rickety step that led to the front door, rock music blared from inside the house. Sarah's hands were wrapped around her belly, her face a glowering mix of rage and fear. The urge to haul her beautiful ass into the truck and demand she leave was so strong, Bones had to turn away as he said, "Stay there."

He'd spoken to a therapist friend of his about telling Sarah she couldn't go with him, but he'd warned against it. His buddy said *if* Bones could assure her safety, she needed this opportunity to prove to herself—not to Bones or to Lewis—that she could stand up for herself. This was her battle even more than it was theirs.

He got that.

And he fucking hated it.

He filled his lungs and rolled his shoulders back, stretching his neck to either side, loose and ready for whatever went down. With one last glance at his girl, who nodded, suddenly exuding the confidence of Al Capone running a job, he rapped twice on the door—*hard.* A few seconds later he did it again.

The door swung open, and a shadow of the man Bones had seen online when he'd googled the asshole stood before him, roughly five ten, cheeks sunken, and skin sallow. Stringy dark hair hung over cold, dead eyes, and the identifier Bones was watching for—a birthmark on the left side of his jaw, gave him all the confirmation he needed. Bones looked past him, to two half-dressed, drugged-out women on the couch. The thought of Sarah and her children in that house, with that fucked-up piece of shit, sent him barreling forward.

"Who the fuck are you?" Lewis asked.

"Someone you don't want to know," Bones seethed.

Lewis's gaze moved over Bones's shoulder to Sarah. A sardonic grin slid into place. "Look who came crawling back for more. What'd you do? Get yourself knocked up the minute you left?"

Bones grabbed him by the collar and lifted him off his feet, slamming his back against the door. "You don't look at her. You look at me, asshole, and we won't have any trouble. But you look at her, and I'll put your fucking head through the wall."

Bones caught movement out of the corner of his eye. One of the women on the couch reached for something on the table. "Don't move an inch or he's dead," he seethed.

She sank back against the cushions.

He sensed Sarah coming closer and said, "Sarah, stay back."

Lewis struggled, "What the fuck, dude? You knocked her up and now you don't want her?"

Bones loosened his grip enough for Lewis to slide an inch forward. Then he crashed the back of his head into the door. While Lewis tried to blink his vision clear, Bones spoke through gritted teeth. "You don't talk. You listen." He waited for a beat, giving Sarah a chance to say her piece, and when she didn't, he said, "We're here for one reason. You're going to sign papers terminating your parental rights, and then you're never going to think about Sarah or her children again."

Lewis scoffed. "That's what you want? The way I see it, those dipshits are worth at least ten grand a piece."

"Motherfucker—" Bones drew back to land a punch.

"Wait!"

Bones stilled at Sarah's plea, his knuckles digging into Lewis's chest. It took everything he had not to break the asshole's jaw. Lewis trembled despite his cocky attitude. His eyes shifted, and Bones shifted with them, blocking his view of Sarah.

"Eyes on me, assfuck."

"You want *money*?" Sarah yelled. "You *spent* my savings. You *sold* my car. You *stole* my dignity. You had hundreds of chances to do the right thing, to be someone other than the person your father was, and you fucked it up. Now you want to *sell* your children? Their *only* chance at a happy life is without you in it."

"Ten grand each," Lewis said, eyes on Bones.

"You're not getting a penny, you son of a bitch," Sarah hollered, and Bones heard the tears in her voice. "I thought you might do one decent thing in your pitiful life, but I guess not."

"I did the decent thing. I took your whoring ass in."

The crack that sounded when Bones's fist landed on his jaw was drowned out by the smack of Lewis's head against the door and the women screaming.

Blood poured from Lewis's mouth as he lifted his head, his eyes rolling as he said, "Oh, you didn't know she spread her legs for every Tom, Dick, or Harry who had a few bucks? That's right. She sold herself for—"

His words were lost in a flurry of punches. Blinded by rage, Bones didn't think, feel, or *care* as he landed one punch after another until Lewis lay limp and bloody on the living room floor and the women's screams broke through his fury. As he cocked his fist for another hit, he realized he couldn't hear Sarah and forced himself upright and out the door.

He spotted her hurrying down the driveway with Bullet walking beside her. *Fuck.* He jumped into the truck and sped toward them, grinding his teeth, wondering how the hell Bullet had found out what was going down.

He slammed the truck into park and jumped out.

"I'll take care of that piece of shit," Bullet ground out. "Get your girl home, but, man, I think she needs some space."

Bullet took off toward the house, and Bones put an arm around Sarah, but she shrugged him off. "Sarah, baby, get in the truck."

She shook her head, tears streaming down her cheeks.

"Sarah, get in, please. What he said doesn't matter."

She opened her mouth to speak, but sobs burst out. He gathered her in his arms, and this time she didn't pull away. He guided her into the passenger seat and buckled her in. Then he got them the hell out of there.

When they hit the main road, he reached for Sarah's hand, but she shrank away from him, huddling against the door. He spotted Bullet's motorcycle parked in the bushes. *Fucking Bullet. How'd I miss seeing his bike on the way in?*

He didn't have time to worry about that. He needed to get through to Sarah. He thought distance would help her calm down, but even twenty minutes out, as they hit the highway, she was still sobbing.

"Sarah, darlin', please don't let that asshole's words come between us. There is *nothing* that will change how I feel about you."

She didn't look at him as she shook her head.

"Sarah—"

"Don't. *Please,*" she choked out. "I can't do this right now. I'm sorry, but I just *can't.* I need to be alone with my babies. Please just take me home."

He didn't know if Sarah was upset with him for suggesting this fucking debacle, hurt over what that son of a bitch had said about her, or appalled at how he'd lost it with Lewis. Bones had never felt such all-consuming rage in his life. He'd been so fueled by hatred and hungry for blood, had it not been for the frightened screams of the drugged-out women on the couch, he wasn't sure he would have stopped.

He'd lost his mind.

He just hoped he hadn't also lost Sarah.

Chapter Twenty-Three

SARAH RAN THROUGH the front door, remembered the kids were asleep, and closed it as quietly as she could, a barrier between her and all that had happened—a barrier between her and Bones. She pressed her hands flat against the door. Her forehead touched the cool wood as tears poured down her cheeks. She closed her eyes against them, but the pain of Lewis's accusation cut too deep.

"Sarah?" Scott said from behind her, bringing more tears.

She gasped to try to break free from the gut-wrenching anguish, but it just made her cry harder. Scott reached for her, but she shrugged away and ducked her head in a futile effort to hide her sobs.

"Don't. I'm sorry, but I can't talk right now." *I need my babies.* She stumbled shakily down the hall, the word *why* repeating in her mind like a plea.

"What happened?"

Still unable to face him, she said, "The other shoe dropped."

"I'm calling Bones," Scott said.

Sarah spun around and said, "Don't. This is *my* mess, not his. Just…just give me time. Please, Scott."

She walked into the kids' room and closed the door, needing to be near them even if they were sleeping. She leaned back against the door and closed her eyes. If only she'd told Bones the truth, then she wouldn't be in this mess. But how could she tell him? She hadn't even told Reagan or Scott.

How much pain and mortification could one person survive?

She tried to slip into mommy mode, her go-to strength builder, but fuck…

She wasn't sure she could do it.

She ground her teeth together and let her head fall back. *Please give me strength. Please.* She didn't even know what or who she was asking. How could there be a higher power when *this* had happened?

There was no one else to rely on. She'd known it forever. If she was going to survive, it had to come from within. She wiped her eyes, telling herself she could get through this even if she wasn't sure how.

She went to the crib, where Lila was fast asleep, her hedgehog lying by her legs. Sarah's heart ached as she reached into the crib and stroked her baby's cheek. *I'll never let you be in the position to deal with this type of thing. I'll never let anyone hurt you.*

Bones's voice ran firmly through her mind—*I will never let him near you. Do you hear me, Sarah? No matter what he does, I'm your shield, your firepower*—bringing more tears.

He kept his promise. He always kept his promises.

How could he ever look at her the same again? She knew she'd never look at him the same. She'd had no idea he was capable of the rage he'd given in to tonight.

For me.

And yet somehow when Bones had come for her after she'd fled to try to escape the humiliation and pain of Lewis's verbal attack, Bones had been calm and protective, not angry or uncontrollable, despite the blood on his clothing and hands and his corded muscles. He'd *protected* her, put himself in danger *for* her, without a lick of hesitation or fear. Knowing what he was capable of should scare Sarah, but it didn't. She knew how good Bones was at his core. Truth be told, she'd felt brave not only *because* of his belief in her but because of his will and desire to protect her. And because of the sheer power he so expertly harnessed, the power she'd caught glimpses of over the past few weeks each and every time they'd talked about Lewis and her parents.

She pulled the blanket over Lila and went to the bed where her little man slept clutching the toy stethoscope from the doctor kit Bones had given him at Lila's birthday celebration. She sank down to the edge of the bed, praying Bradley would stay as innocent and good-natured as he was now and hoping his father's blood wouldn't ruin him. She lay down beside him and told herself that Scott had turned out wonderful, so Bradley could, too. She thought of Josie and wondered what she was like as a mother, as a person. Did she give in to anger like their parents did? Did she demean her son? She seemed protective, but what if she'd picked up their parents' nastiness and tempers and she didn't want anything to do with Sarah or Scott because she didn't want them to know?

She closed her eyes to try to stave off more tears. Bones's compassionate gaze stared back at her through the darkness. *Please don't let that asshole's words come between us. There is nothing that will change how I feel about you.*

Lewis *was* an asshole. A lying, raping, *pimp* of an asshole.

But Bones wasn't, and he deserved to know the truth.

She opened her eyes, looking at her little boy. Was Bones right? Should she tell them about the ugliness of her past when they got older? How could she look into their trusting eyes and burst their bubble about who they thought she was?

How can I live a lie with them?

Life isn't fair.

And there it was, the thing she'd been trying to escape forever. *Self-pity.* Didn't she deserve some modicum of it? Hadn't she been through enough? When, if ever, would this nightmare end?

Her phone vibrated in her pocket. Knowing it would be a text from Bones, she pulled it out and read the message. *I'm sorry if I scared you. Please talk to me.*

Guilt and pain moved through her like a razor's edge.

Another text bubble popped up. *I meant what I said. Nothing will change my love for you.*

She sat up, staring at the screen, wanting desperately to send him a message, but what could she say? *You'll never look at me the same until you know the truth?* There was too much to type, but she knew what she had to do. With another deep inhalation—and another, because her lungs simply refused to fill—she kissed her babies one last time and crossed the hall to her bedroom.

She grabbed a pen and the notebook with *Let your dreams be bigger than your fears* on the front, and then she propped pillows up by the headboard and settled in, putting pen to paper.

Figuring out where to start was easy.

I came into this world Sarah Marie Beckley. My mother once said I was seven pounds, two ounces of trouble. I think from her perspective it was the truth, because babies are trouble. They're messy, noisy, and they sure don't listen. But you know how they say one person's nightmare is another's dream? What my parents saw as trouble, I see as the most glorious aspects of being a baby, seeing and doing things for the first time and relying on others to keep them alive, safe, and happy, to teach them about life and love, loss, and grief. I don't think my parents were meant to have children. Unfortunately, they did, and they taught me things like how not to treat a child and that the human spirit can overcome anything—even if others try their hardest to beat them down.

She wrote for hours, pouring the details of her life onto the pages. The loathsomeness of stripping and the joy she got from talking with the other girls in the back room between dances. The girls who knew what it meant to be upset that a guy pawed at her even if she was showing off her body. Because stripping *was* a choice, but being manhandled wasn't.

She wrote about the fear she tried so hard to hide every day when she was out in public and the way she used to hide her face in the pillow at night in her parents' house so they wouldn't hear her crying. The way she went to bed every night as a kid praying her parents would wake up to be better people and that they wouldn't kill Scott in the process. She detailed her hunt for Josie and how empty she felt at every turn, along with her childlike excitement at connecting with Lewis, how that connection had withered and frayed. She described her insurmountable joy at the birth of her babies. She'd never known it was possible to love someone so deeply and so instantly. She didn't leave out anything, writing about how things deteriorated with Lewis and how she'd spent hours trying to plot an escape with the children. She'd never felt as helpless as she had during those painful months.

She wrote about how she didn't know until too late that she'd only scratched the surface of helplessness.

Page after miserable page came to life as she wrote about the awful night she'd finally left Lewis, revealing what the murky depths of helplessness really looked like. Her phone vibrated a few times, but she ignored it, needing to get this out once and for all.

> *I remember the noise of the party, the smell of drugs and sweat, and how hard I prayed for the night to end because I couldn't take it anymore. I was done. Even if I had to walk all the way to town, I was leaving the second they passed out or left the house. When the noise quieted, hope swelled inside me that maybe they'd left or were getting ready to leave. The kids were asleep, and I was pacing in their bedroom, thinking of the things I wanted to grab from our bedroom, planning our final escape. Then Lewis opened the bedroom door, and I thought he was going to tell me he was leaving, because he had this demonic grin on his face. And I was happy, so very happy I think I might have smiled, too. And then he said he needed me, and I thought he meant sexually, so I refused. I said I was sick and needed to stay with the kids. That's when three guys appeared behind him. They were gross, sweaty, unshaven, and dirty. Everything changed in an instant. He grabbed my arm and yanked me from the room. I struggled, and he said if I wanted to see my kids again, I'd do what he said. There was no choice in my mind. They were my babies.*

Tears fell onto the page, and she leaned back so they wouldn't drip on the ink, but she didn't—*couldn't*—stop writing.

> *He threw me into the bedroom and told me to take my pants off. I was numb, scared, in shock. And I was angry. So angry I was crying and fighting even though he'd threatened the kids. Everything happened so fast after that. He tore off my pants as another guy held me still, and then I was on the bed, and he demanded money from each of them. He tossed it on the dresser and told them they couldn't fuck me unless they used condoms because he didn't want another fucking mouth to feed. I was pleading, cursing, trying to get away, but they were big and it was awful, and I finally closed my eyes and told myself to take it so it would end, so I could get the kids to safety. The whole thing didn't last long. Or maybe it did. I don't know. It felt like hours and a blink at the same time. I think I blacked out or made myself detach from the event. Afterward, I hurt and I was afraid to move. I didn't know if this was it. If this was where my life would end, or who else would walk through that door and do horrible things to me. And I lay there waiting in the empty room for so long. And then something inside me snapped. I could feel it, like one of those light sticks that are lifeless until you crack something inside them. I wasn't going to die by his hand, and I sure as hell wasn't going to let him go near my babies ever again. I ran into the kids' bedroom. I still remember those pigs laughing and drinking in the living room as I pushed a dresser in front of the bedroom door. And then I waited for silence, only this time I wasn't numb or scared. I was ready. When there had been no noise for a long stretch of time, I cracked open the*

bedroom door and heard snoring. I tiptoed out, and they were all asleep. I ran into the bedroom where they'd raped me and got the cash from the dresser. I grabbed the first set of keys I found and more cash from the coffee table. Then I propped open the front door so I wouldn't struggle with it, grabbed my kids, and left.

She was breathing so hard, her writing was almost illegible, but she didn't care. She was getting the truth out, and she felt the weight of her secret easing from her soul. It felt so good, she continued writing about how she'd thought about burning the house down, but she wasn't a whore and she wasn't a killer. She wrote about the drive with the kids seat belted into the back seat, because she'd taken some guy's car—not Lewis's—and she had no car seats.

Writing about the aftermath was as uplifting as it was scary. Finding Scott—and then nearly losing him and the kids—took up many pages of tears. The words on the page blurred as she wrote about Josie showing up at the hospital, how they'd stared silently at each other for a full minute or two before either said a word. How disconnected she'd felt from the girl with whom she'd once shared everything, and how, when Josie walked out of the hospital, Sarah was thrown right back to years earlier, to the day she'd realized Josie was really gone.

As dawn broke, she detailed her feelings from the first time she'd seen Bones in his white lab coat, with devastatingly compassionate eyes and a smile that made her feel inexplicably safe. The way he'd taken her hand, listening without judgment and comforting her while she wept. And how he'd continued visiting, brightening and bringing hope to those awful, scary days when her family lay in hospital beds, and after, when he'd come by the house with treats for the kids. She went on to write about how it felt to have him by her side when they were out with everyone before they started dating. He was always there with them, helping with the babies, caring about them and her in ways no one ever had.

And then she wrote about what Bones had witnessed, because some things were easier to write than to say out loud.

> *When Lewis said those awful things, my first thought wasn't that they were ugly lies. It was that he'd said them in front of you. I know what he said will never be forgotten. Ugliness and lies have a way of staining our minds the way truths don't need to. When I left with my children, I wanted to leave everything about that awful night behind. That's why I didn't tell you what he'd done to me. I talk about people shedding their skin, and I usually relate it to them revealing their hidden monsters. When I left Lewis, I shed mine, but in my case, I was shedding the horribleness of those monsters.*
>
> *I've done a lot of things I'm not proud of in my life, but I have never sold my body. And I have never loved a man the way I love you. I hope you can forgive me.*

She leaned back, catching a glimpse of the clock. *5:58.*

She closed her eyes for long enough to take a few deep breaths. She couldn't believe she'd gotten it all out, every ugly bit of her life. Now it was time to see if she could save the beautiful parts.

She picked up her phone, seeing messages from Bones but not taking the time to read them. She called him instead, and he answered on the first ring.

"Sarah," he said anxiously.

"I'm sorry—"

"Just tell me you're okay."

She closed her eyes against the burn of tears. "I'm not okay yet, but I'm trying to get there. If you're willing, I'd really like to see you."

"Open your front door, darlin'."

THE DOOR OPENED, and Sarah stood in the same clothes she'd worn last night, holding one of the notebooks he'd given her. Her nose was pink, her cheeks puffy. Dark crescents underscored bloodshot, damp eyes. When she opened her mouth to speak, tears tumbled down her cheeks. Bones's chest constricted as he stepped inside and wrapped his arms around her.

"I'm sorry," she choked out.

"No, darlin'. I'm sorry for suggesting we go, for losing my cool, and for causing you pain."

Bullet's strong arms circled them, startling Bones, though it shouldn't have. Bullet had shown up last night about forty minutes after Sarah had gone inside, and he'd sat vigil with Bones the entire night.

Bullet released them and turned to leave.

"Hey, B?" Bones called after him.

Bullet glanced over his shoulder, his coal-black eyes filled with concern.

"Thank you," Bones said.

Bullet nodded, and Bones watched him leave, still embracing Sarah. He didn't want to let go. "I didn't tell him anything," he reassured her. "He knew I had spoken to Court—*Charlie*—

at a club meeting, and he's been watching me ever since. He did some nosing around, figured things out, and got there hours before we did to see what we were up against. I'm sorry. You can take the soldier out of the military, but I don't think it ever really leaves them."

She looked up at him with wet eyes and said, "Don't apologize for being loved so much. I was so scared yesterday. I didn't know who was in the house or what would happen to you, and when he showed up, I was glad he was there, even though I was too much of a mess to show it."

"Talk to me, baby. Please."

"I can't." She shook her head, and his heart hit the floor. She handed him the notebook and said, "It's too hard to say, but it's all in here. Thanks to you, my dreams are bigger than my fears."

"I don't want to leave, Sarah. Not like this."

"That's good, because I really need you to hold me. Think you can read and hold me at the same time?"

Bones took off his boots and jacket, and they went to the bedroom. The sight of Sarah's bed, still made from the morning before, her pillows propped up at the head, made him ache even more. He got situated, and then she crawled onto the mattress. Lying perpendicular to his body, she rested her head on his stomach and wrapped her arms around him.

"Can you read like this?" she asked sweetly.

"Of course."

He ran his fingers through her hair, and she sighed sleepily, dozing off within minutes. Bones steeled himself for whatever lay inside the notebook. He leaned forward, pressed a kiss to her forehead, and whispered, "It doesn't matter what this says. Nothing will change my feelings for you."

More than an hour later Bones heard Bradley say something, and Lila babbled in response. He pried his eyes from the notebook, unashamed of his tears, as Scott peered into Sarah's bedroom, taking in his sister sleeping with her arms still locked around Bones.

"You okay?" Scott asked.

"We will be," Bones said.

"I've got the kids. You just take care of Sarah." Scott closed the door.

Bones had texted Scott last night to say he was out front and wasn't leaving. Scott had said Sarah was a mess, to which Bones had responded that it was to be expected. He didn't tell Scott why; he just said they'd deal with it in time and to give her space if she needed it.

Bones continued reading. The more he read, the harder it became to see the words and to accept that his precious Sarah had endured such violence.

> *I've done a lot of things I'm not proud of in my life, but I have never sold my body. And I have never loved a man the way I love you. I hope you can forgive me.*

He pressed another kiss to her forehead, tears slipping from his eyes. Needing to be closer, to let her *feel* his love, he moved behind her. She shimmied closer, nestling against the confines of his body, and he curled around her.

For the second time in his life, he struggled with doing the right thing. Every iota of his being wanted to kill Lewis slowly and painfully and then track down each of the motherfuckers who had hurt Sarah and torture them until they breathed their last breath.

Sarah whimpered in her sleep, and he held her tighter.

He should have forced that asshole to sign the papers. He'd gotten so lost in rage, the papers had totally slipped his mind. But that was a worry for another day.

All that mattered was that Sarah was there with him. *Safe.* And nobody would ever hurt her again.

Epilogue

"I THINK I see a penis." Dixie squinted at the framed image of Sarah's sonogram. "Yup. I'm pretty sure the radiology tech was wrong and this Whiskey's got *junk*."

"Give me that." Crystal snagged it from her hands and studied the grainy picture. "She does not." Penny and Gemma both leaned in to check it out.

"My daughter does not have *junk*," Sarah insisted. She took the frame from Crystal, remembering how she and Bones had both teared up when the tech showed them they were having a girl. Bones had studied the monitor during the sonogram, repeating, *Isn't she beautiful?* so many times the tech said she'd never seen a father get so emotional. Sarah hadn't corrected her about Bones's relationship to the baby, because he already felt like her children's father.

She rearranged a few Christmas decorations on the mantel and set the frame there, below the picture the kids had given Bones for his birthday, which as promised, he'd proudly framed and mounted on the wall. The baby kicked, and she ran her hand over her belly, thinking about how supportive Bones had been since they'd confronted Lewis nearly three weeks ago.

Bones had connected her with a therapist the very next day. She'd already seen him five times, and she planned to continue going twice a week because he was helping tremendously. Bones had also helped her tell Scott the truth about what Lewis had done, and then he had calmed Scott down when Scott had flown off the handle. Bones had later confessed to Sarah that he'd wished he'd killed Lewis. She'd had a good cry over that, and Bones had been teary eyed, too, because how could one awful man make two good people wish they could have done something so heinous?

It felt like that nightmare had happened a lifetime ago, especially now that it was Christmas and they were surrounded by the delicious scents of their holiday dinner and friends and family who brought so much happiness into their lives.

"Do you think it will feel weird being in Whiskey Bro's when I'm pregnant?" Finlay asked, bringing Sarah back to their conversation.

"No," Crystal and Sarah said in unison.

"Why would it feel weird?" Crystal asked. "It's not like you can get drunk from secondhand beer fumes. Otherwise Dixie would be drunk all the time."

They glanced across the room at Dixie, who was pointing to something out the window with Isabel, Quincy, Jed, and Penny. Scott approached from behind, put an arm around Dixie, and said something that made Dixie say, "Ha! In your dreams!"

Red strode out of the kitchen and announced, "The Whiskey boys and our surrogate Whiskey, Tru, are in the garage in case you're looking for them." She looked beautiful in a pair of black slacks and a black sweater with a chunky green, red, and gold necklace. She scooped Lincoln up as he toddled toward the kitchen and pressed a kiss to his cheek. "You are not big enough to play with motorcycles." She set him on his feet, and he toddled back toward the other kids by the Christmas tree.

"Come on, Linc. Bradley's teaching us how to make bike helmets." Kennedy patted the floor beside her. She looked cute with her hair in pigtails and wearing a Christmas Princess dress Crystal had made for her.

"Look," Finlay said from behind her hand.

Bradley was dragging a bag of diapers down the steps. Sarah and the kids hadn't *officially* moved in with Bones, but they'd been staying there since the day after the awful night with Lewis. She was pretty sure Scott was glad to have his bachelor pad mostly to himself. He'd been hanging out with Dixie a lot more lately, making Sarah wonder if there was something brewing between them, but he'd brought her kids treats from Cassie's bakery twice in the last week, which made her curious about the two of them, too. She was just happy he was spending time with women. He was too good a man to be alone.

"Look." Finlay nudged her, nodding toward Bradley again as he tugged the diaper bag beside the tree and squatted on his heels beside it. "He's so determined."

Bradley took out several diapers and said, "Everybody needs one." He opened a diaper and set it on Lila's head, making the other kids giggle, and said, "One." Then he opened another diaper and plopped it on Lincoln's head. "Two."

Red touched the sleeve of Sarah's blouse. "Oh my goodness, Sarah. Look at that little darling."

Lincoln took the diaper off his head.

"Linc, you need a helmet or you can't ride the motorcycle." Kennedy set the diaper on his head, and Lincoln looked at Lila as if she could fix his bossy sister.

Bradley placed a diaper on Kennedy's head and said, "Three." Then he scooted Lila behind Lincoln and said, "Kennedy you sit behind Lila."

"Good idea. Then she won't fall off," Kennedy said.

The kids held the adults' rapt attention as they whispered about the cuteness playing out before them.

Bradley plopped down in front of Lincoln. He put a diaper on his own head and said, "Four." Then he held his hands up, as if he were holding handlebars, and began making motorcycle-engine noises.

Sarah grabbed her phone and took pictures, as the kids all joined in making engine noises and swaying whichever way Bradley did. She texted a picture to Bones with the caption *I think you have a mini-me.*

"I think I'm going to cry," Finlay said. "That's the sweetest thing I've ever seen."

Gemma put her arm around Finlay and said, "I think you have baby fever. You should borrow Lincoln sometime when he's overtired. It might cure you of it."

"Don't believe her," Red said with a shake of her head. "Once you have the baby bug, you can't escape it until you've got your own little one in your arms."

Sarah's phone vibrated with a response from Bones. *Good boy, taking charge of the pack. Think anyone would notice if I carried you upstairs for another lovefest?* Before she could reply, she heard the guys coming through the garage door. They headed straight for the refrigerator, with Tinkerbell trotting beside Bullet. Sarah was still stuffed from Christmas dinner, but she'd learned a lot about Bones by staying at his place every night. He ate *a lot.* He had to. The man worked out six days a week. He had a gym in the basement and another at the office.

When he couldn't work out before work, he worked out at lunchtime. It was no wonder he looked so good. And she *loved* watching him work out. Her very own eye candy.

"I think Dixie was right about you on Halloween," Gemma said. "The way you're looking at Bones, you definitely have Whiskey fever."

"That I do," she admitted happily. It was wonderful to be so in love, and she had no intention of hiding it.

Crystal glanced at the men, who were heading back out to the garage with beers and a plate of leftover turkey. "Sarah, you seem really good. Are you? I mean, is it true? Because we're here for you if you need to talk."

"I know you are, but it *is* real. I'm happy." Her therapist had suggested she tell her closest friends the truth about what she'd gone through, to build a support network, move past the shame that had plagued her, and to focus on the way she'd grown and become stronger from what she'd gone through. Although she still couldn't go to the shelter, and Camille and Ebony had gone to stay with relatives, she'd kept in touch with the girls, and she'd told them first, because they had all been through something similar. And then she and Bones told his family. They told each couple separately, and every time she told her story, it got a little easier to talk about. When she shared her story with Bear and Crystal, Crystal told her how she'd been raped in college. They'd talked for hours, and it had brought them even closer.

"My therapist suggested I put my story into the blessing bags at the shelter. Bones arranged it with Sunny, and we're using one of the pictures Hawk took of me and the kids on the front of the booklet, and on the last page, there's a picture of all of us, including Bones. Bones delivered a bunch to the shelter last week." She secretly hoped Josie would see it.

"That's wonderful," Crystal said. "You'll probably help a lot of women see that they can get past whatever they've been through."

"How does it feel?" Gemma asked.

"It felt funny at first to have me and the kids on the cover. But while *From Homeless to Happy* started out as my story, it became their story, too. And even though it felt a little presumptuous to have Bones in there, since we're not married or anything, he's a big, important part of our lives that neither of us wanted to leave out."

"Wayne gave me one of the booklets, and I've never seen my son so proud to be included in anything." Red hugged her and said, "He never seemed content with where he was in life until he found you and the kids. It's a miracle."

The guys came back into the kitchen, and Sarah glanced over, catching Bones watching her. He winked and mouthed, *I love you.*

"No, Red," Sarah said dreamily. "He's *our* miracle."

"WHAT DO YOU think the sweethearts are talking about?" Bullet leaned on the kitchen counter, eyeing the girls in the living room.

"Kids," Truman said.

Bear scoffed. "Sex."

"How hot we are, obviously," Bones joked.

Bullet chuckled and took a swig of his beer. "How's your girl holding up, Bones?"

"She's great." The more Bones and Sarah talked about what

she'd been through, the easier it seemed to be for her. "The therapist is helping a lot. I'm thinking about going to see him."

"What's going on?" Bear asked.

"I've got issues, man." Bones watched Sarah laughing with the girls and said, "I can't stop thinking about taking vengeance on that fuckface and hunting down the assholes who hurt her." He met Bullet's uneasy gaze. "I want to destroy them the way they tried to destroy her. I want to humiliate them, torture them, and—"

"Stop," Truman said. "I've been to prison. You *don't* want to go there, man."

"He's *not* going to prison," Bullet said, locking a death stare on Bones. "You're not doing *shit*, you understand?"

"It's eating away at me, B. I'm trying to channel it into other things, but I fucked up. I should have forced him to sign those papers."

"Go see the therapist," Truman urged. "Talk this shit out. Get it out of your system. We'll find another way to get the papers signed."

Bullet clenched his jaw, standing up to his full height, as if trying to intimidate Bones into agreeing to back off.

"I don't want that baby born without those papers signed," Bones said. "Sarah and her kids need protection."

"They have it," Bear reminded him. "There isn't a Knight around who hasn't taken a turn patrolling town, watching out for that asshole. One wrong move and we'll take him down. But you can't do it like you did. You're lucky he didn't press charges."

"Not that he'd win, because I saw that fucker come at you with a knife." Bullet nodded with a wink and a wry grin. "We've got your back."

"Too bad having my back can't clear my head." Bones headed toward the living room.

"Bones." His father's deep voice stopped him in his tracks. Biggs sidled up to him and put a hand on his shoulder, gazing into the living room. "You see those children? That pretty blonde with the baby in her belly?"

"Yeah, I see them, old man. Hell, I *feel* them even when they're not around." Sarah and the kids were not only part of his life, they'd become a part of *him*. They'd become his world.

The other guys brushed past them on their way into the living room. Bullet mouthed, *Everything cool?* and Bones nodded.

"You got your vengeance," Biggs reminded him. "You got away with it, and you kept the woman and children you love safe. If you go to prison, what happens to that little sweetheart who makes your heart feel like it's on speed? The one who was strong enough to live through hell time and time again." He shook his head, took a drink, and then he said, "There are different types of hell, son. Seeing the person you love behind bars? Taking your children to prison to visit the man who made all sorts of promises and can't fulfill them? That's the worst kind of hell there is, and there's no guarantee she'll be waiting for you when you get out. Remember that the next time you want to take that fucker's life."

Bones had struggled with this very debate his whole life, and he was unable to hold in his frustration for a second longer. "How can you say that, when you're the one who taught us to do whatever it takes to make things right? You confuse the hell out of me."

His father's beard twitched, like he was trying to smile but couldn't quite finish it. "You're confused because you don't realize you've already *done* the right thing, son. I didn't raise killers. You catch a man in the act, you do whatever it takes to end it and to keep it from ever happening again. It leads wherever it leads. But after the fact is a whole different situation."

"And what about this anger? How do I fix *that* so it doesn't eat me alive?"

Biggs glanced at Bullet, who had his arms around Finlay and a goofy grin on his face. "Seems to me you knew just what to do when Bullet came back from overseas with PTSD."

Bullet had returned to the States more than six years ago unsure if he'd live or die. Lying in a military hospital, he'd confided in Bones and asked him not to tell anyone he was there. He hadn't wanted their family to worry over him. Bones had kept his secret, and he had hooked Bullet up with a therapist who, in time, had done wonders for his PTSD. But Bullet had still seemed filled with rage, and Bones had worried about him right up until the time he'd fallen in love with Finlay. After that all of Bullet's demons seemed to be laid to rest. They'd found out only recently that Biggs had known about Bullet's brush with death the whole time. Bones was still shocked that their father wasn't pissed at him for keeping Bullet's secret.

"I know your heart has led you every step of the way with Sarah, and I know that's been strange and new for you. Exciting as fuck, I'm sure," Biggs said with a wink. "But this time you've got to lead with your head. Go see that therapist so you can be the father those babies deserve and the man Sarah and I both know you to be."

Biggs limped toward Red as if he hadn't just made Bones feel like he finally understood his father a little better—and proved he fit in after all.

Sarah glanced over, flashing the sweet smile he saw in his dreams. She always looked beautiful, but against the backdrop of the Christmas tree, with her blond hair framing her face, she looked angelic. Dixie said something, and Sarah turned that smile on her. The din of his family and friends mixed with the Christmas music someone must have just turned on. He stepped into the living room and decided his father was right. He'd make an appointment with the therapist, because there was no way in hell he wanted anything but happiness for Sarah and the children.

"Dadada," Lila babbled as she toddled across the room, reaching for Bones with one hand and holding the last unopened Christmas present—the one he'd hung by its bow on the bottom of the tree for later. "Dadadada."

Silence fell over the room, and all eyes locked on Lila and Bones. He didn't think it was possible for his heart to be fuller than it was right then.

"Dadadada," Lila repeated as Bones lifted her into his arms and glanced at Sarah, whose mouth was hanging open.

Dixie was taking a picture. Red had tears in her eyes.

"Dada!" Lila patted his cheek.

He looked at Sarah and said, "It's your call, darlin'. Is this okay with you, or should I correct her?"

"It's perfect," Sarah said a little breathlessly.

"Thank God, because if it wasn't, I'd be worried about doing this." He dropped down to one knee, and Bradley ran to his side, yelling, "Yay!"

Sarah's eyes filled with tears as Bones took her trembling hand in his. The charm bracelet he'd given her for Christmas slid down her wrist, the little pink and blue charms, one for each child, shimmering beneath the lights.

"Hurry! Give her the ring!" Bradley grabbed the box from Lila's hand, causing her to shriek. He shoved it back in Lila's hand, scrambled away, picked up Lila's new doll, and shoved it toward her. "Trade?"

Lila dropped the box in lieu of the toy, and Bones caught it midair, making everyone laugh—and Sarah cry. Bones handed the box to Bradley, trying his hardest not to skip their plan and rush to say what he'd been dying to for weeks.

Bradley opened the box, and Bones said, "Sarah, from the moment—"

"Isn't it pretty, Mommy? I helped pick it out while you were at work!" Bradley thrust the box with the elegant two-carat diamond ring at her.

She laughed, which brought more tears. "It is beautiful."

"This isn't really going as planned," Bones said with a smile.

"Does anything with children?" Gemma said softly.

Bear pulled Crystal against his side and said, "I can't wait to find out."

Bones rose to his feet with Lila in his arms, gazing deeply into Sarah's eyes, and said, "I had a whole speech planned, but, darlin', now I can't remember most of it. Sarah, I want sleepless nights—because of our lovin' *and* because of the children. I want baby barf on my shirts and our best-laid plans ruined because the kids are too excited to wait."

"Put the ring on, Mommy!" Bradley yelled.

"Dadadada!" Lila rested her cheek on Bones's shoulder.

This was...*heaven*. "Darlin', it's you. It's been you since the moment I set eyes on you."

Sarah gasped. "That's it! Our baby's name! Maggie Rose, after our first dance at Bullet and Fin's wedding."

He chuckled, thinking he'd never get the proposal out, and then he realized she said *our* baby. "That's perfect," he choked out.

"I'm sorry! I'm just so happy!" She pressed her lips together, but her smile broke free.

"Me too, Mommy!" Bradley shouted. "We're gonna get married!"

"Uncle Boney is getting *mawied*?" Kennedy squealed and clapped her hands.

Bear nudged Bones. "Dude, hurry up."

"Sarah, you are, and always will be, my one and only love," he said as fast as he could. "Will you marry me?"

"Yes," she said in a half laugh, half cry. She threw one arm around his neck, the other around Lila, pushed up on her toes, and they sealed their promises with a kiss, while Bradley tugged on her shirt and everyone cheered and clapped.

When their lips parted, Red took Lila from his arms. He slipped the ring on Sarah's finger, and then he cradled her face between his hands and brushed her tears away. "I love you, Sarah. I have loved you from the very moment I met you, which could have turned out really bad if you were married." That earned him a sweet laugh. "I'll always make sure you have safe foods to eat, and if we find out you're no longer allergic, we'll take the kids to the best restaurants and find all your new favorites. Darlin', I want to give you the world. I love you more with every passing second, and I will love you well beyond our natural lives."

Her smile lit up the room as she said, "I love you, too. So, *so* much!"

Everyone crowded in, hugging and congratulating them at once.

Dixie hugged Bones and said, "Can it be my turn now?"

"Dix, there's nothing I want more for you than happiness. But it's not me you have to worry about." He glanced at Bullet, who was hugging Sarah, and said, "Good luck with that."

Eventually the kids went back to their toys, and Sarah finally landed back in Bones's arms. "Hello, my beautiful future wife. I missed you."

"Not half as much as I missed you." She went up on her toes and pressed her lips to his. "I have one last present for you, too." She handed him an envelope.

"What's this?" He opened the envelope and scanned the voluntary termination of parental rights form, which was signed by Lewis, witnessed by Bullet, and notarized. *Holy shit.* "You went *back* there?"

"No. I promise," she said quickly. "I was afraid to ask you to go back and try again because I worried that seeing him might flip a switch that was better off left unflipped. So I did the next best thing. I called Bullet."

"I'm not sure if I should be happy or disturbed that I frightened you," he said honestly.

"You didn't," she said. "You love me, and with that love comes a level of protectiveness that is hard to rein in when faced with...*that.*"

Bones glanced at Bullet. He didn't know what to say. *Thank you* didn't seem big enough, and *You asshole, you should have told me*, seemed inappropriate. The truth was, he was just glad the papers were signed.

Bullet shrugged and said, "Told you I had your back. You'd given him a glimpse of what holding out would get him. That, the threat of jail time for what he'd done to Sarah, and a little shove in the right direction was all it took for him to sign the papers *and* give up the names of the other three cretins. I took care of them, too. You won't have to worry about any of them ever again."

Bones opened his mouth to ask what had gone down, but Bullet narrowed his eyes and said, "Don't ask what you don't want to know."

There was a knock at the door, and everyone looked curiously around the room.

"Who are we missing?" Red asked.

"It might be my friend Tracey," Sarah said on her way to the door. "I invited her. I hope you don't mind."

Bones followed her to the door.

Bullet joined him and said, "He's not dead. But this was all you, dude. He was shaking in his boots the second he saw me."

"Good to know. Thanks, man. I owe you one."

"No, man. I owed you big-time. We're even."

Sarah opened the door, and her face blanched at the sight of Josie, looking waiflike on the expansive front porch, wearing a thick green coat with the hood pulled up over her head.

"Josie—"

Bones slipped an arm around Sarah's waist just in time to feel her legs give out. He guided her onto the front porch.

"Dude, stop staring," Bullet snapped at Jed, whose eyes were locked on Josie, and shooed Jed and the others away as he closed the door.

Josie held up a copy of *From Homeless to Happy*, her eyes shifting nervously between Bones and Sarah. "He gave this to me with this address and said to come by anytime. I didn't know you were having a party."

"We're not," Sarah said. "Stay, please. Scott is right inside and I know he's dying to talk to you."

Josie looked over her shoulder at a car idling in the driveway. "I can't. My friend's waiting with Hail in the car."

"Invite them in," Sarah suggested. "I'd love to meet them."

The hope in Sarah's voice had Bones praying Josie would accept.

"No," Josie said quickly. "I just wanted to talk for a minute. I'm not ready to..." Her brows knitted. "I just wanted to say that I read your story. I didn't know...I'm sorry." She hurried down the porch steps, stopping abruptly on the walkway. Her shoulders rounded forward, and she shoved her hands deep in her coat pockets as she faced them again and said, "Merry Christmas. Maybe we can talk after the holidays."

"I'd like that," Sarah said.

Tears streamed down Sarah's cheeks as Josie climbed into the car, and Bones gathered her in his arms as her sister drove away.

"She was here," Sarah said with awe. "You brought Josie to me."

"No, darlin'. You did, by being brave enough to share your story. All I did was deliver your message."

"I'm so happy right now I want to cry," she whispered. "I'm scared to hope and terrified not to."

"*Hope*, baby. Hope is good. This is a start. She did the hardest part; she came to you, and she apologized. The rest will come."

"She read my story. She knows I didn't have a perfect life." Sarah looked up at the sky as snow began to fall and said, "Maybe Thomas sprinkled a little extra miracle dust on us tonight."

"Darlin'," he said as her eyes found his again, "he must have been sprinkling miracle dust on me since the day he passed away, because my whole life has been leading up to you. Let's go get our babies, bundle them up, and let them catch snowflakes on their tongues."

"Catch *miracles,*" she said. "Because we can never have enough of them."

Ready for More Whiskeys?

Dixie and the rest of our Whiskey friends will each have their own stories!

Come along for the sexy, emotional ride as Jed and Josie find their happily ever after in MAD ABOUT MOON, the next book in the Whiskeys series!

The following Whiskey-related books are waiting for you at all book retailers:

River of Love (First introduction to the Whiskey family)

Tru Blue (Truman and Gemma)

Truly, Madly, Whiskey (Bear and Crystal)

Driving Whiskey Wild (Bullet and Finlay)

Sign up for Melissa's newsletter to be alerted when Dixie and the rest of the Whiskey friends' books are available.
www.MelissaFoster.com/Newsletter

Love Melissa's Writing?

Discover more of the magic behind *New York Times* bestselling and award-winning author Melissa Foster with the series that started the phenomenon:

LOVE IN BLOOM
Big-Family Romance Collection

The Whiskeys are just one of the many family series in the Love in Bloom collection featuring fiercely loyal heroes, sassy, sexy heroines, and stories that go above and beyond your expectations! Find downloadable series checklists, reading orders, and more on the Reader Goodies page of Melissa's website. www.MelissaFoster.com

Book List

LOVE IN BLOOM SERIES

SNOW SISTERS

Sisters in Love
Sisters in Bloom
Sisters in White

THE BRADENS at Weston

Lovers at Heart, Reimagined
Destined for Love
Friendship on Fire
Sea of Love
Bursting with Love
Hearts at Play

THE BRADENS at Trusty

Taken by Love
Fated for Love
Romancing My Love
Flirting with Love
Dreaming of Love
Crashing into Love

THE BRADENS at Peaceful Harbor

Healed by Love
Surrender My Love
River of Love
Crushing on Love
Whisper of Love
Thrill of Love

THE BRADENS & MONTGOMERYS at Pleasant Hill – Oak Falls

Embracing Her Heart
Anything For Love
Trails of Love

THE BRADEN NOVELLAS

Promise My Love
Our New Love
Daring Her Love
Story of Love
Love at Last

THE REMINGTONS

Game of Love
Stroke of Love
Flames of Love
Slope of Love
Read, Write, Love
Touched by Love

SEASIDE SUMMERS

Seaside Dreams
Seaside Hearts
Seaside Sunsets
Seaside Secrets
Seaside Nights
Seaside Embrace
Seaside Lovers
Seaside Whispers

BAYSIDE SUMMERS

Bayside Desires
Bayside Passions
Bayside Heat
Bayside Escape

THE RYDERS

Seized by Love
Claimed by Love
Chased by Love
Rescued by Love
Swept Into Love

SEXY STANDALONE ROMANCE

Tru Blue

Truly, Madly, Whiskey

Driving Whiskey Wild

Wicked Whiskey Love

Mad About Moon

BILLIONAIRES AFTER DARK SERIES

WILD BOYS AFTER DARK

Logan

Heath

Jackson

Cooper

BAD BOYS AFTER DARK

Mick

Dylan

Carson

Brett

HARBORSIDE NIGHTS SERIES

Includes characters from the Love in Bloom series

Catching Cassidy

Discovering Delilah

Tempting Tristan

More Books by Melissa

Chasing Amanda (mystery/suspense)

Come Back to Me (mystery/suspense)

Have No Shame (historical fiction/romance)

Love, Lies & Mystery (3-book bundle)

Megan's Way (literary fiction)

Traces of Kara (psychological thriller)

Where Petals Fall (suspense)

Acknowledgments

Thank you for reading Bones and Sarah's story. This was such a tough story to write, given Sarah's background. But Bones made it a little easier, leading the way with his compassionate heart and protective nature. I hope you loved them as much as I do. I'm excited to explore happily ever afters for Josie, Dixie, Penny, and the rest of our friends in the Whiskey world.

A special thank-you goes out to Rosalie Perez, who was kind enough to share with me her personal battle with cancer. I have taken great literary liberties, and I truly appreciate you trusting me with your story. Thank you, Terren Hoeksema, for helping me with details about life in certain parts of Florida. Lisa Bardonski and Lisa Filipe, you were life-savers with this book. Thanks for talking me off the ledge.

If this is your first introduction to my work, please note that every Melissa Foster book can be read as a stand-alone novel, and characters appear in other family series, so you never miss out on an engagement, wedding, or birth. You can find information about the Love in Bloom series and my books here: www.melissafoster.com/melissas-books

I chat with fans often in my fan club on Facebook. If you haven't joined my fan club yet, please do! www.facebook.com/groups/MelissaFosterFans

Follow my author page on Facebook for fun giveaways and updates of what's going on in our fictional boyfriends' worlds. www.Facebook.com/MelissaFosterAuthor

If you prefer sweet romance, with no explicit scenes or graphic language, please try the Sweet with Heat series written under my pen name, Addison Cole. You'll find the same great love stories with toned-down heat levels.

Thank you to my awesome editorial team, Kristen Weber and Penina Lopez, and my meticulous proofreaders, Elaini Caruso, Juliette Hill, Marlene Engel, Lynn Mullan, and Justinn Harrison. And last but never least, a huge thank-you to my family for their patience, support, and inspiration.

Meet Melissa

Melissa Foster is a *New York Times* and *USA Today* bestselling and award-winning author. Her books have been recommended by *USA Today's* book blog, *Hagerstown* magazine, *The Patriot*, and several other print venues. Melissa has painted and donated several murals to the Hospital for Sick Children in Washington, DC.

Visit Melissa on her website or chat with her on social media. Melissa enjoys discussing her books with book clubs and reader groups and welcomes an invitation to your event. Melissa's books are available through most online retailers in paperback and digital formats.

Melissa also writes sweet romance under the pen name Addison Cole.

www.MelissaFoster.com
Free Reader Goodies:
www.MelissaFoster.com/Reader-Goodies

Printed in Great Britain
by Amazon